CINCINNATUS

CINCINNATUS

The Secret Plot to Save America

Rusty McClure & David Stern

TERNARY PUBLISHING

CINCINNATUS

The Secret Plot to Save America

Ternary Publishing

Library of Congress Cataloging-in-Publication Data

McClure, Rusty, 1950-
Cincinnatus / by Rusty McClure and Dave Stern.
p. cm.
ISBN-13: 978-0-9842132-0-7
I. Stern, Dave. II. Title.

PS3613.C363C56 2009
813'.6--dc22

2009030134

Edited by Jack Heffron
Designed by Stephen Sullivan

Cover illustration by Tom Lynch. Tom is a renowned watercolorist and teacher.
He has been the featured artist at the Men's, Women's, and Senior's U.S. Open Golf Championships
and several PGA events and tournaments. Visit www.tomlynch.com for additional information.

Back over illustration of Coral Castle by Tony Greco. An award-winning illustrator and designer,
Tony can be reached at www.tonygrecodesign.com.

Distributed by The BookMasters Group
ATLAS BOOKS

Dedication

To this principle:

Successful defenses of Jeffersonian democracy
shall not forsake its moral compass;

To this aspiration:

All who cope with lost love will not lose their souls.

we dedicate this book.

Contents

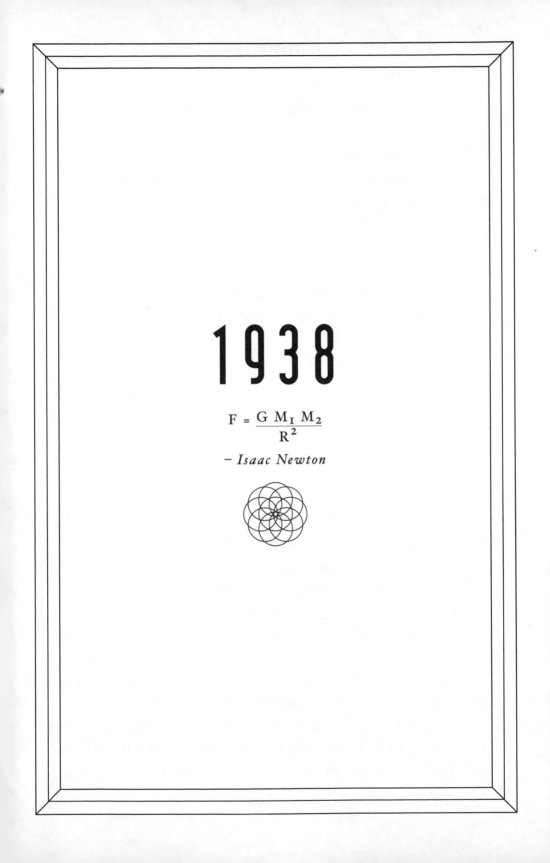

1938

$$F = \frac{G\,M_1\,M_2}{R^2}$$

— Isaac Newton

CINCINNATUS

LA GUARDIA was on the radio.

A recorded broadcast, a speech he'd given a week earlier. Scratchy and barely audible over the wind rushing by.

"...we have to quarantine...the germs of Fascism, of Nazism..."

The man at the wheel of the car fiddled with the tuner to no effect. He turned up the volume.

"...there is nothing a democracy can or wants to learn from a dictatorship in Europe. There is nothing that these countries can give any of our countries. There is—"

A burst of static cut off the mayor's voice. The man fiddled again and gave up.

He was driving a dark green 1938 Buick Sport Coupe, heading south on Biscayne Boulevard, the tan canvas top down, the sun shining on his arms, the ocean breeze blowing back his hair. Miami lay behind him, Key West ahead, his destination somewhere in between.

The man's name was Lewis Crosley. He had the build of a football player turned workingman, the hands of the farmer and dam engineer he'd once been. He wore a businessman's suit now, a summer-weight gray suit that felt sticky against his skin.

He wore the suit because at the morning meeting he represented the Crosley Corporation. The afternoon meeting toward which he drove was personal. He had mixed feelings about it, suspecting it was a fool's errand but hoping, for his brother's sake, that he was wrong.

Biscayne Boulevard became Route 1. Four lanes narrowed to two as the road curved inland. Bugs splattered on the windshield. Lewis turned on the wipers, but the bugs kept coming. He kept driving, turned his mind away from his brother's troubles to La Guardia's speech about the Nazis and the approaching war. Any fool could see it was coming. Anyone

2

who thought the trouble in Europe wasn't America's business was kidding themselves. Europe today. America tomorrow.

Bullets. Tanks. Bombs. War.

Good versus evil. It was that simple.

Lewis had done his part, enlisting in the Great War at twenty-seven despite having a wife and young daughter. He'd gone overseas, taken fire in the Argonne. Serve your country, serve the cause of freedom. It was an obligation, like Thomas Jefferson had said. Eternal vigilance, that was freedom's price, one the founding fathers had gladly paid. Lewis's great-grandfather had paid it with them, in 1776. Two of his uncles had paid it in the War Between the States. Each generation had to pay it anew.

He was so busy thinking about America's obligations to the free world he almost missed his destination. He noticed, just in time, a red house on his left, not much more than a shack, which was one of the landmarks Benny had mentioned. "The guy don't make it easy to find, I'll tell you that much," Benny had said as he gave Lewis directions and the keys to the Buick. True enough. The next landmark was a Key West highway sign a few hundred feet past the red house, same side of the road, and Lewis almost missed that one too, buried as it was in the scrub that passed for forest in this part of Florida.

Then Lewis looked to his right, and saw, coming into view...

Edward Leedskalnin's home.

Huge coral stones standing on end, placed together to form what looked like a castle or fortress—stones as heavy as ten tons, as tall as twenty feet, according to the newspaper article, which had called Leedskalnin an eccentric. Benny had said he was a real character. Lewis was beginning to agree. And he was beginning to think Powel, his brother, was going to be terribly disappointed.

Lewis pulled off the road. As he set the parking brake and opened his door, he glanced across the street, which was when he saw the other car—a black Ford Coupe, parked along the shoulder of the highway, up on the dirt, in a little canopy made by the low-hanging Florida scrub. Two men sat inside, staring at him.

The driver wore a dark suit and a Fedora. The man in the passenger seat wore a shirt and tie, no jacket, no hat. The Ford was twenty feet away, close enough for him to see their faces.

They stared so long Lewis felt compelled to speak.

"Morning," he called out.

The driver started the car, and the Ford sped away.

Before Lewis could think about the strangeness of the encounter, he heard a new sound. Someone was coming.

He raised a hand to shield his eyes and squinted into the sun.

The someone, wearing a white shirt and dark pants, was coming on a bicycle, wobbling down a dirt path next to the road. He was still a hundred yards away, passing by a vegetable garden. He sat erect in his seat, looking straight ahead.

He sees me. He's wondering who I am, what I'm doing here.

Which Lewis, not for the first time that morning, wondered himself.

He drained the last of his soda and waited. He normally didn't drink soda, but while driving from Miami with the sun on his neck, the heat roiling from the leather seats, he found himself craving one. When he stopped to ask directions, he'd picked up a bottle of Double Cola. Jacksonville D.C. Bottling Company. Your Local Flavor, Your Local Favorite.

Lewis looked from the soda bottle to a sign announcing "NO TOURS TODAY," then turned to watch the man on the bike, who he felt sure was Edward Leedskalnin.

The man stopped ten feet shy of Lewis and climbed off the bike. He was, as the article had promised, all of five feet tall. And skinny. Wiry-looking though—muscular, not frail. But even if he was all muscle, he couldn't have weighed much more than a hundred ten pounds.

Smaller, Lewis realized, than his wife, Lucy, whose voice he now heard in his head once again: *Fool's errand.*

Lewis stepped forward to greet Leedskalnin.

Which was when he saw the bicycle's tires. They were metal. Bent in spots, accounting for the wobbliness. Who, in this day and age, rode a bike with metal tires?

"Good afternoon," Lewis said. "I hope you don't mind—"

"No tours today, I am sorry. You see sign?" The little man spoke in a high-pitched voice and a heavy European accent, something close to German, with long, sibilant 's's and rolled 'r's that made 'sorry' come out sounding almost like 'soddy.'

He had dark, thinning hair, combed back from his forehead, bright, piercingly blue eyes set in a rectangle of a face with prominent cheekbones, a prominent jaw, and what looked to be permanent frown lines at the corners of his mouth.

Not a man who did a lot of smiling.

"I'm not looking for a tour," Lewis said. "I was hoping to ask you a few questions—Mr. Leedskalnin, isn't it?"

Leedskalnin grabbed the books from the wire basket on the front of the bike—three thick volumes with brown cloth bindings, paper flaking at the edges.

"Yes. I am Edward Leedskalnin." He pronounced the 'w' in Edward like a 'v': *Edvard.* The 'nin' at the end of his last name with a 'y': *nyin.* Edvard Leedskalnyin. "But I am busy today, I am sorry. Come back tomorrow. I give tour. Excuse me."

"But—"

Leedskalnin headed for the building beyond. The soles of his shoes clanged against the rock path as he went. They were metal too.

Lewis watched the little man walk to the front door of his home, which looked even stranger up close than it looked from the road. An eight-foot rock wall surrounded the place. A two-story tower at one corner looked down on the vegetable garden outside the wall and the field and scrub beyond. The place looked like a miniature version of a European castle, one that had been picked up whole out of the French countryside and dropped in the middle of tropical Florida.

A castle, forty-five minutes south of Miami.

Lewis had a hard time believing it. And he wanted nothing more than to turn his back on his brother's errand, on the odd collection of stones lying in the yard and the little man who'd gathered them.

He had a bad feeling. A feeling like none of this was going to come to any good.

In the shadow of the giant stones, Lewis remembered the first time he'd heard Leedskalnin's name. A week ago, back in Cincinnati. His brother, Powel, had sent for him, and Lewis dutifully headed from the factory to the executive offices on the eighth floor.

"Got something I want to show you," Powel said, and stood up from behind his big cherry desk. He handed Lewis a newspaper, the *Redland District News*.

The headline read: MAN BUILDS CORAL CASTLE FOR LOST LOVE

In the photo below it, Leedskalnin wore a suit, stood in this very yard, and gestured toward the stones behind him.

Lewis looked up from the newspaper. "Okay," he said. "This fellow built a castle."

"Read it," Powel said. "The whole thing."

Lewis continued, learning about Edward Leedskalnin and the monument he'd spent the last twenty years of his life constructing. The article talked about the huge stones and how Leedskalnin had quarried and moved them all on his own. Lewis scoffed; such a thing wasn't possible. To get rocks that big out of the ground cleanly you'd not only need heavy equipment, you'd need some highly skilled workmen. Coral was prone to breaking. No way for one man to work that much stone.

The article moved on from Leedskalnin's construction methods to his past. He was born in Latvia, where he'd spent his first quarter-century before coming to America. He'd begun building his castle for the 'lost love' mentioned in the headline, a girl named Agnes Scuffs. Leedskalnin apparently built his castle in the hope—in the belief—that she would be so moved by the gesture that she would return to him.

"This part," Powel said, pointing to the paragraph Lewis was reading. "You see?"

"Yes," Lewis said, the reason for Powel's interest coming clear. The eccentric man had cured himself of tuberculosis.

"I called Dr. Vorregend," Powel said. "He'd never heard of anything like it. Said it sounded like some kind of mumbo-jumbo."

"I've never heard of anything like it either," Lewis said.

"But if it's true, if this Leedskalnin fellow really did manage to find a cure..."

Lewis heard the anxiety in his brother's voice. It wasn't a note Powel often sounded.

"We should talk to him."

"I've tried," Powel said. "He doesn't have a phone. I'd send a letter, but I don't know if he can read and write English."

Powel walked behind his desk and dropped the article on top of the blotter. Sighed, put his hands into fists, put his fists on the desk, and leaned forward, getting ready to speak again.

He looks old, Lewis thought. Old and tired. It wasn't just the strain of running the corporation, because truth be told, Lewis, as the number two man, did as much of the actual running, if not more, than Powel. They'd been in business together for nearly twenty years, and that was how they'd split up responsibilities from the start. Powel dreamed up the big ideas, Lewis implemented them. The combination had worked out pretty well. Crosley was the largest company in Cincinnati now, bigger than Procter and Gamble. They were into radios, refrigerators, household appliances, about to launch a car. A lot of stress for both men.

But Powel's worries went deeper than the company these days.

"Still...sending a letter...it's worth a try," Lewis said. "I'll have Dorothea type one up."

Powel looked at his brother, and all at once, Lewis understood what Powel really wanted done. Why he'd called Lewis up to his office.

Lewis cleared his throat. "The new parts supplier in Miami," he said, "Benny Merino. I probably should go down there and meet with him to review the specs." Lewis, in truth, rarely made these kinds of trips, but if it would ease Powel's mind, he would go.

Powel smiled. "Homestead—where this fellow is—it's not far from Miami. Twenty miles south, I think."

"While I'm down there...I could take a drive, talk to Leedskalnin. See if there's anything to what the article says."

Powel's smile broadened.

❖ ❖ ❖ ❖ ❖

Lewis came back to the present. He walked past Leedskalnin's garden and was tempted to grab a tomato off the vine. They looked good. Leedskalnin was walking back from the castle, heading straight toward him. Waving a finger.

"What are you doing?" he called out.

"You have mildew," Lewis announced.

Leedskalnin frowned. "I have what?"

"Powdery mildew. On your collards. See?" Lewis plucked a leaf and showed it to Leedskalnin.

"Ah," Leedskalnin nodded. "I have this last year too. All my greens—ruined." The last word sounded like 'ruint.'

"You might try spacing the plants out a little more. Let them get a little more sun. Don't water quite as much."

"You are farmer?"

"Long time ago I was. Now I just keep a garden. Start my day out there, five-thirty in the morning. Get my hands in the soil, get the blood flowing...."

Leedskalnin nodded and smiled.

Lewis smiled too. "These days I work in an office. In Cincinnati. With my brother. Which is what I want to talk to you about." He brushed his hands together to clear off the dust. "My name's Crosley, by the way. Lewis Crosley."

When they shook hands, Lewis was surprised at the strength in the smaller man's grip—like a pair of pliers. Rough, callused hands.

"I am please-ed to meet you, Mr. Cross-ley. I will give you tour now. To show my thanks."

"I really just want to talk to you."

But Leedskalnin hurried ahead to the main gate and then to the metal door, pushing it open. Stepped inside and waited for Lewis to follow.

❖ ❖ ❖ ❖ ❖

The yard inside the castle walls was roughly the shape of a square. Roughly a hundred feet per side. Filled with huge stone sculptures, all of the same gray coral as the walls. Crescent moons, obelisks.

"One thousand tons of coral, Mr. Crosley. Many years of my life to build these."

"Impressive," Lewis said.

"Do it all myself," Leedskalnin said. "Use center of gravity, the place where energy of stone gathers. You understand?"

Lewis nodded. "Center of gravity," he said. "Yes. I understand."

Although the bit about energy of stone...he didn't quite get that.

With each new sculpture, Leedskalnin told a story, often involving his lost love, Agnes Scuffs. His bright blue eyes twinkled at times, as if he were seeing the sculpture's beauty through Agnes's eyes, assessing its power to rekindle her feelings for him. At other times, he looked almost defeated, maybe surrendering to the heartbreak he obviously felt every day. Lewis began to realize that Leedskalnin was not only an eccentric man, he was also a sad one. As he proudly presented each piece, he sprinkled in mentions of "my Agnes" and "my sweet sixteen."

He told Lewis that Agnes, who was ten years younger than Edward, had left him on the day before their wedding. Everything from the heart-shaped dining table to the bathtub to the rocker was made of coral and all had been fashioned with Agnes in mind. Though the sculptures were, in their way, remarkable, Lewis couldn't help but feel the futility of building this monument for a woman who would never see it. He tried not to feel that his mission for Powel was equally hopeless.

"Now," Leedskalnin said, walking to the back wall of the castle, "I show you Rock Gate."

Lewis followed him, stepping past a hole in the ground—a pit, surrounded by a low rock wall—a regular rock wall, not coral, the purpose of which wasn't clear until he caught the faintest scent of a smell, coming from below.

Water.

The little pit was a well.

Lewis peered over the edge...

And at that instant, he felt something.

It made the hairs on his arm tingle.

It made the bones in his jaw vibrate.

The feeling lasted for a split-second, and then it was gone. Like a wind of some sort, rushing through him. Familiar somehow, as if he'd experienced it, or something like it, before. He tried to remember where and when.

They continued the tour, with the nine-ton Rock Gate that guarded the back of the castle, a massive slab of coral that spun on its axis with astounding ease. Center of gravity, Leedskalnin explained again. He showed Lewis the obelisk, the tallest sculpture on the grounds, with a hole in the top shaped like the star on the Latvian flag.

They stood under the chain hoist. Leedskalnin was on Lewis's left; to Lewis's right was a stone that stood fifteen feet tall. Another coral stone, a slab, really, standing straight on end. Maybe four feet across, two feet thick. Huge. It hadn't looked this big from the road, standing next to the log tripod, but up close...

The carvings on the face of it looked almost like writing, but a kind Lewis couldn't recall seeing before. Symbols, more than letters. Like hieroglyphics.

"I raised it last night," Leedskalnin said.

"This stone?" Lewis said. "With that tripod?"

"Quite a task, as you might imagine."

Lewis looked from the stone and then up at the hoist.

Truth was, he couldn't imagine it. He'd been with the Army Corps of Engineers in France, done more than his share of quarrying stone. Using the same kind of makeshift equipment Leedskalnin used. No way that tripod could handle more than a few hundred pounds. Spindly thing like that.

"Perhaps you're wondering how I managed it on my own," Leedskalnin said. "My grandfather was a mason, you see. Taught me—how do you Americans say it?—the tricks of the trade."

It'd take quite a trick to raise that much rock, Lewis thought. But if Leedskalnin wanted to pretend he'd done it all by himself, so be it. Lewis didn't want to offend the man when he'd come here to ask for his help.

"Very impressive," Lewis said.

The tour ended at the two-story tower, but first they went to the ground-floor room—Leedskalnin's workshop, filled with all sorts of tools, most of them laughably primitive. But Lewis couldn't laugh, because they were all so cleverly fashioned, all so clearly designed with a specific purpose, that they were beyond ingenious, they were genius, period. The man was a gifted mechanic, at the least. An intuitive engineer, definitely, but he was more than that. Scattered among the tools were other pieces of equipment—a turbine, gleaned from a junkyard somewhere, judging by the rust; a fan belt assembly from a car engine; dozens of horseshoes (magnets, Lewis assumed, judging from the nails stuck to a few of them); springs large and small; coils of metal wire, thick and thin—which told Lewis that Leedskalnin had not just an engineer's mentality, but an experimenter's.

A flight of stone coral steps led up the outside of the tower. "We finish tour here," Leedskalnin said, turning. "Where I live in."

It looked more like a medieval prison cell to Lewis. But then his eyes fastened on a small metal shelf (one of several built into the coral walls) at the far left corner of the room. On it sat a half dozen Ball Mason Jars, wrapped in copper wire that ran to a car battery and what looked like a telegraph key.

"That's a radio," he said, suddenly, speaking for the first time since Leedskalnin had joined him at the well.

Leedskalnin blinked, surprised at being interrupted.

"Yes," he said. "I build myself."

"A crystal set." Lewis touched it gently. "Spark transmitter, galena crystal…"

Leedskalnin said, "You know radio?"

"Yes," Lewis said. "I know radio."

Radio had started the Crosley company's fortunes. They'd moved on to broadcasting, from broadcasting to appliances, from appliances to cars, but radio was at the heart of it. How many hours had he and Powel spent together, trying to puzzle out its secrets, at his brother's house, in the labs?

Leedskalnin stared at Lewis, an odd expression on his face.

"Crosley," he said, pronouncing it 'Crossley' once more. "Radio," he said, rolling the 'r.' Crosley Radio, this is you? You are that Crosley?"

"One of them," Lewis admitted.

Leedskalnin smiled, a smile of genuine pleasure, the first one Lewis had seen from him all afternoon.

"Hah," he said. "You have question for me—now I have questions for you, too."

❖ ❖ ❖ ❖ ❖

They talked about the history of Crosley Radio. Crosley Broadcasting. They talked about the technology and about the people and even about the politics. As they talked, Lewis realized the man was starved for conversation. When Lewis mentioned Powel, Leedskalnin's face lit up.

"Ah. The famous Powel Crosley," he said.

Lewis nodded. Powel was as well known as any industrialist in the country. Not just his name, but his face, had come to be associated with everything the company did—the Shelvador refrigerator, Crosley radios, WLW broadcasting, the Cincinnati Reds, and the soon-to-be Crosley Car.

But Lewis saw a side of his brother that no one else got to see. The family man. The loving husband.

"It's because of Powel I'm here," Lewis said. "He needs your help."

"What could I do for your brother that he could not hire ten other men to do?"

"Not for him. For his wife. Her name is Gwendolyn. They've been married almost thirty years. Childhood sweethearts, you could say."

Leedskalnin's expression changed, from puzzlement to something else, a flash of anger, another of sadness, of melancholy.

Man Builds Coral Castle for Lost Love

"She has tuberculosis," Lewis said. "She's very sick. The doctors won't come right out and say it, but it's clear she's dying."

Leedskalnin was silent a moment, perhaps making the connection between Powel's wife and his own lost love. "I'm very sorry to hear this," he said. "Sorry for your brother and his wife. It is a terrible disease."

"You had it, as I understand. A terminal case, the papers said. The doctors told you to go home and get your affairs in order."

"Correct."

"You were supposed to die. But you didn't. You lived. Cured yourself. A miracle cure, they said."

Leedskalnin said nothing.

"So that's why I'm here," Lewis went on. "To find out how you did it."

Leedskalnin remained silent. Lost in thought.

"In the paper they mentioned something about magnets," Lewis said.

"Magnetic therapy." Leedskalnin nodded. "That is what I told the reporters, yes."

Told the reporters. Lewis's heart sank. "So that wasn't true?"

The ghost of a smile flitted across Leedskalnin's face. "Oh it's true. As far as it goes. But not the whole truth."

"I don't understand."

"Do you really want to?" Leedskalnin asked with a spark in his eyes. "They called it a miracle, Mr. Crosley, but it's no miracle. There is nothing supernatural about what I did. In the hospital or what I did here."

"What you did here?"

"How I moved the stones," Leedskalnin said. "How I took this obelisk whole, from the ground, and raised it to where you see it now. How I rid my body of the illness—the energies invading it. All the same. It's about recognizing the forces around us. Seeing them for what they truly are and learning how to manipulate them."

Lewis tried to mask his disbelief but knew it showed on his face. The little man wasn't just eccentric. He was crazy.

Leedskalnin said, "I can prove to you the truth of what I am saying. I can demonstrate my knowledge of these things in a way that will make you reconsider everything you know."

❖ ❖ ❖ ❖ ❖

Leedskalnin took another drink from his shot glass, draining it. He smacked his lips. He smiled at Lewis, picked up the dusty bottle he'd pulled from his trunk, pulled out the rubber stopper, and poured a refill of the thick, dark liquid. Riga Black Balsam, he'd called it. A Latvian drink. Smelled like medicine to Lewis; tasted like it too.

"After the tsar's police came for me the first time," the little man went on, picking up where he'd left off, "I knew it was no longer safe in Latvia. Word had gotten out, about the things I had done. The Valleyrs." He practically spat the last word. "They enjoyed seeing my family suffer. Seeing my grandfather grovel. You understand, yes?"

He jabbed his little glass at Lewis for emphasis. Lewis nodded, and to avoid answering the man's question took a sip from his own. He was on his second glass of the stuff; thankfully, they were small glasses.

The two men sat side-by-side. An old seaman's chest rested on a slab nearby. Leedskalnin had taken the Black Balsam and the glasses from inside that chest, which had been covered with a pale green tarp to protect it from the weather. A second tarp covered what Lewis assumed was another chest.

Leedskalnin continued his story until, at last, he came to the only subject Lewis cared about: tuberculosis.

"The look on the doctor's face, the first time he examined me..." Leedskalnin giggled. "He was surprised I could live, with the damage to my lungs he found. But I was not surprised. I knew of them, the energies that had invaded my body..."

"That's the second time you've used that phrase—energies," Lewis said, trying not to sound as impatient as he felt. "Could you be more specific?"

"Agonic lines," he said. "Do you know?"

"Agonic lines?" The term came back to Lewis from somewhere—probably in school, maybe from working in the Corps. "Something to do with the earth's magnetic field."

"Exactly. Magnetic fields. Lines that tell us how these energies are distributed all over the world. There are maps in books, but there are better maps here." Leedskalnin tapped the side of his head. "More accurate maps. Maps that have never been written down anywhere. I know things the books don't. You can believe that. What my grandfather showed me..." The man continued talking, but his words went by without Lewis hearing them.

Finally, Lewis leaned across the table and said, "How did you cure it? That's my question. My brother's wife is dying and he'll do anything to save her."

Leedskalnin nodded. "I understand. Such a loss. Who could bear it?"

"Then tell me how you did it." His tone, Lewis knew, had shown the impatience he was feeling. He added, "Please."

The hint of a smile tugged at Leedskalnin face. "You felt it." His eyes lit up again. "The well. You felt it, yes?"

Lewis's heart jumped in his chest.

The well.

The tingling on his arms.

"I saw," Leedskalnin said. "You felt it. Energy. From earth, from water. This, I used to build my castle. To lift the coral from the ground. As easy as I lift this book."

Lewis stared at him.

"My secret, Lewis Cross-ley, I tell you. First person I share this with. *Gurutvakarshan*. Energy. Power."

And in that instant, Lewis remembered when he'd felt that tingling sensation before. It had been seven or eight years ago. WLW, Crosley's flagship station, had broadcast at half a million watts. Ten times more power than any other radio station before or since—power enough to be heard across the globe, from Brazil to Australia.

Lewis was there the night they switched on those tubes, fed the signal through the relays and the amplifiers, fed it to that huge antenna. He felt the current passing through the ground under his feet, crackling through the air around him.

The hair on his arms had stood on end.

The bones in his body had tingled.

"I..." He shook his head, searched for words. "What does this have to do with curing my brother's wife?"

"All the same," Leedskalnin said. He walked to the wall and slapped the rock. "Energy here. Energy here." He punched his chest. "No difference. Once you understand..." and he went off again on an explanation that made no sense, that was not an explanation at all. Perhaps sensing he had lost his audience, the little man stopped abruptly. "Forgive me," he said, standing up. "This is all talking, and anyone can talk. I will show you that I am more than just talk."

Leedskalnin scurried to the nearest wall and peered through a small hole in the rock that apparently was designed for that purpose. "Gone," he said. "Good. I can show you."

"Those guys in the car were watching you?" Lewis asked.

"People are interested to know how I do such things."

"What people?"

"Government perhaps. Such power is not for all to have. The tsar's police hurt my father, as I told you. I face similar dangers."

"Well, there isn't a tsar here in America," Lewis said.

"People are the same no matter where in the world. Good and bad."

Eccentric, heartbroken, lonely, and apparently a little paranoid too, Lewis thought. His face must have betrayed his thoughts, because Leedskalnin said, "You saw them too, the men in the car, so you know I'm not imagining."

"That's true," Lewis conceded.

"Always someone is watching. Maybe government. Sometimes just curious neighbors."

Leedskalnin walked to the second tarp and pulled it aside.

The tarp had hidden some kind of strange machine.

It looked like a type of generator. There was an armature at the center, wound at least two inches thick with copper wire—maybe not copper, maybe some kind of alloy. Three metal rods, bright silver, tapering to a point, rose off a triangular faceplate fastened just above the armature.

Leedskalnin bent down, pulled on something, pressed on something else, and all at once, Lewis heard a low-pitched humming, barely audible.

Lewis couldn't see any wires coming from the machine. "Where's that drawing power from?"

"Where indeed," Leedskalnin said, and again flashed his impish smile.

The armature began to spin, slowly at first, then faster. Much, much faster, till the individual wires disappeared into a blur. The tips of the three rods began to glow—yellow at first, then shading toward pink.

Lewis looked at the glow, and for the second time that day wanted to run away from Edward Leedskalnin and his Coral Castle as fast as he could. This time, though, that feeling had less to do with the man and more to do with the sensation he felt looking at the strange machine, at the armature as it turned, at the metal rods as they shone.

He realized he was in the presence of power that didn't hew to the laws of physics—power not entirely of this world.

Leedskalnin knelt next to the machine and gingerly moved the three rods so that they all pointed in the same direction—toward the huge coral stone Leedskalnin had called the obelisk.

"Now," the little man said, "please watch."

The glow at the tip of each rod brightened. Grew stronger. Expanded.

Lewis blinked to make sure of what he was seeing. When he was sure, he blinked again.

He couldn't find his voice. And even if he could find it, he didn't know what to say.

Book One

GAMBIT

Put none but Americans on guard tonight.
– *George Washington*

CINCINNATUS

AS long as you had something else to concentrate on, the pain did not exist. That's what the guy had told Matt, and he may have been right. What Matt Thurman was concentrating on right now was the flag on the thirteenth green, four hundred and fifty five yards away, barely visible in the gathering twilight. He was in the teebox, driver in hand, about to hit from the same spot, give or take a few yards, that Tiger Woods had hit from last week, when the PGA tour had come through Columbus for the annual Labor Day Classic.

Next year, he'd be with them. He was sure of it. He had a new focus, a renewed commitment. No more screwing around, no more drinking, no more anything that could be detrimental to his game. And as far as the shoulder went...

That was only pain. Plenty of golfers played with pain. Tiger won the U.S. Open one year, playing on a knee most people wouldn't have been able to walk on. Tim Clark, Jason Saturday, they had back problems. Bad back problems. And then there was Casey Martin. Who played through pain every hole of his life. Whose motto Matt had adopted as his own these last few months: Give yourself something else to concentrate on, and the pain would go away.

Matt Thurman squinted into the gathering darkness. Looked down the long rolling carpet of green, blocking out the hazards to either side of the fairway, the staggered clumps of pine, the sandtraps positioned where the hole dog-legged to the right. He focused on the promised land beyond, the long narrow green and the flag. The numbers came into his head almost automatically: par four and 455 yards. Pin placement today had been toward the back, near the right bunker. Ideal shot would be a downhill drive to the right side of the fairway. Five-iron to the green. Two putts for par.

The kind of hole he ate for breakfast, back in the day. Now...

Well. Four. If he was lucky. If the light held. Matt checked his watch: 7:51. Checked the sky. The light fading. No doubt about it; this was his last hole. Lucky thirteen. Something fitting about that.

He pulled the flask from his back pocket, took a swig, and put it back. Gave the shot a final look, and stepped forward. Put the tee in the ground, put the ball on the tee, and straightened. Rolled his neck. Tugged his glove. His lucky routine. The same routine he'd used since he was a kid and won the Ohio Amateur. "Matt Thurman, 15-Year-Old Phenom, Stuns Field to Take Trophy." Front page of the *Columbus Dispatch*. Fifteen years ago. Hadn't changed it since then. He was never going to change it.

As long as he could swing a golf club. Which was the question, wasn't it?

As if in answer, his shoulder pinged.

Matt ignored it, and the voice in his head. Wait six months. It had been almost five. No real pain in all that time. So he was fine, wasn't he? Fine enough to shoot a few holes. He wouldn't push it. First sign of a problem, he would shut it down. Absolutely.

He secured his grip, positioned his club...

And started his backswing. Drew the club up and away from the ball. The shoulder pinged again—not so much an ouch as a twinge—as he started to bring the club forward, but that was all right. Then he sensed movement out of the corner of his eye, movement where there shouldn't be any, and he glanced up, saw someone walking on the fairway, walking right toward him, right where he was about to put the ball, and that wasn't all right at all, too late to stop his swing though, so he drove the ball, smacked it like he was nineteen again and made of muscle.

It flew off into the trees to his left.

His shoulder screamed in agony.

Matt screamed too. He dropped the club and bit his lip.

"Damn it," he said, walking in a circle. "Ow. Damn it."

He rubbed the shoulder as he paced. Back and forth, back and forth. The bursa sack. He'd never even heard of a bursa sack before, and now the freaking thing had ruined his life. The bursa sack. Two years of specialists and none of them helped. Dr. Leffel, the latest, was going to be mad. Didn't I tell you? Six months? Now you've done it. You've really done it.

"Bob?"

He looked up. The person he'd seen coming up the fairway now stood ten feet in front of him.

A woman. Dressed in a business suit. Gray slacks, gray jacket, white blouse. A good-looking woman. Hispanic, with something else mixed in. Olive skin, long dark hair, pulled back in a bun.

"Are you Bob Kazmir?" she asked.

"No." Good-looking or not, Matt was angry. "I'm not Bob Kazmir."

"Do you know where he is?"

"Do you know where *you* are? You're on a golf course." Matt stepped closer. "And there are rules that need to be followed when you're on a golf course. One of these rules being, you don't walk on the fairways when the course is in play."

"I didn't realize—"

"You don't walk on the fairways. I was in the middle of my swing, and I had to stop when I saw you, and I hurt my shoulder."

The woman tightened her lips. "I'm sorry," she said. "So you haven't seen him? Bob Kazmir?"

"No."

"This is thirteen, right? He told me he would meet me on the thirteenth green."

"This is the thirteenth tee." Matt rubbed his shoulder. "I haven't seen him in a couple weeks. Since the tournament." He added, "And no great loss."

"Meaning?"

"Meaning Kazmir's a jerk." Which Matt knew from first-hand experience. Kazmir was a golfer too, a local boy made sort-of-good, good enough to play on the tour for a couple years, good enough to be the club pro here at The Pines for a few years after that, good enough so that when the new local boy, Matt, was trying to make it, the papers kept comparing them, a comparison Kazmir himself made, pointing out that yes, Matt Thurman had a lot of potential, but he'd have to work to realize that potential, the same way I did. He never missed a chance to put Matt in his place. This year had been no different.

"So you don't know where he is?" the woman asked.

"Went back to Florida, for all I know. He's got some hot-shot job down there. Likes to lord it over us locals." He'd lorded it over Matt a couple weeks back. Matt was checking distances on the greens when he ran into Kazmir on the twelfth. Kazmir charged up, veins popping on his forehead like he was going to have a heart attack. 'Who do you think you are, Thurman? You think you're still a player? You're a caddy. Caddies don't belong on the greens.' Never mind that it had been six in the morning and the hole was getting a complete makeover courtesy of Kazmir's company right before the Classic.

"So you don't know where he is?" the woman prompted.

"Don't know. Don't care." Matt smiled. "What do you need? Maybe I can help."

The woman shook her head. "I don't think so, thanks."

She started off down the fairway the way she'd come.

"Wait!" Matt called out. "What's your name?"

She kept walking.

"How do I find you, if I find him?"

She turned slightly and looked over her shoulder.

"You don't," she said, and kept walking.

❖ ❖ ❖ ❖ ❖

Matt watched her go and then decided to look for his ball, even though the sun had set and the course was getting dark. Play out the hole, if he could. Sundays were the only nights that caddies could play the course.

He went into the trees, carrying his driver, and almost immediately spotted a flash of white on the ground. Not his ball, though. A scrap of paper. He was surprised the grounds crew had missed it. Shocked, really. Those guys never missed anything.

He snatched it off the ground and saw that it was part of the spectator's handbook from last week's tournament. The Pines Labor Day Classic. A little pamphlet with information on the course and the players. There were pictures of the tournament's past champions on the cover, four of them, anyway. Lee Trevino, who won back-to-back in the seventies. Tiger Woods, who'd won it in 2003. Sergio Garcia. And, in the bottom right, Jack Nicklaus in his prime, looking like a movie star, blond hair blowing back, wearing a yellow turtleneck, staring at a ball he'd just hit, a fierce look on his face, like he was sending out magic brainwaves, telling the ball exactly where to go.

Matt smiled and remembered—that day in April 1986. He'd been nine years old. Huge football fan. Huge Cleveland Browns fan—posters of Bernie Kosar and Ernest Byner on his bedroom wall. He'd gone to stay with his grandparents for the weekend. Sunday afternoon, he walked into the living room. His grandfather was leaning forward in his chair, staring at the TV screen, shaking his head.

"He's going to do it, Matt. He's really going to do it."

Matt turned to see the TV screen. Golf. The Masters.

Matt hated golf. Golf was slow. Golf was boring. Golf wasn't really a sport. No golfer should ever be on a Wheaties box.

The man on the screen was Matt's dad's age, maybe a little older.

Blond hair, yellow shirt, checkered slacks. Jack Nicklaus, though Matt didn't know that at the time. The man was leaning over a golf ball. Preparing to putt.

"This is for birdie," the announcer said. "For a share of the lead."

The man drew back his club and tapped the ball. It scooted along the ground on a perfectly straight line; the camera pulled back to show the ball heading toward the hole. Had to be thirty feet away.

"Oh my," the TV announcer said. "Oh my."

The crowd, silent until that second, began to make noise.

The man who'd hit the ball stared after it, pumped his fist.

The crowd got louder. And louder.

"Come on," his grandfather said. "Come on..."

The camera zoomed in.

The ball rolled closer—a foot, six inches.

Come on, Matt found himself saying too. Come on.

The ball went into the hole.

The crowd cheered.

A man screamed.

Matt blinked, came back to the present.

The same man screamed again.

The scream came from the left—from the twelfth green, which was separated from the thirteenth tee by the little patch of trees surrounding Matt.

Matt shoved the pamphlet into his back pocket, next to the flask, and pushed forward. He heard voices.

"...because it's very serious, Bob."

"I get your point, it's serious. It won't happen again, I promise."

Bob, Matt thought. Bob Kazmir?

Matt crept to the edge of the woods, still holding his driver.

He gazed down on the twelfth green, where three men stood. One was indeed Bob Kazmir, dressed, like Kazmir always dressed, to the nines—

flamboyant, black slacks and an iridescent blue button-down shirt, a little touch of Florida here in Ohio. Another guy had his back to Matt, and it was a big back. The guy was huge, buffed up like a bodybuilder. Wearing a tight green polo shirt that showed off his muscles. Matt couldn't see his face.

The third man glared at Kazmir. He was older—fifties, maybe sixties, Matt couldn't quite tell. The guy was in great shape. Six feet maybe, a little taller, close-cropped gray hair, like a military cut. His arms were folded across his chest.

"What did you say?" the older guy asked Kazmir.

"I said I promise," Kazmir said, rubbing his jaw.

"You promised already," the older man said. "We went into business with you on the basis of that promise. And what happened? You broke your promise."

"I got greedy, okay? I mean, it's not like I hurt anybody, I just—"

"You did get greedy. And now they're on to you. And if they find out what's going on—"

"They won't. I promise."

The older man shook his head. "And here we are at promises again."

Kazmir ran a hand through his hair. He looked a mess. Matt had never seen him look a mess before.

"Why can't you just go away?" Kazmir said. "Go away and leave me alone." He looked like he was about to cry.

The older man's face tightened into anger as he took a step closer to Kazmir, who flinched and backed up. "That's how I'm starting to feel about you. I'm wishing you would just go away."

Some kind of deal gone bad, Matt realized. Something between Kazmir and the older guy. It was none of his business. He ought to just walk away. Kazmir was a jerk and probably whatever had gone wrong was his fault. Still...

Matt's heart went out to the guy. He wondered if he could help him.

The older man said something under his breath, and Matt took a step forward, straining to hear.

He stepped on a branch. It cracked like a gunshot.

The older man's head whipped around. So did Kazmir's. And the bodybuilder's.

"Who's there?" the old man said, more an order than a question.

Matt froze where he stood.

The bodybuilder took a step toward him. He was even scarier-looking from the front. He had no eyebrows. A big head. A round, squashed-in face. He looked like one of those wrestlers on TV. Craggy, exaggerated features. Matt knew what gave people that look: steroids. They gave you muscles, too.

They also made you a little bit crazy.

All thoughts of doing something to help Kazmir flew out of Matt's head. All he wanted was to get far, far away.

"Mr. Rawson," the older man said, and the big guy took another step forward. A very quick step, heading toward Matt. The guy wasn't just big, he was fast. Matt knew he would never be able to outrun him.

There was only one thing to do.

Bluff.

He took a deep breath and stepped forward, out of the woods.

The bodybuilder, halfway up the hill from the green, stopped and stared. So did the older guy on the green.

Matt smiled. "Hey, Bob," he said, looking right at Kazmir. He pulled the flask from his back pocket and took a sip. "What's up?"

"Thurman." Kazmir shook his head. "What the hell are you doing here?"

Matt held up the driver. "Got my ball in the trees here, so I was—"

The older guy said, "And you are?"

"Matt Thurman, a caddy," Kazmir said, in a tone that suggested caddies were the rough equivalent of pond scum. "Get out of here,

Thurman. This is none of your business."

"Okay," he said. He screwed the cap back on the flask, put it back in his pocket, and turned to leave.

"One moment please," the older man said. "Mr. Thurman, could you come here a moment?"

No, Matt wanted to say, but then he looked at the bodybuilder—Mr. Rawson—who stood poised about ten feet away, ready to strike. Matt walked down the hill onto the green. Rawson followed.

The older man looked him up and down. "So you're a caddy at The Pines?" he asked.

"That's right."

"And I take it you know my friend Bob Kazmir."

"I do." He and Kazmir peered at each other.

The older man smiled. "Would I be correct in assuming you don't like each other very much? I sense there's a history between you two."

Matt was going to deny it, then said, "Yeah. Some."

"A stroke of luck." The man offered a smile that was more like a slash across his face. "Of course, I don't really believe in luck, as it were. What people call luck is nothing more than preparation meeting opportunity. That's how I got to where I am today. By learning to recognize opportunity. By preparing to take full advantage of it. It's the same in golf. You practice, practice, practice, so that when the moment comes..."

The old man looked toward Matt expectantly.

"Right," Matt said, after a few seconds of uncomfortable silence. "Practice, practice, practice."

"I play a bit myself, so I know how important time on the course is. Time at the tee." The older man held out his hand. "Can I borrow your club for a moment?"

"My driver?"

"Yes. Your driver. May I?"

Rawson, right behind Matt, took a step closer.

Matt held out the driver.

The older man took it.

Which was when Matt noticed that he was wearing gloves—a golf glove on each hand. Nobody wears two golf gloves.

"Thank you." The man gripped the club handle, squeezing it. Took a step back from Matt, positioned himself, and took a practice swing. "You see," he said, "I haven't had time to get on a course these last few weeks, and my swing has suffered. Wouldn't you agree?"

Matt shrugged. It wasn't so much the guy's swing as his stance. His feet were too far apart, his arms not extended enough, his wrists...

The older man smiled. Though dusk had settled onto the course, Matt could see a hard glint in the man's eyes that contradicted the smile. "Perhaps I need to hit first. Before you give me the benefit of your opinion." He pulled a ball from his pocket, plopped it on the ground, and positioned the club. "Am I forgetting anything?"

Matt couldn't muster a reply.

"Something you're supposed to say before you swing?" The older guy looked to the bodybuilder.

"Fore," the big man said.

The older man turned around and stared at Kazmir.

"Fore," he said, and swung.

Not like Jack Nicklaus.

Like Barry Bonds.

He swung right at Kazmir. Hit him square in the side of the head.

Kazmir dropped to the ground without a sound.

Matt stood frozen in shock.

The older man brought the club down a second time. Brought it right down on Kazmir's head.

It made a sound like a pumpkin smashing on concrete.

31

"What the hell," Matt said, stepping forward.

A steel band constricted around his waist.

The big guy's arms. The bodybuilder. Mr. Rawson.

Matt gasped for breath. There was no air left in his lungs.

Rawson squeezed. He kept squeezing. Matt groaned, tried to pry the fingers apart. Useless. He couldn't do anything. All he could do was watch. The older guy, swinging the club. Again, and again, and again. He didn't look angry. He looked focused—intensely focused.

Matt kicked Rawson. Got him a good one on an ankle. Didn't seem to hurt him at all. The big man just squeezed harder. Tighter.

The world spun in front of Matt's eyes. Oxygen. He needed oxygen.

Then the ground reached up and smacked him in the face. He lay on the green, gasping for air.

He looked up and saw the older guy handing him the driver.

The clubface glistened with something wet. Something red.

"You can have this back."

The club fell on the ground next to him.

"What..." Matt's voice caught in his throat; he couldn't manage more than a whisper. "What are you doing?"

"I thought it was fairly obvious." The older man crouched down next to him. "I'm framing you for murder."

BOOK ONE: GAMBIT

MATT tried to focus.

He looked at the older man, and past him at Kazmir's body lying on the green, at the moon shimmering on the lake, and the hill covered with flowers beyond that, and the tee box on top of that hill, and lights in the distance beyond, maybe lights from the clubhouse, from the dining room that looked out over the course, and the caddies locker room behind that, where Kyle Fukanaga was probably waiting to close up, wondering how much longer Matt was going to play. On Sunday nights, Kyle liked to be out of there by nine.

Hey, Kyle, Matt thought to himself. I'm here, on twelve. I'm done playing. Come and get me. Come quick.

I'm being framed for murder.

"He dropped this."

Rawson held out something silver in his hand so the older man could see it. The flask, Matt realized.

The older man took it, unscrewed the top, and sniffed.

"Get him on his feet."

Matt was up before the older man finished talking, up and running, stumbling in the direction of the lake.

He made it all of four steps before Rawson grabbed him from behind.

Matt started to scream for help, but then one of the big man's arms wrapped around his throat, and he could barely breathe again, much less talk.

Rawson spun him around, and dragged him till he was face-to-face with the older man, who raised the flask, bringing it toward Matt.

Matt's eyes widened as he realized what the older man intended to do.

33

He squeezed his mouth shut and turned away, shaking his head.

"Mr. Thurman," the older man said. "Don't make this any harder than it has to be. Let it be over. The sooner the better. Wouldn't you agree?"

Matt shook his head again. No, no, no, no. He tried to think of something to do, tried to break free of Rawson's grip, and he couldn't. He couldn't do anything but turn his head away, and then he couldn't even do that, Rawson forced it back around till he was facing the older man again, six inches away.

The older man and the open flask.

"Open wide, and then it will be over. We'll leave you alone."

Framed for murder.

Matt managed a half-scream, a cry for help instantly choked off by Rawson.

"Open."

Matt looked away, squeezed his mouth shut. Then he felt a hand on the bridge of his nose, fingers on his face, fingers squeezing his nostrils shut.

He couldn't breathe.

He tried not to panic. Counted to five. Eight. Ten. Writhing in Rawson's grip, kicking out, twisting, all to no effect.

He heard someone moaning and realized it was himself. Tears stung his eyes.

Opened his mouth and gasped for air.

Metal slammed into his teeth. Hard. The flask jammed into his mouth. He cried out in pain; someone grabbed his hair and yanked his head backward, and liquor—Jack Daniels Tennessee Whiskey—spilled down his throat.

He coughed.

Rawson's voice in his ear—"Throw up, and I'll make you eat it."

Matt's throat burned. He looked up and saw stars in the sky

above him. Rawson's face above him. Showing no emotion at all, like a sphinx.

How full was the flask? It was a pint; it was full before he came to the course, he'd had a few sips, definitely a few good-sized shots left. How drunk could you get on a few good-size shots?

Drunk enough to fail a breathalyzer. Drunk enough to make it look like...

He gagged, and coughed.

The older man pulled out the flask.

"Breathe," he said

And Matt took a deep breath. "Wait," he gasped. "Please, I—"

The flask was back in his mouth, the taste of liquor back in his throat. It kept coming and coming.

"Good," the older man said. "Very good."

And then the liquor stopped. The older man pulled the flask out of his throat and dropped it on the ground.

There was a fire in Matt's chest. The liquor burned. It wasn't hitting his head yet; give it a few more minutes.

Rawson let him go. Matt wobbled on his feet and stood straight.

His head spun in dizzy circles. He opened his mouth. Rawson clamped an arm around his neck again.

"Can't have him screaming," Rawson said. "Not just yet."

"You're right of course." That was the older man's voice.

Rawson squeezed.

Matt grabbed at the man's one arm with both of his hands. Tried to pry it loose, just a little. He couldn't. Couldn't breathe. Rawson was too strong.

They were going to kill him. No. The whole point of this was the frame. I wish you'd go away, that's what Kazmir said to the older man, that's what the older man said back to him, luck equals preparation plus opportunity—

Matt saw stars.

Then he was down on the ground, coughing, gasping.

Looking up at the older man, who shook his head.

He had, Matt saw now, remarkable eyes. Cobalt blue.

"Almost," the older man said. "Almost."

Rawson's arm closed around his neck again.

The world faded to black.

Matt went with it.

❖ ❖ ❖ ❖ ❖

He was having a nice dream.

He was lying on an examining table, in Dr. Leffel's office. Leffel was smiling, and Matt found himself smiling too.

I was wrong, Leffel said. It was just a muscle pull. Nothing to do with the bursa sack.

So I'm good to go? Matt asked.

You're good to go.

The dream scene shifted to The Pines. The thirteenth green. No, the twelfth.

It all rushed back to him.

He sat up and coughed, and then threw up on the grass.

Pitch dark now. How long had he been out? How much time had passed?

He could see Kazmir's body, off to his right. The bloody club between them.

Framed for murder.

It had happened. It had really happened.

Phlegm dribbled from the corner of his mouth. He wiped it away, tried to get to his feet, stumbled, and went to his knees, just barely missing the vomit.

He could smell it though. His stomach rolled.

He was woozy. No, he was drunk. The world wouldn't stop spinning.

What do I do, Matt thought. What do I do?

He looked at Kazmir, at the club. Moonlight glinted off the metal shaft.

Throw it in the lake. Get rid of the evidence. Did that make sense? No. He could hear Jake's voice in his head. Jake, his older brother, a cop in Columbus. Call the police. Tell them what happened. Tell them about Rawson and the older guy. Would they believe him? They'd have to, it was the truth. Cops were good guys, his brother was a good guy, what to do, what to do—

"Matt!"

He froze.

"Matt! Where are you?"

The voice floated from behind him, from the trees between twelve and thirteen. He recognized it. Kyle Fukanaga.

Come and save me, Kyle, I'm on twelve, he remembered thinking that, and now Kyle was here. Kyle was his friend. Kyle had been working at The Pines ever since Matt could remember, from the time he was a teenager and used to come watch the Classic with his grandfather. Kyle gave him the job as a caddy after the shoulder injury. He could tell Kyle what had happened: couldn't he? Good old Kyle.

"Good old Kyle," Matt said aloud. Everything was going to be all right. He knew it now.

"Matt?"

He looked up the hill and saw Kyle framed in the moonlight, looking down on the green.

"Yeah," he said, and took a step forward and stumbled.

"You all right?" Kyle asked.

He smiled and met Kyle's eyes. "I'm drunk, but it's not my fault.

37

It's these two guys, they..."

He shook his head. This wasn't coming out right.

"Something crazy happened, Kyle. Something bad. These two guys—one of them was like a wrestler or a bodybuilder. They framed me."

His tongue felt thick in his mouth.

"Flamed you?" Kyle peered at Matt.

Another figure stepped out from the trees behind Kyle.

Matt recognized him too. The night guard at the gate. Harvey. Retired Air Force MP. Military guy. Like those guys who framed him.

"You found him," Harvey said.

Kyle nodded. "He's a mess."

"Not my fault," Matt said. "These two guys—"

"We got a call," Harvey said, stepping past Kyle, toward Matt. Down the hill, toward the green. "Something about a fight."

"Not a fight," Matt said. "Murder." The second the word came out of his mouth, he wanted it back.

Harvey stopped on the hill, and looked past Matt, at Kazmir's body, face down on the green. Matt stepped toward him, trying not to slur his words. "Everything gonna be all right. Listen, Kyle, me and you, we go way back, right, we..."

He tried to smile, but that warm feeling he'd had in his gut a few minutes ago was suddenly gone.

"Oh, Matt," Kyle said. "What did you do?"

Harvey pulled a walkie-talkie off his belt. Pressed a button on it. "Fourteen two, over," he said. "Fourteen two."

A voice crackled, "This is two, over."

"Yeah," Harvey said. "I'm at twelve, I need you to call the police. Right now. That report we got. No, just get them here. Right to twelve. They can come in on Augusta."

Harvey walked past him, still talking. Walked up to Kazmir,

looked at the body, at the club. Looked back at Matt, who blurted, "I didn't do anything, I was playing on thirteen and they took my driver, hit Kazmir with it." He looked at Kyle. It was dark, but Matt could read his body language.

He didn't believe a word Matt was saying.

Harvey clearly felt the same way.

Framed for murder.

What to do?

He ran.

❖ ❖ ❖ ❖ ❖

It was more like a stumble; he felt Kyle grab at him as he went past.

Matt shoved him away. Heard Kyle fall backward down the slope.

"Hey!" Harvey yelled after him. "Don't make it worse!"

Harvey kept yelling. So did Kyle. But Matt kept running, up into the trees, pushing away branches, running back the way he'd come, his mind racing along with his legs, trying to think, and the main thing he was thinking was Jake, get in touch with Jake, and he reached into his pocket and felt for his cell phone.

It wasn't there.

Of course it wasn't there, it was back in his locker. No cell phones on the golf course, hard and fast rule. Back to his locker, that's where he had to go. Back to the clubhouse. He had to get there before the cops arrived, get on the phone to Jake, get him to straighten out this whole mess.

He remembered Jake talking about some movie he'd seen where the main character got framed. Put in prison for five years. Cops wouldn't fall for that in real life, Jake had said. Cops aren't that stupid. Criminals aren't that smart.

Except that guy on the golf course had seemed pretty smart.

We got a call, Harvey had said. No doubt part of the frame. How else had they set him up? Could he count on the cops figuring it out?

No. He could count on Jake. That was the only thing he was sure of. He had to get to Jake. Had to get to his phone, get to the clubhouse.

Only one way to do that now.

He ran. Staying in the shadows, sticking close to the low stone wall that separated the course from the real estate development that surrounded it. Stumbling, tripping sometimes, paralleling the cart path downhill, trying to stay quiet, one foot in front of the other, tasting the whiskey in his throat, seeing the older guy in his mind swinging the club, seeing Kazmir fall...

He stopped running.

The clubhouse was right in front of him.

There were police cars—six at least, seven, eight, too many to count—parked in front, lights flashing.

He doubled back till he was parallel with the eighteenth green, looking up at the back of the clubhouse, at the dining room and the big bay windows, the pro shop underneath, and around the corner, just out of sight from where he stood, the rear entrance to the caddies' locker room.

He had to cross about four hundred yards of open space to reach it.

Four hundred yards of cart path, cutting uphill first, running between the green at seventeen and the eighteenth tee, then jogging left, paralleling the eighteenth fairway, leading right up to the clubhouse. Four hundred yards.

He could do it. He had to do it.

Framed for murder.

He walked out of the trees, out of the shadows, onto the cart path path. Started up the rise, not running now, walking, trying not to look out of place, just another employee, black pants, green shirt, coming from the course at the end of another long Sunday, getting ready to head home.

When he reached the top of the hill, he turned. Streetlights lined the path, every few hundred feet. The clubhouse was right in front of him, the course on his left, more houses on his right. Almost there.

He walked faster, past the houses, past a backhoe in the middle of the eighteenth fairway, a tarp stretched over part of the turf, where they were working on one of the bunkers, like they were always working on something, trying to improve the course, that was The Pines for you, that was why after the shoulder injury he'd come back here rather than stay in Florida.

A couple hundred feet in front of him, figures stepped out of the shadows of the clubhouse. Matt stopped, peered into the darkness. No way to tell who they were, what they were doing. Could just be some of the members, taking a stroll. Could be some of the staff, taking a cigarette break. No reason to panic.

Two broke off from the group. One gestured, pointing down the hill, onto the course. A familiar silhouette.

Harvey.

He looked again and saw that the second man was a cop.

Any second now, they could look his way.

Matt ran.

He pushed through the rear entrance, shoved through a second door and entered the caddy locker room. Lockers on the wall to his left, the showers right ahead of him, sinks and stalls to his right. Water hissed in the shower—somebody was in there, two somebodies, but he was alone in the locker area. He hurried to his locker, twirled the combination lock, and pulled out his phone.

He switched on the phone and punched the speed dial, number seven. Jake. He held the phone to his ear, listened to it ring.

He looked up and saw himself in a mirror.

The dark stain on his shirt was some combination of dirt and puke and blood. He had a scrape on his forehead, and a dry white crust covered half of one cheek.

The ringing in his ear stopped. A voice sounded.

"This is Jake Thurman."

"Jake!" Matt almost shouted. "Listen, I need your—"

"I can't get to the phone right now," the voice went on.

A recording. Damn. Matt waited for it to finish, so he could leave a message.

He wet a paper towel and wiped the crud off his face. Smoothed back his hair.

Footsteps sounded in the hall.

So did voices.

"Matt!"

That was Kyle.

"Matt Thurman!"

He didn't recognize that voice.

He shoved his phone into his pocket and ran out the back entrance of the locker room, up a set of stairs, and then through a pair of swinging wood doors into the main area of the clubhouse.

He hustled through the lounge, past leather chairs, a leather sofa, a coffee table in front of a big screen TV. A baseball game lit the screen. Two older guys sat on the couch watching the game. Matt recognized their faces but couldn't place their names. Past the lounge was the entranceway, the clubhouse foyer, past that, directly across from where he stood, was the members' locker room. Cut through there, Matt thought, take the stairs up a flight, and he could get outside again. Get back down to the ground, fade into the trees. Find another place to call Jake.

He took two steps forward—and froze.

Through a window behind the TV, he saw the front entrance to the club, where a dozen or so cops milled around. One of those cops held a walkie-talkie to his mouth then put it down and barked an order. He grabbed the front door and yanked it open. The others followed.

Matt looked to his right. There was a half-flight of stairs, leading up to the mixed grill. Stan, who'd been at The Pines forever, carried a pitcher of water toward the kitchen. Behind Stan a table full of club members, more than he'd ever seen in the place on Sunday evening, talked loudly, animatedly, and he didn't need to be a mind reader to know the topic of conversation.

He looked left. A door. He had no idea where it went.

He spun around and took a step toward the door he'd just come through, the door to the stairway, and grabbed...

And heard voices—headed his way.

Matt looked at the door to his left again and then at the cops walking into the building. The one in front stopped in the foyer to scan the room, looking left, to the locker room, then up the stairs to the mixed grill.

Matt took two quick steps, opened the door in front of him, and stepped inside.

He was in the card room. Empty. Card tables in front of him, a TV in the near corner. A bar across the room. Framed pictures on the wall. Past Classic champions: Trevino, Nicklaus, Woods, Hale Irwin, Tom Watson, the Shark, Vijay, Carl Petersson.

And Craig Driscoll.

Last week's winner. Luckiest golfer in America, Matt thought, remembering the shots the guy had hit. His putt the last day on thirteen, for an eagle. Unbelievable. Matt had never seen a ball move like that. Like a guided missile, straight to the hole.

He heard noises outside the door, bolted across the room, and knelt down behind the small bar in the corner.

And waited.

Thirty seconds. A minute. Two. Nothing. Quiet again.

He pulled out his phone and dialed.

Jake answered on the first ring.

"Matt."

Matt whispered, "Oh damn, Jake, I—"

"Calm down, buddy. Calm down."

"You don't understand," Matt said. He bit his lip. "They're after me."

"I know."

Matt paused. "You know?"

"I picked it up on the scanner. Talk to me. What happened?"

Matt told him about playing on the course, about the woman looking for Kazmir, about hearing the voices coming from the twelfth green, about the bodybuilder, and the older man, and how they took his driver, and they did what they did, and then they attacked him, tried to blame him.

"It's crazy," Matt said. "It's so damn crazy I can't even ... I don't know what to say."

"Yeah," Jake said, and fell silent.

Matt heard voices. At first he thought they were coming from the hall then realized they were on the phone. Voices on the line with Jake.

Matt said, "Where are you?"

"At the station." Jake cleared his throat. "Listen, kid. I'm sorry."

"What? What do you mean you're sorry?"

"I mean you've got to come in. We got reports. You have a gun, you were threatening some of the staff."

Stood up without realizing it. "That's crazy, I don't..."

Then he stopped talking. Voices outside the card room. Footsteps, too. A lot of them.

"Jake," he said, his voice trembling.

The door to the card room burst open.

A cop charged in, weapon drawn, pointing at Matt. Another cop right behind him.

"On the floor!" the first cop yelled. "On the floor, now!"

"Do it," the second one said, as the room filled. More cops, more guns.

Matt's heart raced.

Jake's voice in his ear: "Now, Matt. Do it."

Matt dropped the phone and went to his knees.

Franklin County Detention Center
South Front Street
Columbus, OH
Monday, September 10, 3:30 A.M.

HE rubbed his eyes.

He heard a ticking sound and looked up.

The minute hand—black against the white clock face—had moved again.

3:31 A.M.

"Matt."

Matt turned to the voice. His brother's voice.

Jake was sitting opposite him, on one side of a gray metal table in a folding metal chair. Next to Jake sat David Abraham.

"Focus, buddy. Focus." Jake looked a little angry, which was how Jake always looked. A bigger, angrier version of Matt. Two years older, two inches taller, thirty pounds heavier. Hair cut short. Military. Like the guys on the twelfth green. Jake had always been the clean-cut one of the pair. Matt's hair had always been longer, a wild tangle of curls, the wild little brother to straight-laced Jake. Otherwise, they looked like brothers, same light-brown hair and dark eyes, similar features.

"Anything else you remember about them? Those two guys?" David scribbled notes on a yellow legal pad on the table in front of him. He'd been a friend of Jake's and Matt's since they were kids, and even though now David was a hot-shot lawyer, Matt still saw him as the guy who played ball with them, discovered girls with them, a kid from the neighborhood.

"I can't think of anything," Matt said.

David flipped back a page on his pad.

"The older guy."

"Yeah."

"He was wearing gloves when he took the club from you."

"Yeah."

"Did he have them on when you first showed up? Did he put them on while you were talking?"

Matt shook his head. "I can't remember, really. It was dark."

"Because if he put them on while you were talking—if he put them on to take the club from you – it's possible he might've touched something we can lift prints from."

"Like what? The grass?"

"Like he might've dropped something, smartass," Jake said. "A pencil, a piece of paper, a gum wrapper."

David nodded. "We can get somebody out there tonight—this morning, I mean—go over the grounds."

Jake nodded. "I'll do it myself."

"If he didn't have those gloves on the whole time," David continued. "That's the only way it makes sense to do that, to spend that time and energy."

"I don't know," Matt said. "I really don't."

David tapped the pencil on the pad.

"If he had those gloves on the whole time," he said, and stood up, "then there's a good chance he went there intending to kill Kazmir. They were in business together, you said."

Matt opened his mouth to reply, and realized that David wasn't expecting an answer, that he was just talking to himself.

"So we have to ask what kind of business," David went on. "Doubtful it had anything to do with golf, so we have to file some kind of motion to get Kazmir's banking records, find out what else he was into. He was married, right, so we'll have to get his wife's permission, get her records too, in fact, and that'll mean…"

David went on. Matt took a deep breath and rubbed his left wrist. The skin was still raw from the handcuffs. His shoulder ached too, from what the cops had done after charging into the card room. Put him down on the ground, yanked both arms behind his back and cuffed his wrists. Then they stood him up, marched him through the clubhouse, past Kyle and the members in the dining room, the members in the lounge, everyone staring, Matt staring back, trying to decide what to say, whether to say anything at all, and then it was too late, he was out the front door, he was gone.

Framed for murder.

He shut his eyes, shook his head.

He pictured the older guy, taking his driver. Swinging it. Kazmir hitting the ground.

Kyle, staring at him. Harvey too.

"Kid."

Matt opened his eyes. Jake and David staring at him.

There was a policewoman in the room now. Husky woman with curly dark hair. She was staring at Matt too. He read the clock over her shoulder. 3:44.

Whoa, Matt thought. I fell asleep.

"You want anything? From White Castle?" Jake jerked his head in the woman's direction. "Officer Sherrill's going."

Matt shook his head. "No. I'm good."

As far as coffee went, at least, he was good. He'd drunk half a pot after they brought him in, after the fingerprinting and the mug shot. They sat him down in the interrogation room and tried to pry loose a confession. Matt had heard enough stories from Jake to know that's how they did it, not even good-cop bad-cop just good cop, guy coming in with the coffee, hot, fresh, smelling good, pouring Matt a cup, saying hey, something went bad out there, something happened you never meant to have happen, I don't know how it went down but the important thing is that you get your side of the story in front of the judge, let them see what it was really like, I mean we're talking manslaughter, not murder, maybe even involuntary manslaughter if the guy pushed you, and I hear this guy Kazmir was an asshole, is that it, is that what happened, talk to me, Matt, did he push you, provoke you, threaten you maybe, did he, did he, did he, and the whole time Matt stayed quiet, waiting for Jake. Zipped his lip.

The detective just kept shaking his head. "I can't help you, Matt, if you won't help yourself. You want to help yourself out here, don't you? Don't you, Matt? Matt?"

Matt just stared at the wall.

"Matt?"

He looked up.

The clock read 3:59.

The woman was gone. Jake and David sat across from him at the table. Staring expectantly.

He'd zoned out again.

"The woman," David flipped back a page on the pad. "The one who was looking for Kazmir. You got a good look at her, right? Brown hair, early thirties, maybe Hispanic."

"A pretty good look." Matt shrugged. "I guess."

"You guess?" Jake said. "What does that mean?"

"It means I'm tired, all right?"

"No. Not all right." Jake leaned forward into Matt's face. "You don't have time to be tired. You have to focus. Think about what happened, what you saw, what you heard...think about it now, while it's still fresh in your mind."

"My mind is shot."

"Then have more coffee," he said. "Have a donut. Suck it up, kid. This is your life on the line."

Jake glared, a vein in his temple throbbing.

"It's all right." David put his pencil down. "We can pick up tomorrow, after the arraignment. I have more than enough to get started."

He gathered his pencils and pads and stood. Jake stood too.

"Thanks again, David," Matt said, getting to his feet. "I appreciate this."

He and David shook hands.

"Hang in there," David said, and then buzzed for the cop to let him out.

"He's a good guy," Matt said after the door shut.

"Best lawyer in Franklin County," Jake said. "If there's a way to get you out of this, he'll find it. As long as you don't keep us in the dark."

"What are you talking about?"

"I'm talking about the DUI. Why didn't you tell me about that?"

"The DUI," he said. "I..."

Jake stared at him. Like a cop hearing one more story. Six months ago. Dead of winter, an icy road, he'd had a few beers, the car ahead slammed on its brakes, he couldn't stop in time, skidded into a snow bank on 270, the cops came, made him walk the white line. "What does that have to do with anything?" he managed.

Jake shook his head. "That's prior evidence of a drinking problem. If the sergeant hadn't given me a peek at your record, the D.A. would've sandbagged us with that. Made us look like idiots."

Matt nodded.

"Listen. This whole thing is a wake-up call, you understand? You got to make some changes in your life. You wanted to be a golfer, you gave it a shot, fine, but now—"

Matt gave him a dry laugh. "We're going to have this conversation now? In the middle of the worst night of my life?"

"There's a reason you're here, a reason you hit rock bottom. A reason why Nancy left you, why you're—"

"I'M HERE BECAUSE SOMEBODY FRAMED ME FOR MURDER!" Matt yelled. "THAT'S WHY I'M HERE!"

Jake glared at him a moment longer.

Matt ran a hand through his mop of curls and sat down. "We need to find those guys."

"Them and that woman whose name you didn't get."

"Meaning what? You think I've been making this up?"

"I believe you met them. I'm not sure you just weren't too drunk to remember their names."

Jake shoved his chair in, slamming it against the desk. Then he kicked it.

Then he left the room.

❖ ❖ ❖ ❖ ❖

The next day started just as badly.

It felt like he'd hardly had time to get comfortable on the skinny holding-cell mattress before the cops came back. New ones, blond-haired, square-jawed, freshly scrubbed, freshly shaven cops.

"Time to see the judge," the first guy snapped. He smelled of aftershave and soap.

"Could I get a shower maybe, before we—"

"On your feet," the other one said sharply. They cuffed him, hands behind his back, and marched him out of the holding cell, onto an elevator, and into a courtroom that looked more like a train station waiting room than a hall of justice.

David stood at a long wooden table. He smiled. "You all right?"

Matt nodded and looked around the courtroom. "Where's Jake?"

"Working." David avoided his eyes.

Before Matt could ask any questions, the judge—black man, black robe, white hair—slammed his gavel. "Next case."

The bailiff stepped forward. "People versus Matthew Thurman." He handed the judge a folder. The judge flipped through it, then looked at David.

"And how does your client plead, Mr. Abraham?"

"Not guilty, your honor."

The prosecutor, a young man who looked to be all of nineteen years old, stepped forward. "People ask for bail in the amount of one million dollars."

Matt's eyes widened. "Whoa." He turned to David. "You said fifty would be the most they'd—"

David put a hand on Matt's arm.

He smiled at the judge. "The amount is excessive, your honor. My client is hardly a risk for flight. He has ties to the community."

"He's got a one-room efficiency in Grandview," the young prosecutor said. "He's got $321 in his bank account. There is the possibility of premeditation, as well as a history of—"

"If I could finish," David said, looking at the judge as if they were together in indulging an overly enthusiastic boy. "His brother is a highly decorated police officer, as was his father." David moved a step closer to the judge. "He's a lifelong resident of the area."

The judge held up his hand. "I can read, gentlemen, I can read." Then he banged his gavel again. "Bail is set at five hundred thousand dollars."

The cop standing behind Matt said, "Let's go, buddy."

"Half a million dollars?" Matt came close to shouting it. He looked at the judge, then at the bailiff, then back at David.

The cop's hand tightened on his arm.

David turned and said, "Not now, Matt," with his teeth clenched.

The cops stepped forward, one on either side.

Each grabbed an arm and led Matt away.

❖ ❖ ❖ ❖ ❖

There was a clock on the wall outside the holding cell. Black hands, white clock face, exactly like the one in the interrogation room.

11:25.

Matt sat on the edge of his bunk. Where he'd been for the last half hour. Thinking.

Half a million dollars. What now?

"I'm sorry."

He looked up and saw David standing outside his cell.

"You never know, with bail."

Matt sighed. "I'm sorry for flying off the handle."

"I can get a $500,000 bond for about fifty grand. Is that a possibility?"

"Sure, if you can lend me fifty grand."

David managed a slight smile. "I just talked to Jake. He doesn't have it either."

Matt paced the little cell. Ten feet, end to end, five feet, side to side. Not a lot of room. "So what's that mean?" he asked. "If I don't make bail?"

"It means you have to stay in jail. Until the trial."

"And how long till the trial?"

"Depends. How long discovery takes, how many motions they file, how many we file, the judge's calendar, a lot of factors."

Matt stopped pacing, put his hands on the bars, and stood face to face with David. "But how long? Ballpark? A couple weeks?"

David sighed. "Case like this...I can't lie to you. Six months, minimum."

"Six months?"

He sat back down on the bunk.

"You won't do the time here," David added quickly. "You'll be in one of the county facilities—minimum security, I'll push for that, and you'll have things to do, they have a gym, they've got cable, live entertainment sometimes..."

Matt stood up and started to pace again.

"You've got to find those guys, David. Rawson, and the old guy, and that woman. Find that woman."

"We're working on it. I'm getting videotape from the guardhouse at The Pines. They tape every car going in and out. We'll look at it together, soon as I have it in my hands. Later today, maybe tomorrow."

"Good." He hesitated a second. "So where's Jake?"

"He's working." David said. This time, he met Matt's eyes. "He's out there, Matt. Took a couple days off from the job, he's calling in a few favors, he's on it."

"Tell him thanks."

"You can tell him yourself. He'll come in with me when I bring the tapes."

Matt nodded weakly. "Listen, I can't tell you how much I appreciate this."

"Just don't go mouthing off to the judge anymore. All right?" David was smiling, but there was a little steel in his voice and his eyes.

Matt nodded. "No more mouthing off to the judge."

David smiled again, and this time it reached his eyes. He made his hand into a fist, put it through the bars. Matt made his into a fist too, and knocked it against David's. Just like when they were kids.

"We'll beat this thing," David said. "Just a matter of time."

"Right."

David left. Matt plopped on the bunk and looked up at the ceiling. Just a matter of time.

About six months.

He closed his eyes.

❖ ❖ ❖ ❖ ❖

Somehow he fell asleep.

He woke up when they brought lunch. Hamburger, fries, and a salad. Cold, greasy, wilted. Matt took a few bites and pushed the plate aside.

When the guard came to take it, he asked for something to read.

The guard snorted. "I got a Bible. You want that?"

Matt shook his head and went back to staring at the ceiling. Thinking about Kazmir, and Jake, and Nancy. The DUI, and his shoulder, and the murder, and the last three years of his life. He should be playing pro golf, not sitting in a jail cell.

He rubbed the shoulder.

Dinner came. Spaghetti and meatballs. Rubbery meatballs. Just like momma used to make. He wondered if momma was going to show up. If Jake had called her. Earliest she could get here, he figured, was tomorrow, so he decided not to worry about that conversation yet.

He ate the meatballs. He got indigestion. He lay on the hard, thin, rubber mattress and willed his stomach to stop rumbling. Eventually it did.

Eventually—despite the light right outside his door, shining into the cell—he fell asleep.

The sound of the cell door swinging open woke him.

He saw a man standing in the doorway.

"Three minutes," the man said, and stepped inside.

Franklin County Detention Center
South Front Street
Columbus, OH
Tuesday, September 11, 1:58:30 A.M.

MATT sat up. Tried to get his brain working.

"Three minutes." The man looked at his watch. The face glowed light blue in the darkness. "Make that two minutes and fifty-two seconds."

He had a deep voice, a faint accent of some kind. Hispanic?

He was shorter than Matt and stocky. Wearing a dark shirt, dark pants, a coat of some kind, a little shiny in the darkness, maybe a windbreaker.

"Who are you?" Matt asked, still groggy with sleep.

"I set this up so we would have three minutes. How much more of that time do you want to waste?" The man moved closer. Matt squinted, tried to make out his features. He couldn't see much. The cell was close to pitch-dark, the only light coming from the exit sign down the hall, a faint reddish glow.

The light bulb directly opposite the cell, he realized, had somehow gone out.

"Set what up? I don't understand."

The man reached into his pocket and tossed something onto the cot next to Matt. It bounced and landed on the floor.

"Ten thousand dollars," the man said.

Matt's pulse quickened. He reached down and picked it up. It was an envelope. Loosely sealed. He opened it.

It was money, all right. A lot of it.

Ten thousand dollars?

"There's a red Camry in the parking lot to your right, as you leave the building. Indiana plates. The keys are in it. The tank is full."

"I don't get it."

"You're being framed," the man said. "I'm offering you a way out."

Matt looked up at the stranger in his cell. He felt the money in his hand. Ten thousand dollars. A red Camry. A way out.

This was all happening too fast.

"Wait a second." Matt got to his feet. This didn't make sense. Then he smiled. "Jake." He took a step back. "You're one of Jake's friends. He sent you, right?"

"No." The man looked at his watch. "Two minutes. Then the lights come back on, the guards come back on duty."

"But if Jake didn't send you—"

"One minute fifty-one seconds. I'll leave you alone for the last thirty. Let you make up your mind. But that last half-minute is always a little iffy. Somebody counts wrong, somebody comes back too soon...I wouldn't walk out of the cell at zero and expect it all to go smoothly."

"Wait a second!" Matt yelled.

The man's hand was suddenly around his throat. His fingers clamped down hard. The guy was strong—a lot stronger than he looked.

Before Matt could even react, the grip relaxed.

"Do that again, and we're both in deep shit," the man said.

Matt pulled back and took a deep breath. "Who are you?" he said. "Why are you doing this?"

"I don't have time to explain."

"But if I run, it's as good as saying I'm guilty. If I run, I got to keep running."

"One hundred seconds. I'll give you sixty of them." He looked at his watch again. "Starting now."

He began to talk.

❖ ❖ ❖ ❖ ❖

"Kazmir was mixed up with some bad people. They're the ones who killed him."

"The guys on the golf course."

The man nodded. "They're part of it."

"It?"

"Something we've been looking into the last few months."

"You're a cop?"

"Close enough."

"FBI, CIA, something else?"

The man shook his head. "I can't tell you that."

"But you know I'm being framed. Why don't you just tell the judge?"

"I have nothing to offer in the way of evidence."

"But you know who those guys are."

"I know *what* they are. Not who."

"What they are? What does that mean?"

"Harper will fill you in."

"Who's Harper?"

"That's thirty seconds gone," the man said.

Matt turned around and walked to the far wall of the cell. He almost ran into it. He turned and walked back. "What happens after I get out?"

"You help us fill in the blanks. Harper will tell you about it."

"Yeah, right. Harper."

"Forty seconds gone," the man said.

Matt turned away again. This was crazy. Who was this guy? How had he gotten in here, gotten the cops away from their posts? Had he drugged them? Hurt them? Killed them? Was he really a cop himself? Was there really a red Camry to go along with the money, was it really ten thousand dollars or just an envelope full of singles? Too many questions and no answers whatsoever.

He turned back. "I can't do it." He shook his head. "I'll risk a trial."

"There's not going to be a trial."

"No trial?"

"You're being transferred to county jail number two tomorrow afternoon. We have an informant there." The man stepped closer. "He told me there's already a price on your head. A very big price."

"Somebody wants to kill me?"

"Your friends from the golf course. They aren't going to let you stand up in a courtroom and identify them."

Matt felt the envelope in his hand.

Ten thousand dollars. A price on his head. The guys from the golf course.

He snapped his fingers. "There's a videotape," he said. "The gatehouse at The Pines, they keep track of every car coming in and out, those guys must be on it, Rawson and the other one."

"I've seen it. There's nothing on it you'd be interested in. You or your lawyer." He stepped out of the cell. "Forty seconds. I have to go."

"Wait. No. You got to give me more."

"I'll give you a phone number," the man said. "588-5377. Area code 513. That's Cincinnati. Got it?"

Matt nodded.

"Repeat it to me."

"513-588-5377."

"You drive to Cincinnati, you call that number, you ask for Harper."

"What happens after that?"

"You don't call anyone else," the man said, ignoring Matt's question. "Not your lawyer, not your brother. Give me the number again."

"513-588-5377. In Cincinnati. Harper."

"Good. Your thirty seconds starts now."

The man crossed to the wall opposite the cell door.

"Cover your eyes," he said, and Matt did, and a split-second later the light came on—sudden, sharp, blinding.

Matt blinked. Tried to focus and couldn't.

When his vision came back, the guy was gone.

And the cell door stood open.

Thirty seconds. Make it twenty-five now.

I wouldn't walk out of the cell at zero and expect it all to go smoothly.

He felt the envelope in his hand.

Ten thousand dollars.

A red Camry.

Jake, and David, and his mom. And Nancy. What would they think if he ran? That he'd done it, and bribed a cop to get out? That Jake had bribed someone?

That was how it was going to go down, Matt realized. Jake would take the fall. He couldn't run.

The guy said there's not going to be a trial.

This was crazy.

He started to turn and pace, only he realized he didn't have time to do any pacing, he had to decide now. This instant. Did he believe the guy or not?

He looked around the cell. Five by ten. For six months. If he was lucky.

There's not going to be a trial.

Maybe just a few days of it before somebody in the jail killed him.

Fifteen seconds. Maybe ten, who the hell knew.

He heard a metallic click down the hall. Almost like a light switch being thrown on—or coming on automatically.

That last half-minute is always a little iffy. Somebody counts wrong, somebody comes back too soon...

He ran.

The Carlyle Residences
Wilshire Boulevard
Beverly Hills, CA
Tuesday, September 11, 12:02 A.M.

EVERYBODY in L.A. was obsessed with their bodies—sculpting them, toning them, making them look sleek and sexy. Shurig had never seen anything like it. Not in New York, not in Miami, not in Rome, certainly not in Turkey or Nairobi or any of the other places he'd lived.

Sam Hernandez had a theory: inbreeding.

"These people," he would say as they came back from lunch, walking down Westwood or Gayley, "these movie stars, singers, whatever, they come here, make a ton of money and marry each other. Right? You read about it in the papers all the time. That's what they do, marry each other?"

He'd look at Shurig and then go on without waiting for an answer.

"Okay, maybe they don't get married. Either way, they have sex, have beautiful kids, who then marry other beautiful kids, who have even more beautiful kids, who are so obsessed with how they look they spend the whole day going from hair stylist to clothes stylist to personal trainer."

Shurig would shake his head or cluck his tongue, unconvinced.

"Let's find out," Sam would say, and walk up to the nearest perfect-looking person—nine times out of ten a woman, because Hernandez, never mind his age and crooked teeth, had an eye for the ladies, knew how to talk to them—and ask where they were coming from, where they were going, and more often than not...

The gym.

But Shurig knew that as perfectly sculpted as their bodies looked, these people weren't hard at all. They were butter. Gym muscle was window dressing.

The guy standing in front of him now had gym muscle. Biceps

bursting under his short-sleeve shirt. Light blue. Matched his eyes. Went perfectly with his slacks. And the black nameplate pinned to the shirt pocket: Ethan.

"Hi, Ethan," Shurig said, stepping forward.

The doorman, though half a foot taller and sixty pounds heavier, stepped back.

Shurig had that effect on people. He had muscle, and it wasn't just gym muscle. Muscle he'd used on more than one occasion and would use again. People could sense that sort of thing.

"Good evening, sir." Ethan said, using the podium he stood behind to reassert himself. He put his hands on it and looked down on Shurig. "Can I help you?"

"We're here to see Mr. Njomo."

Ethan picked up a phone attached to the podium, and scanned the rows of buttons in front of him. There was a sign on the marble wall behind him:

BY ORDER OF CARLYLE BOARD OF DIRECTORS:
EFFECTIVE IMMEDIATELY:
ALL VISITORS MUST BE ANNOUNCED

"Mr. Manny Njomo," Ethan said. "Suite 3F."

"That's right," Shurig said.

"And who should I say is calling?"

"You shouldn't say anything. You should just buzz us in."

Ethan, his finger poised over one of the buttons, looked up. "It is almost midnight, sir," Ethan said. "Is Mr. Njomo expecting you?"

Shurig said, "I doubt it."

"I'm sorry, but we have regulations that forbid—"

"Excuse me," said the man behind Shurig. "This ought to clear things up."

He pulled out his billfold and slapped it on the podium in front of Ethan. "FBI," he said. "I'm Agent Kauffman, this is Agent Shurig." Kauffman nodded toward the glass door that led into the building. "Buzz us in, will you?"

Ethan did as he was told.

❖ ❖ ❖ ❖ ❖

The stair rail was some kind of dark wood, polished to an almost metallic sheen. There was gold leaf along the wall moldings. The carpet on the stairs was an inch thick, deep red, and very, very clean.

"Nice place," Shurig said, following Kauffman up the stairs. "Can't say much for the help, though."

Kauffman shook his head without turning. "Anybody ever tell you that you have an attitude problem, Mike?"

"Lots of people. But only once."

"Funny," Kauffman said.

But he didn't laugh. The man didn't seem to find anything funny. He'd been a banker in his previous life and still had a banker's demeanor. Very by-the-book. Which made him one of the office's favorite agents. They liked guys by the book, liked to know what they were doing today and what they would be doing tomorrow. Shurig didn't operate that way, a remnant of how he worked in his old job.

But Hernandez loved him. In the two months since Shurig joined the squad, he'd become one of Hernandez's favorites. Hernandez was the squad supervisor, and they had even become friends. He and Shurig liked to find humor in even the blackest situations. Hernandez would see the humor in Ethan. Figure an address like this, in the heart of Beverly Hills, the guy probably pulled down forty, maybe fifty thousand a year to look pretty and press a button once in a while. You'd think he'd feel a little obligation to the people who paid his salary, but the first time things get difficult—he's face-to-face with two FBI guys who want in—and he gives in like a wuss. That was the problem with the country; nobody had any regard for anything beside themselves.

At the third-floor landing, Kauffman turned right and stopped in front of 3F.

He turned to Shurig. "All set?"

"Absolutely."

Kauffman pressed the buzzer. No response. He pressed it again.

Shurig heard footsteps approaching the door. The sound of a peephole cover being flipped.

"Who is it?"

"Mr. Manny Njomo?"

"Who wants to know?"

Kauffman held his badge up to the peephole. "FBI. We have a few questions."

Silence.

"Isn't this a little late for a visit? Could we perhaps talk tomorrow? I'd be happy to come to your office, if you like."

Shurig stepped to the door. "Mr. Njomo, we're doing you the favor of asking. But we don't have to. We have a little thing called the Patriot Act now. We don't need a judge, we don't need a warrant."

"You have no cause to threaten me. I've done nothing wrong."

"Then you won't mind us coming in," Shurig said.

"We just have a few questions," Kauffman said. "We can talk and be on our way."

More silence.

Then the doorknob turned. A second later, the door opened—a crack at first, and then a little wider.

Shurig shoved it wide and stepped through.

❖ ❖ ❖ ❖ ❖

Njomo was skinny. Jet-black hair cut fashionably short, thin nose, olive skin—middle Eastern. More Persian than Semitic. He wore khakis, a plain black t-shirt, and a Rolex on his left wrist. No shoes or socks. Shurig would have gone barefoot too if he had a carpet like the one on the living room floor. White, spotless, even thicker than the one in the hall. Five hundred square feet of it, Shurig guessed. Probably cost as much as Shurig's car.

Njomo sat down on a long brown leather couch in front of a bay window that fronted Wilshire. Kauffman sat on a matching armchair opposite him. Shurig stood behind his partner.

"Can I get you anything to drink?" Njomo asked.

Shurig said, "No thanks."

"Then I suppose we should get to your questions. I have work to do."

"You work here, then?" Shurig asked.

"My office is right through that door." He pointed. Shurig turned reflexively, but he'd already caught a glimpse of the room after Njomo let them in. It was a pretty bare-bones office: a desk, a computer, a chair. The whole apartment was pretty bare bones, in fact: the couch and chair, a coffee table in front of them, and that was it for the living room. Bare walls. No TV.

"What kind of work do you do, Mr. Njomo?" Kauffman asked.

"I'm sure you know. Why else would you be here?"

"Humor me."

"I'm a technology consultant."

"Which means...?"

"Different things, depending on the client's needs."

Kauffman waited for more.

"I provide small to medium-sized corporations with software and hardware solutions appropriate to their budgets and requirements."

"You're a problem solver."

"Exactly."

"Good," Kauffman said, "because I have a problem."

"Let me guess. You have a question about the work I do for the AAAL."

"Yes I do."

Njomo gave a theatrical sigh. "I've had a dozen visits from the bureau in the last few years about this."

Kauffman pulled out his Blackberry, punched a few buttons, studied the screen, and then said, "You've been working for the Arab-American Amity League for...looks like about ten years."

"Twelve. Since the group was formed. I believe in the work they're doing."

"Arab-American Amity," Shurig scoffed. "We should all just get along."

Njomo glared at him and stood up. "I think I've had enough, gentlemen. I'm calling my lawyer."

Shurig blocked his path. Njomo slowly sat back down.

"So could you describe the work you do for the Arab-American Amity League?" Kauffman asked.

"I set up databases, recommended the purchase of certain pieces of hardware. Specific servers; workstations. A lot of my work involves simultaneous coding for both Arabic and English."

"And that's the extent of it?"

"I'm sure I haven't remembered every detail, but...yes."

Kauffman nodded. "Now I have another problem. You just lied to me. You want to try again? Tell me what it is you do for the AAAL."

"As I said, I may have forgotten certain details," Njomo said, "but my work for the Arab-American Amity League—"

"You hear about the raid in Denmark a few days ago?" Kauffman asked. "Oh no. You wouldn't have, that's right. We kept it quiet."

Njomo said, "I have no idea what you're talking about."

"The Icepack systems," Kauffman said.

Njomo stiffened.

"We finally got the Danish government to give us the okay to shut them down. Because they were a threat to national security. People would log in from their computers to Icepack and then, presto, they were anonymous. No way to track them. Terrorists could communicate by e-mail, could talk to each other in chat rooms, send each other money..."

"I want to talk to my lawyer," Njomo said, and started to stand up again.

This time, Shurig didn't even give him a chance. Just put a hand on the man's shoulder and sat him back down.

"We've had those servers for a few days," Kauffman said. "We've found a lot of interesting stuff—reconstructed things people thought would never see the light of day. For example..."

Kauffman pulled out his Blackerry and punched a few buttons. "On August fourteenth you sent a long list of instructions to a Mr. Thomas Hand of the Sayeed-Pearson bank in Riyadh, Saudi Arabia. The instructions included details on a series of wire transfers to be sent from the AAAL's account at Sayeed-Pearson, transfers totaling roughly eight million in U.S. dollars."

"I won't speak without a lawyer present." Njomo looked down at the thick white carpet. "I am not a terrorist," Njomo said. "These people are not—"

He shook his head.

"These people are not what?" Kauffman said.

Njomo remained silent.

"What were you going to say?" Kauffman asked. "These people are not what?"

Njomo remained silent.

"You're being stupid," Kauffman said. "We could be looking at the death penalty here. Treason. You understand? And if you think that after what happened to those kids at Long Beach any jury's going to hesitate to recommend the death penalty, you are sadly mistaken."

Njomo raked his fingers through his hair.

Kauffman leaned closer. "We know you're not the guy giving orders. You're not who we're after. Tell me what you know, Manny. I'll try and get you a deal. I'll help you if I can. If you help me."

Njomo started to hyperventilate.

He's going to cave, Shurig thought. Just like Ethan downstairs. No backbone whatsoever.

A buzzer sounded.

Kauffman frowned. "You expecting anyone?"

Njomo said, "No."

Shurig and Kauffman exchanged a glance. Shurig went to the intercom and pressed the button.

"This is Ethan downstairs. There's a Mr. Rawson here now."

"Rawson?" Shurig said.

"Oh my god," Njomo said. "Oh my god."

The man had looked scared before. Now he looked positively terrified.

"Who's Rawson?" Kauffman asked.

Njomo looked away, whispered, "He'll kill me."

"Then I think we ought to talk to him." Kauffman looked at Shurig, who told Ethan to send up Mr. Rawson.

Njomo put his head in his hands and started to cry.

❖ ❖ ❖ ❖ ❖

Kauffman moved to the couch next to Njomo, talking softly. Trying to get him to say something about Rawson. The man just kept shaking his head.

The bell rang.

Shurig opened the door and took a step backward.

The man entering the apartment was huge. Six four, maybe two hundred fifty pounds, most of it muscle. Not gym muscle. Blond hair buzzed in a marine cut, a nose that looked like it had been broken more than once.

Shurig held up his badge.

"FBI." Rawson stared at Shurig a second, and then shook his head.

Kauffman stepped forward. "You have some ID, Mr. Rawson?"

"Sure." Rawson wore a navy blazer over a black t-shirt and jeans; he reached into the inside pocket of the coat and frowned. "I left my wallet in the car."

"In the car."

"In the glove compartment. You want me to go get it?"

"Not right this second. Can you tell us why you're here?"

"To talk to Manny." The man took a few steps into the living room so he could get a look at Njomo.

"Talk to him about what?"

"It's personal. You all right, Manny?"

Njomo stared at the floor.

"Personal?" Kauffman said.

"Like private. Like not your business."

"Everything to do with Mr. Njomo is my business."

The four men were arranged in a circle now, like points on a compass. Shurig standing opposite Njomo, who sat on the couch, Rawson to his left, Kauffman to his right.

"I didn't get your first name, Mr. Rawson," Kauffman said.

"Everybody just calls me Rawson."

"For the record," Kauffman said, putting a little edge in his voice. "Your first name."

Rawson smiled. "That's for my friends."

Kauffman shook his head. "Legally, under terms of the Patriot Act we—"

"You don't look like a lawyer," Rawson interrupted. "You a lawyer?"

Kauffman's eyes narrowed. The man had a thing about being interrupted. It made him angry, and a little careless.

Shurig reached inside his coat pocket; his fingertips brushed against the handle of his gun.

"All right," Kauffman said. "You don't like that question, I have another for you. Why is your good friend Manny here so afraid of you?"

"Of me?" Rawson shook his head.

"I didn't say anything," Njomo said. "Not a word." He looked up at Rawson like a little boy expecting to be disciplined by his father.

"He said," Kauffman continued, "that you were going to kill him."

Rawson laughed.

"Why would he say that?" Kauffman asked.

"I have no idea."

"What's your connection with Mr. Njomo?"

"Like I said. We're friends."

"You in business together?"

Rawson said nothing.

"What line of work you in, Mr. Rawson?"

Still nothing.

"I changed my mind," Kauffman said. "I would like you to get your driver's license. I want to see it. I'll send Agent Shurig with you, to make sure you don't get lost on the way back."

Rawson looked at Kauffman and then at Shurig. Then he shrugged. "John, okay? My first name's John."

"I'd like to see that license." Kauffman folded his arms across his chest. "Now."

Rawson smiled and put his hands up in the air, as if surrendering. "All right," he said. "I lied. I got the license right here." Rawson grabbed the lapel of his coat with his left hand and reached toward his inside pocket with his right.

"Stop," Kauffman said, and Rawson looked up and didn't just stop, he froze.

Kauffman had drawn his gun.

Shurig drew his weapon as well.

"Oh god," Njomo said. "Oh god, oh god."

Kauffman said, "Take it nice and easy."

"You're the one with the gun, chief. You take it easy."

Shurig kept his gun level.

"You want to see the license or not?" Rawson asked.

"Slowly," Kauffman said. "Reach into your pocket and hand it to me."

Rawson pulled out a long, black billfold and held it up in the air. "Satisfied?"

Kauffman lowered his weapon, holding out his hand.

Rawson stretched out his right hand with the billfold in it.

Njomo screamed. "Look out!"

As Rawson's right hand stretched toward Kauffman, the left hand reached behind him, pulling something out of the waistband of his pants, something metal. Something shiny.

A gun.

Kauffman started to raise his weapon. So did Shurig, who was moving too.

Rawson, though, was faster than either of them.

BOOK ONE: GAMBIT

Interstate 71
Ten miles south of Columbus, OH
Tuesday, September 11, 3:05 A.M.

THE guy in the cell had left a grocery bag in the passenger seat. Matt opened it after reaching the highway. Clothes. A gray sweatshirt and sweat pants. Running shoes. White socks. As he drove, he struggled into the sweatshirt, covering the bright orange jailhouse jumpsuit. A few miles outside Columbus he pulled off the highway, found a dark road and changed clothes—not easy to do in the front seat of the car. The clothes didn't exactly fit—too loose in the waist, too short in the arms and legs, but they worked well enough. He wadded the jailhouse jumpsuit and stuffed it in the grocery bag.

Never mind what the guy in the jail cell told him, Matt decided to call Jake. He stopped at a United Dairy Farmers, gave the clerk a twenty (the envelope was crammed full with them, used twenties and fifties, ten thousand dollars worth, maybe, who knew, he didn't have time to count), bought a prepaid cell phone, went into the rest room, and dialed his brother's number. He got the recording, not Jake. He didn't leave a message. He thought about calling David but decided against it.

He got back on the highway.

Drive to Cincinnati. Call 513-588-5377. Ask for Harper. 513-588-5377. Ask for Harper.

He chanted it as he drove.

❖ ❖ ❖ ❖ ❖

A half hour outside Cincinnati, he started to get paranoid. The driver in every car that passed him seemed to be staring at him. He got off the highway, got on Route 42, took it all the way to Hamilton County, south and west, reached the outskirts of Cincinnati at 4:31 A.M., by the dashboard clock. He had till nine o'clock, he figured, before he could call Harper. Four and a half hours. He could find a motel, leave a wake-up call, take a shower, get a few hours of sleep.

He found a Days Inn and parked. Sat in the car and drummed his fingers on the steering wheel.

He saw Kazmir, lying on the twelfth green. Kyle and Harvey staring at him as he tried to explain what had really happened.

David and Jake in the interview room, staring too.

The judge, banging his gavel.

The cop, bringing him dinner.

The guy who'd given him the car and the money, standing in his cell door.

There's not going to be a trial.

He saw his fingers still drumming on the steering wheel, faster than before. He knew he was too wired to sleep.

He pulled out of the parking lot and back onto 42. He passed the city limits sign—Welcome to Cincinnati, the Queen City—and kept going until the road ended. It dumped him into a deserted section of town, with wide boulevards, run-down old factory buildings on either side of them. He had no idea where he was: he'd only been to Cincinnati a couple times before, to see the Reds play. The ballpark was by the river; the river was nowhere in sight.

The picture on a Burger King billboard made him hungry. He drove around for ten minutes, looking for food, passing shuttered storefronts, darkened gas stations, a McDonald's that claimed a 24-hour drive-up window but police sawhorses blocked the entrance. He finally found a brightly lit white building near an entrance ramp to I-75. The sign above the entrance, red letters on white alphabet-block cubes three feet square, spelled out C-H-I-L-I. Below it: Camp Washington Chili. Chili was the last thing he felt like eating at five in the morning, but he stopped anyway, figuring they had other things on the menu.

The décor was classic diner—black and white linoleum floor, white formica tables, metal chairs with red cushions. A lot of chrome. The lights were very bright; the whole place was very bright. And clean. Spotlessly clean. It seemed to emphasize the stink of the jailhouse that covered his body. He needed a shower.

"Wherever you want to sit, honey."

Matt turned and saw a little dark-haired woman standing behind the counter, reading a newspaper spread in front of her. She looked at him and smiled.

He looked at her, at the paper, and his heart skipped a beat.

He pictured his mug shot splashed across the front page.

He did his best to smile anyway; he supposed he was being paranoid. The woman went back to reading. He saw a man at the rear of the restaurant, brewing the day's chili. He looked nice enough—gray hair, glasses, even gave Matt a friendly smile.

He chose a table at the front of the diner, a seat facing the front door. The woman brought a paper napkin and a menu. After he ordered breakfast, he bought a paper from the vending machine outside, brought it back to the table, and flipped through it. He skimmed headlines about gas prices, a lot about terrorism, nothing about jailbreaks or missing prisoners in Columbus.

Breakfast came. Matt cleaned his plate. Drained his coffee cup half a dozen times. Flipped to the sports section, found an AP story on the Lexus Championship being played next week at Bellevue. Tiger had a wrist injury. Phil was coming off a poor showing at the Deutsche Bank the week before. The field was wide open. Listed among the leading contenders was The Pines Classic winner, Craig Driscoll.

Matt sighed. Driscoll had been lucky. Maybe there was a little jealousy in that assessment, he knew, given that he felt he should be at the Open himself, but a few of Driscoll's putts were too good to be purely skill.

He was rubbing his shoulder, the one that had ruined his hopes, when two cops walked in.

"That your red Camry in the lot?" the one in front asked him.

Matt opened his mouth, and tried to make words come out. "Uh," was the best he could manage.

He was done. Trapped.

He looked at the guns on their belt. He was an escaped fugitive; that gave them license to shoot, didn't it? He was going back to jail.

"Yeah. That's mine," Matt said, and started to stand.

"You left your lights on," the cop said and turned to the take-out counter. He said, "Morning, John," to the man working in the back of the restaurant.

Matt eased back into the seat, his heart hammering in his chest.

❖ ❖ ❖ ❖ ❖

He drove around in circles for the next two hours, the coffee and adrenaline gradually wearing off. He started to shiver and cranked the heat. He started to nod off and opened a window.

He turned on the radio, searching for news of his escape. Ended up on WLW. A morning drive-time show hosted by a guy named Jim Scott. Lots of news, weather, upcoming events in the city. No mention of a manhunt for Matt Thurman. He checked the dashboard clock: 7:58. Another hour to go.

He fell asleep at a traffic light—jarred awake by a chorus of horns honking behind him.

He finally stopped at a United Dairy Farmers store and bought another pay-as-you-go phone, went back to his car, took a deep breath, and dialed the number: 513-588-5377.

Someone picked it up halfway through the first ring.

"This is Harper."

Matt blinked.

Harper was a woman.

"Hello?" she said.

Why hadn't the guy told him Harper was a woman? Did he even have the right Harper?

"Yes, I'm here." He hesitated again. What was he supposed to say now? Hi, you don't know me, but this guy who helped me break out of jail last night gave me your number.

"Thurman?"

He blinked again.

"Yes."

"Where have you been? I've been up since four this morning waiting for you to call."

"I didn't think—"

"You were given the number and told to call when you reached Cincinnati." He heard her sigh. "Never mind. Where are you?"

"I'm not sure. A parking lot. Looks like a park across the street."

"You see any street signs?"

Matt craned his neck. "I'm on Clifton. Near the intersection with Ludlow."

"Head south on Clifton. Close to where you are now you'll see a tower above the trees in the park. That's the Crosley Tower. Drive to it. I'll meet you on the street in front of it."

"Okay," he said.

"Repeat it back to me."

He did. Then he asked, "How will I know who—"

But the woman hung up before he could finish his question.

❖ ❖ ❖ ❖ ❖

He pulled next to the curb under the shadow of the imposing

Crosley Tower, a tall, gray monolithic building on the campus of the University of Cincinnati. He gazed up at the sixteen-story concrete tower, which widened at the top like a plant in bloom. School apparently had not begun yet as only a scattering of students walked by. He drummed his fingers on the steering wheel, waiting for Harper, anticipating some answers.

Harper will fill you in.

A car pulled behind him on the street, a little blue sedan, a woman in the driver's seat. She had olive skin, dark hair pulled back in a bun. She wore a gray business suit with a white blouse.

It was the woman from the golf course, the one who had been looking for Kazmir.

She beckoned to him. He got out of his car and hustled back to her as she lowered the window.

"You were at The Pines," he said.

She barely glanced at him before saying, "Let's go."

"You want me to get in your car?"

"Leave the keys to the Camry under the front seat."

He did as he was told.

"You have the money?" she asked.

He patted his waist, or rather, the envelope under his belt. "I spent about sixty dollars of it," he said.

As she pulled into traffic, Matt turned in his seat and watched the red Camry disappear in the distance.

"Tell me what you've been doing these last few hours," Harper said.

"Not much." He settled back in his seat. "Waiting to call you."

She shook her head, as if both amazed and disgusted. "Tell me details. Where you've been, who saw you."

He obliged. When he was finished, she said, "Good on the cell phones, bad on the highway, terrible on stopping to eat."

"Well, it's not like I do this kind of thing every day." He was still surprised that the woman from the golf course now sat next to him. She looked as good as she did that night—dark eyes, olive skin, dark hair pulled back. She tilted her head slightly as she drove so that her chin jutted forward, as if daring the other drivers to get in her way. Seeing her so close and in the light of morning, she looked a little older than he remembered—maybe early thirties. She was petite, but there was a steely quality about her. Someone who could stand her ground.

"You got lucky," she said. "Very, very lucky. Those two officers must have just missed the APB."

"The APB?"

"Columbus PD sent it out around six this morning. You're a wanted man, Mr. Thurman. Your picture's going to be on the news tonight. In the papers tomorrow. It's all over the Internet now. No harm done yet. But we'll have to keep you under wraps."

His picture in the paper. Wanted. He knew that was coming, but still...

"What about Jake? Do they think he had anything to do with the escape?"

Her expression softened. "I imagine they're talking to him."

"You got to tell them he didn't."

"They'll find that out soon enough, don't worry."

But what if they don't, Matt was about to ask, and then the adrenaline coursing through his veins, all at once, ran out.

He sat back and sighed, suddenly exhausted.

"So how did you do it?" he asked. "Get me out?"

"I can't answer that."

"So who was the guy in the cell?"

"Somebody who knows how to do a lot of things," she said, a note of defensiveness in her voice. "Getting you out of a county lockup wasn't much of a problem for him."

"Well that sure clears it up. You're doing a great job of filling me in."

Harper turned in her seat and pointed a finger at him. "We saved your life, Mr. Thurman. If we hadn't gotten you out of that cell, you'd be dead in a week. So the main thing you ought to be feeling toward me—and that man in the cell—is gratitude. Understand?"

Matt opened his mouth to respond, but she kept going.

"Furthermore, right this second, as I'm talking to you, I'm risking my life too. My whole career, everything I've worked for in the last ten years. Okay? So you're not the only one who's out on a limb."

A mile down the road, Matt said, "I just want to know what's going on."

"I'm not going to be able to tell you some things. Not now. Maybe not ever. You have to accept that."

He nodded. "Okay."

They drove on in silence a little longer.

"What I can tell you," Harper said, "is that a number of us are involved in a very important investigation. Something we've been working on a long time."

"Something to do with Bob Kazmir. Obviously."

"That's right."

And what's your role in this investigation, Matt was about to ask, when he saw a little plastic ID card clipped to the front of her jacket.

Cincinnati DOJ.

"DOJ. Department of Justice."

Harper shot him a glance.

"Are you a lawyer or something?" Matt asked.

She didn't respond, but Matt could read the answer in her eyes. She was a lawyer, all right. A government lawyer. That fit.

"We arranged for your escape," she continued, "because we thought you might be able to help us with our investigation."

Matt nodded, remembering what the guy in the cell had told him. Fill in the blanks.

"I'll help if I can," Matt said. "Only—and don't take this the wrong way—how can I help without knowing what this is about?"

"You can give us the benefit of your expertise."

"My expertise?"

"Let me start with a hypothetical question—one we've been kicking around for some time now."

Matt turned in his seat to face her. She shot him a sidelong glance, and then turned her attention back to the road.

"How—hypothetically speaking—would somebody go about fixing a golf tournament?"

CINCINNATUS

One Lytle Place
East Mehring Way
Cincinnati, OH
Tuesday, September 11, 10:14 A.M.

HARPER was a book person; her apartment was full of them. Living room walls lined with shelves that ran floor to ceiling, wall to wall on three sides. Big thick leather-bound volumes on the lower shelves, legal books, newer-looking, more colorful volumes higher up. There was another bookcase in the kitchen, and a little white one in the small half-bath. Books everywhere. Papers too—yellow legal pads, manila folders, stacks of printout piled neatly wherever he looked. A lawyer's apartment. Despite all the stuff crammed into it, though, the place looked neat. Immaculate. Not like his apartment, Matt thought.

He sat on a wooden stool, behind a yellow counter that separated kitchen from living room. Harper stood by the stove, her back to him, making a cup of tea. She was big on tea: the cabinet to the right of the stove was full of it in various colored boxes. She'd put water on to boil as soon as she walked in the door.

"You sure you don't want any?" she asked

"No thanks."

Matt didn't want tea or coffee or anything to eat. He wanted to take a shower and go to sleep for a long, long time. Wanted to wake up and have this all be a bad dream.

Harper reached up to put away the box of tea. Her suit jacket rode up. Her pants stretched tight across her butt. Nice butt.

Harper turned around and faced him. He noticed again the tilt of her head, slightly back, her chin slightly forward. "You were saying."

They were continuing the conversation they'd begun in the car; Matt trying to explain the answer he'd given to her question. Fix a golf tournament?

Impossible.

"I don't know what else to tell you. You're talking about making sure who wins. I don't see how you can do it."

"It's hypothetical. Use your imagination."

"My imagination. Yeah. Okay." He leaned on the counter, and thought for a minute. "No." He shook his head. "Take the Classic, for example. The tournament they just had up at The Pines?"

Harper took a sip of her tea, her dark eyes riveted on him.

"There were a hundred and five golfers in the field. Maybe two-thirds of them make the cut. So you're talking about bribing at least fifty people."

"Maybe not. At the start of the last round, there were ten with a realistic chance to win. Within five strokes of Sergio."

"You've been doing your homework." He smiled.

She didn't.

"But you're wrong," he said. "Five strokes is nothing. Crazy things can happen on a golf course." He remembered his grandfather. The 1986 Masters. Nicklaus coming from five shots back on the back nine alone. "And even if it is just ten guys—some of them make millions a year. How could you bribe them? Tiger Woods? How can you bribe Tiger Woods?" He laughed. "It can't be done."

"Okay," she said, matter-of-factly. "So you can't bribe the players. Could you fix the course?"

Matt snorted. "You mean fix it so it played differently for different people? No way. You try and mess with any top-level course like The Pines and somebody'll know it right away. There are fifty people on the grounds crew, there's always somebody out there, leveling the fairways, trimming the greens..."

His voice trailed off.

"Kazmir," he said. "This is why you wanted to talk to Kazmir."

Harper took a sip of her tea.

Her phone rang.

She put down the mug and pulled out her cell.

"Harper." A pause as she listened. "No, it's all in the file. Absolutely everything I had."

She frowned.

"Which we've gone over half a dozen times already. I don't see the point in—"

She sighed.

"All right. No. Nothing urgent. I'll be there in half an hour. All right." She snapped the phone shut. "I have to go back to work."

"You didn't answer my question," he said.

She looked him in the eye, her dark eyes even sharper than normal. "Yes, that's why I wanted to talk to Kazmir."

"I'm getting the feeling this isn't a hypothetical question—whether or not you can fix a golf tournament."

Harper emptied the rest of her tea into the sink. "Somebody's been doing it. He was involved."

"Bob Kazmir was fixing golf tournaments?"

"He knew Driscoll was going to win the Classic."

Matt shook his head. "He couldn't have known that."

"He won seven thousand dollars on him."

"Whoa," he said. He nearly added "You're kidding" but Harper didn't seem like much of a kidder.

"He won ten on the Southwest Pro-Am," she said. "Six more on the Lexus Invitational. He's won maybe a quarter million dollars over the last three years."

"That's a lot of money," he said. Something about the Southwest rang a bell.

"It's peanuts. Hundreds of millions of dollars is being won on these tournaments. Maybe more."

Matt gave a low whistle.

"That's why they killed him," she said.

"Those guys at The Pines," Matt said.

"That's right."

"Who are they?"

She shook her head.

"You don't know. Right." Matt remembered what the guy in his cell had said. "But you know *what* they are, whatever that means. What does that mean?"

"I'm not ready to talk about that yet. There's a lot at stake here. A lot of money, a lot of lives, potentially. Not just yours."

Her phone rang again. She pulled it out of her purse, saw who was calling, and rolled her eyes.

"I have to go." She put the phone away without answering. "I don't know when I can get back. Maybe six tonight. Seven. We'll talk more then."

"Okay."

"Don't leave the apartment. Don't answer the phone." She pointed a finger at him. "Don't call your brother."

Did she know about the call he'd tried to make last night?

"His phone is probably tapped," Harper went on. "They'll trace the call here, and then I'm screwed. And so are you."

"I understand," Matt said.

"Help yourself to whatever," she said, heading for the apartment door. "Take a shower. Towels under the sink. Those clothes okay?"

"Not a perfect fit but okay."

She nodded and started to leave.

"Hey," he called after her.

She turned, thrusting her chin even a bit more forward.

"I just wanted to say thanks. I mean, for getting me out. For letting me stay here. I appreciate what you and that guy—"

"Think about the tournaments, okay? After you get some sleep."

He smiled. "So what am I supposed to call you?"

She stood in the open doorway. "What do you mean?"

"I mean, what's your name?"

"Harper." She looked at him like he was an idiot.

"Your first name." Matt felt himself flushing, just a little. "It seems strange just calling you Harper."

"Everybody calls me Harper," she said, and shut the door behind her.

❖ ❖ ❖ ❖ ❖

He found it stamped in one of the big leather-bound books on the bottom living room bookshelf: *Key Constitutional Law Cases of the Marshall Court, Volume III.* From the library of Esperanza Marcelina Harper.

Esperanza Marcelina...what a mouthful. No wonder she went by Harper.

Matt had pulled the book at random. He was fresh from the shower, a towel wrapped around his waist.

Most of the titles on the higher shelves were non-fiction. History. Biography. A lot about the Revolutionary War. Washington, Jefferson. A lot of Jefferson. *Jefferson and the Muslim Pirates* sounded interesting. The rest—boring. He wondered if Harper had read them. He hated reading anything but the sports page.

He moved to another wall. More serious stuff. Tolstoy. Dickens. Shakespeare. The classics. Leather-bound editions. He pulled *Don Quixote* off the shelf and flipped it open to the inside front cover.

From the library of Esperanza Marcelina Harper. Strange. Harper didn't like her first name, but she had it stamped in all her books.

He pulled another—a little paperback wedged in among the big ones. *The Great Gatsby.* The spine was nearly cracked in half, the edges worn. She must have read that one a hundred times. He'd seen the movie—an old classic with Robert Redford and Mia Farrow. Guy gets dumped by his girlfriend and so he becomes a rich bootlegger to win her back. Buys a big mansion to show her he's worthy. Throws huge parties. Eventually gets himself killed because of her.

"Should have moved on, bro," he said to Gatsby. "When it's over, it's over."

He rubbed his shoulder, which had begun to throb.

He squatted to look at the bottom shelf, which held a half-dozen oversized volumes with black leather bindings. Dates on the sides, in white stick-on numbers: 1980-1990. 1991-1998. Right up to this year.

Photo albums. Harper's life, in pictures.

The first page, an old-fashioned baby portrait, black and white. A chubby little kid in a crib, looking very serious; Esperanza, in fancy gold script, running along the bottom of the picture. He flipped through color snapshots of Harper looking uncomfortable in various baby out-fits. Harper, still chubby, still looking serious, sitting on a woman's lap, the woman clapping the baby's hands together. Harper crawling toward the same woman, who sat cross-legged on the floor, holding out her arms.

Harper's mother?

The two didn't look alike. The woman was blond, thin, classic movie-star features. Ski-slope nose, bright blue eyes. Scandinavian. In the pictures she was barefoot, wearing jeans and a white turtleneck. She looked about nineteen; she didn't have that harried look of most of the young mothers he knew. She looked like she didn't have a care in the world.

The perfect mom. Perfectly posed.

The photos were staged, Matt realized. Studio shots.

Which made the woman Harper's mom for sure.

So where was dad?

Nowhere in the first album. There were more pictures of Harper and her mother, some of Harper and her friends. Birthday party shots of Harper and some family members, who all resembled mom. Maybe dad took the pictures. Maybe he'd run off.

In the second album: Pre-teen Harper, wearing glasses, mugging for the camera with a friend. Harper at her high school graduation, with more of her friends, and then, still in her graduation robe, looking serious, arm-in-arm with her mother. Harper in a white dress standing next to a tall boy in a tuxedo. The glasses were gone, her hair pulled back in a bun.

She looked, for the first time, like the woman he'd just met.

He moved on to college. Ohio State. Harper the Buckeye, sitting in the neatest dorm room Matt had ever seen. Neat stacks of paper, neat piles of books. No beer cans anywhere.

He kept flipping pages: a series of shots of Harper at a political rally. The Young Republicans. The last in the series was Harper standing next to an older man, a dark-haired guy in his mid-thirties. He wore khakis and a sport coat, a white turtleneck. He had perfect, bright white teeth.

He had his arm around Harper's shoulders.

On the next page, Harper with the same guy, holding hands in front of the Eiffel Tower. On the facing page was a postcard, turned over so you could read the back: Espy, You are going to love the apartment I found us.

Matt shut the album with a thwack.

He went to the kitchen looking for cereal and found packets of granola-looking stuff. No Cocoa Puffs. No Frosted Flakes. Not even Wheaties. He made himself a sandwich of all-natural peanut butter and organic jelly. In the freezer he found a box of all-natural, organic popsicles called Fruitique.

He wandered into the living room and sat down on the couch.

Harper didn't have a TV.

There was a glass coffee table in front of him. Another neat stack of magazines on top of it. More law journals. Matt pulled out *The Journal of Law and Religion* and flipped through it as he ate.

He came on an article Harper had dog-eared. And highlighted. Something about the founders' intent regarding "moral instruction for the American citizenry," which was not supposed to come exclusively from the Bible, but from "studious study, of the lives of great men, and the manner in which they conducted themselves."

Matt yawned and tossed the magazine back on the table.

He finished his sandwich and the popsicle, which was actually very tasty.

He closed his eyes.

❖ ❖ ❖ ❖ ❖

But his brain wouldn't shut off.

He was a wanted man. APB. Would they come after Jake? Arrest him? And someone was fixing golf tournaments. Winning hundreds of millions of dollars. How was that possible?

Kazmir won seven grand on the Classic. Six more on the Lexus Invitational. Another ten betting on the Southwest.

"Gary Wadman," he said out loud, and sat up on the couch.

That was why the bell had rung in his head when Harper mentioned the Southwest. Gary won it this year, Gary Wadman, who'd been with Matt on the Nationwide Tour. The guy drove like Bubba Watson, putted like Hulk Hogan. Gary had finally made it to the PGA tour this past January. And won, his third tournament out. The Southwest. Matt had seen the last round on TV. Gary's short game looked completely different that day. He looked like Tom Kite on the green. When they'd been on the Nationwide, Gary completely forgot how to putt, was all over Matt every day. Watch me, Matt. Tell me what I'm doing wrong. Is it my stance, is it my left hand, is it my right hand, should I change my grip, should I change my putter, what do you hear about the graphites, blah, blah, blah, and now...

Gary Wadman, PGA tour winner.

Matt started pacing.

No one could have seen that coming. Not Bob Kazmir, not even Gary himself. Gary had barely made the cut out of Q school, tied with ten others to get on the big tour. So how had he won the Southwest? How had Driscoll won the Classic? And how had Kazmir known to put money on them? How could you fix one golf tournament, never mind three?

He ran those questions over and over in his head until he suddenly realized that some of them he could, in fact, actually answer.

It took him almost three hours, and two long phone calls. Phone calls to the same person, an hour and a half in between. Then he made another. 588-5377.

"Harper."

"It's Matt."

Silence.

"Mom. I can't talk right now."

She was someplace she couldn't speak freely.

"Okay. Call me back when you can."

"It'll be awhile. Another couple hours. At least."

"You'll be interested in what I have to say."

"I'm sure I will. I can't wait to get caught up."

"I have some answers for you."

Silence. Then. "I'll get free for lunch. We can meet at my apartment."

"I'll be here."

"See you then. Mom."

He smiled. "See you then. Espy."

Silence.

Harper hung up.

CINCINNATUS

St. Andrews Health Care
West Washington Boulevard
Los Angeles, CA
Tuesday, September 11, 7:48 A.M.

WARM sun on his face. A throbbing pain in his shoulder, a terrible taste in his mouth. The low hum of machinery, punctuated by intermittent electronic beeping. The whispered hush of conversation—several conversations—going on nearby. Shoes squeaking on linoleum.

Shurig opened his eyes.

He was in a hospital. Staring up at a white paneled ceiling. White walls all around him. His arm was in a sling.

He saw Hernandez, sitting in a chair next to his bed, looking concerned but very much under control. It took a lot to rattle that guy, the hero of the now famous incident in Long Beach. In fact, he didn't look a whole lot different than he did sitting at one of the many lunches they had eaten together. His dark hair, peppered with gray, combed back with precision, his large dark eyes taking in everything while revealing nothing.

Shurig was happy to see him. And then it all came rushing back.

Njomo screaming. Kauffman reaching for the billfold with one hand, raising his gun with the other.

Rawson's finger, already on the trigger. The spark, the sound of shots being fired. The blood on Kauffman's neck. Seeping through his shirt collar, welling on the plush, white carpet.

Rawson's face, as he turned to Shurig and smiled—and fired again.

The pain in his shoulder.

And then, blackness.

Shurig squeezed his eyes shut and opened them again.

Hernandez was staring at him with those big, all-knowing eyes.

92

"When you're ready," he said. "I'd like to hear about it."

❖ ❖ ❖ ❖ ❖

Shurig took a minute to compose himself, and then ran it down. Mission debriefing. Just like the old days, the Phoenix Bravo days. Short and sweet. He kept the emotion out of his voice. He left out his thoughts—what had been going through his mind at each step of the way, from Njomo's denial to Rawson's arrival to the shooting itself. He took Hernandez through the whole thing, and then he lay back on the pillow and closed his eyes.

"I blew it, Sam," he said. "I had the drop on the guy."

"You both blew it," Hernandez said. "You and Kauffman. You should have searched him. The second he didn't show ID."

"I know."

"The second he mouthed off. You should have put a gun right up against his head and made him eat that carpet."

Shurig said nothing.

"Kauffman was careless. You were that and worse. Overconfident."

"The guy was fast. He was so big, so bulked up, you wouldn't think..."

He opened his eyes again.

Hernandez gazed at him with nothing remotely resembling sympathy.

"How's Kauffman?" Shurig asked, knowing the answer even as he spoke.

Hernandez shook his head. "Njomo is gone. Rawson too."

There was a knock on the door. A woman peered in. A red-haired woman in a white lab coat, stethoscope around her neck.

"All right to come in?"

Shurig composed himself. "Sure," he said.

"I'm Doctor Elizabeth Haileigh. I worked on that shoulder of yours last night, Mr. Shurig."

"Thank you."

"You're welcome." She walked around the side of the bed, looked at a few of the machines, then at Shurig again. "How are you feeling?"

"Sore as hell. But okay, otherwise."

"When can he leave?" Hernandez asked, fixing the doctor in his powerful gaze.

She looked at Hernandez. "Who are you?"

"His boss."

"The FBI." She nodded ruefully. "You guys aren't any different than other people, you know."

"Yes we are," Hernandez said.

Haileigh started to laugh, then saw he was serious. She got serious too.

"Your man took a bullet at close range, Mr...?"

"Hernandez."

"Mr. Hernandez. He's lucky to be alive."

Shurig and Hernandez looked at each other with the same thought: No such thing as luck. You make your own luck.

"Incredibly lucky," she went on, "that every bone in his shoulder wasn't fractured, a weapon fired at that distance."

"A small caliber weapon," Hernandez said. "A thirty-eight. Not that surprising."

"A twenty-two can fracture bone at five feet."

"Sometimes." He smiled. "You know your weapons, doc."

"I have a lot of experience with them, unfortunately."

Hernandez nodded. "So when can he leave?"

Haileigh smiled and put her fist on her hip. "When I'm sure the danger of infection has passed."

"What's that mean, a week?"

"I don't know. Maybe."

"Not that high a risk of infection in wounds like these, though, am I right? When the bullet passes through soft tissue. What is it, like one, two percent, something like that?"

"You know your gunshot wounds, Mr. Hernandez."

"I've had some experience with them. Unfortunately."

She brushed a few strands of hair from her forehead in a way that seemed, to Shurig, almost flirtatious. Old Sam had a way with the ladies, even, apparently, lady doctors.

"Let's see how he's doing later this morning, all right?" she said. Then she turned to Shurig. "You need anything like more painkiller or to get rid of this guy" she nodded in Hernandez's direction "just buzz for the nurse."

"Okay."

"I'll see you later." She turned to Hernandez. "I have a feeling I'll be seeing you as well."

Hernandez said, "I have that same feeling."

The two of them shared a look.

Dr. Haileigh left the room smiling.

"You know," Shurig said, when she was gone, "when a guy gets shot, he's the one supposed to—"

"You don't have time to mess around," Hernandez said. "Kennedy wants the paperwork on this ASAP."

"All right."

"I want it too. I'll have Jackie do the forms. You'll have to do the reports from home when you get out of here. Quick as you can."

"I could do them now if I had my laptop."

"With that on?" Hernandez nodded at the sling.

Shurig held up his left hand. "Nothing wrong with this hand."

"I'll get it for you. I want that paperwork done as soon as possible."

"I heard you," Shurig said. "What happens after the paperwork?"

"What do you mean?"

"I mean are we back to square one? No Njomo, no money trail...."

Hernandez shook his head. "Tell you the truth, I don't know where we are," he said. "Get that paperwork done. I'll be back."

He left the room.

❖ ❖ ❖ ❖ ❖

The laptop arrived an hour later; Burghart came with it. She rapped once on the open door, and walked in without waiting for a response.

"Jackie," Shurig said.

"Mike." She sat in the chair Hernandez had vacated, sat without looking at him, and put the case on her lap.

"I'm sorry," he said. "My fault."

"No." She answered without looking up, without meeting his eyes. "You heard it from Hernandez, I'm sure. You don't need to hear it from me."

Burghart was tall and lanky with dull, shoulder-length brown hair and a perpetually knit brow, as if she were always confused about something or just near sighted, a look that contradicted her determined nature. Her tenacity and focus made her a good agent, though she and Shurig had never quite connected.

Burghart had been Kauffman's best friend on the squad. Best friend in the L.A. office. She'd been a lawyer before joining the bureau; she and Kauffman had the same kind of minds, same approach to casework. They traveled in the same circles, socialized outside of work. Their families were close too. There were rumors she and Kauffman had an affair, once upon a time. Shurig wasn't sure about that, but there was no denying their closeness.

And looking at her now—the set of her jaw, the circles under her eyes, the way she kept looking past him, not at him—there was no denying how devastated she was by Kauffman's death.

She finished unpacking the laptop, set it on Shurig's lap.

"Hospital has an open network. You can log on as a guest, and you're good to go." She took a pencil and a pad of paper out of her pocket. "The guy at the apartment—Rawson. We're spelling it R-a-w-s-o-n. That sound right?"

"Sounds right."

"No first name."

Shurig shook his head. "No first name."

"Six two, two hundred ten pounds. That's the doorman's guess."

"A couple inches taller, twenty pounds heavier. Maybe thirty."

"Blond hair."

"Not much of it. Buzz cut."

"Blue eyes."

"Yeah."

"Nothing else?"

"He was a bodybuilder. Maybe on drugs..."

"The doorman said that too. We're cross-referencing HGH, steroids, those kind of things."

"Good."

"Of course, it's possible Rawson's not his real name."

"Likely," he said.

Burghart tapped the pencil on the paper a few times, then stood.

"Anyway. Jalen's out on a kidnap thing right now. When he's done with that, he's coming here."

Jalen was their sketch artist, the best in the area. He'd sit with Shurig for twenty minutes and do a sketch they'd circulate to every bureau office, every post office, every police station in the country. Rawson's face—the best rendition they could get of it—would be everywhere.

"Good," Shurig said.

"We'll get him, Mike," she said.

"I know we will." He tried to sound as certain as she had, but he knew it wouldn't be easy. Hide in plain sight—a skill Shurig had picked up in Phoenix Bravo. Rawson was clearly a pro. He'd know how to make himself invisible.

Burghart met his eyes for the first time. She was close to six feet tall. Solid. Unflappable in the most pressure-filled situations. Shurig had never seen her upset before. There were tears in her eyes now.

"What the hell happened, Mike?"

She turned around and left before he could answer.

❖ ❖ ❖ ❖ ❖

The casework took Shurig longer than he thought, nearly two hours. Part of the problem was the one-handed typing. Harder to do on a bed, with the computer shifting all over his lap, than he'd foreseen.

Part of the problem, though, was the images that kept flashing through his mind. The shooting, yes, but everything that had led up to it as well—the work he'd been doing the past couple of months, since arriving in L.A., running all over the city with Hernandez or Kauffman, following a money trail here, an informant's tip there. Hitting the mosques, the community centers, sitting at his computer reading e-mails and lurking on forum chats full of hate speech spewing from both ends of the spectrum, all in search of a terrorist group that seemed literally to have vanished from the face of the Earth after its single, horrific act.

Al-Hasra. The Unconquerable. One minute no one had even heard the name. And then...

Long Beach.

A group of terrorists took over a school, lined up kids against a wall. Killed adults too. The most heinous act of terrorism since 9/11. It would have been worse—much worse—if FBI agent Sam Hernandez hadn't swooped in and saved the day like some middle-aged Batman.

After that, everyone in America knew the name Al-Hasra. The group became lead demon in the hellish war that had been going on for a decade—or, actually, for centuries.

Was there a connection between the group and the Arab-American Amity League? Sam obviously thought so, which is why he sent Shurig and Kauffman to see Njomo. The nature of that connection—and what had turned Sam onto the AAAL and the Sayeed-Pearson bank through which funds had been transferring from one group to the other—they were still trying to figure out.

He finished the forms and sent them—encrypted, of course, the bureau's e-mail did that automatically—to administration, then on-line a minute longer, doing the electronic equivalent of phoning home; typing a couple of nasty, but necessary, e-mails. Brief. To the point. One-handed.

Dr. Haileigh peeked in on him. She was going off-duty now, she said. She told him he ought to stay at least one more night but assumed he wouldn't and said he should have her number. She scribbled it on a note pad and left.

Shurig turned on the TV but didn't pay much attention to it. He saw Kauffman's face. Kauffman's wife, Kauffman's kid. He was think-ing about what he'd done, what he hadn't done, where the investiga-tion would go from here.

At some point, he saw Hernandez standing in the doorway.

Shurig turned off the TV.

"You did the paperwork," Hernandez said. He seemed distracted, his mind someplace else.

"I did some thinking too," Shurig said. "About the case."

"So did I." Hernandez went to the window. Folded his hands be-hind his back, and looked out on the street.

Shurig waited for him to continue, but he just stood there.

"What I was thinking," Shurig said. "The connection between Al-Hasra and that Amity League. I don't know what put you on them in the first place, but if there's a file, I could take a look at it, and maybe..."

He stopped talking then because Hernandez was shaking his head.

"What?" Shurig asked.

"It won't do any good. I have to rethink this whole thing."

He stood there another minute before turning around, distractedly straightening the knot of his tie. "What did the doc say?"

"I ought to stay one more night."

"And what does the shoulder say?"

Shurig rolled it a little, back and forth. It hurt like hell. But he couldn't tell Hernandez.

"I guess I'm good to go."

Hernandez opened the closet, pulled out Shurig's clothes, and tossed them on the bed. He helped Shurig out of the hospital gown and into his clothes. Gave Shurig a fresh shirt, which he apparently had bought on the way to the hospital.

They sped away in Hernandez's Honda, taking 10 West to 405 North, but Hernandez drove past the Wilshire exit.

"I guess we're not going to the office," Shurig said.

"You guessed right."

He moved to the HOV lane and they drove on in silence. Shurig knew Hernandez well enough by now not to press. The man would tell him where they were going when he was ready.

Shurig shifted in his seat and grimaced.

Hernandez gave him a sidelong glance. "We'll have to get you some painkillers," he said. "Antibiotics too, probably."

Shurig nodded. "Haileigh gave me her number." He pulled the scrip from his pocket and held it out with his good hand.

"Got it, thanks," Hernandez said. "We'll have her call in a few prescriptions, pick them up when we get there."

He had it already. Of course he did, Shurig thought, and lowered his arm. "Get where?" Shurig said. "What's going on?"

"I've been approaching this like any other investigation—assemble a team, find clues, hunt the bad guys."

"That's the way it works," Shurig said.

Sam shook his head. "Not this time. These bad guys have a leg up on us."

"What's that mean?"

Hernandez took so long to answer Shurig thought he hadn't heard the question.

"Think about it," Sam said at last. "How'd they know you and Kauffman were going to see Njomo?"

"They couldn't have known," Shurig said. "I didn't even know till that night. They got lucky."

"Yeah. Lucky. And how'd they know to send Rawson, right then, right there? Was that luck too?"

"These guys are smart. Al-Hasra. Very, very smart."

Hernandez shook his head. "Something else is going on. I think they have somebody inside the bureau."

One Lytle Place
Mehring Way
Cincinnati, OH
Tuesday, September 11, 10:56 A.M.

MATT had taken notes during the two long phone calls he'd made. The notes were numbers, mostly. He sat on the couch, still wrapped in the towel, pondering what those numbers meant on the golf course, what they meant in real life.

A lot of money, for one thing.

Hundreds of millions of dollars. A big-time gambling ring. Rawson and his boss maybe were running it and Kazmir had been in on it but had slipped up somehow, gotten greedy. No surprise.

Matt folded the yellow sheets of paper in half, set them on the coffee table, and headed to the bedroom in search of something he could wear. The bedroom was small, maybe fifteen feet a side. One wall was all closet. On the opposite wall was the bed with a night table next to it. An exercise machine stood next to the bed, one of those multi-use ones that looked very complicated to him.

Facing the exercise machine, on top of a bureau, a TV.

So Harper had some connection to modern civilization after all.

He opened the louvered doors to the closet and found, on one side, two metal filing cabinets. On the other side he found a half-dozen work outfits, a half-dozen dresses, a dozen or so pairs of shoes. Fairly slim pickings for a woman's closet, based on his experiences. That didn't surprise him.

He turned on the TV, surfed for news of his jailbreak. On the local news, he saw David Abraham surrounded by reporters. He looked grim.

"I have no further comment at this time," he said.

Then David's face disappeared, and Matt's filled the screen.

His mug shot, he supposed, taken right after they brought him in. Unshaven, exhausted, a bruise on his forehead, his hair sticking out every which way.

"Matthew Thurman is believed to be armed and extremely dangerous." His picture shrunk to fill the upper-left hand corner of the screen; an anchorwoman filled the rest. "If you have any information about his whereabouts, authorities ask that you contact them immediately."

They gave a phone number; they broke for commercial.

❖ ❖ ❖ ❖ ❖

The reality—and its absurdity—struck him again.

He was a murderer and an escaped fugitive. Armed and dangerous.

He watched the commercials, hoping to hear more about the case when the news returned. He hoped to hear that Jake was okay. When the anchorwoman came back, she talked about the Middle East. Went to a tape made a couple days ago, the president in the Rose Garden, calling on the rebels in Waziristan to accept Premier Hazim's call for a cease-fire for the next thirty days—the next month, the Islamic holy month of Ramadan. So far, the rebels hadn't responded.

Then a commercial.

Matt yawned and slid back on the bed. Propped his head on the pillow and kept watching.

The war. The stock market. The weather. The Reds' winning streak.

He yawned again.

He closed his eyes.

He fell asleep.

He woke to the sound of footsteps in the apartment. Heels against a hard surface.

He bolted upright, looked at the bedside clock. Going on two. He'd been asleep for all of five minutes.

The TV was still on. He reached for the towel and jammed his pinky toe on the metal edge of Harper's workout machine.

He cursed out loud.

"Esperanza? Are you home?"

Matt froze.

A woman's voice, but not Harper's.

"What are you doing home in the middle of the day, sweetheart?"

Matt shut off the TV and slipped the towel around his waist.

The clicking heels stopped outside the bedroom door.

"Esperanza? Are you in there?" The woman's voice had a nervous edge to it: whoever she was, Matt knew he had to say something or she'd start jumping to a lot of wrong conclusions.

"Hi." He stood behind the half-open door. "It's, um, not Esperanza." He poked his head around the edge of the door "I'm a friend of hers."

He recognized the woman. She was Harper's mother.

❖ ❖ ❖ ❖ ❖

Other than a few wrinkles around the eyes, she hadn't changed much since the pictures in the photo album were taken. Tall and thin, straight blond hair, shoulder length. Classic movie-star features. A beautiful woman, in a beautiful—and very expensive-looking—blue dress.

And he was wearing a towel, his clothes still in a pile in the bathroom where he'd left them after taking a shower.

She took two steps into the bedroom, saw it, and stopped.

"I was taking a nap," Matt said, holding the towel around his waist.

Harper's mother raised an eyebrow.

"I'm a friend of Esperanza's," he said.

The woman smiled and held out a hand for him to shake. "I'm her mother. Penelope."

Matt was using his right hand to hold up the towel; he shook awkwardly with his left. "Pleased to meet you, Mrs. Harper. Ms. Harper."

"Penelope. Or Penny. Whichever you prefer. And you are...?"

"Matt," he said without thinking. "Matt Thurman."

And he felt the blood drain from his face.

He'd just given her his real name, the name that was all over the news. And the Internet too, no doubt; and the papers, and the radio. It had slipped out reflexively, his mouth working faster than his brain.

"I'm sorry. I shouldn't have barged in. Why don't I let you get dressed, and then we can talk. You can tell me how you know Esperanza." She smiled and gave him a penetrating look.

The same look that Nancy's dad had given him, back in the day.

"I'll put some water on," Harper's mother said. "Would you like some tea?"

"Sure," he said.

"Esperanza loves tea, as I'm sure you know. She got that from me. From my side of the family. My grandfather was twenty years in Bombay, with the East India Company. The Harpers all love tea." She shut the bedroom door behind her.

❖ ❖ ❖ ❖ ❖

He put on his clothes, which seemed to have shrunk, looking more like someone else's clothes than they had before. When he walked into the living room, Harper's mother was standing at the stove, her back to him, two steaming mugs in front of her.

"I made my special blend," she said. "Earl Grey and a mystery tea.

See if you can guess what it is."

She handed him his tea. "I imagine Esperanza's told you a lot about me."

"She talks about you all the time."

"We're very close," she said. "Always have been." She took a sip of tea. "And yet...she's never mentioned your name."

He cleared his throat. "Well, Espy can be kind of... um... secretive at times."

Harper's mother smiled. "Gets that from her father. So how did you two meet?"

"Through friends. Friends introduced us."

"Esperanza's been telling me she doesn't have any friends here. Doesn't have time, she's too busy working."

"Friends from work, is what I meant," Matt said. "Colleagues."

"So you're a lawyer too?"

"Yes. Absolutely. I'm a lawyer."

Her smile broadened. "What firm are you with?"

Matt took a sip of his tea. He looked around the room, and his eyes fell on the coffee table. And the journals spread out across it.

"I teach," he said. "Constitutional Law."

"You're a professor." She frowned. "Does that pay well?"

The phone rang.

She picked up the receiver. "Esperanza Harper's Residence."

Her face, all at once, brightened.

"Esperanza," she said. "You naughty girl. You've been keeping se-crets again."

❖ ❖ ❖ ❖ ❖

Harper tucked the phone in the crook of her neck while she gath-ered files from her desk for the meeting that was going to keep her from getting back to the apartment and finding out what Thurman knew about the golf tournaments. The meeting involved Bob Kazmir, and she would have to not only lie her way through, she would hear more talk about her incompetence.

She called to tell Thurman she wouldn't be home for lunch and maybe not for dinner.

"Mom," Harper said. "What are you doing there?"

"Dropping off a few things." Her mother had a key to the apartment—in case of emergency but used significantly more often. "I was at Saks this morning. Saw a couple dresses I thought might work for the reception."

Harper sighed. "I can buy my own clothes." And in fact, she'd picked up a lime-green dress last week that seemed perfect for the occasion.

"I just thought, well, honestly you haven't been to a lot of these before, and I have, so—"

"Mom."

"I just want you to fit in. Feel comfortable."

No sense in arguing with her mother about clothes. And her mother had a point. It was important to look good at the reception. A lot more important than her mother knew.

But she had more important things to worry about right now. Like Thurman, who was probably hiding in the bathtub. Or her bedroom closet.

"Thanks. Just leave the clothes in the hall closet."

"If you're worried about me waking Matt, I'm afraid it's too late."

Harper's heart skipped a beat. "You met Matt?"

"Well of course. You didn't think you could keep your Mr. Thurman secret forever, did you?"

The idiot had told her his real name.

"Is he there?" she asked.

"Right here."

"Could you put him on for a second?"

She was about to carve up Thurman when she heard someone at the door.

Leonard.

U.S. Attorney Leonard Kennebeck. Her boss. Her mentor. Her friend, too, up until about five months ago. When she started digging into the Kazmir case. When everything between them changed. When Espy pulled back, Leonard had been hurt. Then confused. Then resigned.

Right now, he was angry, his blue eyes more penetrating than usual behind his rimless glasses, his face flushed all the way across his balding scalp. Though of average height and build, Leonard had an authoritative, almost patrician, bearing that made him seem larger.

She punched the hold button. "I'm sorry. Personal emergency. Be right there."

Leonard said, "We're on a tight schedule."

"I know."

"You found the files?"

She tapped the stack on her desk.

"Bring them. We'll be waiting."

Leonard left. She put Thurman back on.

"Thurman?"

"I'm here. I'm in the bedroom. I didn't mean to tell her my name. I just—you have to talk to her."

"I can't do that now."

"But my picture's on TV. I saw it."

Harper squeezed her eyes shut. The whole thing was falling apart. It had been a stupid idea. Help the guy escape, maybe he knows something about Kazmir, about the tournaments, about the people behind it, save him from a frame up.

She opened her eyes and saw Leonard in front of the conference room door down the hall. His hand on the doorknob, staring at her.

"Do the best you can," she said. "I have to go."

"I'll call you if something goes wrong."

"Only if you have to. Emergencies only."

"Emergencies only. Got it."

Emergencies only.

Exactly what she'd told her mother about the spare key.

Golden State Freeway
Just north of Los Angeles, CA
Tuesday, September 11, 12:56 P.M.

405 ended, dumped them onto 5. Hernandez kept going north. A sign said Santa Clarita.

Hernandez had said all of twenty words since making his announcement: These guys have somebody inside the bureau. Shurig had waited for more and finally opened the subject again.

"You've got to be kidding, Sam," Shurig said. "Al-Hasra?"

Hernandez stared straight ahead.

"A data entry guy?" Shurig asked. "One of the clerical staff?"

"No. They don't have that kind of access."

"You think somebody in the squad is working for them?" Shurig had a sudden, sick, sinking feeling in his stomach. "Is that what this little trip is about? You think it's me?"

Hernandez smiled. "No," he said. "I don't."

"Then who?"

There were seven in the squad—no, six, now. Kincaid and Dilts, Burghart and Pramaggiore, and the two of them. Sam thought it was one of those four? He thought it was someone from another squad? What did he think?

Shurig waited for an answer to his question.

But Hernandez didn't say a word.

I should say something, Shurig thought. Tell Sam he's crazy. Remind him how long he's been with everyone in the squad. How often every agent in the office got vetted as a matter of course, how people don't switch sides in this war, because the guys on the other side don't do deals with infidels, don't offer money for information the way Ivan did back in the day, back before the Wall fell. It was a different game now.

But Sam knew that. Just like he had to know his theory was crazy, on the face of it.

Yet, clearly, he knew something else too. The question was what.

❖ ❖ ❖ ❖ ❖

They took 14 East. After twenty minutes, they pulled off the highway, into a little town called Canyon Country. Hernandez parked across the street from a Jack in the Box. Since Shurig joined the Al-Hasra squad, he must have watched Hernandez eat a hundred Jumbo Jacks.

Sam got the usual—Jumbo Jack with cheese, jalapeno poppers, and a Coke. Shurig got the same, minus the poppers. His stomach felt a little squirrelly.

It was a little after three in the afternoon, and the place was practically empty. A guy in a UPS uniform, reading the paper; an old woman nursing a coffee. A teenage boy up front, flirting with the counter girl.

They took a table by the front window. Hernandez unwrapped his burger and took a couple bites. Shurig sipped his drink.

"First leak was back in June," Hernandez said, out of the blue. "That's how I know it's not you. We had a name, we had a money trail, and then all of a sudden we had nothing." Hernandez wiped his fingers with a napkin. "That's how I know it's not you. Because in June you were still training at Quantico."

"That's true."

"Plus, well, I've seen you work, I know how you think. It's not you."

"So who? Kincaid? Dilts? Burghart?"

"Not Burghart." Hernandez bit into his burger.

"This other money trail—back in June. That was related to Al-Hasra?"

"No," Hernandez said. Then he smiled and looked over Shurig's shoulder. "Jackie," he said, and put down his burger. "You got it?"

Shurig turned to see Burghart holding a big leather briefcase.

"I got it," she said.

❖ ❖ ❖ ❖ ❖

"You're not eating?" Hernandez asked her.

"This crap?" She shook her head. Set the briefcase down on the table between the two trays.

Hernandez patted the briefcase. "The hard drive off Njomo's machine. He and Rawson were in too much of a hurry, apparently, to bring it with them. I want you to examine this very carefully."

"Me?" Shurig asked. "I'm not a tech guy."

"I'll get you tech guys, don't worry." He frowned then and reached inside his coat pocket. Pulled out his phone, which was vibrating, and looked at the screen. "Doctor Haileigh," he said. "I was just going to call you." He got up from the table and walked out of earshot.

"What's going on here, Jackie?" Shurig asked.

"He'll tell you what he wants you to know." She slid the hard drive back into the briefcase, snapped the latches shut, and put it next to his chair. "There's a folder in there too. Copies of pictures, inventory of stuff we found at Njomo's apartment."

"Thanks."

"One more thing." Her eyes narrowed. "He's convinced it's not you. I'm not."

Shurig nodded. Burghart obviously was upset about Kauffman, maybe blamed everything on Shurig.

She leaned across the table. "Far as I'm concerned, the only ones in the clear are me and Hernandez. Until I see proof, everybody else is suspect. Including you. Especially you. You were there with Kauffman.

When it all went down."

Shurig let a little anger creep into his voice. "I messed up. I told you that before. I'm sorry."

"I heard you. But if I find out you're lying, if I find out you were involved..."

"Then I guess I ought to keep an open mind too. Not rule you out, either."

They glared at each other.

Hernandez sat down. "The doc is going to phone in the prescriptions," he said. "We'll get them when we get where we're going."

"Thanks," Shurig said, not breaking eye contact with Burghart.

Hernandez looked from one to the other. "You guys all right?"

"I'm out of here." Burghart nodded to him, glanced at Shurig, and left.

"It's going to take her awhile," Hernandez said. "To get over Kauffman."

"Yeah, well, the same goes for me."

"She's probably always going to blame you. A little. Which is why she doesn't trust you now—am I right?"

"Something like that."

"Give her time." He bit into a jalapeno popper.

Shurig leaned forward. "She said you'd tell me what was going on."

"As far as she's concerned?" Hernandez sipped his drink. "It's Al-Hasra. A terrorist investigation, plain and simple. We were chasing a money trail, now we're chasing the people who killed Kauffman."

"Who have someone inside the bureau," Shurig said.

Hernandez nodded. "That's exactly what she thinks."

"And as far as I'm concerned?"

Hernandez finished eating, crumpled the papers on his tray into a ball. "It's not about terrorists. At least not the kind we're used to chasing."

Hernandez leaned back in his chair, smoothed his hair into place. "It's a long story. I'm not sure where to begin."

"The first leak," Shurig said. "In June, right? Start there."

"Oh." A knowing smile crept across Hernandez's face. "It goes back a little further than that."

"So start as far back as you need to go."

Hernandez reached into his pocket and pulled out a handful of change and a few loose bills. He picked through the bills, set one on the table, and put the rest back in his pocket. "Let's go back two hundred years," he said, and smoothed the bill flat on the table. "Let's go back to this guy." He pointed to the portrait on the front of the dollar.

Shurig said, "George Washington."

"That's where the story starts."

"You lost me already."

"*Omne reliquat servare republicam*." Hernandez smiled. "He gave up everything to serve the republic."

"Still lost."

"When he decided to go to war, with the British. Became commander of the Continental Army. Later, too, when he became president." Hernandez turned over the bill and pointed to the back of it. "You see that?"

"The pyramid?" He shook his head. "Oh, no. This isn't one of those secret society things, is it?"

"I'm not talking about the pyramid. This."

Shurig looked again.

"The eagle?"

Hernandez nodded, and shoved the bill back into his pocket. "Now let me tell you something about George Washington that you didn't learn in grade school."

BOOK ONE: GAMBIT

Fountain Square
Corner of Fifth and Vine streets
Cincinnati, OH
Tuesday, September 11, 4:15 P.M.

THURMAN peered over his sunglasses to watch the people on Fountain Square. He wore a Bengals jersey, baggy jeans, and a silver hoop in one ear. A clip-on. He had lifts in his shoes, the right higher than the other, which made him walk with a slight hitch. All things Harper had picked up on her walk back to the apartment—a half-assed disguise but the best she could do on short notice. Enough to fool a casual passerby.

They had gone out for a late lunch. The area wasn't crowded, but active enough that Thurman had asked her why she picked the spot. Her father, she said, had taught her the value of hiding in public, of becoming invisible in a crowd.

The dad who was invisible in her photo album.

She moved away from talk of her dad and plunged into questions about what he had figured out.

"You could look, for example, at how he hit the ball off the tee," he told her. "How many yards." He pointed to the numbers on the legal paper he'd used to scribble his notes. "We looked at his average before the Southwest and how he hit the ball there. You can see the numbers are about the same."

Harper looked at the numbers—284.5, 280.1.

The 'he' was Gary Wadman. Thurman was trying to explain what he'd discovered; she was trying to decide how much of a pain her mother was going to be. Mom wasn't going to call the police. The explanation and plea for silence had gone well enough—"if Espy is convinced of your innocence, Matt, then I am too"—but Thurman had let slip that other people were involved in the jailbreak, and Espy knew her mother had a feeling about who one of those people might be.

115

But her mother seemed less interested in the jailbreak than in the 'hideous lime-green dress' she'd seen hanging in Espy's closet: "What on earth," her mother had said, "do you intend to do with that?"

Matt said, "You look at his driving accuracy, that's similar too. This column here. And this one—how many greens he reached in regulation. That's the same as well." Thurman pointed to some other numbers. "We pulled down a bunch of other statistics and they all came out pretty much the same."

She said, "*We* pulled down a dozen other statistics?"

"Right. Scoring average—"

"Who's *we*?" She'd been so busy thinking about everything else, she hadn't focused on what Thurman was telling her. "Where did you get these numbers?"

He shrugged. "I made a couple calls. A friend of mine at PGA headquarters in Palm Beach."

Harper took a deep breath. "Tell me you didn't call a friend of yours from my apartment. From my phone. Tell me you didn't do that, please."

"Of course not. Do you think I'm stupid?"

She folded her arms across her chest.

"For your information, I used one of those cell phones I bought."

"But you called a friend."

"Before my picture was on the news."

"Before *you* saw it on the news. How do you know your friend didn't see it?"

"He didn't."

"But he will. They'll trace the call."

"No way they can trace the call."

"We don't know what they can do. We don't even know who they are." Harper grabbed her purse and stood to leave. "Like I keep telling you, it's not just your ass on the line."

"But it is mostly my ass," Thurman snapped. "I'm the one the cops are after. If we don't figure this out, I'm the one who goes to jail. Gets killed in jail."

She shook her head. "That's not going to happen. I promise you."

"Is that what you promised Kazmir?"

She looked at the people on the square, a few families, a boy dipping his hand in the fountain, groups of colleagues heading home early or to a happy hour.

"I'm sorry," Matt said. "I didn't mean that."

"That's all right." She made a half-hearted attempt at a smile. "So what do these numbers tell you? How did your friend win this tournament?"

Thurman cleared his throat and seemed to be trying to calm down. "Short answer? He putted better. A lot better." Thurman pointed to his notes. "Look at the numbers here."

She looked at the numbers. 1.858; 1.704. She had no idea what they meant.

"These are putts per hole. 1.704? That's lights out. Tiger, the last two years, he went 1.723, 1.725, something like that. My best year, the year I won the Dover, I was 1.93. 1.84 at the Dover."

Harper looked up from the paper. "You won a golf tournament?"

"Yeah," he said. "Why?"

"Nothing," she said. "I just must've missed it on the background check."

"You did a background check?"

"Of course. We're not going to bust you out of jail without taking the time to see what kind of guy you are."

He managed a little smile. "So I guess I passed."

"Yeah. You passed." She almost mentioned the DUI but decided against it. "So your friend's stroke average was the difference, between winning and losing."

"Not stroke average. Average putts per hole." Thurman looked at the numbers. "Gary was .154 better at the Southwest."

"That doesn't seem like a big deal."

"Do the math. .154 strokes per hole, eighteen holes, that's 2.7 strokes per round, about eleven strokes over the course of a tournament."

Harper nodded. "That is a big deal." Which still left the million-dollar question. "So are you saying it's possible to fix a golf tournament?"

"I don't know," Thurman said. "Maybe. But get this." He pulled out another sheet of yellow legal paper, covered with more numbers. Two identical tables of numbers, one stacked on top of the other. "This is where it gets interesting."

❖ ❖ ❖ ❖ ❖

They were Gary's scores, from the Southwest. Matt had written them down, round by round, hole by hole, as his buddy at the PGA had dictated them to him. Like a scorecard.

HOLE	1	2	3	4	5	6	7	8	9	OUT
PAR	4	3	4	5	4	4	4	3	5	36
ROUND										
1	4	3	3	5	4	4	4	3	4	34
2	4	3	3	4	3	4	5	4	3	33
3	4	3	3	4	3	4	3	3	5	32
4	3	3	3	5	4	3	5	2	4	32

HOLE	10	11	12	13	14	15	16	17	18	IN	OUT	TOT
PAR	4	4	3	5	4	4	4	3	5	36	36	72
ROUND												
1	4	4	4	5	4	4	4	3	5	37	34	71
2	4	3	3	6	4	4	4	3	5	36	33	69
3	3	4	3	7	4	4	3	4	4	36	32	68
4	3	4	3	6	4	4	4	3	4	35	32	67

Even before he'd finished taking the information, Matt noticed patterns. For one, Gary had been much better on the front nine than on the back: thirteen under versus even par. And much better on certain holes. Gary had birdied number three every day with a single putt. Ten feet the first day, five feet the second, a thirty footer in the third, and a twenty footer in the fourth.

Matt had started thinking, how would you fix a golf tournament? Well, you'd make sure it wasn't obvious. You'd do whatever you were doing when people weren't watching, and they weren't watching as much on the front nine as on the back. So three was a good hole to do something on, but what could you do?

You could landscape it somehow, so that it played a certain way, so if Gary knew exactly where and how hard to hit the green, he'd have a pretty good sense of how his putt would travel and what he'd have to do to make it go in the hole.

Matt asked his friend to find out the pin placement on three, where they'd put the flag each day. If it was in the same place, maybe there was a sweet spot to the green, meaning whoever was responsible for pin placement had to be in on the scam.

But it turned out that the flag on three had been in a different spot each round. Which totally destroyed Matt's theory.

But the pattern was still there.

He was about to show it to Harper when her phone rang.

She looked at the number and answered quickly. She walked out of earshot for a short, intense conversation.

She came back looking very upset.

"We have to get you back to the apartment."

"But I want to show you—"

"Show me on the way," she said, and started down the steps, heading toward the far side of the plaza, toward the fountain and the flagpole.

Matt cursed under his breath, snatched the papers, and started to follow.

Then he stopped.

"No," he said.

Harper turned around.

Matt held up the papers. "The first time you said fix a golf tournament I thought no way is that possible, but looking at Gary's scores, maybe you're right. I want to find out for sure."

Harper took a deep breath. "What do you want to do?"

"Get on the PGA website. Look at Gary's scores again—look at the Classic too, how Driscoll did there."

"Okay. I'll bring my laptop home tonight," Harper said.

"I don't want to wait until tonight."

She jabbed a finger in his direction. "You cannot," she said, lowering her voice, clenching her teeth, "risk blowing this investigation because you have ants in your pants. We are in this together."

"In this together?" he said. "Okay then. Fill me in."

"What?"

"Harper will fill you in. That's what the guy in the cell said. So fill me in. On what you're investigating and why your boss doesn't know about it."

"I can't."

"Then we're not really together. I have to solve this myself."

She sighed. "If I tell you something, you go back to the apartment."

Matt nodded. "Deal."

She walked away. Fast. Matt had to quicken his stride to catch up with her. She stopped in front of a flagpole and waited for Matt to catch up. "You see the flag there?" she asked.

He looked up. The American flag fluttered in the breeze at the top of the pole. Two others hung beneath it.

"I see three flags," Matt said.

"The one on the bottom."

It had blue and white stripes and a circle of stars set off in a box in the upper left hand corner, like the stars in the American flag. Blue stars, surrounding an image. Looked like a bird of some kind.

"What's that in the corner?" he asked. "An eagle?"

❖ ❖ ❖ ❖ ❖

While Matt and Harper gazed up at the flags, a man a block away watched them. A big man. A bodybuilder type.

He pulled a phone out of his pocket and hit three on speed-dial.

"Me. Guess who the attorney is having lunch with. No. The golfer. That's right. And guess where they are?" He went on without waiting for an answer. "The square. She's showing him the flag."

He listened for a moment, then nodded.

"Right. No, I understand. I agree completely."

He nodded one more time and then ended the call.

The colonel had a point. Bodies were piling up. More on the way. Some publicity was unavoidable, but still...

This one could be quick.

This one could be quiet.

The body could disappear and never be found, and no one would know the difference.

Antelope Valley Freeway
Eastbound
Southern California
Tuesday, September 11, 2:05 P.M.

"AFTER the war, Washington was in a lot of trouble, financially," Hernandez said. "His estate, his farm...that's what he was going to concentrate on."

They were back on 14, heading east again, into Antelope Valley. Shurig knew where they were headed now, though he didn't entirely know what to expect when they got there. Sam was still being mysterious. He had made and received another phone call, in private. Pulled onto the shoulder and got out of the car to take the calls. Something related to what was happening here.

"Of course he ended up leaving the farm again anyway, a couple years later. Becoming president."

Shurig looked at Hernandez. "We're a long way from Njomo and that sixty million dollars he was moving around."

"He was fifty-seven years old," Hernandez continued. "That was pretty old back then. Not really the point in your life you want to start a new career. Thing is, Washington saw the country was in trouble. Everything they'd fought for would come to nothing if he didn't step in. *Omne reliquat servare rempublicam.*"

"You said that before."

"It means he gave up everything to serve the Republic. They made it their motto. Put it on their flag, along with the eagle. Right along with his portrait."

"Washington's portrait—"

"Not Washington," Hernandez interrupted. "His role model. Cincinnatus."

Fountain Square
Corner of Fifth and Vine Streets
Cincinnati, OH
Tuesday, September 11, 4:45 P.M.

ESPY tried to keep it simple. She didn't know how much Thurman would be able to handle. She'd been studying it too long, was way too wrapped up in it.

"This was before the emperors," she said. "When Rome was a republic. Rome was at war and in trouble," she said. "The senate gave Cincinnatus dictatorial authority and begged him to come out of retirement."

They had left Fountain Square and the flag behind, heading back to her apartment.

"They gave him absolute power," Harper said. "It took him about two weeks to win the war, and then he returned the power to the senate. Went back to his farm. *Omne reliquat servare republicam.* He put the republic first. That's what made him a hero to Washington and his circle."

She explained how in the first few years after the war ended the new American experiment was a disaster. Not quite anarchy but not far from it. There was talk about scrapping the republic, going back to a monarchy, and making George Washington king. They had just fought a long war to get rid of a king, so a group of officers from the military and political elite got together and formed a secret society to preserve the ideals for which they'd fought.

Then somebody darted into a store behind them—there, and then gone. A man. Somebody following them?

She watched the store entrance for another moment.

No one appeared.

She decided she'd been imagining things.

"Not that I object to a history lesson," Thurman said, "but what does this have to do with fixing golf tournaments? With the guys at The Pines? You think they're members of this Cincinnatus group?"

"Society of the Cincinnati," Espy corrected.

"And they're the ones running the gambling ring."

"That's what I think, yes."

"Why don't you turn them in?"

"For one thing, we don't have proof."

"They're winning millions of dollars on hundred-to-one shots and you don't have proof?"

"As far as the law is concerned, all they are right now is very, very lucky."

"How'd you find out about the gambling in the first place?"

"Kazmir," she said. "I got an SAR, Suspicious Activity Report. It's how bankers red-flag something that doesn't seem on the up-and-up. Cash transactions, usually. Things that don't fit the usual pattern. We got one on Kazmir back in April. And he wasn't the only person to bet on your friend to win. So did a man named Charles Knox. Another named Edward Hand. And there was Arthur St. Claire and Thomas Pickering."

"Friends of his?"

"They're names of founding members of the society."

"Names of dead guys."

"Exactly. Another name on the list was William Rawson."

Thurman stopped walking. "As in Rawson from the golf course. The guy who almost killed me."

Harper nodded. "It doesn't prove anything by itself. After I got the SAR, I checked Kazmir's records pretty thoroughly. He bet on a lot of longshots in the past couple of years. All of them came in. It didn't make sense. I spent a couple weeks learning about bets on golf. All the ways you can do it."

"There are a lot of ways," Matt said. "People bet this guy will beat that guy by so many strokes, this guy will break par…"

"Lots of ways to make money if you know the results in advance. And these guys are smart about it. They didn't bet a lot of longshots and they never hit the same place twice. They made a thousand little bets instead of a few big ones. So they made hundreds of millions of dollars without calling attention to themselves."

"Until Bob bet too big."

They stopped at the corner of Broadway and Fifth. Espy needed to go three blocks east to her office while Matt walked the next block to her apartment. She pulled out her keys. "Remember where I live?"

"That way." Matt pointed.

"You ought to get some sleep."

"You should too. Didn't you get up at four?"

"I always get up at four."

She smiled then, and turned, and crossed the street.

Matt watched her go, noticing the way she moved in a tight, firm gait, her chin high, as if daring someone to mess with her. Her dark hair shimmered in the late-afternoon sun, and he wondered what that hair would look like if she didn't tie it back, if she let if fall free.

Then he headed down the street, thoughts of secret societies and Roman generals and George Washington dancing in his head.

A car horn sounded. Brakes squealed.

Matt stood ten feet off the curb, in the middle of the crosswalk, a little yellow car stopped inches from his knees, the car's driver yelling at him, cursing, then adding, "Who do you think you are?"

The phrase echoed in his head. Familiar.

The driver shot off down the street.

Matt watched him go.

Who do you think you are?

And then he remembered Kazmir, red-faced, screaming at him to get off the green. Who do you think you are, Thurman? You're not a player anymore. You're a caddy. Caddies don't belong on the green.

It had been early in the morning. Barely dawn. He'd walked toward Kazmir, who was crouched down, measuring distances. Using his PDA. The grass had been ripped back, the pipes and sprinklers and hoses exposed.

Maintenance work, in preparation for the Classic.

Maybe Kazmir hadn't been measuring distances. Maybe he was doing a little repair work of his own. Fix it so that he and his friends would know how to bet on the tournament.

What kind of work could he have done?

Matt couldn't go near The Pines to find out.

But...he could call Jake, ask him to do it.

First, though, he would call Harper on the 588-5377 line, tell her the idea.

A hand fell on his shoulder.

A very big hand.

Something jabbed into his side at the same instant.

He looked down and saw the gun.

He looked up and saw Rawson.

BOOK ONE: GAMBIT

TEN minutes north of the Walgreen's where they'd stopped to pick up Shurig's prescriptions, they turned down a side street and drove along a chain-link fence fifteen feet tall, with barbed-wire at the top. Signs every few feet proclaiming:

AUTHORIZED PERSONNEL ONLY

TRESPASSERS WILL BE SHOT ON SIGHT

There was a break in the fence a quarter mile down the road—a guardhouse, and another, much bigger version of the same sign.

Hernandez turned in.

"I hope to hell we're authorized personnel," Shurig said.

"They won't shoot you as long as you're with me."

A man in an Air Security Police uniform—dark camo, navy beret, black boots—stepped to the car. Took their badges, asked them to step out of the car. He patted them down, while another guard searched the car and their possessions. Took a close look at Shurig's computer and the hard drive Burghart had brought them. Njomo's hard drive. Evidence, Hernandez said.

The guard didn't take his word for it. They waited at the gate until a tech guy came to not only boot up the laptop, but hook up Njomo's drive, make sure it was legit.

Finally, they were waved into the base. They drove along a freshly tarred road, paralleling a runway, itself recently lengthened, recently widened, judging from the different colors and the wear on the tarmac. Shurig could feel the painkillers starting to kick in, making him a little woozy. He needed a clear head, to concentrate.

A lot of things that he'd been wondering about the last few weeks were, he had a feeling, about to be made clear.

They parked in front of a long, low building, with a banner reading JTTF SOCAL stretched across the top of it.

"Bring that stuff," Hernandez said, nodding at the computer gear on the seat between them.

Inside, they showed ID to a young man in a suit. Two more air police guards stood at attention behind him.

"Good to see you again, sir," said the suit, who gave Hernandez two blue badges to pin on their shirts.

They moved on, past the desk, on into a long narrow hallway. Construction noises came from somewhere in the building—the buzz of saws, the pounding of hammers.

As they walked through the building, Shurig observed as much as he could. JTTF SOCAL. Joint Terrorism Task Force. This was temporary headquarters for the force, which was made up of local and national law enforcement and intelligence personnel, working off the new network feed from DC. Once the server system was installed in LA, the force would relocate there. At the moment, they shared space with the Air Force.

Hernandez led Shurig through an open set of double doors into a huge room, sixty or seventy feet square. New construction. Only partially dry-walled, maybe half a dozen people at work at free-standing desks, electrical wires and cables dangling everywhere.

They walked past two skinny guys in suits staring at a map of Saudi Arabia on what had to be a forty-inch LCD monitor, past a woman wearing headphones who turned at their approach, saw Hernandez, and smiled like she'd won the lottery.

"Agent Hernandez," she said. "Where have you been all week?"

"Busy." He returned her smile.

"Tonight too?"

"Tonight too. But we'll talk."

She smiled again and returned to her work.

They came to a glass door with a big FBI decal and the letters JIT on it. Hernandez pushed through and into the small room beyond. A row of servers filled the far wall and two standard office cubicles occupied either side.

A man knelt on the floor, a clump of cable in one hand. When they entered he looked up. "Sam," he said, and dropped the cable.

"Goran."

The man brushed his hands off and stood up. He and Hernandez shook.

"Problem?" Hernandez asked, nodding toward the wires on the floor.

"More of the same. System is very sluggish." The man had a slight accent: Eastern European. Goran, Hernandez had said. Slavic name. Which made him Croatian, maybe Serbian. He was thin, pale-skinned, thin dark hair that he wore unfashionably long, to go with his unfashionable clothes. First generation immigrant, Shurig guessed.

"I think I have solved the problem now, though," Goran said. "We will see."

"Let's hope so." Hernandez turned. "This is Agent Michael Shurig. He's going to be working here the next few days."

"Goran Tomasevic." The two shook hands. Tomasevic had a strong grip, and a stronger body odor.

Not a good thing in such closed quarters.

"Give us a few minutes, will you, Goran?" Hernandez asked. "A couple things I need to explain to Agent Shurig."

"Of course." He smiled. "If you are here tonight, you will come to dinner? Maya, I know, would—"

"Sorry," Hernandez shook his head. "Tonight's not going to work."

"Of course," he said. "Another time. You too, Agent Shurig. You will come to my house for dinner?"

"Be a pleasure," Shurig said. "Thanks."

Goran left.

"Do not accept any dinner invitations," Hernandez said. "His wife...beautiful woman. Can't cook worth a lick."

He took a seat at one of the cubicles, set down the briefcase. Shurig pulled up a chair.

"So what am I doing here, Sam?"

"As far as the rest of the squad is concerned, you're taking the intel as it comes in from DIA, NSA, wherever, and reading through it. Whatever looks like it might be relevant to Al-Hasra, you flag for the data guys downtown."

"Sounds simple enough."

He took out Njomo's hard drive. "See what you can find on here. We're looking for more on the bank."

"Sayeed-Pearson," Shurig said.

"Right. And more on the Arab-American Amity League."

"I'm not a tech guy."

"Goran can help. But whatever you find, you two are the only ones who see it."

Shurig nodded.

Hernandez pulled his chair closer to the desk and powered on the computer. Began typing. The way they were sitting, Shurig couldn't see the monitor without leaning over Sam's shoulder and making it obvious he was snooping. He thought about doing it anyway.

"Catch this when it comes out of the printer," Sam said, nodding toward the other side of the room.

Sam had printed a copy of a memo. The heading alone caught Shurig's eyes.

MI-5 INTERNAL MEMORANDUM
RE: ALDERNEY FINANCIAL GROUP

Half the document was blacked-out.

The word 'CONFIDENTIAL' was stamped all across it.

MI-5. British Intelligence.

Shurig looked at Hernandez. "How'd you get this? Where'd you get this?"

"Friend of a friend," Sam said. "Not important."

Shurig read the memo.

Per JTAC's memo of 7 November, following our 'best-guess' list of questionable transactions funneled through AFG (Alderney Financial Group).

The list was split in two: Domestic and Foreign. Every domestic entry was blacked-out. Most of the foreign ones were too. All but four.

Consolidated Oil (COR) - $413.1M
MGT - $344.6M
McCormick/Bailey International - $25.4M
Kandini Aerospace - $3.1M

"Alderney Financial is a bank in the Channel Islands," Sam explained. "Off the English coast. Under the jurisdiction of the British government but not subject to the same rules and regulations. Not subject to our rules and regulations either, so...a good place to do business if you need to keep that business confidential."

Which you'd need to do if that business was at all illegal, or even 'questionable,' as the memo put it. Hence MI-5's interest. Shurig got that part. But.

"What does all this have to do with the Society of Cincinnati?" he asked.

"What you're looking at is a memo written in response to a big scandal last year; big over in Britain at least. Reports that a lot of Saudi money was being used to unduly influence military contracting procedures."

Shurig vaguely remembered hearing about the scandal. "So you think—what? Saudi money is going to these American groups too? Influencing our contracting procedures?"

"This is not about Saudi money. Mostly it's about Alderney. And MGT. It's a piece of the puzzle, one of the first I found."

"What puzzle?"

"The society, the Cincinnati, of course. And what they're doing with several billion dollars in gambling money they've won over the past ten years."

Shurig gave a low whistle.

"Which they've gone to a lot of trouble to hide." Hernandez put his hands behind his head and sat back. "The question is why."

"And how does this tie into Njomo? What you had Ben and me looking for?"

Hernandez smiled. "That's going to have to wait till I get back."

A young man in an air force uniform knocked at the door.

"Thank you." Hernandez stood and powered down the computer. Shurig got a quick look at the LCD screen—blue text, on a white background, a list of some kind—before everything went to black. "Walk with me?" Hernandez asked

"Sure," Shurig said, getting to his feet. "Where are we going?"

Hernandez pointed out the door, to the window beyond, through which the runway was visible.

"Out there," he said. "I have a plane to catch."

❖ ❖ ❖ ❖ ❖

An Air Force officer escorted them onto the runway, left them standing in front of a small white plane with a USAF decal on the side. Not a jet, not much more than twenty feet long. Range of a few hundred miles or so, Shurig guessed.

"Where are you headed?" Shurig asked.

"A little research."

"Sam. Come on. Tell me something. At least tell me why this isn't an official investigation, why we can't tell Kennedy."

"Our Assistant Director does things by the book. You know that. If I go to him...." Hernandez shook his head. "Reports will be filed. A lot of reports."

"Let him file his reports. In the meantime, we set up a sting operation, and—"

Hernandez held up a silencing finger.

A guy in an orange jumpsuit walked past them, lugging a hose as thick as a jungle snake. He carried it around to the back of the plane, hooked it up to a port at the back. Refueling.

"...an undercover operation," Shurig said. "There's precedent for that."

"Kennedy'll never approve it on his own. He'll go to Washington."

"So?"

"I don't want anyone in Washington knowing about this."

Shurig's eyes widened. "You think they have someone in the DC office too? "

"It's a possibility."

"What are these guys doing? What do they want?"

Hernandez shrugged.

"You're not going to tell me."

"Later."

"You don't trust me."

"You're one of about two people I do trust at this point."

"Then..."

"I don't want you going off half-cocked. Look, Kauffman's dead. You didn't get the guy who did it. I know what you're thinking. You want revenge. You want to find Rawson, find the guys who put him on you. But we've been working on this for months now. The point is, I appreciate your energy. Your enthusiasm. But we don't need any heroes at this point. Understand?"

"I wasn't offering to be a hero," Shurig said. "I was offering to do my job."

"I appreciate that. But this isn't a war zone. This is Los Angeles. Hernandez put a hand on Shurig's shoulder. "I'll be back tomorrow. We'll talk then."

He turned for the plane...

And a second later, turned back around.

"Almost forgot."

He reached down, and pulled his keys off his belt.

"You probably want to use my car to get home tonight," he said, holding out his hand.

Two things happened then.

First was the impact.

Then came the blood.

Blood and more.

Splashing onto his face, his neck, his shirt, in his eyes.

Sam was covered in blood too, he saw. Parts of him, at least.

Parts of him were gone entirely.

Specifically, his head.

"Down!" someone yelled. "Everybody get down!"

Shurig didn't move. He couldn't move.

Somebody tackled him around the waist, taking him down to the tarmac. He hit hard but didn't feel a thing.

"Sam," he said, and watched as what was left of his boss, his friend, toppled slowly, almost gracefully, to the tarmac.

CINCINNATUS

U.S. Department of Justice
Federal Building
Cincinnati, OH
Tuesday, September 11, 8:45 P.M.

AT 8:45, another pink envelope showed up. A courier delivery, brought from downstairs by the building staff. Second one of the evening. Harper went to the front desk to get it; everybody else was gone.

It was thinner than the first, which had been a fifty-page brief filed on behalf of a restaurant owner named Rico Mandini, who DOJ was taking to court for fraud. An attempt by Mandini's law firm to bog her down in minutae. Harper didn't need any help getting bogged down. She had a stack of work on her desk, the cases she'd let slide these last two days, while she focused on bringing everyone in the office up to speed on Bob Kazmir and the investigation she'd launched into his finances, the investigation she'd stopped working on months back according to official records, only of course she hadn't really stopped working on it at all, because that little investigation into whether or not Kazmir had paid taxes on a few hundred thousand dollars worth of offshore gambling proceeds had turned into a monster. A monster that had sucked up her life.

She was going to have to call Thurman, let him know she was running late. He wouldn't like that, but it couldn't be helped. Mandini's pink envelope, and now this one. No return address.

She wondered what it was.

She sat down at her desk, set the envelope down in front of her, and reached for the phone. Dialed her home number.

The machine picked up after five rings. She tucked the phone under her neck, and waited for the beep.

"Matt," she said, reaching for her letter opener. "Pick up."

But he didn't.

Where the hell was he? She should've gone with him, made sure he went to the apartment. Made sure he stayed there.

"Matt, pick up. It's me." She waited a few seconds longer, then hung up. Maybe he fell asleep. She hoped so. If he'd gone back on their deal; worse yet, if he'd bolted entirely...

She didn't want to think about it now. She reached inside the envelope and pulled out two sheets of paper. A good thing, she thought. No fifty-page brief here.

Then she frowned.

The top sheet consisted of a single typewritten word in the middle of the page. All caps.

STOP

The second sheet was a computer print-out of a black and white photograph.

A man lying on the ground somewhere. Lying on his back. Little dark stains all around. The man was lying on a road. A wide road. Car wheels in the background. No. Plane wheels.

It wasn't a road; it was a runway.

She looked closer at the body.

There was something wrong with it—the shape. Something familiar about it too. The clothes. She knew this guy.

She brought the picture closer, squinting, trying to make out his face, but the angle the picture had been snapped at—

Oh god.

She set down the paper, the realization dawning that her inability to see the man's face had nothing to do with the camera angle. And the stains on the ground all around him, on his clothes—they weren't oil.

She looked at the first sheet of paper again.

STOP

A chill shot through her.

"Oh no," she said out loud. "Oh no, no, NO!"

She screamed the last, and shoved away from the desk, slamming her chair against the filing cabinet behind her, standing up, pushing herself as far away from the photo as she could get, a second, much more horrible realization dawning, the realization that she didn't need to see the man's face to know who he was.

"Dad," she said, in a voice that sounded like it was coming from far away. "Dad."

She felt like she was going to faint. And then she did.

Book Two

SOLDIERS

Every man must be for the United States
or against it.
— Stephen Douglas

CINCINNATUS

Federal Bureau of Investigation
Los Angeles Field Office Headquarters
Wilshire Boulevard
Los Angeles, CA
Wednesday, September 12, 10:24 A.M.

SHURIG sat on an orange plastic chair, one of a half-dozen lined up against the wall outside the conference room. Drinking lukewarm coffee out of a Styrofoam cup—what seemed like his eight hundredth cup of the day. He was buzzing like he hadn't buzzed since those last few weeks in Baghdad, when their unit was pulling out, when he and the rest of Bravo stayed up around the clock guarding the airports and the evac routes, scouring the bad parts of the city.

During that time, Shurig kept a vial of blue pills in his pocket to keep him going—awake, alert, paranoid. The only way to be in that kind of situation, the only way to make sure you got out alive. He'd barely gotten out alive. Lucky. But luck he'd made himself.

The rest of the squad hadn't been so fortunate. Spetko, Chmielewski, Duncan, Batanovic, four out of fourteen picked off that last week. Deena on the last day. Deena Batanovic. D.B., Shurig would never forget her, never forget that morning, the two of them taking an informational 'stroll' in Ghazaliyah, alongside half a dozen IPS guys, when this little girl—eight years old? seven? younger?—walked from behind a fruit stand, carrying a basket, a big smile on her face.

"*Salaam*," she said, holding out the basket filled with dates, oranges, naana kaasi, a couple cans of Sprite, a couple bottles of water. "*Salaam aleikum.*" Ninety-five degrees and not even noon yet, who wouldn't want to pick from a basket like that? The IPS guys exchanged smiles and walked toward her. D.B. went with them. Shurig, the sickly sweet taste of a blue pill still on his tongue, slowed down, just a bit. Suspicious, as always.

He remembered thinking the little girl was a real cutie. Jet-black hair, big dark eyes, big smile frozen on her face. *Frozen* was exactly the word that came to mind, and the instant it did, he tensed. "D.B.," he said, "hang on a..."

Next thing Shurig knew, he was flying. Literally flying, backward through the air, his ears ringing, the oranges and reds of the explosion seared into his retinas. The back of his head slammed into a brick wall. He slumped to the ground, stunned, a little deaf, a little blind, but all in one piece. He'd had his helmet securely fastened, procedure was procedure, Ghazaliyah was still Ghazaliyah, and so he was still alive. Eating dust, eating smoke, smelling fire, hearing screams, seeing bodies, but still alive.

"D.B!" he shouted, staggering to his feet.

No answer.

"D.B.! Come on! Come on! Where are you?"

No, he remembered thinking. No, no, no, this is not happening, ten hours before we pull out. No.

He stumbled forward, shoving people out of the way with his hands, the butt of his gun. Screaming her name, screaming himself hoarse, knowing after the first thirty seconds that he probably was better off not finding her, better off not messing with the memories running through his head that instant, better off remembering her intact, whole, alive.

But he kept going anyway.

Kept picturing the little girl. Kept trying to imagine what that kid must have felt. On her way to paradise, on her way to martyrdom? Happy to be going? Or maybe she hadn't known the bomb was in the basket. Maybe they'd planted it and sent her off. What kind of person could do something like that?

He stopped in the middle of the street.

Felt a hundred pairs of eyes on him. Staring. Glaring. Like what had happened was his fault, as if just by being here he'd triggered the bomb. Which was absolutely untrue. These people had spent centuries fighting—dragging each other into dark alleys and doing unmentionable things in the name of...

And there was his answer, Shurig realized.

What kind of person could send a little girl off to die with a smile on her face?

He was surrounded by them.

Right then, right there, he made a decision.

No more reasoning with these people. No more trying to protect them from themselves. No more negotiating. It was them or us.

"Them or us," he said quietly, taking a last swig of his coffee. Picturing D.B.

Picturing Sam.

The door to the conference room opened. Kincaid emerged, looking ashen-faced. He disappeared down the hall without noticing Shurig. A second later, an agent ushered him in.

❖ ❖ ❖ ❖ ❖

Kennedy was at one end of the table, a manila folder spread in front of him. He didn't even look up as Shurig entered the room. A coat hung over the back of the chair to his right. A guy in an air force uniform sat in the chair to his left, his lips pursed in what looked like a smirk, like he smelled something foul.

"This is Lieutenant O'Neill. Air Police. He's assisting on the investigation," Kennedy said, still not looking up.

"Agent Shurig," O'Neill said, rising, holding out his hand, that odd smirk on his face.

"Lieutenant." They shook across the table.

O'Neill was a little guy. Thinning hair, wire-frame glasses. Didn't look like much, but he was Air Police, and they were the Air Force version of an Army M.P., toughest guys in the service, so he could handle himself in a fight.

He had to be a top-notch investigator too. The Air Force would send their best on something like this—an FBI agent shot on an Air Force base. O'Neill would look into everything.

The bureau would let him, up to a point. But it was one of theirs who had gone down and they would take the lead. Cooperate as best they could, but if push came to shove...

Kennedy was in his shirt sleeves. His shirt sleeves looked expensive. Kennedy dressed for success. And it had worked. Two years into the job here and already they were grooming him for a big position back east. The biggest, eventually. Consensus had been that his chances were good, if he could control his temper. But with two agents dead in two days...

Kennedy apologized to Shurig for making him wait, introduced himself, added that he wished they had met under different circumstances. At the first opportunity, Shurig said he wanted to be in on the investigation.

"I understand," Kennedy said. "We all want to get these bastards. One step at a time." He gave Shurig a politician's smile. In fact, he looked like a politician. Perfectly groomed hair, graying at the temples, nice teeth, square jaw.

"The clothes are window dressing," Sammy had said during Shurig's first week on the job. "He's the toughest sonuvabitch I ever met in my life. Be straight with him and you'll be fine. Mess with him, he'll cut your throat."

"I want it in your own words," Kennedy said.

"Sir?"

"I want to know what you were thinking. What you were feeling." Kennedy held up the papers he'd been reading. "What you wrote here..."

"It's thin," O'Neill said.

Shurig straightened up.

"Like you left something out," Kennedy said. "Not deliberately. But your thought process is missing."

"My thought process."

"What you were thinking when Sam pulled you out of the hospital even before doing the sketch, when he gave Njomo's hard drive to you instead of the RCFL. Multi-million-dollar computer forensics lab. Did that make any sense to you? Asking you to examine that data?"

"It all happened pretty quickly, sir," Shurig said. "Kauffman getting shot, Sam driving me to the base. I wasn't focused, I guess."

"You guess," Kennedy said, and looked Shurig right in the eye.

Shurig met his gaze head-on.

Be straight with him. Or he'll cut your throat.

But he couldn't be straight. There was a traitor in the bureau.

"Looking back," Shurig said, "I should have asked those questions."

"I want to know why Agent Hernandez broke procedure," Kennedy snapped. "Why he took you up to Fox, put you on the Intel station. Why he was taking a plane to Kirtland Air Force Base."

Shurig blinked. "He was what?"

"Taking a plane to Kirtland Air Force Base in New Mexico," Kennedy said. "Any idea why he was going there?"

"First I heard of it."

"He didn't tell you he was going to New Mexico? Didn't tell you why?"

"No, sir."

Kennedy waited. Staring at him.

Shurig resisted the urge to say more. Because he did know. But he couldn't say. He resisted the temptation to reach in his back pocket and pull out a dollar bill.

"You see the *Times* this morning?" Kennedy asked.

"Yes sir." Hard to miss it. Half-page headline: "FBI Hero Assassinated." A picture of Sammy with the vice president six months after Long Beach, at the school's rededication. The two of them surrounded by a bunch of smiling kids and teachers.

"A hundred twenty-six people dead that day," Kennedy said. "If it hadn't been for Hernandez, it would have been a thousand. He was a symbol."

"Yes, sir."

"Him getting shot on an Air Force base in broad daylight...I won't allow it. You understand?"

"Yes, sir."

Kennedy held up the folder. "This is not good enough." He leaned across the desk, not looking remotely like a smooth politician. Shurig thought the man might take a swing at him. "I want to go through what happened from the beginning. I want to know what Hernandez said word for word. I want you to describe the expression on his face, the inflection in his voice."

Someone knocked on the door and a woman stuck her head inside.

"Washington called again, sir," she said. "The Director."

Kennedy sighed. "Damn it. You remind her we have a conference call in an hour?"

"Yes, sir. She needs to talk to you before that."

"For God's sake." He stood up and gathered his papers. "Agent Shurig, you'll give your information to these gentlemen. All of it." He met Shurig's eyes.

"Yes, sir."

"We need to know who did this. Because we are going to retaliate. If it was Hamas or Al-Hasra or Hezbollah or someone else entirely... we are going to retaliate. But we can't start shooting in the dark hoping to hit the right target."

❖ ❖ ❖ ❖ ❖

Shurig spent the next two hours answering questions. Telling stories, mixing lies with truths and half-truths, hoping he hadn't contradicted himself or anything the other guys in the squad had said.

O'Neill was a good interrogator.

He kept going over the timeline—when they left the hospital, what time they got to the base. Shurig skipped the trip to Jack in the Box, figuring Burghart didn't mention it, but the omission left a gap of at least a half hour. He filled it with a stop at a gas station and Hernandez's mysterious phone call.

O'Neill didn't seem to be buying it, but Shurig couldn't read him. They broke for coffee twice, which helped, but Shurig kept wishing for his vial of little blue pills. The ones that had kept him on point in Ghazaliyah. They were prescription, and the only one he had was the one Haileigh gave him for painkillers. And that wouldn't do—unless he resurrected his forgery skills.

Finally, they finished. Shook hands, and walked out of the stuffy conference room.

To find Burghart sitting in one of the orange chairs.

"That took awhile," she said. She wore a business suit, as usual, this one a dark blue. Her posture was all business too, her chin slightly tilted at him.

"What are you doing here?" Shurig said.

"Waiting for you. Come on."

They fell into step alongside each other.

"Kennedy made me acting supervisor," Burghart said.

"Congratulations."

"It's nothing to celebrate, obviously," she said. "We need to talk."

"I was thinking the same thing." He'd been thinking it since the shooting. She was the only other person who knew why the whole thing with Njomo had gone sour and that there was a traitor inside the bureau.

"So we'll talk," she said. "After you finish." She pointed to Jalen's lab.

"Let's get that sketch done first."

❖ ❖ ❖ ❖ ❖

Jalen did two versions—one by computer, one by hand. Shurig didn't see much difference between them. Though both looked like Rawson, neither captured the essence of the man. They worked for an hour, and Jalen was still tinkering as Shurig left. The final would go out to every Bureau office worldwide, would go up on the ten most wanted list. For all the good it would do. Rawson was gone.

Shurig and Burghart left the building a half hour later, heading into Westwood. They stopped at Mongol's for barbeque, sat on a concrete bench in front of a parking garage, ate while watching the college students go by.

"Kirtland Air Force Base," Burghart said. "Why?"

Shurig shrugged.

"He didn't say anything to you in the car? Who he suspected?"

"Not me. Not you. And he didn't trust anyone else."

Burghart sighed. "I don't know what to do here, Mike. Do we tell Kennedy?"

"Sam didn't."

"But why? Because he didn't trust him?" Burghart sipped her drink through a straw, the plate of barbeque perched awkwardly on her lap.

Shurig did know, but Sam hadn't told Burghart about the society, what he was afraid would happen if he told Kennedy about his suspicions, and Shurig wasn't going to tell her either.

"So what do we do now?" Shurig asked.

"We keep looking," Burghart said. "See if we can pick up the trail again."

"Al-Hasra."

"And the traitor."

"What do you know that I don't? What sort of evidence did Sam have?"

Burghart shook her head. "He played it very close to the vest."

"Find anything on Njomo's computer?"

"Nothing yet. Not in any of Sam's stuff. At least nothing I know of."

"Can we get a look at what they've found?"

"I can ask," Burghart said. "Point out that we might spot things they wouldn't."

"It's a good idea. I bet they go for it."

"I bet they will."

They talked a few more minutes; then Burghart stood up.

"I've got to get back," she said. She tossed what was left of her food into a nearby garbage can. "So we keep this to ourselves for now?"

"Absolutely."

She shook her head. "A traitor in the bureau." She walked away and disappeared into the crowd.

Shurig sat and watched the girls go by. Imagined Sam was sitting with him, seeing the California girls strutting their stuff, on their way to the beach. On their way to the gym.

Girls gone wild, while the world went wild around them.

Rome, before the fall.

BOOK TWO: SOLDIERS

THE next few days were a blur.

Burghart had the squad looking for clues Shurig knew didn't exist. Proof that Al-Hasra was behind the shooting. Proof that they had planted someone in the office. Shurig and his new partner, John Huston, a tall, stick-thin guy, a transfer from the Hezbollah squad, ran from source to source, hoping to pick up on something.

They put three hundred miles on Shurig's car in three days—Thursday, Friday, Saturday. Everybody was working. Nothing mattered but finding Sam's murderer. They visited mosques, community centers, local police. They got nothing.

On Saturday night, they ended up in a bar called The Blu Monkey, talking to a writer named Russell Pinto, a journalist who'd been one of Hernandez's sources. Pinto had been one of the first into Waziristan after the revolt and had gotten footage of bin Laden and the new republic's first president. Pinto had his ear to the ground in hot spots all around the world. Ridiculously accomplished, ridiculously good-looking, like a rock star. Scruff on his face, tousled hair, gym-built body.

Shurig knew Pinto was not only a good guy (he'd sent a card to the office the day after Hernandez was killed), but he knew what it was like over there. Even though he laid a little of that chickens-coming-home-to-roost crap that journalists used when talking about terrorists, he drew a line at apologizing for their actions.

The fact that his nephew was killed at Long Beach probably had something to do with that.

"Imam Husayn al-Rani," Russell said, taking a seat. They were in a booth against the far wall of the bar, beat-up red leather cushions, beat-

149

up wooden table, Shurig and Huston on one side, Pinto on the other.

Huston said, "Never heard of him."

"You will." He lifted his bottle. "Cheers." They were all drinking Red Stripe. "He gave the khutba at the Islamic Center yesterday—over on Vermont?"

"That huge place," Huston said.

"It wasn't exactly a packed house." Pinto swigged his beer. "The guy is completely off his rocker."

"Muslim cleric off his rocker," Shurig said. "What a surprise."

"He's the fundamentalist's fundamentalist," Pinto said. "An end-of-days type. Muslims mend your evil ways, or God will smite you down."

"And people buy that?"

"Not here," Pinto said. "In Egypt, though, the guy's a draw." He took a long swig, set his beer on the table. "So. You ready to do that article yet?"

"Not on your life." Shurig shook his head.

"Just give me background," Pinto said. "Training, mission parameters, that sort of thing. I'll get stories from the other guys."

"No one's going to to talk to you. Code of silence."

"Time out," Huston said. "What are you guys talking about?"

"Soldier boy's old unit," Pinto said. "Phoenix Bravo. Mike here was Special Forces. The Special Forces special forces," Pinto said.

Shurig said, "I'm not talking about it."

"Why not?" Pinto asked. "What'd you do that was so bad?"

Shurig smiled and waved away the subject. "Why don't you tell us some things. Like things about Al-Hasra."

"You guys are beating a dead horse there," Pinto said. "I've been telling Sammy that for a while. You hit them so hard after Long Beach, they're done. Pinto stood, held up his Red Stripe. "One more?"

Shurig said no, Huston said yes, Shurig changed his mind. They had one more round, and then another, and another, and another.

Shurig called a cab home. Managed to sleep till 11:30. The best sleep he'd had all week—the only dreamless sleep. The only sleep where a headless Sam didn't keep running after him, yelling things at him— you forgot the car keys, Kauffman's dead, it's your fault.

When he woke up, he went straight to the office and started look- ing through copies of what they'd found—files from Hernandez's computer, copies of letters found in his apartment, call logs for his cell phone. Some interesting leads, Shurig thought, but nothing re- motely resembling the evidence that he and Burghart had hoped to find. Nothing remotely resembling the evidence he knew ought to be there. Nothing on Alderney Financial Trust or where Sam thought that missing billions had gone and what the society might be planning to do with it. Nothing useful at all, really.

On Monday, he and Huston drove around looking for information. Around four o'clock on Tuesday afternoon, Shurig went for a walk in Westwood to clear his head of the minutiae he'd been sucking in and spitting out for the last few hours. He headed to the UCLA campus, thinking, trying to put himself in Sam's head. You've got evidence on this secret society, you're not sure who's on your side and who's not, you're an FBI agent, anything happens to you, you know everything you own is going to be gone through with the finest of fine-tooth combs...

How do you hide it? Who do you give it to? Who do you trust?

You're one of about two people I know I can count on.

Shurig stopped in his tracks.

Right there, he had his answer.

❖ ❖ ❖ ❖ ❖

On the way back to the office, walking through the campus, he saw a group of young people setting up a table on the sidewalk. Bearded young men, some in robes, young women too, all in headscarves and long dresses. A banner hanging off the front of the table: ISLAMIC STUDENTS FOR PEACE

Shurig picked up a brochure from the table and flipped through it.

Help Stop Imperialist Aggression In Afghanistan

He snorted and shook his head.

"You find this funny?" A young woman glared at him.

"I find it wrong," he said.

"You should read more about the situation. Learn what's really happening."

"Trust me. I know what's happening." He flipped through the brochure. "This is nice work, though. Expensive little piece. Who paid for it?"

Her eyes narrowed. "You're a cop."

Shurig shook his head. "FBI."

"You think because we wear the hijab we are terrorists?"

"Khimar," Shurig said. He pointed. "Your head-dress. Khimar, not hijab."

The young woman rolled her eyes and jabbed a hand on her hip.

He dropped the brochure back on the table.

"Is there a problem here, Ayah?" A female voice came from over his shoulder. Shurig turned and his jaw dropped.

A woman who looked almost exactly like Deena—D.B., from Special Forces, who he'd last seen alive seconds before the little girl offered the squad refreshments and then blew them all to bits. D.B., back from the dead.

"This man is an FBI agent," Ayah said, but Shurig wasn't listening. He stared at the woman, who of course wasn't Deena but looked remarkably like her—the shape of her face, the cut of her hair. But Deena's hair had been dark-brown; this woman's was jet-black. Deena's skin had been caramel; this woman's was toffee, Deena had been slim but muscular; this woman was just plain skinny.

"Did he show you his badge?" the woman asked.

"No," Ayah said.

"Let me see your badge," the woman said, holding out her hand. She reminded him of D.B. mostly because of her presence. Defiant. Spoiling for a fight.

Shurig looked at her outstretched hand and then at her face again. And smiled.

"Ayah, please call campus security," the woman said. Her eyes burned into him. "Tell them we have a suspicious intruder on campus."

Shurig handed over his badge. "Special Agent Michael Shurig. FBI."

She examined it. "What are you doing here?" she asked.

"Just taking a stroll."

"Harassing my students."

"You're a professor."

"That's right."

He waited for a name; she didn't give it.

"Well, professor, I was just assisting in your pupil's education here."

The professor smirked at him.

"Ayah here didn't know the difference between khimar and hijab."

"Why don't you just move along, Agent Shurig. You don't belong here."

A nasty retort bubbled into his mind, but he said, "No problem," and walked away.

Ended up back at the office, where he stayed the rest of the afternoon. And beyond. Doing paperwork. Running down leads. Making phone calls.

Wishing he'd gotten that professor's name. Her number. So he could call her. Stupid to think about that when the whole world was going crazy, but it somehow gave him comfort, forced him to think about something else, even brought D.B. back to life. Sort of.

By 9:30 everyone else in the squad—Huston, Kincaid, Dilts—was gone, and Burghart stopped by to talk. She perched her lanky frame on the corner of his desk, her normally impeccable business suit looking wrinkled and askew.

Both admitted they had made no progress.

"I'm beginning to think your buddy Pinto was right," Burghart said.

"You don't think it's Al-Hasra?" Shurig asked.

She raked her fingers through her hair. "I've been thinking about it all day. Trying to remember what Sammy said to me exactly, and I don't think he ever said Al-Hasra specifically. He just said terrorists. Which opens up the field a lot."

Shurig nodded. "You have any other group in mind?"

"I can't think of any other group it could be." She stood up to leave.

"I was thinking about going down to Long Beach tomorrow. Huston and I could..."

Burghart shook her head.

"Not Long Beach?"

"Not tomorrow." She smiled, a half-smile, a wistful, sad smile. "Tomorrow's the funeral."

❖ ❖ ❖ ❖ ❖

It was a big deal. Not as big as the dedication ceremony for the new school at Long Beach—where Sam had been called to the podium, the hero who had saved the lives of hundreds during the terrorist attack—but big enough. The vice president didn't show, but the governor did. Along with his security people. And the mayor of Long Beach, and the school principal, and a bunch of families and kids, who came in a school bus, each of them wearing the green ribbon that had become a commemorative symbol of the attack.

There were plenty of other bigwigs too. The FBI Director, for one. She and Kennedy walked in, side by side, stone-faced, which Shurig suspected had as much to do with their mutual dislike as anything else. The Los Angeles chief of police was there too, and so were a couple dozen uniformed cops, and a half-dozen women that Shurig vaguely recognized.

He saw Hernandez's family, his kids from both marriages, both his ex-wives, and all his friends. And half the agents in the Bureau, the whole Al-Hasra squad, others from the local office, all squeezed into a little East L.A. Chapel. The service was short and sweet, the sweet coming from words spoken by Hernandez's older brother, and one of his daughters.

He wanted to meet the daughter and tried to squeeze onto the receiving line to say hello, but the wait was so long, the little church so crowded, he decided to hold off.

They moved on to the cemetery, where a priest sprinkled dirt on the coffin and offered words Shurig was too far away to hear. The priest ended by asking for a moment of silent prayer for Samuel Hernandez's immortal soul. Then everyone congregated around the family, offered their condolences, and began to drift away.

The family drifted too, breaking into smaller clusters. Shurig made his way toward two women who stood apart from the rest— one tall, one short; one blond, fair-skinned, the other brunette, with a darker complexion.

The woman with her—not unattractive by any means and a good bit younger—paled by comparison. She was petite, early thirties, dark hair pulled back in a tight ponytail. She looked like she had a degree in posture—ramrod straight, her shoulders thrown back, her chin slightly raised. Though a small woman, she exuded an air of 'don't mess with me.'

Shurig walked up to them and cleared his throat. "Excuse me."

The dark-haired woman stepped in front of the other, as if to protect her. She said, "Yes?" Her dark eyes peered at him with suspicion.

"My name is Mike Shurig. I'm—I worked with your father."

"Yes. Shurig. You were there. When he was shot."

"That's right. I'm wondering if I could have a few minutes of your time. I also..." He cleared his throat. "I also wanted to let you know how sorry I am for your loss, Ms. Hernandez."

The woman shook her head. "My name is Harper."

BOOK TWO: SOLDIERS

Calvary Cemetery

West Temple Ave.

Los Angeles, CA

Wednesday, September 19, 11:46 A.M.

SHE had fainted.

Damn lucky no one found her lying on the office floor. When she regained consciousness a minute later, she put away the photo, the sheet of paper with STOP on it, and the envelope (very carefully away, had them checked by a friend at the Bureau crime lab for fingerprints, trace oils, anything, the next day, nothing—all clean). She had gone home and awaited the phone call, which came a little before eleven, though not from the Bureau but from her mother, hysterical, sobbing. Her mom's reaction surprised her. You would have thought she was still married to him, instead of thirty years divorced.

Espy had done her share of crying, too. Not right away, but when her mother called, when she heard her mother falling apart...

She fell apart too. But she needed to take care of her mom, who showed up looking a mess, the first time Espy had ever seen her that way. Her mom was not a terribly happy person most of the time, not terribly stable either, and things worsened as friends called, as the media picked up the story and twisted it into some sort of new shot in the war on terror, when it was really something else entirely, something only Espy knew about.

STOP

Like hell.

They thought she was going to fall apart? They thought she was going to run and hide? No way. Her father needed her now, maybe more now than ever. It was her case. And it had brought them closer than at any time in her life. She had grown up without him, for the most part, and suddenly he had needed her, as she had needed him for so many years. She was his daughter and she would honor him, show him how much she loved him, by nailing the people who had killed him. She felt cheated that after all the years with him not around, suddenly he was there every day. And people had taken him away from her. It wasn't fair.

Stop?

Hardly.

She was through with crying. She focused on something else now. Justice. With a lot of revenge thrown into the mix.

Of course, it had been hard to stay focused these last few days. Flying from Ohio to California, dealing with her mom, wondering what had happened to Matt, with work, with the well-wishers this morning at the church. Now she wanted only to get back to the hotel room and review what she'd learned about the shooting, see if she could get past the photos and the gory details of the investigative report the FBI guys had passed on when they talked to her. She wanted to focus on the facts, what they might tell her about the connection between Rawson and Njomo and the society and what her father had been up to the last few days and why he hadn't told her about any of it.

She'd thought they were a team.

"Everything I have, you have," he'd said to her. Almost the very last thing he'd said to her, the day he died. Called her from the road somewhere, she could hear cars whizzing past, she could hear the strain in his voice. Kauffman dead, Kazmir dead, he wanted her to get Thurman and head out there right this second, leave Cincinnati and come to him so they could figure this thing out together. He sounded worried. He sounded a little bit scared.

Which was completely unlike him.

"Dad," she said. "Is something going on? Is there something you're not telling me?"

"No," he said.

Everything I have, you have.

"Ms. Harper?"

She looked up and saw Agent Shurig staring at her. Waiting for an answer to his question.

"I'm sorry," she said.

"No problem. Just wondered if we could talk at some point, before you leave." He was a youngish guy, around her age, not especially big, but he had an intimidating presence. Solid build, sandy hair, fair complexion, with hazel eyes that seemed older than his face, as if he'd seen a lot in a relatively young life, maybe seen too much. He looked powerful, even dangerous, and yet there was a melancholy quality about him.

"Yes, we can talk," she said. "I'm flying back on the red-eye tonight," she said. "I could do early evening. Around six?"

"Whatever works." He gave her his card. "Just give me a call."

"Sure," Espy said. "I will."

Shurig stood there, as if he wanted to say more.

Over his shoulder, Espy saw two women in their sixties, maybe seventies, dressed in plain black dresses walking toward them. One looked vaguely familiar, but then her view of the woman was blocked as her mom stepped past her, crying all over again, and fell into the woman's arms.

Shurig cleared his throat. "I just wanted to say," he began, and stopped again, and over his shoulder, the older woman who'd been talking to her mother suddenly turned toward Espy, and looked straight at her. And smiled.

And Espy's heart jumped.

"Esperanza," the woman said, or maybe Espy just imagined her saying it, but in any case, the woman came toward her.

"It's a loss to all of us at the Bureau," Shurig went on. "The whole department. We're going to miss him."

"Yes," Espy said.

"He was..." Shurig shook his head. "I mean, there's only a certain number of guys you meet in your life, who become like—family, and your father, I kind of came to feel like he..."

"Yes," she said again, and then, "excuse me," and she stepped by Shurig and fell into the older woman's arms.

"Abuela," she said. "Abuela."

And as her grandmother held her close, stroked her hair, Espy discovered that she wasn't through with crying after all.

Not by a long shot.

❖ ❖ ❖ ❖ ❖

She should have left it at that, the family reunion. The tearful hug with Grandma Rosa, her *abuela*, at least the closest thing to an *abuela* she'd ever have in her life, the only person on her father's side of the family who'd ever treated her like anything other than an outsider.

Instead, she let her mother talk her into going back to her sister's house for the reception, which had proved to be as uncomfortable as she'd expected. The small house was packed with family and friends who sustained a hum of quiet conversations, nibbled on the food that had been laid out on rickety tables.

Carli was her half-sister, her father's daughter by his first wife, the wife he'd left when he met her mother, the wife whose name Espy couldn't even remember, whose picture Espy was staring at now, pinned to the lime-green refrigerator in her half-sister's kitchen by a Central High School magnet. Olivia, Espy thought. That was it. Her father's first wife's name was Olivia.

"That's my grandma."

Espy, standing in the kitchen and trying not to look completely out of place, turned to see a little girl in a white dress. Straight black hair, brown skin, brown eyes, arms folded behind her back.

"That's who I'm named after," the girl said.

"That makes you Olivia. Am I right?"

"Hey!" The girl's eyes widened in surprise. "How'd you know that?"

"I've heard about you," Espy said. Her father had sent pictures of the little girl a few months back, attaching them to his e-mails, telling Espy about how smart she was, how cute...

What he hadn't mentioned: little Olivia looked exactly like Espy when she was a kid. Not that big a surprise.

"You heard about me how?" the girl asked.

I'm your aunt, Espy was about to say.

And then the bathroom door opened and her sister Carli stepped out.

Carli had gained a lot of weight. Fifty pounds, easy. She was a few inches taller than Espy and wore a black dress at least two sizes too tight. Tottering around on heels at least an inch too tall. Panty-hose bunching at the knee, skin folding over at the waist, too much makeup, especially around the eyes.

She was two years older than Espy but looked at least forty.

"Go find your father," Carli snapped at Olivia.

"But I gotta use the bathroom," Olivia said.

"Quick, then." Carli held the door open for her daughter and pulled the door shut behind her. The little girl gave Espy one last smile before disappearing from sight.

"She's beautiful," Espy said.

Carli nodded. "Wasn't sure I'd see you here."

For a second Espy thought she was talking about the funeral and was about to say how could I not come to my own father's funeral, what kind of person do you think I am, especially since it's my fault he's dead, I'm the one who got him into all this, then she realized Carli was talking about the reception.

"I wasn't sure I was going to come myself," Espy said. "But..."

"So you're a lawyer now," Carli said.

"That's right. I work for the government."

"Yeah. Pop said."

Pop. Carli had always called their father by that name. Espy remembered thinking that was funny, the one summer she'd come out here to stay with her dad, to try and be part of his world too. She and Carli spent the better part of a week together, when her dad got called on a case. The two of them got on each other's nerves. Started with arguments, but then one day Carli smacked Espy in the face, gave her a black eye, and when it happened again Espy had called her mom, who had come on the next plane and taken her back to Cincinnati.

"How about you?" Espy asked. "How are you doing?"

"We're doing good," Carli said. "Hernan's still working at the Vons, Olivia's starting kindergarten. Friend of mine and I are opening a salon."

She said it with an attitude, arms folded across her chest, like she was daring Espy to make some kind of snide comment. Like she wanted to start another fight.

"That's great," Espy said, trying to sound enthusiastic. Happy for Carli. This was her sister, after all. Her brother-in-law. Her niece. Her family.

Complete strangers.

Olivia came out of the bathroom. Smiled at Espy.

"Go find your father," Carli reminded her.

"Yes, mama." She turned to Espy. "Bye."

Espy nodded and smiled. "Bye."

She watched the little girl scamper into the living room, which continued to fill with people. Espy didn't see her mother anywhere.

"Do me a favor," Carli said. "Don't go telling her you're my sister."

"Why not?" Espy asked, though she thought she knew the answer.

Carli obviously was jealous of her and didn't want Olivia to compare them.

"I don't want her thinking she's got an aunt that pays no attention to her," Carli said. "That don't remember her birthday, that's not really part of the family. Might make her think she done something wrong."

"Carli, even if you and I don't get along...I'm still family."

Carli smirked. "Family? You and your shit-don't-stink mother come out here once every ten years, that's not family. You don't come to my wedding, you don't come to Livvy's christening, that's not family."

"I haven't seen you in Cincinnati, either."

"I don't think I ever got no invitation to Cincinnati," Carli said.

Espy figured that was true. But she hadn't received a wedding invitation, had she? Her father had said something once, would you like to come, and she had said something along the lines of are you kidding, if I showed up she'd probably kick my ass.

"You telling me I'm wrong?" Carli said. "You telling me you're gonna move out here and be part of Livvy's life?"

"Move here? No, of course not, but I—"

Carli pushed past her into the living room.

Espy watched her go, saw her pass by Olivia, who stood near the food table, who then turned around and looked at Espy. And smiled.

Espy smiled back. Waved.

Goodbye, Livvy.

She walked out the back door and called Shurig.

❖ ❖ ❖ ❖ ❖

On the way back to the hotel, her mother, a little drunk, gave advice. Don't make the same mistakes I made. You have a great career that gives you personal satisfaction, but I don't see you with friends, and I worry about that. If you sacrifice everything, you'll end up lonely—like me.

The whole ride back—through the heart of East L.A., past the dollar stores and liquor stores and the cheap furniture outlets and the fast-food knock-offs, on the freeway and into Malibu, where they were staying, where her mother always stayed, at the Taj Mahal Hotel—her mother dispensed advice while Espy nodded.

Of course, her mother was drunk.

Espy gave the car to the valet and helped her mother upstairs to their room. Settled her into bed, and then went down to the bar.

Shurig sat at one end of the bar by himself. Looked like he'd been there awhile. A half-eaten plate of nachos in front of him, a half-empty beer.

"Ms. Harper," he said, getting up from his stool. "Thanks for making time."

She took the stool next to him and ordered a Coke. The bartender asked Shurig if he wanted another beer.

"No, no." Shurig shook his head. "One's my limit."

They made small talk about the funeral and then got down to business.

"There's a case I'm working on," Shurig said, "and I wondered if maybe you could help me."

Espy said nothing, waiting to find out about this guy. She noticed the odd mix of aggression and wistfulness that had struck her at the cemetery. His eyes looked sad, but his firm jaw suggested that he'd have no problem, if the situation required, with knocking someone out.

"Actually, it's not my case," he said. "It's one of your father's."

"My father and I didn't talk about his work. We had a firm rule about that."

"Surprising," he said. "Him being in the Bureau, you being in Justice."

"That was the way he wanted it," Espy said.

"Okay." Shurig sipped at a glass of ice water like he had all the time in the world. Which she didn't. She had about an hour and a half to pack and get to the airport. She wanted him to get on with it, ask his questions so she could ask him what her dad had said that last day, give it to her word for word or as close as he could get it, something that might give her a clue about what he'd found out, why he was flying to New Mexico.

Then Shurig said, "513-588-5377."

Espy coughed, cleared her throat. "Come again?" she said.

"It's the number that showed up on Sam's phone reports. An encrypted cell phone that disappeared out of an evidence locker a couple months ago."

"I don't know anything about it. How would I?"

"The area code is Cincinnati. Your father made a call to that number at 5:20 A.M. the day he was killed."

"If you're asking me who he was calling," Espy said, "I'm afraid I don't know."

Five twenty A.M. the day he was killed. He was at the Columbus airport, heading back to L.A. after springing Matt from jail. Something's happened, he had said. Something terrible.

"There was an agent killed that day," Shurig said. "My partner."

"Ben Kauffman," Espy said. "I know. Those other agents told me about that. They said they thought the two deaths were connected. Something to do with Al-Hasra."

"Al-Hasra's not involved," Shurig said.

Espy looked at his eyes, his face, trying to get a clue about this guy. "You sound pretty sure about that."

"I am. Aren't you?"

"I don't know anything about it."

"Or the phone number."

"That's right," she said.

Shurig shook his head. "You're a terrible liar, Ms. Harper."

Espy sat up straight. "I beg your pardon?"

"I wouldn't get in any high-stakes poker games if I were you."

Espy glared at him, then climbed off the stool, pulled a few singles out of her purse, and threw them on the bar. "Nice meeting you, Agent Shurig. Good luck on your case."

She turned to go.

"Listen, I understand if you're scared," he said. "These are very dangerous people we're dealing with."

"Al-Hasra," she said.

"You know who." He picked up one of the dollars she'd put on the bar. Held it up so the eagle on the back faced her.

Espy stared at him a good long minute.

"He told you," she said.

Shurig nodded.

"Let's walk," she said. "I need to walk."

BOOK TWO: SOLDIERS

Palisades Park
Ocean Avenue
Santa Monica, CA
Wednesday, September 19, 6:05 P.M.

THEY walked along a sidewalk near the hotel, the California sky beginning to turn pink. Shurig told her what Sam had told him and told her some of what he suspected. She told him about the note she'd received and the picture that came with it.

STOP.

"But you're not going to," Shurig said.

"No." She stopped in the middle of the sidewalk and looked him head-on. "I want to make sure we're clear on this," she said. "If we're going to work together."

"Okay," he said, unsure where she was heading.

"The scope of what we're talking about. What you're getting involved in."

"These guys walked onto an Air Force base and killed your dad," Shurig said. "I think I get it."

"Do you? Do you have any idea who these people are?"

"Some kind of secret society."

"They're terrorists, that's who they are. No different from Al-Hasra or Hezbollah. The ends justify the means. They don't care who gets hurt or who gets killed. As long as they get what they want."

"Which is what?" Shurig asked.

She looked away, down the street, where traffic lights gleamed in the dusk. Shurig was about to ask the question again but noticed her eyes glistening and realized she wasn't thinking about the Society of Cincinnati right that second. She was thinking about her dad.

Shurig couldn't help thinking about him too.

"Sorry," she said, and wiped her eyes.

"No need to apologize," Shurig said. He pointed across Ocean Avenue to one of the little parks that dotted the beach side of the street overlooking the ocean and the cliffs leading down to it. "Over there. We can sit. Talk it through."

She nodded, still looking a little lost. A little bit shell-shocked. He understood.

He took her arm, and led her across the street.

❖ ❖ ❖ ❖ ❖

They sat on a bench under a palm tree. And started in on what she knew—the history first, George Washington and his role model, and the organization he'd inspired. She told him about the Cincinnati, the officers, the suspicions they'd aroused after the war. Shurig let her go on even though he knew the story. He wanted her to get comfortable, so she'd be at ease talking to him. Though he wasn't sure how capable she was of relaxing. In some ways, it was hard to believe she was Sam's kid. Not so much physically—she was from the same gene pool obviously—but mentally.

A whole lot of Sam's charm flowed from his easy-going nature. He was at home in the world. His daughter seemed just the opposite. Wary. Rigid. Wrapped tighter than her ponytail, which yanked back from her face like it was held with a vise.

"... that's what they were, really," she was saying. "A veterans rights organization."

"That's not all they were, though," Shurig said. "People thought they were gearing up to take over the country."

"Making George Washington king, you mean?" She shook her head. "That was never going to happen."

"Why not?"

"Because Washington wouldn't have allowed it. He wanted to be

Cincinnatus, remember? Not Caesar. Retire to his farm, not sit on a throne."

"But that was then. What about now? What is the society now?"

"They're headquartered in Washington, D.C., they have state chapters in each of the original thirteen colonies, they sponsor a lot of educational programs. Patriotic programs, teach students about the Revolutionary War, why it was fought, that sort of thing. On the surface, anyway."

"So what makes you so sure they're involved in all this?"

"What did my father tell you?"

"Not much. He didn't have time." Shurig filled her in. Alderney. MGT. The missing money.

"The gambling money." Harper nodded. "That's where this all started."

"A billion dollars?"

"More. I'm not sure exactly how much."

"Which they're getting how? Casinos, that sort of thing?"

She shook her head. "We think they're fixing golf tournaments."

Shurig knit his brow. "Fixing golf tournaments? Is that possible?"

"I'm not entirely sure, to tell you the truth. We had a guy..."

She fell silent then. Trying to collect her thoughts, Shurig figured at first, but then realized she was trying to get her emotions under control.

"You had a guy..." he prompted.

"A golfer. Matt Thurman. He was trying to help figure it out."

"And?"

"Gone. I think they killed him too," she said.

❖ ❖ ❖ ❖ ❖

Espy didn't know why she was getting choked up about it. She'd known Thurman for all of a day. Maybe she just felt sorry for him, the mess he'd found himself in. Or maybe she felt guilty for breaking him out. If they hadn't, he might still be alive.

Accent on the might. The society had hired someone to kill him in prison. By breaking him out, they'd just delayed the inevitable. Or hastened it.

"He's dead?" Shurig looked surprised. "You sure about that?"

She nodded. "It's what they do."

She'd been sure that first night, that horrible night, the image of her father lying on the runway still fresh in her mind, sure as soon as she walked up to her apartment door and realized she didn't have her keys, Matt had her keys, and where was Matt, he hadn't answered the phone before, he wasn't here now, he was gone. Run off? No, she'd decided instantly. She'd only known Thurman those few hours, but she knew that even if there had been a reason for him not being at her apartment, he would have called. So something had happened to him. And, logically, what was that something?

They found him, killed him, and taken the body, put it someplace where it would never be found. It was the only reasonable conclusion. Call it a fact.

She explained her reasoning to Shurig. She explained their history with Thurman too, what he'd been accused of doing, how they knew he was innocent, how her father had arranged the escape.

"Rawson," Shurig said. "Same guy?"

"Sounds like."

"And the other guy on the course—no name?"

"None."

"Fixing golf tournaments." Shurig shook his head. "Are you sure about that?"

"It's how this whole thing started."

"Go on," Shurig said.

And she did.

❖ ❖ ❖ ❖ ❖

It had all begun five months ago, almost to the day. A Tuesday. Tuesday afternoons were the time when Espy worked on her Suspicious Activity Reports, filed by bankers and stockbrokers and anyone involved in the financial industry who came across transactions in excess of ten thousand dollars that seemed, well, suspicious. The reports were mandated by law in those instances, and thousands of them gummed up the works at FINCEN, the Financial Crimes Enforcement Network, waiting to be reviewed. Someone in the Justice Department had gotten the bright idea that local enforcement might be able to lend a hand with that mountain of paper, and so for the last six months Espy had been a (mostly) unwilling participant in a pilot program to see if that bright idea had any merit.

So far her vote was no.

The one in front of her seemed unlikely to change her vote. It was from the compliance officer at Fifth Third Bank. The offending party was Bob Kazmir, of Powell, Ohio. The amount in question: $10,048. Just over the legally mandated reporting threshold.

Espy took one look at it and sighed. $10,048? The kinds of cases the department took on involved hundreds of thousands at a minimum, everyone knew that, why had this report even been filed? She flipped through the document, saw right away that it was less about the single transaction than a pattern, a series of wires for smaller, under-the-radar amounts—five or six thousand dollars, dozens of them over the last few years, that added up to a couple hundred thousand dollars. It looked like small potatoes, like the guy at Fifth Third was just being careful by reporting the amount the law required.

She learned that Kazmir was an ex-PGA golfer from the Columbus area, who ran a business called Kazmir Associates, which had something to do with golf. The $10,048 had been paid into his account by a Costa Rican sportsbook called High Roller's Haven—gambling money, obviously. So were the other amounts, which had all come from various sportsbooks and internet gambling sites. Odds were good he hadn't reported every bit of that gambling income, but so what? These days, gambling offenses were low on the priority list.

Of course, it was possible that Kazmir's 'winnings' weren't that at all, that the 'sportsbooks' weren't real sportsbooks, that they were paying off Kazmir with dirty money—drug money or terrorist funds—which came out of his accounts clean. Possible, she supposed. But unlikely. Still...

Due diligence.

She called High Roller's Haven, whose COO (and CEO, and majority owner, she saw from the incorporation papers) was a man named George Babyak, who was too busy to talk until she mentioned she was from the Department of Justice. Then he listened.

"I'm calling about Bob Kazmir," Espy said. "On April eleven of this year you paid $10,048 to his account at the Fifth Third Bank. Do you recall that transaction?"

She could almost see Babyak shaking his head. "That was like a month ago. You think I remember paying off a single bet from a month ago?" Then he said, "The golf guy. Sonuvabitch. Him and his friend, I lost fifteen grand. On a golf tournament? Never happens. Tell me they're in trouble. Please tell me they're in trouble."

"I just have a few questions."

"What'd this guy do? Kneecap somebody? Because he's a cheat, I can tell you that. Without a doubt, he's a cheat."

Espy scribbled notes. "Why do you say that?"

"Come on. He bets a hundred to one shot to win, and it comes through? The fix was in, obviously."

She'd been on the periphery of a few gambling investigations, enough to know that the big betting money wasn't on golf. It was on football and basketball, pro and college. And none of the high rollers bet long shots. So Kazmir wasn't a high roller unless the bet was an aberration.

"Hey, I'm kidding, right?" Babyak said. "Not making any official allegations here. Come on, how could you fix a golf tournament?"

"I have no idea," Espy said, which was the truth. She knew nothing about golf. "Does Mr. Kazmir bet with you frequently?"

Espy heard fingers typing on a keyboard. "No. That was it. First and only time."

"You mentioned something about his friend..."

"I don't know if the guy was his friend. They made the same bet, that's all I know, they bet this same longshot."

"You have a name?"

More typing. "Charles Knox."

The name was familiar to her, for some reason.

"He bet with you a lot, this Charles Knox?"

"Only time for him too."

"And how'd you pay him?"

"Paid the money right to the card he placed the bet with."

"Which was on what bank?"

"Let's see...Alderney Financial Trust."

Hearing that, Espy's radar went up, just a little bit.

Alderney was one of the Channel Islands. There were only a handful of jurisdictions that didn't comply to the letter with U.S. banking regulations. Even places like Switzerland and the Caymans were cooperating now with the new rules about client confidentiality and customer identification. The Channel Islands were one of the last places on the planet where financial institutions still fought to preserve their customers' right to operate in as close to total secrecy as possible.

She thanked Babyak and hung up. Instead of throwing the SAR on the 'no' pile, she moved it to the stack of 'maybes,' for follow-up.

In early May, she ran Kazmir's credit report. He had accounts at two other banks besides Fifth Third. One in his hometown of Powell, an affluent Columbus suburb, and another in Florida, in a place called Wilton Manors, which sounded like money too, though both his homes were mortgaged to the hilt. He was also in the middle of a fight with a local Mercedes dealership over late lease payments, and he'd fallen well behind on his credit cards, though the balances were so high and the interest rates so exorbitant, that the card companies were cutting him and his wife a great deal of slack.

Which fit nicely with another piece of information: Kazmir's wife came from big family money. Family as in Constantine Petropolos, as in Petropolos Construction. Millions of dollars in a trust fund, houses in Nantucket and the Bahamas, apartments in New York and South Beach. She was used to a certain lifestyle, and it looked like Bob was spending well beyond his means to keep her in it. Which probably accounted for the gambling. Probably.

She looked for more information on Kazmir Associates. Net worth, net income. She couldn't find it. She called Fifth Third. They didn't have it either. Kazmir's company banked overseas. In the Channel Islands.

With Alderney Financial Trust.

"Coincidence," Shurig said.

They had gotten up from the bench, moved to the cliff overlooking the beach and the Pacific beyond.

"That was my first thought too," she said. "Except I don't really believe in coincidences when it comes to this kind of thing. Besides which, there was more."

She told him about it. More names: Hand and Pickering and Shaw and a dozen others she finally recognized. Original members of the Society of the Cincinnati. That couldn't be coincidence; somebody was a history buff. Somebody was running all those accounts, but she couldn't find out who. The trail dead-ended at Alderney.

She called her father. First thing he found was the MI-5 memo. That sent them looking for more information, not just on Alderney, but on the companies the memo listed. MGT, in particular. Which had its own connections to the Cincinnati and to a half-dozen other companies. A web, Harper called it. With the society at the center.

Shurig listened as she reeled off the names, but the information flew by too fast for him to really absorb. He was tired.

He looked down at the highway and the beach beyond. The sand. Ghaziliyah.

Salaam. Salaam aleikum.

D.B., reaching for an orange.

He thought back to her funeral, back to his first few days stateside, how lost he'd felt, how he'd decided then to keep fighting the war, only in a different way. He wanted to join the Bureau. People thought he was crazy and tried to talk him out of it, saying the Bureau's not looking for soldiers or cops anymore, they're looking for lawyers and data analysts and bankers and computer programmers. They turned out be right. It had been next to impossible to get an interview. Strings had to be pulled, and even after that, it wasn't easy.

But eventually he got in. His mind drifted to his first few days in L.A., on the front lines of the war alongside one of that war's true heroes, and he pictured that hero in his mind's eye—Sam putting a hand on his shoulder, telling him we don't need any heroes at this point.

"I'm not boring you, am I?" Harper asked.

Shurig woke from his reverie. "Sorry. Just trying to follow the thread."

"What aren't you following?"

He had to get back on track here. Focus.

"The SAR got you to Kazmir, who got you to the Channel Islands—"

"To Alderney Financial."

"Right. Which got you to the Cincinnati."

"Basically."

"Okay." He nodded. "So where does Kirtland fit in?"

"I don't know."

"You don't know why Sam was going to Kirtland?"

"No."

"But you were working together. Your number is all over his phone records."

"He never said anything about New Mexico."

Shurig pushed back from the railing. She didn't know why Sam was going to Kirtland?

This was a problem.

"I must have missed something," she said. "I'll go through everything I have when I get home."

"I'm not sure that's a good idea."

"What do you mean?"

"That note, for one thing. They obviously know you're on to them."

"I'm not scared, if that's what you're saying."

"That's part of what I'm saying." He turned to face her. "There's more, though."

BOOK TWO: SOLDIERS

The Hotel Taj Mahal America
Ocean Avenue
Santa Monica, CA
Wednesday, September 19, 8:15 P.M.

A traitor in the bureau.

It was all she could think about as they headed back to the hotel.

It wasn't possible. But it explained a lot, her father's behavior these last few weeks, for one thing. It explained why he held back whatever information led him to Kirtland.

Which didn't make it any easier for her to forgive him for keeping her in the dark. They'd shared everything. They'd sent encrypted files back and forth to each other as the investigation unfolded. Via e-mail, via CD, via cloud-based storage programs. Duplicate copies of their work, so that in case one of them was unavailable, the other didn't have to wait. So that in case something happened to one copy, they'd have another.

So that if, worst case scenario, something happened to one of them...

Everything I have, you have.

But he'd lied.

They reached the door of her hotel room and as she unlocked it she heard voices. A man's and a woman's.

"Esperanza, we're in here."

She walked into the living room of their suite, Shurig a step behind.

Her mom sat on the couch, looking wide awake. A man sat on a chair opposite her. A small man with glasses, wearing a military uniform. Air Force.

"You're up," Espy said to her mother.

"I'm up and packed. And I packed your things. We have to leave

177

in ten minutes, don't we?" Harper's mother gestured toward the man rising from his seat. "I told the lieutenant you'd be back sooner."

"O'Neill. Air Force Security Services. I'm part of the investigation into your father's death."

"Esperanza Harper," she said.

As they shook hands, O'Neill nodded at Shurig.

Shurig nodded back.

Old friends?

She didn't think so.

❖ ❖ ❖ ❖ ❖

O'Neill wanted to talk to Harper alone. No offense, Agent Shurig. I'm sure you understand. Shurig did. The guy didn't entirely trust him. And it probably looked like he was horning in on the case.

He went to the hotel lobby and waited, thumbing through a decorative book about vintage American cars he found on an end table—Studebakers, Packards, Crosleys. Read the newspaper, a little piece on Husayn al-Rani, the Muslim leader, and reactions to his visit here.

Fifteen minutes passed.

The elevator door opened, and the two Harpers walked out, O'Neill a step behind them. After the goodbyes, O'Neill and Shurig turned to face each other.

"You want to talk?" the lieutenant asked, his lips pursed in what looked like a smirk.

"Absolutely."

They went into the bar and took seats. The same seats he and Harper had vacated a couple hours before. They both ordered Coke. Then O'Neill got to his point.

"What are you doing here?"

"Same thing you are," Shurig said. "Investigating."

"I wasn't aware you were officially part of the investigation."

"I want to find out who killed my friend."

"You think your guys missed something when they talked to her?"

"Maybe," he said. "Obviously you think the same thing."

O'Neill pulled over a bowl of peanuts, popped a few in his mouth. "The mother's a piece of work," he said. "Nice house. But nobody's home."

"I wouldn't know," Shurig said.

"You didn't recognize her?" O'Neill asked. "I guess you're too young. She was an actress, back in the eighties. Had a couple guest spots on some networks shows—*Magnum, P.I.?*"

"Never heard of it."

"My wife loved that show. There was this one episode, Magnum had to judge a bikini contest...she was in it. Penelope Harper." He took a sip of his soda.

Shurig decided not to wait for O'Neill to ask; he'd volunteer the information. "Her number was all over his phone records. The daughter."

O'Neill nodded. "You ask her about it?"

"She said as far as she was aware, they weren't talking any more than usual. What'd she tell you?"

O'Neill rolled an ice cube around his mouth. Made a non-committal noise.

Fine, Shurig thought. He'd get the real story later.

"What about his work?" the lieutenant asked. "They talk about his work at all?"

Shurig shook his head again. "She had a general idea what the squad was up to, but no real specifics."

"And she had no idea why he was going to Kirtland?"

"None."

"What do you know about Kirtland?" O'Neill asked.

"It's in New Mexico, right?"

"Albuquerque. The place is huge. Fifty thousand acres. Air Force base doesn't really describe it. It's a research facility. Sandia National Laboratory, Space Vehicle Development, Directed Energy, Nuclear Weapons Center..."

"High security stuff."

"High tech stuff. Not just military. A lot of private sector too. Over a hundred companies with some kind of presence there. I made a list of those companies. Maybe you could take a look, see if any of the names ring a bell."

Down at the end of the bar, a woman's laugh rang out. Shurig turned and looked at her—close-cropped hair, dark-skinned...vaguely Middle Eastern looking. He was reminded of the professor.

"You heard we found the casings, right? The shells?" O'Neill asked.

Shurig turned back to him. "I did."

"Shoved into a storm drain on top of a parking garage. About a thousand yards from the runway." He shook his head. "That's a hell of a shot. You think Al-Hasra has someone who can pull that off?"

"Possible," Shurig said. "There were training ranges at the camps. A busted-up crate of Black Arrow M-93s..."

"Yeah. I saw the report." O'Neill nodded, chomped down on another cube. "Thing is, I was talking to some guys I know in Air Force Intelligence. Guys with their ears to the ground. They haven't heard a peep out of Al-Hasra in six months. Since the raids on Waziristan. They think they're finished."

"I don't know about that."

"Al-Hasra," O'Neill said. "They got the name from a fort, right?"

"In Northern Iran. Adabril province."

"A fort no one could ever conquer."

Shurig smiled. "You've been doing your homework."

"So is that what they've been doing since Waziristan—holing up in their fort? Plotting their revenge on the guy who took them down? Hernandez ruined their big moment at the school in Long Beach so they take him out?"

"Maybe," Shurig said again.

"What did Hernandez think?"

Shurig shook his head, and told the whole truth for the second time during their conversation. "I wish I knew."

They sat in silence a moment.

"An Al-Hasra revenge killing," O'Neill said, but didn't seem convinced.

"What do Kennedy and the others think?" Shurig asked.

"They don't see it like I do." He fixed his eyes on Shurig. "But I'm thinking you do. I'm thinking that's why you're here."

Shurig took a deep breath. "I'm thinking you might be right."

"And what else are you thinking?"

They locked eyes.

Windows to the soul, that's what they taught him in Bravo, when they were telling him how to stay safe, how to spot trouble on patrol in a potentially threatening area, a hostile neighborhood. Find the eyes. Read the eyes—several pairs, if you can. They'll tell you intent. Attitude. Windows to the soul. Poetic phrase. Ironically, Arabic in origin.

Unfortunately, O'Neill's eyes weren't telling him a damn thing. The guy offered only that smirk, which had begun to get under Shurig's skin.

"I'm thinking there are a lot of possibilities," Shurig said. "Which I intend to spend the next few days running down."

"You'll keep me posted?"

"If you'll do the same."

O'Neill nodded. "Deal."

Shurig got to his car and pulled out his cell phone. Two missed calls; both from Harper.

He punched in her number.

"Agent Shurig. I've been trying to reach you."

"I was with the lieutenant. He suspects something."

"That he does." She lowered her voice. "Maybe we ought to tell him."

"Why?"

"He seems honest. Plus, the military connection. We'd have someone on the inside."

Shurig thought for a moment. "Maybe," he said. "Let's not rush into anything. In the meantime, can I get a look at those files you were talking about?"

"Sure." They were on a remote server; she gave him the site and password. She said she'd review her notes when she got back to see if she'd overlooked something about the investigation.

"Just be careful," he told her. When the people they were chasing said "STOP," they meant it.

Delta Flight 787
En Route Cincinnati/Northern Kentucky International Airport
Thursday, September 20, 2:42 A.M.

HER mom slept.

Espy worked.

Half an hour's worth of housekeeping on her DOJ cases. Then she got down to business. Pulled a network card from a zippered pocket inside her purse, popped it in the cardbus slot, which the DOJ tech-support guys had disabled, of course, which her dad's tech guys had 'fixed' for her. She accessed a web proxy service to hide her IP address, and logged on to the account she and her father had shared at cloudbytes.

She pulled up the MI-5 memo and the note her father had sent with it.

Espy -

MGT. Big military contractor. Practically running the war. Chairman of the Board is Stuart Crane.

Who had also, for the last fifteen years, been president of the Society of the Cincinnati.

She pulled up a bunch of information on MGT; stuff from Bloomberg, Factiva, some articles on Crane. Skimmed through it, noted something she had missed the first time around in one of the articles. A picture. Crane and three other men, sport-fishing in the Bahamas. Actually, Crane and two of the other men were fishing. The caption identified the one who wasn't as Jed Seagrave. The other two were Kent Holwadel and Garrett Crandall.

All members of the Society.

More to the point, Crandall was the founder of the Democratic

Fund for Direct Action. And in about two months, he was going to be a senator.

At 5:30 they turned on the cabin lights in the plane. Ten minutes later, her mom popped awake in the seat next to her.

"I had the most wonderful dream," she said.

Espy shut down the laptop and put it away.

Her mother frowned. "You're working. Well, I won't bother you then. But I'm starving. I wonder what's for breakfast."

Espy held up the rock-hard bran muffin they'd brought around when the lights went on.

"That doesn't look good," her mom said, and raised a hand. The flight attendant (a guy in his late thirties who was clearly smitten) trotted right over. He and her mom chatted, Espy trying hard not to listen, to stay focused on her work. Then he walked to the front of the plane and returned a minute later with a mug of tea and an omelette from first class. "Extras," he said, without bothering to ask Espy if she wanted anything.

They were on the ground at 6:40, she was in her office at 8:50.

Amy Anderson, the office manager, walked in carrying a stack of files, humming to herself. She got two steps inside the door before she realized Espy was there.

Her jaw dropped. "Aren't you in Los Angeles?"

"Good morning to you too."

Amy put the files down on the corner of the desk, took a closer look at Espy. "Word to the wise," Amy said. "Take a few minutes, get yourself together. You look terrible."

Espy combed her fingers through her hair, wet her lips. When Amy left she pulled a compact from her purse, looked at herself in the mirror. She did the best she could to look presentable. Her mother always made this kind of thing look easy. Use the eyeliner here, and here; a thin line. Careful. That color's completely wrong. You bought what?

Honey, please, please next time... just come with me to the Clinique counter. One trip, we'll find what works and you'll be all set. Won't that be great? Won't that be a load off your mind?

Espy sighed. Another reason not to look forward to Friday night—getting the once/twice/thrice-over from her mother, getting lectures on her make-up skills, her fashion sense.

Amy came back in a few minutes. "That's...better," Amy said with a fake smile. "You know, one of these days at lunch you ought to come with me to the Aveda counter and we'll figure out which colors work best for you."

"Sure." Espy snapped her make-up kit shut. "Love to."

"You want some tea? I could bring you a cup."

"Thanks, no. I'll get one myself."

"You don't have time," Amy said. "Leonard wants to see you."

❖ ❖ ❖ ❖ ❖

She headed down the hall to Leonard's office. The Cincinnati Department of Justice (a satellite to the main Columbus office, just three attorneys and a half-dozen support staff) had half a floor in the new Federal Building. Leonard was at the far end of their floor, with half the department's windows. They used to joke about it.

They didn't make jokes anymore. They barely spoke to each other.

She knocked on the door.

"Come."

She edged it open and stepped inside.

Leonard sat behind his desk, reading. Head down.

"Good morning," she said.

"Morning." He tried to smile. But his heart wasn't in it. Unlike the smile he wore in the picture behind his desk. Leonard and Tunde, his wife, and their son, Franklin, who looked about two in the picture, but was more like three now. No wait, four.

His birthday was July third. She'd missed it, and felt the same sickening sensation in her stomach she'd felt the first time Garrett Crandall's name had popped up in connection with the society.

"You know," Leonard said, peering over the tops his glasses, "you didn't have to come in today."

"Better to have something to do than just sit around at home."

"All right," he said. "Well. Let's go over a few things."

"Sure."

"The Mandini case. We're ready for trial?"

"Yes," she said. "Thanks to Dan."

Her colleague had covered a court appearance for her last week. She wanted to review the files again, but she had till tomorrow.

"And United Apparel?"

"United Apparel," she said, trying to remember.

"I forwarded the papers a couple weeks ago."

"Oh. Right, right," she said. "Yes. United Apparel."

The file sat in her bottom desk drawer, untouched since Leonard had passed it to her. No rush, he'd said, and she'd taken him at his word, because she had a lot of other things to do. Not just Mandini. The investigation.

"I'll move it up to the top of my list," she said.

He shifted in his chair, suddenly uncomfortable. "The files on Kazmir are back in your office," he continued. "I have copies of everything. Just in case."

"Thanks. I'll catch up on what's happening, see if I can pitch in a little. I'm sure it's been a scene."

Leonard managed a smile. "I guess you could call it that."

Ever since Kazmir's murder, when news broke that the man had been the target of a gambling investigation, the whole office, but Leonard in particular, had felt a lot of pressure. Never mind that the investigation ended, at least as far as everyone but Espy was concerned, people were still up in arms. Especially the people at The Pines, who were not without political clout. A gambler on their golf course. Why weren't we notified? Why did you let him go? Why this, why that?

"Listen," Leonard said. "I know it's late in the day to be talking about this, but I want to go over some of the work you did."

"Sure," she said, suddenly uncomfortable herself.

"I was looking at the original SAR. From Fifth Third."

"Uh-huh."

"Kazmir's company. You didn't follow up on them."

"What do you mean?"

"I mean you didn't check the source of their funds. I was curious as to why."

"Why I didn't follow up on Kazmir's company?" she repeated, stalling for time, because of course she had followed the money trail from Kazmir to Alderney to MGT to Garrett Crandall to the Democratic Fund for Direct Action, and right back here, to Cincinnati, and the man sitting in the chair across from her and his wife. That was why she teamed with her father and not Leonard to investigate the society.

Leonard said, "I'd like to know what you were thinking."

Amy walked in the room.

"Excuse me," she said. "You have a visitor."

"Not now," Leonard snapped.

"Not you," Amy said. "Her." She pointed at Espy. "A lawyer named David Abraham. He's waiting out front."

"David Abraham?" Espy asked, and then stopped talking as her brain caught up to her mouth.

David Abraham.

Matt's lawyer.

❖ ❖ ❖ ❖ ❖

Leonard came with Espy to the reception area. Abraham stood up as they arrived. He was medium height. Fit-looking. And young looking for such a successful attorney. His boyish face didn't fit his track record in the courtroom.

He got quickly to the point, stating he'd been reviewing the Kazmir case while assembling Matt's defense.

"Forgive me for being blunt, sir, but don't you need a client to assemble a defense?" Leonard said.

Abraham nodded. "I have every confidence my client will surface."

More likely his body will, Espy thought.

"In the meantime," Abraham continued, "there are some things I wanted to get clear with you."

"I understood the Columbus office provided you with copies of all our files," Leonard said.

"They did." He shifted his gaze from Leonard to Espy. "But I have some questions."

"Fine." Leonard indicated the way to his office.

"I was hoping to speak with Ms. Harper alone."

"Fine," Leonard said. "It was her case." He offered a smile, a terribly false one.

Espy led Abraham to her office and shut the door behind them.

"Before we start," she said, "you're aware that anything material you say to me, I'm going to relay to my boss."

He sat down in a chair on the other side of her desk. "I don't think you'll want to repeat what I have to say."

"Okay." She leaned back in her chair. "And why is that?"

He tugged at the crease in his pants, then looked directly at her and said, "The night Bob Kazmir was killed, you were at The Pines."

BOOK TWO: SOLDIERS

U.S. Department of Justice
Federal Building
Cincinnati, OH
Thursday, September 20, 11:21 A.M.

ESPY hadn't seen that coming. Took her a second to rearrange her expression—and her thoughts.

"I was where?" she asked.

"At The Pines. The golf course."

She shook her head. "No I wasn't."

Abraham smiled again. "You're a terrible liar."

The second person to tell her that in as many days.

"What makes you think I was there?" she asked.

Abraham pulled a sheet of paper from his briefcase. He flipped through a few pages, then settled the stack on his lap.

"A conversation I had with my client. This is part of his rundown of events the night Kazmir was killed." He cleared his throat. "His words. 'It was about eight o'clock P.M., I was on the thirteenth tee, getting ready to swing, saw this woman coming up the fairway.' Could you describe her, I said. 'She was short, five two, maybe. Wearing a pantsuit, gray pantsuit, white blouse.'" Abraham paused and looked at her. "Much like the clothes you have on right now."

Espy snorted. "Marshall's sale rack. You could find a dozen women in this building wearing the same outfit."

"Matching your description?"

"A dozen on this block."

"Maybe." Abraham straightened the papers on his lap, put them back in the folder, back in the briefcase. "But I read this last night and got to thinking. Who had a reason to be there, to meet with Kazmir? Who matches this description?"

"And you thought of me."

"Eventually." He smiled. "The Internet is a wonderful thing."

"I wasn't there."

"I think you were. I can't prove it yet, but you know how easy it is to find that kind of evidence once you get enough people looking. Somebody spotted your car, you stopped someplace to buy gas, get coffee, ask directions..."

Espy met his eyes and continued to offer her mask of ease.

She could have been spotted. Her, or her car. A strange person, a strange vehicle on one of those streets, maybe someone had noticed. Abraham could have found that someone. If she was in his shoes, that's one of the first things she would do, comb the neighborhood for anyone who'd seen anything out of the ordinary. If he had proof, there would be hell to pay. She'd be disbarred for withholding information germane to a murder investigation.

"I think you set up a meeting with Kazmir," Abraham said. "A confidential meeting he obviously never made it to."

"Why would I do that?" Espy asked. "We closed the investigation months earlier. And if I wanted a meeting, why wouldn't I have him come to the office?"

Abraham shrugged. "Maybe The Pines wasn't your idea. He lived near there. Maybe he wanted to meet someplace he felt safe."

Espy almost smiled. Abraham had hit the nail on the head. Almost. Except she had been the one to make the call. She replayed it in her mind.

"You don't know me, but my name is Esperanza Harper. I want to talk to you about High Roller's Haven."

Silence.

And she'd gone on from there. Talking around the truth of what they knew, the gambling and the shell companies and the society, letting him know who she was, implying what might happen to him, working up to the suggestion that he cooperate with her investigation.

He said almost nothing. Except that he needed to think. She said she'd give him an hour, and then she was coming to his house.

He said he wanted to meet at The Pines.

She was early.

He never showed.

"You were there to talk to Kazmir about the gambling," Abraham said. "The men who killed him beat you to it."

"Those mystery men," Espy said. "Which only your client saw."

"Saw, and heard. Enough to know they were involved in it too. The gambling ring. They found out Kazmir was going to talk to you, they shut him up." Abraham took off his glasses and held them loosely in his hand. "Now that is a motive for murder. A much better one than the police are attributing to my client. An early-morning argument about who should be allowed on a putting green and when?" He shook his head. "Please."

"I'll give you that," she said.

"Give me something else. Tell me who those men were."

"I don't know," she said, making sure to meet his eyes straight-on, because now she was telling the truth.

Abraham leaned forward. "You know someone put out a contract on my client's life?"

Espy kept her face neutral. "I wasn't aware of that."

"He was supposed to get transferred to county jail number two. He would have lasted all of two days up there, from what his brother heard."

"His brother?"

"Jake Thurman. A cop. Called me a few hours before my client disappeared."

"You're telling me those two mystery men from the golf course did this?"

He nodded. "Tell me about them, Ms. Harper. My client's out

there, running scared, and he's got good reason to be. I want to bring him in before it's too late."

It's too late already, she knew.

"Obviously you know more than what's in the file," he continued. "Or you have some leads. Give them to me. I won't say where I got the information."

Espy steepled her hands. "I don't know anything that can help you."

Or Matt, she thought. Nothing can help Matt.

Except bringing the people who killed him to justice.

He leaned closer, his voice low, sincere, almost conspiratorial. "I grew up with Matt and Jake. They're like family to me. This can all be off the record. We can meet someplace, I'll put whatever you want in writing—"

"No," she said again. "I'm sorry."

Abraham sat back in his chair. "I'll find that evidence, Ms. Harper. You know I will. And when I do, the first person I go to will be your boss."

"Go to him now, then," she said. "Tell him what you think."

Abraham didn't respond. Instead, he stood, and picked up his briefcase. "Don't bother walking me out. I know the way."

❖ ❖ ❖ ❖ ❖

Leonard, of course, buzzed her as soon as Abraham left, wanting to know what had been so confidential. Espy had no choice but to tell him the truth.

"Thinks you were there?" Leonard said.

With the phone pressed to her ear, Espy leaned back in her chair, suddenly exhausted, feeling like she could shut the door and sleep for a million years.

"That's right."

"Where did he get that idea?"

"Something his client said to him."

"But you weren't."

She shook her head. "I think he was just trying to rattle my cage. See if we were holding something back about Kazmir."

"He knows everything we know."

"As far as I know," she lied again. "Probably more."

"This afternoon we can talk more about Kazmir's company. Your initial investigation."

After they hung up, she thought about shutting her door and lying on the floor under her desk. Taking a quick nap. It wouldn't be the first time. Instead, she walked to the supply room, where she found a case of Red Bull in the refrigerator. She took one back to her office, drank it down, fearing she might throw up.

Then she read through all the Mandini material in an hour, flew through complicated corporate tax issues, caught up on everything she'd missed, even talked to her mother, who wondered if Espy had chosen a dress yet, wondered if Espy wanted to have dinner. No, and no. She was working late. I don't mind eating late, her mom said. Espy almost said no again, but something in her mother's voice changed her mind.

They made a plan.

She hung up and pulled the United Apparel file out of her drawer. Flipped through it quickly, returned one of the half-dozen messages left by their lawyer, Chris Holloway, cHolloway@cummingshasty.com, the e-mail address sparking a realization. Hasty was a good friend of Leonard's, no wonder he was asking about it. She had better keep up with this case. She asked Holloway for additional documentation—obscure documentation relevant to now-expired tax-code regulations that had arguably been in effect during the time period in question.

Arguably. Holloway would have to go back and interpret IRS rulings for a good while to get a handle on what he should and shouldn't supply her. Which ought to keep him out of her hair for at least a day or two.

She also found an e-mail from O'Neill, the Air Force officer investigating her father's murder. He had sent a list of companies located at Kirtland Air Force Base and wanted to know if any names rang a bell. None did. Not that she would tell him.

Who could she trust?

Nobody.

She found the card Shurig had given her and dialed his number.

It took five rings for him to pick up. "Mike Shurig."

"This is Esperanza Harper."

There was a lot of noise in the background.

"We'll have to talk later," he said. "It's a mess down here."

"Where are you?"

"West Hollywood. The Islamic Center."

"What's happening?" she said.

"You don't know?" he asked. "Turn on your TV. I have to go."

He hung up.

She didn't have a television in her office. But Leonard did.

She went down the hall to his office.

Everybody else was in there already, watching.

BOOK TWO: SOLDIERS

Islamic Center of Southern California
South Vermont Ave.
Los Angeles, CA
Thursday, September 20, 9:52 A.M.

SHURIG knew crowd control from his Bravo days, but situations involving American citizens called for a different approach. Subtlety. Restraint. Entitled to their first amendment rights to free speech and protest. Entitled to vent their anger.

A couple thousand people milled around the street, the sidewalks, with a lot more to come. No violence so far. Shurig hoped it stayed that way.

Not his problem, though. Crowd control was LAPD's job.

He and Huston stood on the corner of Fifth and Vermont, a block from the Islamic Center, and watched them work. A knot of men in blue here, another knot there. Staying back. Letting the protesters see them but not interfering. A team of policemen standing in front of a barricade on Vermont, detouring traffic away from the protest. Raising the barricades to let in patrol cars, which seemed to be arriving every thirty seconds, lights flashing. Shurig would have toned that down a bit, would have had the cops park a couple blocks away and walk, adding them slowly so the crowd didn't feel penned in.

You didn't want to agitate them or give them a focus for their anger. They'd gathered so quickly, as soon as the news broke, that the protesters had no plan. Most were kids—college and high school students, maybe even younger. It was a weekday. Everyone else was either at work or on the way there when it happened.

He and Huston were told to lend a hand if necessary, but mainly to observe—see who might show up to incite the crowd.

Shurig pointed across the street to one of the signs. "Stop Zionist Crimes Against Civilization." The girl carrying it couldn't have been

195

more than twelve years old. A teenage boy held a sign that said *Jihad* in English and Arabic. He had splattered red ink all over the sign to represent blood. Shurig sighed. The kid was right—it was coming, one way or another.

Huston pointed across the street to a man standing on the corner. "That's Karim Jabbat," he said. "His father is Rachman Jabbat. The importer?"

Shurig shrugged.

"Before your time," Huston said. "Rachman was one of the main guys in a counterfeit clothing scam a couple years back, selling high-end knock-offs on the street and sending the money to Hezbollah. We worked with the L.A. Sheriff's office, one of our first big busts."

They crossed the street.

Karim was slim, dark skinned, with a neatly trimmed beard. He wore jeans, a loose-fitting white shirt, a cream-colored topi on his head. When they were about fifteen feet away, he recognized Huston and he stiffened.

"Karim," Huston said. "Haven't seen you around. Where you been?"

"LAX," he said. "I like to wait on the ticket lines, see people freak out."

Huston smiled. "So what are you doing here?"

Karim twisted his beard. "How can you even ask that question? After what happened this morning..."

"Nobody knows what happened," Huston said.

Karim snorted. "That's the party line? Freak accident?"

"This is America," Huston said. "There is no party line."

As they jousted back-and-forth, Shurig could tell that Huston wasn't going to get anything useful out of the younger Jabbat. He looked around and saw the crowd growing by the minute, saw a TV truck, where a blond reporter interviewed a woman who looked very familiar—dark-haired, thin, gesturing as she spoke.

"Be right back," Shurig told Huston.

Twenty feet away, he stopped to watch the dark-haired woman, who eventually noticed him but kept talking into the reporter's microphone. When Shurig moved close enough he heard her say, "This is a ridiculous expectation. No one person speaks for all Muslims. Not even the Pope speaks for all Christians, does he?"

"So you disagree with the Imam's statement?"

"Which part?"

"I don't have the whole thing in front of me," the reporter said. "I mean your reaction to the overall tenor of his statement."

"I'm not going to speak in sound bites," the professor said. "If you have something specific you'd like me to comment on, read it to me."

The reporter was straining, Shurig could see, to hold her temper. "Okay. Do we have a copy of the statement, Neil?" she asked the cameraman. She brushed her hair from her face, smiled at the professor—a phonier smile Shurig had never seen—and said, "It'll just be a minute."

The professor turned to Shurig. "What do you want?" she asked.

She reminded him more of D.B. every time he saw her. "Just to say hello, Professor Mifani."

She snapped, "How do you know my name?"

❖ ❖ ❖ ❖ ❖

Shurig had found it online: Leila Mifani, Associate Professor, Near Eastern Languages and Cultures. M.A. from Wesleyan University in Connecticut, Ph.D. from Stanford. Her faculty page included a picture that didn't do her justice. Shurig found a couple more on one of her students' Facebook pages that he liked better. What he also liked—no visible wedding ring.

He'd spent the whole night on the computer—looking up Professor Mifani during a break from reviewing the files Harper and Sam had put on the remote server at cloudbytes.com, account name betsyrossi, files that turned out to be the same list he'd caught a glimpse of earlier. The MI-5 memo, a bunch of banking records, and tax returns, belonging to MGT, to a company called Aiken-Scuffs, to the Democratic Fund for Direct Action, and Garrett Crandall, and Stuart Crane and a dozen other members of the Society of the Cincinnati. Proof of the web Harper had been talking about. But other than that...

Proof of nothing.

And no mention of the Arab-American Amity League, or Sayeed-Pearson. Or Kirtland Air Force Base.

He was in the middle of typing an e-mail relating all of this when he heard a knock at his apartment door.

"Mike! You in there?"

Huston. Shurig checked his watch. 8:05. He'd called into the office and said he was running late. What was Huston doing here?

He yelled back, "Hang on a second."

He'd had a helluva time sleeping and a helluva time waking up, but the little blue pill had helped.

He opened the door to see Huston wearing a dark suit and looking worried.

"What's wrong with your phone?" Huston asked.

"I had it on silent."

"I've been calling you for a half-hour. We got to get down to headquarters, we have a briefing in ten minutes."

"Briefing on what?"

"Al-Aqsa," Huston said.

Shurig's expression hardened. Aqsa Martyrs Brigade. Another attack. Another Long Beach? World Trade Center?

"What did they do?"

"Not the terrorists. Al-Aqsa mosque. In Jerusalem."

"The Dome of the Rock?"

Huston nodded. "It's gone," he said. "They blew it up."

❖ ❖ ❖ ❖ ❖

That information, though, turned out to be wrong.

The mosque had been destroyed, but nobody had blown it up. It was still not clear what had happened. A natural disaster. Of course, those initial reports came from investigators on-scene, who were all Israeli, and if there had been a terrorist attack on the Al-Aqsa mosque, odds were Jewish terrorists had perpetrated it.

He and Huston got to the conference room in time to see the last few minutes of the president's speech on a television that had been rolled in on a cart.

"...urge restraint on the part of all concerned. Initial reports indicate that this is some sort of natural disaster, and we have offered the Israeli government the full use of whatever facilities and equipment they may need to complete their investigation. I have spoken with the Prime Minister at length, and she has already been in touch with officials in Jordan and Egypt and has accepted a Jordanian component within the investigative team...."

Shurig slid into the room, alongside Burghart, who looked at him and shook her head.

"...Our thoughts, our prayers, and our sympathies are with Muslims worldwide, in particular with our fellow Americans of Muslim faith. We—Americans of every creed and persuasion, Christian, Jewish, Mormon, and all others—stand in solidarity with you on this tragic occasion. Our hearts break alongside yours at the loss of this sacred place, and the sacred ground it stood upon."

Kennedy, sitting at the head of the table, shut it off. "What's happening over there is not our concern," he said. "Not at the moment." He told them their task was to assist LAPD when necessary and to gather information about the situation and about any possible retaliatory attacks.

"And put the word out," Kennedy added, "that based on the evidence gathered so far, this was a natural disaster. Not a terrorist attack."

"A pretty well-aimed natural disaster," Mousharraf said. He was on the Hamas squad and the only Arab-American agent in the office.

"Stinks to high heaven of Kahane Chai, you ask me," Kennedy said. "But we don't know anything yet."

"Speak for yourself," Kincaid said, and everyone laughed. The tension in the room eased a little.

"People," Kennedy said, motioning for quiet. "Let's not forget we're in the middle of another investigation here."

Silence fell on the room.

The murders—Kauffman and Hernandez.

"I bring that up because it gives us added incentive to be very sensitive in our inquiries," Kennedy said.

After the meeting broke up, Burghart sent Huston and Shurig to Long Beach—the heart of what had been Al-Hasra territory and what was now a dozen square miles of dead-end. They were almost there when they got a call to turn around and head to the Islamic Center. Felt like busywork to Shurig, but given the appearance of the professor, it hadn't turned out to be a bad thing at all.

He wished they hadn't gotten off to such a rocky start, first with the student group and now her annoyance at his knowing her name.

"How do you think I found out your name?" he replied to her question. "I've been sitting here listening to you go back and forth with this reporter."

The professor's expression softened.

"Oh," she said.

"I'm sorry about all this," he added. "What's happened."

"Do you know anything more than what's being said about it?"

"I wish I did. Some kind of natural disaster is what I've heard."

"Sometimes we don't hear the truth. We're fed a lot of lies."

"This isn't the kind of thing that can get swept under the rug," Shurig said. "It's too important to too many people. The investigative report will be made public the second it's done."

"Unless it turns out to be terrorism after all. Then all we'll see is the edited version."

"Here's a promise," he said. "Whatever that report says, I'll show it to you."

Her dark eyebrows raised over her darker eyes. "Why would you do that?"

"You're a pretty influential person in the community. Part of my job is to keep things calm. You can help me do it."

Which was true. His job as an FBI agent, his job in a larger sense as a citizen of the world, though keeping things calm here wouldn't keep things calm in that wider world—in the Arabian peninsula, in the Phillipines. In Somalia, Manila, Baghdad, rational thought had ceased to matter. Over there people sent little girls into the streets carrying baskets of fruit and semtex.

"That's a generous offer," Mifani said.

"Where are you going to be later?"

She furrowed her brow.

"In case that information comes in. So I can show it to you."

"I have a seminar. The Modern Female Islamic Identity."

"Sounds interesting," Shurig said. "Mind if I sit in?"

U.S. Department of Justice
Federal Building
Cincinnati, OH
Thursday, September 20, 1:21 P.M.

AFTER the president spoke, the talking heads analyzed the accident—some sort of earthquake tremor, had apparently collapsed the dome. First up was a retired general who thought the president's response sent all the wrong signals. He should have waited until the facts were known. By forcing Israel to bow to Arab demands for an investigation, he legitimized their claims of a terrorist attack. And who was he to decide which of the Muslim nations were entitled to have representation in the investigation? Shouldn't the Muslims decide among themselves?

Espy thought the guy had it entirely wrong. The most important thing the president could do now was show the U.S. pushing for an impartial investigation.

"We're seeing another example," the general said, "of this president's inexperience in foreign affairs. Defense Secretary Talbot left after six months because he was continually forced to operate from a position of weakness."

"Excuse me, general," the moderator said. "We're getting word that there is actual footage of the incident. This is a simulcast from Channel One in Israel, a video taken by cell phone at the time."

The screen went black, and then filled with a dark, grainy image. The only thing Espy could see clearly was the Golden Dome itself, atop the mosque, clearly visible against the new moon.

"It's built on the ruins of the old temple," a voice whispered, and then the next second—

The dome imploded, crumbling to the ground.

Then screaming followed by a sound like rain—dust, rocks, and rubble falling from the sky. And then louder screaming and then the screen went black.

It was like 9/11 all over again. The footage that had run on an endless loop, of the towers collapsing, people running, screaming, the curtain of debris coming in like a tsunami, swallowing everyone and everything in its path...

The anchorman came back on.

Leonard shut off the TV.

"I didn't see any explosion," said Sullivan, one of the staff.

"How many were killed?" Espy asked.

"A hundred people, they're estimating," Leonard said. "They don't know for sure."

"Thank God it didn't happen during prayers," Amy said.

"Thank God," Espy echoed. She'd been there once—the Dome of the Rock. Part of a whirlwind tour she'd done with Mark after Paris. She'd seen the Dome right after the restoration, gleaming like a Faberge egg on steroids, the architectural heart and highlight of Jerusalem. She remembered walking through the Western Gate, the only gate non-believers were allowed to use to access the Holy City, staring at the tile, the marble, and the arches on the outside, and then going in, seeing more of the same, and then stopping at the railing surrounding the heart of the Dome, the rock itself, the very stone Mohammed had stood on, when he ascended up to heaven....

Gone.

She couldn't believe it. She wondered if they'd find the stone.

People slowly drifted out of Leonard's office. She had a feeling the two of them would not meet that afternoon to discuss Bob Kazmir and the various ways she'd mishandled her investigation.

❖ ❖ ❖ ❖ ❖

Leonard ended up going to Columbus. He called her from the

road, asking if they could meet for breakfast the next day. They picked a time and place.

She put aside the United Apparel file and thought about what she would say tomorrow morning, came up with ways to reply depending on what questions he asked. I did look at Kazmir Associates and it seemed like a dead end. Or, you're right. I should have looked harder. Why don't we do that now?

She could always try the truth: I did investigate. And you know what I found?

She pictured herself pulling out a dollar bill and putting it on the table in front of him. And then she would tell him about the golfing and the gambling and the money trail she'd traced to the Cincinnati, and the Democratic Fund for Direct Action, and then she'd tell him about the killings, what had really happened, and he would break down and tell her...

No. He wouldn't tell her anything.

Because she didn't have any proof.

They were fixing golf tournaments, yes, but she didn't know how.

They were moving money around illegally, but she couldn't tie that money directly to anyone but Kazmir, and he was dead.

She knew they'd killed him, yes, but the only eyewitness to that murder was dead too. She couldn't prove they'd killed Ben Kauffman or her father.

And she still had no idea why they were doing this.

It wasn't just about money. It couldn't be.

"There's something else going on here," her father had said. Almost the first words out of his mouth, the first time they met to talk about what she'd stumbled upon. "Because the last thing these people need is more money."

They were walking the river path back from the Montgomery Inn Boathouse, past the statue of Cincinnatus a few blocks from her apartment.

"People like this can never have enough money," she said.

Her father shook his head. "Don't stereotype. Stuart Crane—does he need money? He's worth what—a couple billion?"

"Give or take." Espy hadn't pulled his bank records, but he was in the news enough that his net worth (at least his "official" net worth) was public knowledge.

"There you go," her father said. "How many companies has he started? How many charities does he support? Come on. Does this guy work for money? No. Not at this point in his life."

"So why are they fixing these golf tournaments?"

There's something else going on.

What that something was, she still had no idea.

Maybe her father had a clue. Maybe that was why he was going to Kirtland.

As good a place as any to start.

❖ ❖ ❖ ❖ ❖

She shut her office door and called Amy to say she was going to shut her eyes for half an hour. She popped in the network card, anonymized her IP address, and went back to O'Neill's e-mail in which he sent the list of companies at Kirtland. She printed the list and started googling. First name on the list: Altair Technologies.

She found the website—a Silicon Valley software start-up, focused on platform integration within today's new high-technology information systems, whatever that meant. It was enough to convince her that Altair was not the company her father planned to visit.

Next name: Abbott-Merker-McCloy.

They ran oil refineries, specialized in high-quality, high-octane jet fuel and other aviation products. Based in San Antonio.

She moved on to Bateman Optics, speeding through the site until she realized she was moving too fast. She went back to Altair Techolo-gies, checked to see if they were an independent firm, part of a con-glomerate, and if so, which one. She'd spent enough time these last few months chasing shadows to realize these people were smart. She was going to have to dig deeply to find the clues she needed. Not just track companies, but individuals—corporate officers, board members.

The search required some planning.

She opened a new window and logged on to cloudbytes.com. Typed Betsyross1 (her ID) and patriot1776 (her password). Kind of an in-joke, a jab at the society.

She started a new database, set up some fields, and went back to Altair's site. Found some names and plugged them into the fields. Googled around, found out Altair was a subsidiary of Enovation, LLC, a company based in Delaware. Went to Enovation's website, entered more names and companies.

And then she moved on to Abbott-Merker-McCloy. And Bate-man. And on through the alphabet. As she was filling in information on Jet-Air Propulsion Systems, someone knocked on her door.

"You all right in there?"

Amy.

"Fine," Espy called back, as the doorknob turned, and the door started to open.

She slid the United Apparel file closer to her computer, so that it covered up the network card, just as Amy stepped inside. Amy re-minded her about the breakfast with Leonard in the morning and said she was leaving a little early.

Espy checked the clock on her computer: 4:45 p.m.

The whole day was gone. She had to finish checking the list of companies and then she'd better work on United Apparel.

At 6:00 her mother called about dinner and said she'd see her around seven. Espy said let's make it eight. They compromised at 7:30.

Espy told her mom to let herself in the apartment.

Her mother asked if she'd pick up a movie as well.

A movie? Espy didn't have time to watch a movie.

Make it something light, her mother said. A romantic comedy. Something that'll take us away for a couple of hours.

Sure, Espy said. Sounds good.

Unfortunately, she underestimated how long it would take her to get through the S's and the T's, which formed a full quarter of the forty companies on O'Neill's list. By the time she finished, it was already 7:15. She rushed through the last half dozen entries on the list. By then it was 7:30. She called her mother and apologized.

She hung up, and looked over the work she'd just done.

There's something else going on, her father had said.

For the life of her, she couldn't figure out what.

❖ ❖ ❖ ❖ ❖

As she closed her computer, she glanced guiltily at the United Apparel file, and then threw it in her bag. Maybe she'd wake up early and work on it.

No, she was meeting Leonard for breakfast. What could she say to him about Kazmir and why she hadn't followed up? Should she explain the situation? No. That would mean she'd lied not just to him but to Columbus. And to Abraham, for that matter.

What if Abraham came back with proof that she had been at The Pines? She replayed that night in her mind. She'd driven straight to The Pines, avoided the front gate, parked on a side street, gone straight to the thirteenth green, and waited for fifteen minutes before heading up the fairway, which was when she ran into Matt, who had yelled at her and said he hadn't seen Kazmir. At which point she left the way she came in—side streets to the highway and home, no stops. She'd gone to bed thinking Kazmir had chickened out, then woke the next morning to find out that he was dead, Matt was in jail, and their best hope of finding out how golf tournaments were being fixed was gone.

Something tugged at the back of her mind. Something Matt had said about Kazmir. Besides the fact that he was an asshole.

She sat back in her chair, gave it a minute to percolate to the top of her consciousness. Gave it two minutes.

Nothing.

She left the office and headed to her apartment. Stopped to pick up a movie, a light, romantic comedy. When she came out of the store, a man stepped from the shadows and followed her.

Kerckhoff Coffeehouse
Kerckhoff Hall–Second Floor
Westwood, CA
Thursday, September 20, 4:41 P.M.

MIFANI'S seminar was held at Kerckhoff Coffeehouse, which was located a flight of steps up from the streetlevel in Kerckhoff Hall, the first coffeehouse on the UCLA campus, dating back to 1976.

Inside, wood tabletops, copper-counter front with leaded-glass windows, a bulletin board crammed with leaflets announcing concerts, lectures, student events. Walking in, Shurig felt more than a little out of place. He was glad he'd left the suit coat and tie in his office.

He spotted Mifani sitting on a couch in the back, a student on either side of her, three students in chairs nearby. She wore a loose-fitting dress, white, with red stitching at the collar, a nice contrast to her dark hair, which splayed across her shoulders. She looked exotic and languorous, her legs tucked beneath her.

When she spotted him, she raised a hand. He waved back.

He ordered a double espresso from a short, severe-looking young woman with a shaved head and tattoos up and down both arms, and then joined the group.

"Professor," he said.

"Glad you could make it. Everyone, this is Agent Michael Shurig."

"Mike." He looked around the group. "In case the 'agent' part didn't give it away, I'm with the FBI."

"Leila told us," said the girl in the chair to his left—short, chubby, with curly red hair. She smiled. "I'm Judy."

Leila, he thought; the students used her first name. Probably normal at a civilian college, but he'd never have called the Colonel or any of his other Bravo instructors by their first names. It implied a familiarity, an equality, that wouldn't have felt comfortable. Even now.

He went around the group, got names. One of the students he already knew—Ayah, the young woman who he'd given a hard time the day before, still wearing her khimar. Her greeting was decidedly less friendly than the rest.

"We're talking about what happened today," Leila told him. "Maybe you have something to contribute." She offered a challenging smile that reminded him of D.B.

"Leila said you might have more information about what happened," said a student whose name he'd already forgotten.

"Not yet," Shurig said.

"Well, what do you think happened?"

"Slow down, Kate," Leila said. "Let's make sure Agent Shurig is comfortable participating in this discussion."

"I'm fine," he said.

Ayah immediately jumped in. "I am saying my identity today, here and now, who I am, is not about me as a woman. It is about Islam. It is about my religion. It is about all of us, everywhere in the world, stereotyped, ignored, stepped on. Everyday. And now this. Finally they succeed in—"

"Shouldn't say 'they,'" Judy interrupted. "'They' stereotypes."

"Okay, the Israelis."

"Not all Israelis," Judy said. "The extremists. They did this."

"We don't know that anyone did anything yet," Shurig said.

"It is the logical conclusion," Ayah said. "When you consider the evidence."

"It is the logical inference," Leila corrected.

"Evidence?" Shurig said. "You know something I don't?"

"The historical evidence," Leila said. "Fifteen times, since the Israelis took control of Jerusalem, the mosque has been attacked. Fifteen times, they have tried to destroy it. And now they have succeeded. Now they can rebuild their temple. And what can we do? Nothing."

"They," Judy said again.

"They," Ayah snapped. "Extremists make the bomb, but the Israelis stand by and do nothing. They want the temple too. Christians here in America, they want the temple because it is Biblical prophecy. So now everyone can be happy."

"You think the president looked happy today?" Leila said.

"The president." Ayah snorted. "No one cares what he thinks."

"Here's something." Another student spoke up, reading from her cell phone. "No readings on Richter scale reported."

"No earthquake," Ayah said. "See?"

"No explosion, either," Shurig said.

"It must have been a bomb underground," Ayah said.

"Then there would have been a Richter reading," Shurig said.

Before Ayah could respond, Mifani took charge of the conversation. They began talking about lost traditions of Islamic thought, and the role of the Prophet's wife, and horror stories about the Taliban and the Saudi royal family and Muslim treatment of women worldwide, and Shurig listened quietly.

When class ended, the students left and Shurig moved to the couch next to Leila. "Hot-button topic," he said. "Religion."

"Always is."

"Nice to see it discussed without the accompanying holy wars."

She leaned back on the couch. "Where do you stand on the subject?"

Shurig winked. "I decline to answer on the grounds that if it gets back to my mother..."

"Let me guess," she said. "your mother was Catholic, Irish Catholic?"

"Yes, very perceptive. Full-blooded Irish Catholic. How did you guess?"

"That Celtic Cross tattoo on your forearm,"

"Oh yeah, that. A dead giveaway."

"But Shurig? An unusual name."

"Yes, it is. Actually, it's an Americanization of the German name, Schuricht. Great grandpa changed it during World War I. Germans weren't real popular back then." Shurig explained. "Dad was raised German Lutheran. He's dead now."

"Oh. I'm sorry to hear that."

"Happened a long time ago."

"My parents are both gone too." She brushed her hair from her face with one hand, exposing the nape of her neck and a long expanse of caramel-colored skin.

"Where were your parents from?" he asked.

"Lexington, Massachusetts. My great-great grandfather was from Egypt, originally, if that's what you meant. Came to America in 1891 without a dollar to his name. Built a multi-million-dollar business, him and his son. Mifani Import/Export. My four brothers are in Boston running it."

"You never had any interest in the family business?"

She shook her head. "My family is very traditional. A place in the business...that was never an option for me."

Shurig sensed there was more to the story but that it was a sensitive subject.

"And you?" she asked. "Did you always want to be an FBI agent?"

"I'm from a long line of soldiers. My father, grandfather, great-grandfather..."

"I can see that. You have the qualities of a soldier."

"And what would those be?"

She shrugged. "Observant. Assertive. Always...I don't know...not spoiling for a fight but certainly ready for one."

"I was thinking much the same about you." His voice held a flirtatious note, but she didn't seem to hear it.

"Where were you stationed?"

He took a sip of his espresso. "Waziristan," he said. "Baghdad.

Ghazaliyah. Among others."

"And you came back and joined the FBI?"

"The war wasn't over."

She paused before saying, "If you keep thinking about it as a war, then it will never end."

"What other way is there to think about it?"

"A clash of civilizations," she said. "That's the phrase I prefer."

"Clash. Sounds like war to me."

"Clash. Up here"—she touched her head—"and here." She touched her heart. "A war of ideas. Of words."

"It's not just ideas and words," he snapped. "People are dying."

She studied him with her dark eyes, waiting for more or perhaps searching for the source of his anger.

He sighed. "Sorry. I didn't mean for it to come out like that. It's been a tough couple weeks."

"Those murdered agents." She put a spoon in her tea, stirred it. "I've had a tough few weeks too. Not on the same level, but...well...I won't bore you with my personal problems."

"I'll let you know if I'm bored," he said.

She smiled and took a long sip of tea. "My partner," she said, staring at the ground. "Five years we've been together, and last weekend, she just..."

Shurig managed—just barely—to cover his reaction before she met his eyes.

"Just like that, she's gone," she said. "It's why I've been so edgy all week."

"I'm sorry," he managed.

He felt like an idiot.

Leila talked for a while about her girlfriend, as Shurig realized he'd read meaning into her words and gestures that hadn't been there at all. He'd been hallucinating. Seeing D.B. in a woman who was nothing like her, trying to bring D.B. back to life through another person he knew nothing about.

"Anyway," Leila said. "Do you think you will get that report? On what happened at the Dome?"

"Definitely."

"I'd like to see it."

They made small talk for a few more minutes, and then she left. He stayed on the couch, nursing his espresso.

Focus, he told himself. Concentrate. What had he been thinking, chasing after a woman while Rome burned around him? He *hadn't* been thinking. What was it Harper had said—Washington was Cincinnatus, not Caesar? Who did that make him? Caligula?

His phone rang.

"Mike. It's Jackie. Where are you?"

Burghart. Speaking of losing focus...

He hadn't spoken to her since the night before the funeral. Not about anything important, at least. Not about what Sammy had said or about who they were looking for.

"I'm in Westwood," Shurig said. "Coffee place on the UCLA campus."

"We found the gun. The rifle that killed Sammy. Kincaid and Dilts found it. Down in Long Beach. Found a bunch of other things, too."

Shurig was up and moving on the word 'rifle.'

BOOK TWO: SOLDIERS

Federal Bureau of Investigation
Los Angeles Field Office Headquarters
Wilshire Boulevard
Los Angeles, CA
Thursday, September 20, 6:12 P.M.

THE rifle had been planted. Shurig knew that before he walked in the lab. Burghart had to suspect the same thing, except it seemed, on first glance, she didn't. In her gray business suit, her light brown hair freshly washed and styled, she looked confident, authoritative.

"This explains it," she said, keeping her voice low. She'd met him at the elevator. "Everything that Sammy was telling us. Why he thought there was someone inside the bureau."

"I don't understand."

"It's exactly like what happened a few years back—the counterfeit CISCO routers the Chinese were selling. Remember?" She went on without waiting for an answer. "Who knows what the hell snuck out through the backdoor then? This is the same thing. The routers we were using up at Fox Airfield. There's a hole there, too. A vulnerability."

"Time out," Shurig said, struggling to keep up with her, not just the conversation but her pace. Her legs were longer than his, and she was hyped up while he was exhausted—physically, emotionally. "You're talking about computers, right? What does this have to do with the gun that killed Sam?"

"You'll see," she said, and then turned at a door marked 'RCFL Use Only' and pulled it open. Inside it was another door. When he opened it, he walked into another world.

At least it felt that way. Most of bureau headquarters was done to the usual government (a.k.a. lowest bidder) standards: industrial-grade carpet, industrial-grade paint, drop-panel ceilings, particle-board furniture. Only the top people like Kennedy got real desks.

215

They'd spent money on this room, though.

Shurig stepped onto genuine hardwood. Maybe it was a plastic laminate, but it wasn't cheap. The temperature, too, was cooler, and the air smelled clean. And no whirring a.c. noise. It was quiet. Dollars were poured into computer forensics like there was no tomorrow, because it had become an article of faith in Washington that the only way to stop the people who were trying to make sure that, in fact, there was no tomorrow, was to make sure the bureau had the latest, the fastest, the most expensive equipment.

This place was full of it.

The room was split in two by a wall on their immediate left. The wall was glass, maybe plastic, from the waist up. There was a bay of server blades, another bay next to it full of shiny equipment whose purpose he couldn't even begin to guess. A lot of blinking LEDs. Two workstations with flat-screen monitors, numbers scrolling by too fast to follow. A guy wearing headphones, standing in front of them, arms folded across his chest, finger pressed to his lips.

The other half of the room was open space, maybe twenty feet square.

The whole squad was there—Huston, Kincaid, Dilts—standing in a clump behind a woman seated at a long table behind a big computer monitor. Tomasevic, the shaggy haired computer guy from Fox Airfield who had invited Shurig and Sam to dinner, perched on a second, identical table off to the right, looking very unhappy.

Perched next to him was O'Neill.

The woman at the computer was talking. She stopped suddenly as Shurig and Burghart entered the room.

"Mike," Huston said. "We found the gun."

"So I hear."

Huston, his skinny chest bursting with excitement, stood with his hands on his hips. "We're going through the drive now. A lot of files on it, encrypted, of course, but should be able to get at the information without too much trouble."

"This scan's going to weed out the ones we don't need to look at," the woman at the computer said. "Take about five more minutes."

Shurig looked over her shoulder at the screen. A progress bar was about a third of the way filled. While they waited, Shurig got up to speed.

"Echelon II flagged a wire transfer from Algiers, a few weeks back,"

Huston said. "Three thousand dollars to a Western Union in Anaheim. Pick up made by a guy named Bob Patrella. Clerk had a copy of his driver's license and address, it all looked good. But four days ago, another four thousand came in. Same point of origin."

"Algiers," Shurig said.

"Only this time, the money went to a Western Union in San Diego. The system flagged a possible connection. The money was picked up by a woman named Martine Duseau. Her driver's license and address checks out, so we decide it's coincidence, and hang up, except a copy of the paperwork comes through, and Kincaid files it alongside the receipt we already have from Anaheim, which is when he notices the signatures match."

Shurig peered at Kincaid, a member of the squad who he hadn't gotten to know very well. Kincaid had red hair, a sprinkling of freckles, and a loud laugh. He was easier going than the others on the squad but also, Shurig thought, too gullible for the work of an FBI agent. Shurig was surprised that Kincaid had made such a keen discovery.

"The signatures matched?" Shurig asked. "The man up here, and the woman in San Diego?"

"Martine Duseau," Kincaid said, "is a very manly woman."

"Which we find out," Huston says, "because even though the Western Union in Anaheim doesn't have a security camera, the one in San Diego does. We get a copy of the picture sent up. Meanwhile, the licenses—"

"Fakes," Shurig said.

Huston nodded. "Good ones. New photos on top of real information. We're not dealing with amateurs here. That tells me we might be looking at something serious. And then this morning, right after the briefing, it hits me—Algiers. Amal Zougaz."

Zougaz was an Algerian businessman, accent on the *was* because the bureau had eventually sourced a lot of the money used in the Long Beach attack to various enterprises, commercial and charitable, under his control. Right around the time the news broke, Zougaz disappeared—into hiding or an unmarked grave.

"Which is where we came in," Kincaid said.

"Started showing the picture around," Dilts put in. "Gas stations, motels, you know. Driving around all damn day. Finally, a clerk recognizes the lovely Martine. She checked in three nights ago, he says, is paid up through the week. We call for back-up, go in, but the room is empty."

"Martine's car, however," Kincaid said, "is not. We found the laptop in the trunk, the rifle in pieces in the spare tire well, an OM-50 Nemesis."

"Found a bag of trash under the front seat," Dilts added. "A whole bunch of stuff in it. Road maps, bus schedules, a picture of Sam."

O'Neill pushed himself off the desk. "They left the laptop? And the rifle? I have a hard time buying that."

"Maybe he saw us pull up," Kincaid said. "Maybe he didn't have any choice but to ditch the car."

"That's a lot of maybes," O'Neill said.

"The big thing for me," Burghart said, making eye contact with Shurig, "is the network info. The laptop had the same machine access code as one of ours at Fox, so whenever that computer logged on to the network, they were able to log on too. Whatever information we had, they got it."

He knew what she was thinking; they'd found the traitor Sammy was looking for, and it wasn't one of them, it wasn't a person at all, it was a piece of computer equipment. A ghost in the machine, planted by Al-Hasra.

"We haven't changed that code," Burghart said. "Depending on what happens...we may want to use it to our advantage. Feed them false information."

"That's if we catch this Martine guy," Kincaid said. "Otherwise..."

"Odds are he's already told his people that the machine's been lost," Shurig said.

"We should fix the problem now," Tomasevic said. He had been silent, even morose, to that point and everyone turned to look at him. "Make sure nothing else is a problem. If they had that address, maybe they have other things."

"We're being careful," Burghart said. "Nothing else is going to leak out."

Tomasevic glared. "I don't agree."

Burghart patted his shoulder. "Don't feel bad," she told him. "There's no way you would have spotted the problem."

Tomasevic snorted and leaned back against the table with an angry look.

The tech woman, whose name was Kramer, said, "Ready," and the group turned to a list of files on the screen.

"We'll try this one first." She clicked on a file about halfway down. "An image of some kind. Hold on a second."

And then the entire monitor screen filled with a picture of what looked like the mountains on the old Afghanistan/Pakistan border, all rock and sand and dirt, only a medieval-looking fort had been superimposed atop the summit of one of the hills. A banner—a few words of Arabic writing—were superimposed over the sky at the top of the picture.

The image was all too familiar to everyone in the room.

"Al-Hasra," Kincaid said.

"Same picture, new motto," Burghart said. "Am I right?"

Shurig nodded. "The Unconquered," he translated, reading off the banner. "The Unconquerable, maybe.'"

"'Or Invincible," Kramer said. "Depending. Let's look at the rest of it."

There were three paragraphs of smaller text on the screen. When she double-clicked the text, it grew large enough to read.

In the name of Allah, all-merciful, the mercy-giving, the compassionate, in the name of our brother in paradise, Wassim Amawi—

She paused for a second, and Shurig knew why. Amawi was the ringleader of the Long Beach attack, the guy whose image had been carried around the world, the video of him lining up kids up against a classroom wall and...

He had to close his eyes for a second and breathe.

This begins our revenge upon you, defilers of the Holy Land, we are a nation that drinks blood, and there is no better blood than the blood of Jews and Americans, the blood we spill now, the blood we drink today, the blood of the murderer Hernandez—

O'Neill wasn't buying this, Shurig saw, anymore than he bought the rifle or the hard drive or the bag of goodies in the trunk.

"Good work, Kramer." Burghart said. "I'll show this to Kennedy."

"We're taking this at face value?" O'Neill asked.

Halfway to the door, Burghart turned around. "We're taking it with a grain of salt. Doesn't mean Kennedy shouldn't know about it right away."

Burghart looked more relaxed than Shurig had seen her in months.

She was satisfied they'd found the traitor. They'd found Sammy's killer.

But Shurig wasn't satisfied at all. O'Neill wasn't, and Harper wouldn't be either, he knew.

One Lytle Place
Mehring Way
Cincinnati, OH
Thursday, September 20, 9:21 P.M.

"I got two so you could choose," Espy said. *"High Society* or *Gentlemen Prefer Blondes."*

"Gentlemen Prefer Blondes? Why?" her mother asked. Espy looked at her blond, stunning mother, lounging on the bed. They had curled up, a plate of cheese and crackers between them, a glass of wine on either nightstand. Espy wore sweats and a t-shirt, her mother wore designer jeans and a salmon-colored button-down mercilessly pressed.

"Can't imagine what I was thinking," Espy said. "It seemed like it would be good. Marilyn Monroe—"

"I know who's in it." Penny smacked her lips as if tasting something sour. "Too tragic for me."

"It's a romantic comedy."

"Not the movie. Marilyn. Such a sad story. I can't enjoy her movies knowing how her real life turned out."

Espy put in *High Society*, which from the look on her mother's face, wasn't a good choice either.

"This is a classic," Espy said.

"Yes it is," her mother said. "A classic."

She watched in silence as Louis Armstrong and his band set up in Bing Crosby's living room, as Bing did a number with the little girl playing Grace Kelly's sister. It got worse when Grace Kelly came on screen.

"Who decided she could act?" her mother said, and poured another glass of wine.

"She's completely miscast," she said a few minutes later. "No chemistry between her and Bing."

"He's way too old," Espy said.

"It's her as much as him," her mother said, and drained her second glass of wine. She got up off the bed. "They're about to sing," she said. "If I have to watch Grace Kelly sing, I'm going to need something stronger than wine."

"Mom," Espy said, but she was out the door.

Espy followed.

"You have any Scotch?" her mother asked, opening a kitchen cabinet.

Espy came up behind her and slammed the cabinet shut. "I invited you here to relax. Not to drink yourself unconscious."

Her mother stood still. "Fine," she said. "Let's watch the movie."

They got through another half hour.

"It's not a terrible performance," her mother said. "I suppose." And a minute later: "I mean she did it, at least. She had a career. I was on half a dozen wretched TV shows. And then I got pregnant."

"Bad decision?" Espy said.

Her mother sighed. "That's not what I meant. He was married. What was I thinking?"

"You weren't," Espy said. "You fell in love."

"That's right. I fell in love." She ran a finger across each eyebrow. "So did he, you know."

"Yeah," Espy said. "I know."

Her mother filled her glass again. And again ten minutes later. Well before the end of the film, she fell asleep. Espy went into the living room. 11:35. She was restless. Still on L.A. time.

She called Shurig to tell him about the database she'd started on the companies at Kirtland. She got his voicemail. There was nothing she felt comfortable saying on a message, so she didn't leave one.

She thought about calling O'Neill, telling him about the list but decided against it. She and Shurig were in this together. She'd have to check with him first.

She got a spare set of sheets, made up the couch, and sat down.

Sleeping pills? She didn't have any. She could go out and get some or she could go get a drink. There were a half-dozen bars within walking distance of her apartment. That was why she lived downtown, right, so she could go out once in a while? Have fun?

Right.

How much fun would she have sitting in a bar by herself waiting for some loser to hit on her?

Besides...

The image of that sheet of paper with that single word printed on it—

STOP

—kept flashing through her head.

It was like a buzzer going off. Get moving. Get back to work.

She pulled up the Kirtland database, but nothing struck her this time around either. She pulled up the other files on her account, the list of aliases, the banks that went with them, the lists of transactions and companies and non-profits making them. The trail of money she and her father had been following.

They're using it for something. Some purpose. They have a plan.

Why did he think that?

She stared at the numbers and names till her eyes began to blur.

Everything I have, you have.

What she had, Espy realized, was nothing.

❖ ❖ ❖ ❖ ❖

She checked her messages on the DOJ server. One caught her eye immediately—from an address she didn't recognize. Someone named villerosa@vwest.com. It was from Carli.

Esperanza,

If your interested, Livvy's birthday is next Tuesday.

And that was all.

It was some kind of peace offering, her sister's way of opening a place in her life. Maybe she had changed her mind about Espy. Maybe. Or Grandma Rosa had changed it for her.

Livvy's birthday. How old was she? She had said she was in first grade. How old were first-graders? *Abuela* would know. She could call. Carli would know too. She could just send a quick e-mail.

Espy started three times, each time deleting and starting again. She sounded phony in one, distant in another, fawning in the next. Was Carli offering a truce? Just being polite? Hoping for a sisterly connection? She didn't have time to guess. She would call her grandmother tomorrow, find out.

Espy clicked to the next e-mail. It was from cHolloway@cummingshasty.com. Sent at about nine o'clock that night. Hard worker, Mr. Holloway, she thought.

An angry one too. He cited recent Federal tax codes that undermined the ones she had sent him earlier in the day. He also asked that another attorney be assigned to the case.

He obviously felt he was being given the run-around, and, in truth, that is what she'd been doing. She sat back in her chair and tried to keep from screaming.

She typed several replies, deleting each one.

She needed to clear her head of tax precedents and Chris Holloway and the Cincinnati and her father and her mother and Kirtland Air Force Base and Agent Shurig and all of them. What she needed was a complete change of pace.

What she needed, really, was a date.

A good conversation with a man. A romantic walk through downtown.

She clicked back up a few messages, to villerosa@vwest.com, and typed a reply:

Carli:

Thanks for letting me know about Livvy's birthday. I will send something.

Espy

Then she logged off the DOJ server and went shopping.

Online shopping. Took forty-five minutes to find two gifts: a book and a game. The latter was P.U. The Guessing Game of Smells, which was similar to Candyland but with scratch-and-sniff cards and a board called Odorville. What will they think of next?

The book was *Dr. Seuss's Sleep Book*. She had warm memories of reading it with her mom at bedtime. Livvy and Carli could do the same.

The site recommended other selections based on her previous purchases, which most recently had been books on gambling. The little something that had been tugging at her mind earlier at work began tugging again. Something about Matt and Kazmir at The Pines, standing on a green, arguing about who was allowed on it and when. She had a feeling that wasn't what their fight was really about.

She drifted to thoughts on fixing golf tournaments. Which couldn't be done: all the books she'd read, all the people she'd talked to, had assured her of that. Matt had said the same thing...at first.

And then he changed his mind.

Espy pictured those sheets of yellow paper he'd brought to lunch, pictured his scribbled handwriting all over them. The pages, filled with tiny little numbers: yards off the tee; average putts per hole. She wished she had those sheets now. They would tell her something, the something he'd been about to tell her before her phone had rung, before she'd cut him off.

Before he was killed.

She went to bed wondering what that something was.

Federal Bureau of Investigation
Los Angeles Field Office Headquarters
Wilshire Boulevard
Los Angeles, CA
Thursday, September 20, 11:41 P.M.

TECH support pulled apart the hard drive in every way possible. They used six methods to decrypt the files they'd found, used five others to search for ones that hadn't shown up on the initial scan. They found propaganda, the same line of crap Al-Hasra had been spewing since day one. They were the spiritual descendants of the unconquerable Sufavids, heirs to the glories of Persia, the only people in the Middle East to withstand the bastard Caliphate of the Turks, they would drive the Jew monkeys into the ocean, the Long Beach attack and the Hernandez assassination were just preludes to a greater glory yet to come, a Holocaust beyond all imagining.

It would have made Shurig sick if he thought any of it represented a real threat, which of course, it didn't.

He stayed for two hours, long after everyone else had left, Burghart with a pat on the back and a smile, Kincaid shaking his head, cursing under his breath about the accuracy (or lack thereof) of foreign intelligence estimates, Dilts right along with him, Tomasevic a few minutes after that, still looking angry, and last of all, O'Neill, who made a point of telling Shurig he'd be in touch soon.

"What's with him?" Kramer, the technician, asked after the door shut.

Shurig sat in a chair next to her, watching her work.

"He's under a lot of pressure to solve the case."

"Didn't we just do that?"

"He doesn't think so."

"Well, maybe he's right. But if this is all a fake, somebody went to a lot of trouble to do it, because it's very convincing."

Shurig's cell buzzed, the third time since he'd been in the room. First it had been Harper, then Burghart. Now—speak of the devil—it was O'Neill. Shurig let it go to voicemail.

Kramer had another image on the screen—a group of men, super-imposed over the same image they'd looked at a couple hours before—the mountains and fort, the Al-Hasra name and motto splashed across the blue sky.

She pointed to the lower left corner. "You see the rocks here. See how these little splotches of color don't seem to fit? This black, this orange? This could be noise. Digital noise. Might be indicative of an artifact introduced into the file."

"An artifact?" Shurig asked.

"Like a message."

"In the file?"

"Any picture, audio file, video...they're all just strings of binary information, so if you wanted to, you could insert other binary in-formation—a chunk of text, say, encrypted, or not—inside it. And it wouldn't look or sound any different to the casual observer. It's a tech-nique called steganography. Back ten years ago, we ran into a lot of it. Nobody uses it much these days. Kind of old hat."

Shurig remembered hearing about steganography during his train-ing at Quantico. Even then people spoke of it in a 'yesterday's news' kind of way. It had also been referred to, now that he thought about it, in that Computer Security memo that had gone out to all the DOJ-affiliated agencies a few months back.

Kramer opened the raw file and scrolled through it, line by line. As he watched her work, Shurig wondered if they'd been as thorough when they examined Sammy's computers. Somehow, he doubted it.

He went down a floor, to data support, where he found Tomasevic sitting at his cubicle, staring at a computer screen. On the gray fabric cubicle wall Tomasevic had pinned a picture of a woman, apparently his wife, the one Sam had mentioned—gorgeous woman, horrible cook. Sam hadn't been kidding about the gorgeous part. She was beautiful. Looked like a movie star.

Looked somehow familiar.

"You got a minute?" Shurig said, pulling up a chair.

"I am sitting here wondering what to do. They say not to fix the problem, but I can't do any other work because the security flaw is still there. Also...I am sick. Here." He punched his stomach lightly. "Samuel is so good to me, to my wife, and now I find this out, that they kill him because of my mistake."

"Your mistake?"

"System at Fox was running slow, sluggish...yes, my mistake. I should have noticed."

"Once they decided to kill Sam there was nothing you could have done. Nothing any of us could have done."

Tomasevic didn't look convinced. "There is something you wanted?"

"There is. The kind of work Kramer was doing on that hard drive upstairs—did we do the same with Agent Hernandez's machine?"

"Same kind of work, yes," Tomasevic said.

"We ran all those tests?"

"Not all. You think there is something we missed?"

Shurig shrugged. "Sam was a cautious guy. Maybe he had an idea that there was some kind of leak...I'm just guessing."

It sounded half-assed to him, but Tomasevic seemed to buy it. "You think he might have actually hidden some of his files?"

Shurig said, "Might be worth checking out."

"The Evidence Response Team still has the machine. I could check to see—"

"Let me run this by some people first," Shurig said. His mouth, he realized, was outrunning his mind. He had to think about what to do next. Maybe he should get custody of the machine himself, then get someone outside the bureau to pull it apart. How could he make that happen? And who could he get to look at it?

He went back to his desk. There was an e-mail waiting from O'Neill—addressed to Kennedy, with copies to the Al-Hasra squad and the Evidence Response Team—objecting to issuing a press release about a breakthrough in the search for Sam's killers. O'Neill felt his recommendations in the investigation had not been followed. He listed them: Kirtland was number one; Harper was number two. Hernandez's girlfriends were number three.

Shurig scratched his jaw. The first two he understood, but Hernandez's girlfriends? O'Neill mentioned a woman named Deb Huddleston, who worked at Fox, another named Tecki Shackleford, who owned a clothing store in East L.A., another named Marita Thelen, who was a traffic cop in Santa Monica, making the point that Hernandez had spent considerable amounts of time with all those women in the last six months.

As Shurig read, a response from Kennedy popped up.

Lieutenant O'Neill:

My agents continue to explore possible connections between SAC Hernandez's scheduled flight to Kirtland and his murder. DOJ Attorney Esperanza Harper was questioned at length while here in Los Angeles. The women you mentioned have all been interviewed, along with several others not on your list.

Next time you have a complaint to make, you make it to me in person.

J.L. Kennedy, ADIC Los Angeles FBI

Shurig remembered what Sam told him about Kennedy.
Be straight with him, Mike. Or he'll cut your throat.

Too bad O'Neill hadn't heard that advice.

❖ ❖ ❖ ❖ ❖

He sat at his desk staring at Kennedy's e-mail. Eventually, his screen saver came to life. One of the colonel's guys had e-mailed it to him the other day. A cartoon version of Osama bin Laden, popped out of a cave and was blown to bits by a hail of bombs. Osama popped up again a second later. Art imitating life.

He leaned back in his chair. What to do next? Return Harper's call? Return O'Neill's? He could look at the list of companies O'Neill gave him. Because the lieutenant was right that Kirtland was key. Hernandez hadn't decided to go there on a whim. He'd found something, spoken to someone. Who? And when? O'Neill was smart to focus on who else Sam had spent time with. The girlfriends. Family. His daughter in L.A., his grandkids, his mom, though Shurig knew they'd all been interviewed.

Time to go home and get some sleep.

Except he wasn't really sleeping these days. Maybe he ought to grab a drink, take the edge off. What he needed were a few of the red pills they'd all used in Ghazaliyah. That might do the trick, silence the voices in his head.

He could call Dr. Haileigh. She'd take care of him. A lot of pain in the shoulder today, doc—which wasn't far from the truth. You think you can prescribe something to help me get some rest?

He pictured the doctor standing in the door of his hospital room. Good-looking woman, he thought. Then he suddenly realized—take away the freckles, lighten the hair...Haileigh looked a like the girlfriend from the Air Force base. And they both looked a little like Harper's mother. The movie star.

And there was someone else who looked like Harper's mother.

And she wasn't on the list of women the bureau had interviewed. Or on any other list for that matter.

Except—now—his.

U.S. Department of Justice
Federal Building
Cincinnati, OH
Friday, September 21, 4:40 A.M.

THOUGH Espy remembered the broad strokes of the argument between Matt and Kazmir, the details escaped her. They were in the files at her office.

She got dressed, her mom still asleep when she left. It was 4:40 A.M. when she walked into the office. Early, even for her.

She pulled out the Kazmir file, looking for copies of the motions Abraham had filed with the prosecuting attorney. After a long search, she found the relevant passage—a summary of a jailhouse conversation between Abraham and Matt on the night of the arrest. A passage asserting that the facts of the case did not support a charge of premeditation.

'Said premeditation,' Abraham had written, 'is supposedly traced to a single brief encounter between defendant and Mr. Kazmir at approximately 7:30 A.M. the morning of August 17, when defendant, having arrived at the 13th green of The Pines golf course to perform duties related to his job as a member of the caddy staff at said course, was ordered to vacate the green by Mr. Kazmir. Defendant suggested that since the green had been repaired, there was no danger of damaging the putting surface, and that it was unnecessary to protect the grass against repeated trampling. Mr. Kazmir disagreed and became verbally abusive, at which point my defendant placed the pin as he had been directed by the caddy master and left without further discussion."

Kazmir yelled that caddies don't belong on the green. It wasn't much of a motive for murder—or even for a temper tantrum. Why was Kazmir so upset?

She tried to picture the scene—Matt showing up, Kazmir yelling at him, because...

Because caddies don't belong on the green. No.

Because Matt might damage the putting surface. No. The green had been repaired. Because...

She paused.

How did your friend win the tournament, she'd asked Matt.

He putted better. A helluva lot better.

A little tingle went up her spine.

Maybe Kazmir was angry at Matt simply because he was there, on the green, that morning, when Kazmir expected to have time to himself to do...what?

How do you fix a golf tournament?

Espy believed she was getting closer to an answer.

❖ ❖ ❖ ❖ ❖

She called The Pines at 7:15, using the encrypted cell (588-5377) her dad had given her. She called every five minutes or so, figuring sooner or later someone would answer.

At 7:37, her mom called. From Espy's apartment. She let the call go to voicemail.

At 7:44, someone picked up at The Pines: "Corey Tanner speaking, how can I help you?"

Espy smiled. Corey Tanner sounded like he was barely out of high school.

This might be easier than she'd hoped.

"My name is Jodi Alford," she said. "I'm a reporter with the *Lexington Herald-Leader*, in Lexington, Kentucky?"

"Okay," Tanner said.

"I'm doing a story on The Pines Classic, on this year's winner—"

"Craig Driscoll."

"Exactly. He's from Lexington." Espy had no idea where Driscoll was from, but she hoped Tanner didn't either.

"You probably want to talk to our publicity office," Tanner said. "They don't come in till nine or so. Let me switch you to their voicemail."

"No," Espy blurted quickly. "I just have a few basic questions about the Classic. Mostly about the course, the things you do to maintain it."

"You want Gary Blackstone, then," Tanner said. "He'll be in about nine too, I could let him know—"

"Actually, they're very simple questions. Maybe you could help me out."

There was a pause.

"Uh...I don't know if I'm allowed to do that," Tanner said.

"Just basic information," Espy said. "That way I can get start the article, then call back later and talk to Mr. Blackstone."

"Um..."

"What do you do there, Mr. Tanner?"

"Right now? I, uh, I'm working in the locker room. But I've been doing a little caddying, they have some open spots up here."

Matt's face flashed across her mind. She pushed it aside. "I'm interested in the work that's done to keep the course in shape, the greens, in particular. You know about that?"

"Some."

"Perfect," Espy said. "The article is going to talk about how Driscoll played the course...versus how the course usually plays. That sort of thing."

She sounded ridiculous, and she braced herself for Tanner to say something like who do you work for again or to just hang up.

"Focusing on the greens," Tanner replied.

"Exactly."

"So you want to talk about what happened on thirteen."

Espy almost fell out of her chair.

"Yes," she managed. "I definitely do want to talk about what happened on thirteen. How did you know?"

"It's kind of obvious. That was the luckiest putt I ever saw. Sixty-five feet. Most of it downhill? You ask me, he won the tournament right there."

Driscoll hit a miracle putt on thirteen. Matt and Kazmir fought on thirteen.

That couldn't be a coincidence.

"What I heard around the clubhouse," Tanner said, "was that thirteen was playing really fast, all four rounds. Everyone was amazed."

"I heard that repair work was done on that green before the tournament. You know anything about that?"

"That's the kind of thing you'd have to ask Gary. Or someone in his department."

"I see."

"Of course, whatever they did, they're going to have to do it again."

"Why's that?"

"Monday night some jerks tore up the whole green. Going to have to rebuild from scratch, practically. From the drainage system on up."

"Somebody destroyed the green?"

"Kids on dirt bikes, ATVs, something. It's happened before, but they really did a job this time."

Espy drummed a pencil on her desk, trying to absorb the information while keeping the kid talking.

"Now, tell me again about the drainage system. There's a drainage system under the greens?"

"Sure. Pipes, vacuums, hoses." His tone became more assured, almost condescending. "You know, on a green the grass has to be just the right shade of firm. Too dry, and it wilts; too wet and it takes on fungus."

It sounded fairly complicated to her. It also sounded, just a little bit, like a clue.

"Gary knows more about it than I do," Tanner said.

"Okay." She would have to call back, try to fool someone other than a high school kid with her reporter impersonation. "Thanks for your help."

"Or you could call the manufacturer."

Espy, about to hang up, stopped: "The manufacturer?"

"I'm pretty sure they're the ones who installed the system. If you want to know exactly how it works, they'd be the ones to talk to."

"Do you know the name of the manufacturer?"

"You'd have to ask Gary," he said, then paused, then added, "Or I could go check the computer. It's probably in the maintenance log."

Espy smiled. Mr. Tanner was a reporter's dream.

Someone knocked on her door.

She checked the clock on her computer screen: eight exactly. Early for anyone else to be here. Had to be Amy. Sometimes she came in early, a flextime thing, because of her kids.

She said to Tanner, "Could I ask you to hold for one second?"

She punched a button on the phone without waiting for a response.

"Come in," she said.

It wasn't Amy.

It was Leonard.

He didn't look happy at all.

It took another second for her to realize why.

"Oh my God," Espy said. "Breakfast. I completely forgot."

❖ ❖ ❖ ❖ ❖

She hung up on Tanner without a word. She'd call back and apologize later.

Assuming she got through this apology now.

"I'm so sorry," she said.

"Tell me what's happening," he said. His eyes burned behind his glasses. His whole face was flushed and he barely maintained his usual composure.

"What do you mean?"

He sat down. "I mean there's something going on with you. Has been for a few months now." He folded his arms across his chest. "Your work's been suffering. I've been cutting you some slack, because...well, just because. But I can't overlook this thing with Kazmir. This is gross incompetence, you not following up on the source of those funds."

"I should have, I know, I was going to, I just..."

She couldn't recall any of the excuses she'd rehearsed yesterday.

"You know how much hell I'm catching from the Columbus office on this? Not just the fact that we botched the investigation, but that the guy is dead?"

"No," she said. "I mean, I can guess."

"The only silver lining is that the two aren't connected. Kazmir's gambling and his murder."

"Yes," she said. "A silver lining."

"We know who the killer is, even if they don't have him in custody anymore. Of course, David Abraham disagrees. He called me at home last night."

Espy's stomach rolled over.

"We had a long talk." Leonard peered over his glasses at her. "I'm sure you can guess about what."

Abraham had called Leonard. Espy could think of only one reason why. He had found proof that she was at The Pines.

"Is there anything you want to tell me?" Leonard asked.

A lot, she thought. There's a lot I want to tell you. Let's talk about the $140,000 that the Springboro Voter Registration Initiative placed into Garrett Crandall's senate campaign. Your wife, Tunde, is president of the group, which is also part of the Democratic Fund for Direct Action. Let's talk about that.

"I wasn't there," she said. "If that's why he called."

Leonard slapped her desk so hard she jumped an inch out of her chair.

"Of course that's why he called." He stood and glared down at her. "He wouldn't let me off the phone. Kept telling me how long he'd known the Thurman family, that no way was Matt a killer, that I should talk to the brother, get confirmation on this jailhouse contract that was put out on the guy."

"I'm sorry you had to go through—"

"I'm not doing this anymore." He sat down. "I can't," he said, less harshly. "I know the timing stinks, but it can't be helped. We are supposed to be a team. For the last six months you've been shutting your door. This is not how I want to run my department."

"I know I've been...locking myself away..."

"Your review is in two months. I'm going to recommend that before it comes up, you find yourself another job."

"No," she said. "Leonard, I—"

"No?" He actually laughed. "What on earth is the matter with you, Esperanza? I'm trying to help you."

"I don't want another job," she said. "Please. I want to..."

She let her voice trail off, because she didn't know actually what she wanted.

She wanted the last five months of her life back. She wanted never to have heard of Alderney Financial Trust or the Democratic Fund for Direct Action or Garrett Crandall or Stuart Crane, or any of the others in the society.

She wanted her father, alive.

"I'm sorry," she said. "I really am."

Leonard's posture, and his stare, remained firm. "You finish the Mandini case," he said. "You handle United Apparel. And then we'll see. And in the meantime, I want the Kazmir file. Everything you have. I don't want you working on that anymore. Understood?"

"Yes," she said.

"I want your word." He looked her in the eye.

"You have my word."

He walked to the door, put one hand on the knob, and then turned around. "On a personal level," he said, his voice shaking, "I'm hurt by how you've been acting. And Tunde is hurt. She thought you were friends. Whatever your problems are with me, I can't think of a single thing she did to deserve the cold shoulder you've been giving her."

"I," she said, and then stopped, because she could, in fact, think of a hundred and forty thousand things Tunde had done wrong.

But she couldn't say that. Not yet.

Leonard left, looking as angry as when he walked in.

How long Espy sat there, shaking with a dozen different suppressed emotions, she couldn't tell.

A stack of files landed on her desk.

Espy looked up and saw Amy.

"You have court at two," Amy said.

"Right."

"You won't forget?"

Espy shook her head, unable to meet Amy's eyes. Then her phone rang. She looked at the caller's number: her mother.

Espy picked up as Amy left.

"I called you before," her mother said. "You didn't pick up."

"Sorry. I was in the middle of something."

"I hope it was good enough to miss breakfast with your boss."

"Listen, this isn't a good time to talk."

"I only wanted to say I'll see you tonight. At the reception." She also put in some quick advice about what to wear—and what not to wear, which included the green dress that Espy sort of liked—and then hung up.

Espy sighed.

Then opened her eyes wide.

The reception. Good God.

❖ ❖ ❖ ❖ ❖

The reception started at six, she wanted to be there early enough to find out what she could before dinner. When was dinner? She pulled the invitation from her briefcase: eight o'clock. So as long as she was there by seven, she'd be fine.

Her computer dinged. Incoming e-mail. From Chris Holloway.

He wanted a reply to his message: would she please recommend another lawyer to take the case? Would she please respond before three this afternoon, as he would be unavailable after that?

She could picture Leonard's face if she even hinted at the possibility. She sent a terse reply, telling him she'd respond in the morning.

She went on Lexis/Nexis, started making notes, checking precedents, reviewing the file. Losing herself in her work.

At noon, her cell rang.

The encrypted number. Shurig.

"You're up early," she said.

"Been up all night."

He sounded like it—his voice sluggish and husky with fatigue.

She told him about the Kirtland companies and about the golf course and the irrigation system. He told her what they'd found and what everyone seemed to think about it.

Al-Hasra behind her father's shooting?

"They can't be serious," she said. "Finding all that evidence at once...nobody thinks that's a little suspicious?"

"They just want to put this mess behind them. The sooner the better. There's a press release going out today. My guess is they'll start winding things up over the weekend."

"So we'll lose all the bureau's resources."

"All my free time, too," Shurig said. "Come Monday, I have to put this on the back burner."

"So what do we do?"

"We keep looking," Shurig said. "As long as we can. We have to."

"Right," she said. They had to. It wasn't just about the money, after all.

There's something else going on.

She heard her father's voice in her head.

Then she heard Shurig saying goodbye.

Barton Lane
Lancaster, CA
Friday, September 21, 9:15 A.M.

SHURIG was in Lancaster, twenty minutes southeast of Fox Airfield, driving down Barton Lane, searching for house number forty-two. Which was going to be on his right, because here was number twenty-eight, the first house with a street number he'd seen so far, a little tan ranch house, with a little fenced-in yard, a little driveway, and a little concrete walk. Yard was being generous; it was a bunch of scraggly weeds and some dirt. Two houses on, a guy sat on a cinder block in the middle of his yard, sucking on a bottle in a brown paper bag.

As Shurig drove past, the guy belched and gave him the finger.

Garbage overflowed from trashcans. Junked cars on cinder blocks littered half the yards.

Shurig shook his head. He'd heard stories of what was going on up here in Antelope Valley—third-world squalor, ninety minutes from Beverly Hills.

He stopped at number forty-two—Tomasevic's house.

It was the only one that looked halfway decent. Shurig got out and scanned his surroundings. Looking for trouble. He didn't see any. The streets were nearly deserted. Not a surprise, this early in the morning, most of the gang-bangers probably still in bed, sleeping it off.

"Hello?"

Shurig turned.

Tomasevic's wife stood in the doorway of their house. She wore jeans and a short-sleeve t-shirt. Long auburn hair. Long legs. The way she stood, leaning out of the house, one foot on the sill, one foot on the front step, she looked like a model posing for a fashion shoot. Except for her eyes. Suspicion. A little fear.

He took out his badge as he walked toward her. "I'm Mike Shurig.

Agent Shurig. I'm with the FBI."

He stopped a few feet before he reached her, gave her a chance to study the badge. She looked at it, and then warily, back at him. Big emerald eyes.

"Is there a problem?" she asked. "With Goran? At his work?"

Her accent was a lot heavier than her husband's.

"No. No problem. I just wanted to talk to you for a few minutes, if I could."

She put her hands on her hips. "You want to talk to me?"

"I worked closely with Agent Hernandez. I understand you knew him."

Her face brightened. "Sam," she said. "Yes, I knew him."

And if he'd had any doubts in his mind about the wisdom of this trip, about taking the day off, the look on Tomasevic's wife's face erased them from his mind.

She knew him all right. The question was what else she knew.

"May I?" Shurig asked, nodding toward the house.

"Of course," she said, and swung the door all the way open. "Come in."

❖ ❖ ❖ ❖ ❖

Her name was Maya. She was twenty-six, five years younger than Goran. They had grown up together in Rogatica, a little town an hour outside Sarajevo. Their families were friends. Then Goran's family came to America, settled in New Jersey. Goran went to university. Did well. Her family came too, later. She and Goran met again. They got married. They moved here. End of story.

End of life, Shurig thought.

They sat at the kitchen table, which looked like a Wal-Mart special, a round faux-wood, made-in-China piece of crap that had probably looked good for the first two weeks and then started to chip and stain and fade. Like the neighborhood.

Like Tomasevic's wife, eventually. If she didn't get out of here.

"Thank you for this," he said, raising his cup. "For inviting me in."

"I am glad for the company," she said, sipping from her own mug, setting it down next to the still-folded, unread *Times*, which sat next to a little plate of cookies she'd brought out with the coffee. She asked why he wanted to speak to her about Sam.

"We're trying to nail down his movements these last few weeks. Make a timeline."

She nodded but obviously didn't understand. He was struck again by her natural beauty. Auburn hair, green eyes, alabaster skin, a sweetness that charmed him to the point where he felt guilty deceiving her.

"We want to find out where he went. Who he talked to. I understand he was here a few times."

"He come every week, almost."

"For dinner?"

Her eyes started to tear. She dabbed at them and nodded.

Did he come for more than dinner, Shurig wanted to ask.

"And how long did he do this—come here?"

"Three months, maybe. I don't know. Maybe longer."

"And it was just the three of you? Sam and Goran and you?"

"Sometimes, just the two of us."

Shurig nodded. He picked up a cookie and took a bite. Or tried to. It wouldn't give. He bit down again, harder, felt something snap in his mouth. For a second, he thought it was a tooth.

"Good," he managed, crunching away.

Maya smiled. "These are Croatian cookies. Not so sweet. Is enough sugar for you?"

"Definitely," Shurig said.

Her smile lit up her face. Lit up the whole room. God she was beautiful.

Focus, he told himself. "You and Sam spent a lot of time together?"

"He teach me English. Goran, he has no patience for this. Anyone who is not smart like he is, Goran gets upset. Sam is patient. Good teacher. Good man." She leaned across the table toward Shurig. "You catch people who killed him?"

"Not yet. Soon."

"Arabs, yes?" She spat out a curse. "Muslims. They are plague. Cause trouble everywhere. Here, Bosnia-Herzegovina..."

"To tell you the truth, we're not sure yet who—"

"Ah. You need proof. You want to give them trial." Maya shook her head. "I don't give them trial. I give them what they give Sam." She made her right thumb and forefinger into the shape of a pistol. "Eye for eye, like Bible says."

"Maya." He leaned forward. "I have to ask you something. Something personal, and I don't want you to take offense."

She nodded, eager to help.

"Were you and Sam, Agent Hernandez, having an affair?"

She giggled. Cocked an eyebrow and giggled again. "You mean do we...? No," she said. "Me and Sam? No. Sam is my friend, yes? My good friend. But he was...I don't want to insult, but Sam was old. Yes?"

Shurig instantly knew she was telling the truth. Of course they hadn't had an affair. Maya had to be almost thirty years younger than Sam, younger than his own daughters. And Sam would not have an affair with the wife of someone in the bureau. A stupid idea to even think of it.

She stopped smiling and looked at him. "Someone says this at your office? Goran thinks this? That Sam and I—"

"No, nothing like that." He shook his head firmly. "It's just something I needed to ask. A possibility I needed to check out."

She took a cookie from the plate but did not bite into it. Just held it delicately in her hand. Still looking a little unsure.

"So," Shurig said. "Sam was teaching you English."

Maya leaned forward. "I tell you secret. He was teaching to me computer too."

Shurig sat up in his chair.

"Goran thinks I cannot learn." She gestured dismissively with the hand that still held the cookie. "He tells me leave machine alone, I will show you when I come home. But he never does. Sam does. He shows me e-mail, Internet..."

"You have a computer here."

She pointed behind him. "In spare room. Goran never uses. Only me."

"And Sam."

"Sam too. Sometimes I practice English, he does work. I am out here, he is in there."

Shurig stood up. "Could I take a look?"

BOOK TWO: SOLDIERS

U.S. Department of Justice
Federal Building
Cincinnati, OH
Friday, September 21, 12:46 P.M.

ESPY'S office phone rang as she finished the United Apparel memo for Holloway. A nice piece of work, if she did say so herself. Clear and concise, cutting through the legalese and lawyer-speak straight to the heart of the matter.

Your client engaged in a series of corporate transactions that served no legitimate business purpose. That served no purpose other than to lower your client's tax liability.

The law is clear.

Those are improper tax shelters.

The deductions you claim are hereby denied.

We're not settling.

Pay up.

You wanted me to do my work, Mr. Holloway? There you go. Hope you're happy now.

She felt proud of herself as she picked up the phone.

"Ms. Harper. This is Lieutenant O'Neill."

Espy did a quick shift in her mind. "Yes. How are you?"

"A little pissed off, frankly."

She guessed he was about to tell her what Shurig had mentioned earlier. But she figured it was better if he didn't know the two of them had spoken.

"There's a press conference in half an hour," he told her. "The Assistant Director out here is going to announce they found evidence linking your father's murder to Al-Hasra."

"So it was revenge," she said. "The shooting."

"That's horseshit," he snapped. "And you know it."

"Excuse me?"

"There's something else going on. Since Agent Shurig won't tell me, why don't you?"

"I don't know what you're talking about," she said.

O'Neill was silent. She expected him to offer a version of the 'you're-a-terrible-liar' line that everyone seemed to be using these days.

"You're in the middle of another murder investigation, I hear," he said. Coincidence, don't you think? This guy Kazmir—you were investigating some illegal gambling. Might be ties to organized crime or something like that."

"Organized crime? Where'd you get that idea?"

"I talked to a couple people."

"There was no organized crime connection. We decided not to even prosecute, as you might have—"

"The bureau found a book in your father's apartment called *Great Gambling Stories of the Twentieth Century*."

Espy's heart beat faster. "Does that mean something?"

"I don't know. It has 'From the Library of Esperanza Marcelina Harper' stamped inside it."

She didn't remember doing that. Force of habit. "I guess he borrowed it last time he was here. I still don't get your point."

"My point. That's a helluva coincidence, don't you think?"

Now she did laugh. A forced laugh, but she made it sound as natural as she could. "You're stretching, lieutenant. For what, I don't know, but—"

"I'm trying to find out who killed your father. I would think you'd be interested in that too."

Her laughter turned to anger. "Of course I'm interested."

"Then tell me the truth," O'Neill said.

"I'm hanging up now."

"So am I," O'Neill said. "Get your priorities straight, Ms. Harper.

This is not only a murder investigation, it's a matter of national security. You and I ought to be on the same side."

He clicked off before she could.

❖ ❖ ❖ ❖ ❖

Work was impossible after that. Her DOJ work, that is.

She stared at the Holloway memo, which she'd been so proud of minutes before, and felt like erasing the whole page of legalese she'd written and stating her position—stop cheating, pay your taxes—in the same no-bullshit way O'Neill had just stated his.

He was right. She and Shurig had to bring him in. They had to trust someone. Three days of working together, and they'd gotten nowhere. O'Neill was obviously smart. He could help them.

She picked up her cell and started to dial Shurig's number.

We're on the same side here.

But were they?

A traitor in the bureau. Maybe it really was a bug in the computer, the way Shurig's colleagues thought. But that computer was on an Air Force base. So did the Cincinnati have someone in the Air Force too? Maybe not O'Neill but somebody getting O'Neill's reports? Somebody O'Neill trusted?

She put the cell back in her purse and looked at her watch. A little before one. She had court in an hour. She ought to look at the Mandini file one more time.

She spun in her chair and reached for the filing cabinet.

And stopped.

She heard O'Neill's voice in her head again.

Get your priorities straight, Ms. Harper.

She grabbed the cell phone from her purse.

❖ ❖ ❖ ❖ ❖

She shut her door. She dialed. She asked for Corey Tanner, who apparently was caddying. She asked for Gary Blackstone, who was at lunch. She asked for anyone in the grounds crew. Finally got a guy named Bill who told her the name of the company that made the pump system under the greens: Next Century Course Development.

Wow. That was easy.

She disconnected her laptop from the DOJ server, popped in the three-G card, and went online. Googled the company, found a very non-descriptive webpage, looked more like a placeholder than any-thing else, but it had a phone number and an address. Fort Lauderdale, Florida.

She dialed. Got voicemail. A woman's voice. Computer generated.

She hung up and checked her watch: 1:28. Ten-minute walk to the courthouse. Ten minutes in the courtroom to get ready. Which left her ten more here. Time to do a little more googling...

Someone knocked on her door.

She froze.

Leonard, she thought, and suddenly pictured him sitting in her chair this morning, asking for the Kazmir file. Asking for her word that she would stop working on it. Which she'd given.

And which she'd just broken.

The knock came again. She quit the web browser, rearranged her features.

"Come in," she said, and then saw that the three-G card was still plugged into her laptop. The little light on it blinking green. She yanked the card out and dropped it in her lap.

The door opened. Amy—reminding Espy of the court time. Espy said, "Yes, thank you," and waited for Amy to leave.

Then she turned back to her computer.

And found herself staring at the Holloway memo again.

With a little dialog box on top of it: the program Wordworks has encountered an error and needs to close.

"No," Espy said. "Oh no."

She knew right away what had happened. She was supposed to power down the card before she pulled it. By yanking it out, she'd crashed the machine.

Had she saved the file at all this morning? She couldn't remember. She hit key combinations, trying to get the computer to respond, the little dialog box to disappear. Nothing happened.

"Everything okay?" Amy called from her desk.

"Just a computer thing."

"Want me to call tech support?"

She couldn't call tech support. They'd see the modifications her father made to the computer. She'd be escorted off the premises. Plus the evidence would be there, her browsing history, she hadn't cleared that either...

"No. Thanks. Won't be necessary."

She shut down the computer. Slid it to the edge of her desk, slid the Mandini file into her briefcase, and slid out the door.

❖ ❖ ❖ ❖ ❖

Of course it wasn't the Mandini file she'd picked up.

It was the United Apparel material.

Which she discovered when the hearing started.

She had two choices: wing it, or take her medicine. She decided on the second, because she had her own version of the physician's oath—do no harm, and if she screwed up in an official proceeding...

The judge reamed her for not being prepared. She hoped he wouldn't tell Leonard. They rescheduled. She walked back into her office.

There was a guy sitting at her desk—a guy she'd never seen before.
Her laptop was open and running.

"This yours?" he asked.

"Yes."

"Couple things," he said, and stood up.

BOOK TWO: SOLDIERS

Barton Lane

Lancaster, CA

Friday, September 21, 11:48 A.M.

MAYA'S computer was a generic bargain-basement box, the monitor a crappy fifteen-inch LCD screen with a half-inch square of dead pixels in the lower right corner. It was running Vista, for God's sake. Tomasevic was data support, and this was what he gave his wife?

The computer sat on a piece of white countertop six feet long, a couple feet wide. Piles of bills on one side, a printer on the other. Shurig sat behind the monitor, facing the door, on a rolling desk chair that no longer rolled so well.

There was one account on the computer: Maya's. She'd given him her password. He could tell she was a bit suspicious, but he told her he might find evidence to use in a trial. She nodded and pulled the door shut behind her.

He'd come up here certain he was going to find out Sam and Maya had been having an affair, certain she wouldn't want his visit publicized any more than he did. Now, though...

Keeping his trip secret would be impossible. From Goran, at least. Probably from the rest of the squad, too. And if he found anything on the computer...

Maybe he ought to stop right now. Say there was nothing on the machine, leave, then hire one of the local gang-bangers to come back in a couple days and steal it. Crime situation around here was probably such that no one would even notice. Probably the cops wouldn't even investigate.

He was getting ahead of himself, he realized. Imagining worst-case scenarios, when he didn't even know if there was anything on the hard drive worth keeping secret. He entered Maya's password and began checking her folders, her files, but found nothing that looked

255

like it belonged to Sam. He launched a few programs, checked a list of recently opened files. Nothing. He opened the web browser, went through her history, and it really was her history, a lot of Serbian language sites, a few cooking sites. Checked her cookie file. Went to the DOS prompt, checked the list of files. Nothing.

Not a surprise. Sam was no more of a computer expert than he was, but the man was no dummy either. He knew how to hide his tracks.

He wouldn't have had huge chunks of time. What kind of work could he do?

E-mail, Shurig thought.

The computer didn't have a separate e-mail program, so probably they were using a web-based service. He checked the browsing history again, found repeated visits to speedmail.com. He clicked on that page.

Good morning, Tomasevic!
You have 2 unread messages.

Both messages were from the local supermarket. Coupon specials. No other messages in her inbox; her trash folder was empty; no messages in her sent mail. The rest of her e-mail was very precisely organized. Shurig counted twenty-two separate folders. He looked through them, one by one. In the third one, he found a message from shernandez@vwest.com.

Maya:
Just got this from my friend Joe Augustino at Landers Real Estate. As you can see, he's happy to talk to you. Good luck.

Sam

Shurig looked at the address line again.
shernandez@vwest.com.

Vwest. They were a local Internet provider. Most Internet providers gave you e-mail services along with the connection packages.

shernandez@vwest.com.

Shurig didn't recall seeing that e-mail address before.

He called Kramer at the bureau's tech support. She was at lunch, according to the assistant tech, named Osterberg.

He asked if Osterberg had access to the material on Sam's murder. He did. He asked if he had a list of Sam's known e-mail addresses. He did. He asked Osterberg if he could read the list to him. He did.

shernandez@vwest wasn't on it.

"What's going on?" Osterberg asked.

"Just wanted to make sure I had all of them," Shurig said. "I need to find a message he sent me awhile back, so—"

"You're still investigating," Osterberg said out of the blue. "You don't think it's Al-Hasra either. I agree. That evidence was obviously planted. Good luck. Oh, you'll want the password: Princess Grace. One word."

Harper's mother's face flashed across his mind. She'd reminded him of Grace Kelly at the funeral. Seems she reminded Sam of Grace Kelly too.

Shurig thanked Osterberg and hung up, found Vwest's home accounts page, and typed in Sam's user name and password.

Princess Grace. Harper's mother. Some unresolved feelings on Sammy's part. Her part too, given how she broke down at the funeral. Poor Sam. Trying to recapture the past with a lot of other women, trying to fill up the hole in his heart that the loss had left.

Sad. Futile.

That's what people do, Shurig thought. He thought about D.B. and his pathetic attempt to find her in the professor. Lost love. Makes us do crazy things.

The Vwest home page finished loading.

One new message. From two days ago. From cloudbytes.

User: Shernandez

Your account is due for payment.

Shurig scratched his jaw. User shernandez? The username Harper and Sam had shared was betsyross1.

This was a different account. He logged in with the new name and password.

The screen filled with a list of files. Different files; Sam's private files. Arranged alphabetically by title. The one at the top was called Altair.

Altair.

Familiar name, Shurig thought.

Took him a few seconds to realize why.

BOOK TWO: SOLDIERS

U.S. Department of Justice
Federal Building
Cincinnati, OH
Friday, September 21, 4:09 P.M.

THE tech support guy stuck out his hand: "Adam Soltz," he said. "You're Harper, right?"

She set her briefcase on the chair in front of her desk. "Yes," she said.

Soltz sat back down. "We have problems."

Espy nodded, waiting for the hammer to fall. Illegal modifications. Illegally accessed government documents. Dereliction of duty. Guilty, guilty, guilty.

"Come take a look," he said.

She walked behind her desk and immediately saw one of the problems—the 3-G card lying on the floor. It must have fallen from her lap when she yanked it out of the computer.

It was right next to Soltz's feet.

She couldn't reach it or even kick it under the desk without shoving him out of the way.

"I'm running Norton," Soltz said, pointing at the screen, where a progress bar inched slowly from left to right. Seventy-two percent complete. "Your hard drive is a mess. Didn't you get that memo?"

"Memo?" Espy conjured a look of innocent confusion.

"The big one. Computer Security Procedures, sent about six months back?"

"Oh. That." She'd read through a little of it, started with an overview of the whole Homeland Security network structure, how it had been overhauled, how it incorporated the latest security protocols from the private sector, how those protocols were designed to thwart potential threat incursions, what each individual end-user

259

should do to insure those protocols were maintained, what kind of tricks the druglords/terrorists used to evade detection. It went on and on in progressively more mind-numbing detail. Espy had given up after ten pages.

"Yeah. That," Soltz said, and went on in progressively more mind-numbing detail about how she hadn't been following those protocols, because not only was her hard drive ridiculously fragmented but it was almost full, not just with work stuff but these big picture files, which she wasn't supposed to have on the computer because they were obviously personal. Some little girl.

Pictures of Olivia, Espy realized, the photos her father had been sending her the last few months.

He went on to describe more problems, which no doubt had to do with the modifications her dad's guy made. She heard little of what he said, listening only for mention of the hardware modifications. He didn't mention them.

"As for the file you were working on when you crashed, I managed to reconstruct a version of it, but it's from around eleven this morning. Which I guess was the last time you saved. Take a look."

Espy did, and her heart sank.

There was her memo to Chris Holloway—or, rather, the scattered notes for it.

Soltz stood up. "Wish I could have recovered more for you."

His foot just missed the network card.

"I appreciate it."

"Hey." He smiled, showing a mouthful of crooked teeth. "What are friends in data support and network storage for?"

He pushed in her desk chair and ran right over the network card. Espy heard it crunch.

The second he left, she picked it up, saw a hairline crack. Salvageable? She hoped so.

The Holloway memo wasn't. She looked at the notes she'd made and couldn't imagine how they had formed the final version.

She sighed, and logged onto the DOJ server.

More bad news.

An e-mail from Holloway, reiterating his wish that another attorney be assigned to the case. He had cc:'ed his boss.

And Leonard.

Espy went down the hall to explain what happened but Leonard was gone.

"He had to leave early," Amy said. "You want to leave a message?"

"No. That's all right," though of course it wasn't all right, she had to talk to Leonard in person before he fired her. Should she call him at home? Yes. But first...

She had to rewrite that memo.

She went to her office, and stared at the screen. Stared at her notes. Willed her fingers to type something. Anything.

They wouldn't.

The problem wasn't so much the words. She saw a way to reconstruct her thought process, but it all seemed pointless, when she could distill its essence into two sentences: Stop cheating. Pay your taxes.

Why waste the next hour obscuring that simple message with a lot of big words? She had more important things to do with her time, didn't she?

Get your priorities straight, Ms. Harper.

❖ ❖ ❖ ❖ ❖

"You've reached Next Century Course Development, the leader in cutting-edge golf course maintenance equipment. If you know your party's extension..."

Espy hung up.

She logged out of the DOJ server. Popped in the network card. It didn't work.

She pulled it out and logged back on, went straight to Factiva from the DOJ server. There would be a record of what she was doing now. Another thing she'd have to explain to Leonard. But not tonight.

She searched Next Century Course Development, came up with a half-dozen articles. No company profile. She wouldn't find anything on Hoover's or D&B either, she realized. No surprise. If she was really on the right track...information would be difficult to come by.

She scanned the article abstracts: they were all basically the same. So-and-so of such-and-such golf course has engaged Next Century Course Development to upgrade its greens maintenance system. The courses mentioned were big: Pebble Beach, Medinah, Oakmont, many of the top-level PGA courses. Familiar to Espy because of the tournaments on which money had been gambled and won. By the society and by Bob Kazmir.

Bob Kazmir.

Something was ringing a bell there.

Next Century and Bob Kazmir. There had to be some connection between them. Next Century was based in Fort Lauderdale. Kazmir was in Ohio, but he had a bank account in Florida. And she didn't need to look at the file, which Leonard had taken, to remember where: Wilton Manors.

About three miles from Fort Lauderdale.

Espy picked up the phone, called the IRS, her pal Jim Grater. They had worked on a couple of big tax fraud cases, gotten to know each other. They ate lunch together a couple times a month, and he was one of a half-dozen people to call her at home after hearing the news about her father.

"I have a favor," she said. "A company in Fort Lauderdale. Next Century Course Development. I want a look at their 1120."

"Hang on a second."

She heard typing.

"Yeah. Here they are. Next Century Course Development. Huh."

"What?"

"Nothing. It's just that...they filed a paper return. Nobody files paper anymore."

"Is that a problem?"

"It means I can't send it to you electronically. I have to call Florida, have them fax it or send you a scan."

Which meant she couldn't get it today, Espy realized, looking at the clock, already after 4:30.

"If you could do that Monday," Espy said. "I would really appreciate it."

"Sure. But hang on a second. Let me put their tax I.D. into the system, see what else we come up with."

She heard more typing.

"Here we go," Grater said. "Got an M-3."

That form was sort of a shorthand summary of the 1120. The IRS scanned all those as a matter of course but only for corporations with ten million or more in assets. She didn't figure Next Century did that kind of business.

She said, "Next Century has an M-3?"

"Not them. Their corporate parent. Company called Enovation."

Enovation. That sounded familiar.

Then sounded very familiar.

Enovation was associated with Altair Technologies. From the list of companies on Kirtland Air Force Base.

"Can you forward me what you have there?" she asked. "And anything else you have on Enovation?"

Grater had nothing. Enovation's U.S. offices were in Fort Lauderdale, but the company was not only privately held, it had been incorporated in

Turks and Caicos. Good luck getting any information out of there.

Still, it was a starting point. At last. She thanked him and hung up. She called Shurig. No answer.

"Call me right away," she said.

It was a little after five. She still had to go home, pick a dress to wear. What had the invitation said about dress?

She pulled it from her briefcase.

It was fancy. Rectangular. The front was the society's flag—blue and white stripes, with a circle of blue stars in the upper left hand corner.

Inside the circle was an eagle.

The lettering inside was fancy too. Gold leaf script.

THE SOCIETY OF THE CINCINNATI
Invites You to an Anniversary Celebration
The Signing of the Constitution of
the United States of America
September 21
Union Terminal, Cincinnati, OH
Cocktails 6:00 P.M.
Dinner 8:00 P.M.
Festive Dress Suggested
Formal Dress Required

Festive suggested; formal required. Espy had no idea what the former meant. As for the latter...

She'd do her best.

❖ ❖ ❖ ❖ ❖

Two men watched her leave. From a parked car, half a block down. One man at the wheel, a second man in the back.

"What do you think?" the man in back asked. "Tonight?"

The driver watched her cross the street, heading for her apartment building.

"Yeah," he said. "Tonight."

CINCINNATUS

Union Terminal
Western Avenue
Cincinnati, OH
Friday, September 21, 6:20 P.M.

Union Terminal was less than a mile from her apartment. Given the importance of the society and its members, she expected a first-class affair. What she didn't expect were Revolutionary War-era soldiers.

A dozen or so of them milled around the entrance wearing shiny black boots, bright white tights, dark-blue coats with bright red facings and cuffs, and eighteenth century-style white wigs under black tri-corner hats trimmed in white. Not real soldiers, of course, doormen. Parking attendants.

Festive dress suggested—now she got it. It was kind of a costume party. She'd gone for a mixture of festive and formal with her outfit, choosing not the dresses her mother had left in her closet, which were all black and navy blue, but the lime-green she'd picked out weeks earlier. She accessorized it with a scarf that matched. Sort of. She hoped it worked. Certainly her mother would let her know.

"Good evening, madam." One of the soldiers stood by the driver's side door of her Honda. "On behalf of President Washington and the Society of the Cincinnati, I bid you welcome."

Espy stepped out of the car, took a valet ticket, and headed up the steps. On the terminal entrance hung two huge flags. The Stars and Stripes. And the Society's.

She stared up at the eagle in the circle of stars. Stared into its eyes.

Before her father had been killed, attending the event had seemed like a good chance for her to put names to faces, to see the society up close and personal. Now...

Everything had changed.

266

STOP

What were they going to do to her, Espy wondered, if she didn't.

❖ ❖ ❖ ❖ ❖

Union Terminal was an art deco landmark, a recognized architectural masterpiece. It had won awards from countless organizations, both for the original building and for the redesign after its conversion from train station to museum center. The heart of the terminal was the rotunda—the giant dome, the train station waiting room, off which everything else in the station flowed. Since the terminal's conversion, the other rooms—the old station offices, dining rooms, passenger service areas—had been converted into separate museum spaces—the Cincinnati Children's Museum, the Museum of Natural History and Science, the Cincinnati History Museum, an IMAX theater. Espy had been here a handful of times. The impression she'd gotten was of space—a lot of empty space.

Not tonight.

The rotunda was packed with people and tables and decorations. Everywhere Espy looked, she saw red, white, and blue—the American flag, or flags, rather, flying from stanchions set up throughout the rotunda.

As she handed her invitation to a woman wearing a Revolutionary War-era dress, she saw a half-dozen big men dressed in period outfits standing near the entrance. One of them looked like the man Matt had described meeting on the golf course. The bodybuilder. Rawson.

He looked in her direction. She looked quickly away.

Not possible it was really him. The man wouldn't show his face in public after killing two people. Though no one had seen the golf course murder except Matt and no one had seen Kauffman's killer besides—

Shurig. He hadn't called her back. She wondered if something was wrong. It was seven o'clock here, four o'clock there.

"You're all set," the receiving woman said. "Table fourteen."

"Table fourteen. Thanks." Espy moved onto the main floor. Maybe half the crowd wore costumes. The men who weren't in costume wore tuxes. The women mostly wore black or dark blue. She saw a handful of red dresses.

Nothing in lime-green.

"Esperanza!" called an older woman with a powdered wig slightly askew. The woman looked familiar—one of her mother's friends.

"Hello!" Espy said, putting on a smile. "Good to see you."

They hugged.

"It's good to see you too, my dear," the woman said. "You look… lovely."

She said it with a frozen smile that meant 'what in the world are you wearing?'"

Another woman appeared, another of her mother's friends, wearing an even more elaborate Revolutionary War gown.

"Mrs. Claypool," Espy said.

When Mrs. Claypool looked at Espy's dress, her smile wavered.

"Esperanza." The first woman leaned closer. "Robert is here. "

Espy had no idea who Robert was. She looked at the woman again and finally recognized her. Cecily Teresi. Robert was her son.

"Oh." She managed a half-smile. "I haven't talked to him in forever."

"He's in advertising," Mrs. Teresi said. "Doing quite well for himself."

"And he looks wonderful," Mrs. Claypool added. "Lost quite a bit of weight."

"You two will have plenty of time to catch up," Mrs. Teresi said. "You're sitting at our table, I believe. Table fourteen?"

"I sure am," Espy said, keeping the smile frozen on her face.

"He was just here a minute ago," Mrs. Teresi said. She raised a hand to her brow and squinted into the crowd.

Espy scanned the room for a familiar face. Or the bar. She didn't see either. She saw a trio at the far end of the immense space, a piano player, a drummer, a bassist, also dressed in Revolutionary-era garb. She saw a lot of costumed waiters carrying trays of food. She saw a lot of men and women, younger ones mostly, wearing military uniforms.

Then she saw Leonard and Tunde, arm in arm, not twenty feet away, handing over their invitations. Him in costume, her in a long, flowing, multi-colored caftan.

"Is something the matter?" Mrs. Claypool asked.

"No," Espy said. "I see some people I want to...will you excuse me?"

She bolted away without waiting for a reply.

❖ ❖ ❖ ❖ ❖

She found the bar and ordered a cranberry juice, which they didn't have. She settled for a Diet Coke.

Leonard was here. Now she knew why he'd left early today. This was proof, she thought, that whatever the Cincinnati were doing, he and Tunde were in it up to their necks.

Of course, by that logic, so were Mrs. Claypool and Mrs. Teresi.

Someone laughed.

She turned and saw a man smiling at her. A big man with a full head of white hair, neatly trimmed white beard, well-worn tuxedo, in his sixties at least.

"Excuse me young lady," he said. "That dress you're wearing..."

"Oh, for God's sake," Espy said, and pushed past him, heading toward the middle of the room. The point of coming here was to observe without drawing attention to herself. How was she supposed to do that when everyone commented on her dress?

Maybe coming had been a bad idea. It wasn't as if she had a master plan for the evening. Her presence really was a fluke.

She'd been at her mom's house in June (a couple weeks after she and her father had started to dig into the money trail) when the mail arrived. Her mom was in the kitchen, making iced tea. Her special blend. Espy heard the mail slot open, heard paper hitting the parquet floor.

"I'll get it," she said.

Among the letters, Espy noticed the invitation. Her mom got a lot of them. She was involved in many charities and society functions.

The envelope had landed face down. The back of it was stenciled with a flag. A flag of blue and white stripes, with a circle of stars in the corner, and an eagle in the middle. It was, indeed, from the Society of the Cincinnati. Washington D.C. return address. Sent to Penelope Harper.

She felt a pang of paranoia—like a scene in a bad horror film.

"You," she pictured herself saying as she backed away from her mother. "You're one of them."

Of course she'd done nothing of the sort.

Through her mother, a similar invitation arrived at Espy's apartment a few days later. And now, here she was.

And there was her mother, standing near the main entrance talking to a man in a tuxedo. One of several men in tuxedoes clustered around her. She wore black, of course, a long simple dress with a V-cut back. Her hair was pulled back into an old-style chiffon. She wore a silver choker around her neck. She looked beautiful, as always.

Espy headed toward her mother but a waiter suddenly appeared, saying, "Mincemeat pie?" He held a tray in one hand and cocktail napkins in the other. "This is an authentic 1700s recipe. All the food we're serving tonight—"

"No thank you," Espy said, and tried to move past him, but the crowd had suddenly closed in around her. No, she realized. Not around her. The food.

She took a step back and landed on someone's foot.

"Sorry," she said.

The foot she'd stepped on belonged to a man her age. Maybe a little younger. He had longish dark hair and very white teeth. Tortoiseshell glasses.

He was handsome. Very handsome.

"Never get in between people and free food," he said, flashing a smile. "Even rich people."

"My mistake," she said.

"I like your dress," he said. "No reason why everyone has to wear black to these things. It's not a funeral."

She checked his face for the slightest hint of mockery. She didn't see any.

"Thanks," she said. "I like your costume too."

He was wearing a version of the standard Revolutionary War soldier, only the red in his was closer to maroon. The blue was slightly darker as well.

They chatted for a few minutes, trading observations about the crowd. She noticed a lot of security guards—not just the costumed kind, but a good dozen in the standard dark suit, earpieces in place. Not a surprise. She'd read that the governor was expected to attend. The mayor too, as well as the police chief and a number of city councilmen.

The column had mentioned Stuart Crane as well, though he was the only one of the Cincinnati they'd talked about by name. She hoped some of the others would be here: Garrett Crandall, in particular.

Toward the back of the crowded rotunda, behind the musicians and the bar, one of the costumed waiters stood staring at her. Then he waved discreetly.

Why was a waiter waving at her?

He wasn't, obviously, Espy decided. He was trying to flag down someone else. She turned, didn't see any likely candidates.

The handsome man appeared to be waiting for a response.

"Pardon?" she said.

"I don't seem to be holding your attention," he said with a smile. "I asked your name. I'm Chris Holloway."

Espy froze. "Chris Holloway," she said. "You're not a lawyer by any chance."

"Why?" he said, his charming grin in place. "What do you have against lawyers?"

"Nothing," she said.

"Good. Because I am."

Espy sighed. "I see," she said.

As if on cue, Holloway suddenly said, "Leonard."

She turned around and there he was. Tunde stood right beside him.

"Chris," Leonard said. "Esperanza."

"Chris," Tunde said, not looking at Espy.

"Esperanza?" Holloway said.

"Small world," Leonard said. "You two talking about the case?"

Holloway said, "I didn't even know who she was until just now." With a sneer on his face, he looked decidedly less handsome.

"I didn't know who you were either," Espy said in a snide tone.

"Like hell," Holloway said.

"Is there a problem?" Leonard asked.

"Did you see my memo?" Holloway said. "I've been asking Ms. Harper to let another lawyer handle the case."

Leonard's eyes narrowed. "We're talking about United Apparel?"

"Yes," Holloway said. "Ms. Harper has been unable to focus—"

"Not true," Espy interrupted. "I am intimately familiar with the facts—"

"You cited three separate incorrect precedents," Holloway snapped. "You—"

"Stop cheating," Espy blurted out. "Pay your taxes."

Holloway blinked. "What?"

"That's the position I am recommending the department take against you and your client. Your tax shelters are wholly inappropriate."

"Is that so?" Holloway asked.

"That's so," Espy said, and then looked at Leonard and hurriedly added, "pending your approval, of course."

Leonard looked flabbergasted.

"That's an interesting position," Holloway said. "I look forward to discussing it further. Leonard. Tunde."

He nodded curtly and stalked away.

"I'm right," she said to Leonard. "I'll show you the work."

"Fine. You're right. But 'stop cheating, pay your taxes'? For God's sake, Esperanza. We have other cases with these people, we don't need to antagonize them. Excuse me. I'll be right back," he said to Tunde, putting a hand on her arm and then heading off after Holloway.

Which left Espy and Tunde together, doing their best not to look at each other.

Espy cleared her throat. "I'm sorry I wasn't able to make Franklin's birthday party..." she began, but Tunde walked off without a word.

Leaving Espy standing by herself. Angry. Embarrassed. And a little scared.

"Esperanza."

She turned.

And there, of course, was her mother.

❖ ❖ ❖ ❖ ❖

Her mom took her by the arm and led her through the open doors of the Cincinnati History Museum. Away from the din. Espy took a deep breath.

"Is there some kind of trouble?" her mother asked.

She shook her head. "Work stuff. The usual."

"It didn't look like the usual. Leonard looked furious."

"He was."

"Mad at you for missing breakfast?"

"Among other things."

They strolled down the ramp leading to the exhibit floor and turned at a display called "The Founding of a City." A diorama, with scale-model pioneers in buckskins next to a river. According to the display tablet, the city was Cincinnati, only it had been called Losantiville for a year before being renamed. No reason for the name change was given, no explanation of the new name. Nothing about the society or the Roman general who provided their inspiration, which she found odd. Even a little suspicious.

Or maybe she was just being paranoid.

They kept walking, moved past a scale-model of downtown as it had looked in the trolley-car era.

"So," her mother said. "I'm surprised you're here."

"You sent me the invitation," Espy shrugged. "The Revolutionary War. It's what I studied in college, in law school."

"Oh for heaven's sake, don't lie to me. You hate these things."

Espy stopped and faced her mother. "I'm not lying."

Her mother waved away the response. "You've always been a terrible liar."

Espy opened her mouth to respond, and then shut it again.

"You want me to guess?" her mother asked. "All right. It has something to do with that man I found in your apartment. The killer."

Her voice went up on the word 'killer.' Espy looked around. A handful of people strolled through the museum. None of them seemed to have heard.

"Mom. Please." She leaned forward, lowered her voice. "I can't talk about this right now."

Her mom rolled her eyes. "You'll never talk about it. You don't trust me."

"I do trust you."

"I'm very worried."

"You have nothing to worry about."

"They killed your father. I'm afraid they'll kill you too." Her mother's face was flushed, an angry look in her eyes. "You think I'm stupid? You think because I'm not in the almighty FBI I can't add two and two?"

Espy could muster nothing to say. She'd never seen her mother like this.

"You and your father were working together," her mother said. "That's obvious. On what, I don't know. Something dangerous. Something that got him killed. And I can't stop thinking the same thing will—"

"Penelope? Esperanza?"

Mrs. Claypool and Mrs. Teresi stood a few feet away, looking concerned.

"Is everything all right?" Mrs. Claypool asked.

Espy saw her mother's eyes glistening with tears.

"Yes," Espy said. "Everything is fine."

❖ ❖ ❖ ❖

They finished the tour of the museum as a foursome. Mrs. Claypool and Mrs. Teresi provided a running commentary as they passed each exhibit: a display of black and white photographs devoted to the great Cincinnati industrialists who had helped America win World War Two. Procter and Gamble, the Cincinnati Milling Machine Company,

U.S. Playing Cards. There was a scale model of a radio tower built by the Crosley Corporation in the early 1930s, used to broadcast the Voice of America into occupied Europe. There was a car built by the same Crosley Corporation, not a scale model but an actual automobile in a display case, a little yellow two-seater. The display included a picture of the car's very tall inventor, Powel Crosley, squeezing into his brainchild. Crosley's company, according to the text accompanying the photo, had not only built the car and the broadcast tower but at one time had been the largest radio manufacturer in the world.

"He was quite the tycoon," Mrs. Claypool said. "My father knew him. Had box seats at the ballpark for goodness knows how long. Of course he knew the brother better. Lewis. Lewis's daughter, Ellen, is here tonight, sitting with the Castellinis."

Espy was eager to get back to the party, to learn what she could about the society, meet a few members, put faces to names, find out something that might be the least bit helpful. Then she caught a glimpse of her mother, who was on the verge of tears or another explosion.

When they finished the tour they made their way back to the main hall, which was even noisier than before. The musicians had turned up the volume, and the room echoed with a hundred different conversations. Espy thought, for a second, she heard her name being called.

"There's Robert!" Mrs. Teresi said. She waved into the crowd.

A man in the distance waved back. A woman stood next to him wearing the same lime-green dress as hers. Espy smiled. Someone shared her taste in clothes.

Above the din of voices and music, a huge crash sounded—dishes shattering on the floor. A waiter bent down next to the mess holding an empty metal tray at an angle. The crowd around him looked as if he'd exploded a bomb.

Next to her, three men in tuxedoes walked past without breaking stride.

"Westmoreland's point exactly," one said. "The military didn't lose the war, the politicians did. Tied their hands."

"Which is exactly what's happening now," a second put in.

"That's a crock," the third man said. "It was a crock then, and it's a crock now. Let me remind you I was in Vietnam."

"As if you'd ever let us forget," replied the second, and they all laughed.

"Come on," the first said. "He's got to be around here somewhere...."

As they headed for the far side of the hall, Espy stared after them. Interested not so much in their conversation as in the medallions that hung from their necks on red, white, and blue ribbons. Medallions in the shape of eagles.

The men were from the society.

"Excuse me," she said. "I think I see someone I know."

"Of course," Mrs. Claypool said.

"We'll see you at dinner," Mrs. Teresi said.

Her mom said nothing.

Espy knew what she was thinking.

Be careful.

CINCINNATUS

Union Terminal
Western Avenue
Cincinnati, OH
Friday, September 21, 7:47 P. M.

THE three men entered a room off the main hall: GIFT SHOP. Espy stopped at the door, lingering outside, waiting for them to emerge.

She looked down at the floor, pretended to pull something off her shoe.

She looked toward the center of the room and saw a security guard looking back. She turned away.

The men were still inside. Finally, she took a deep breath and walked in.

It was small and very crowded, filled with people and spinning racks of gift cards and tables of souvenirs and books and toys. It was two rooms, really, one directly in front of her, another off to her left.

The three men stood in an archway talking to someone in the other room.

"Can I help you find something?"

A woman stood behind the cash register. Caroline, her nametag said. Manager.

"Just looking," Espy said. "Thanks."

She squeezed past one of the spinning racks, circled around a table of souvenirs, and stopped in front of a chest-high set of bookshelves. The three men were ten feet away, directly in front of her. She still couldn't see to whom they were talking, but at least she could hear bits of the conversation: *Speech. Governor. Head table.*

She picked up a book, flipped through pages, straining to hear more.

All of a sudden a booming voice rang out: "We're not turning this into a political rally."

Someone mumbled something. The booming voice replied, "Don't be ridiculous. I'm not trying to censor anybody. Jed can say whatever he wants, as long as he keeps politics out of it. This is a fundraiser."

"Of course." A woman's voice. "We support a lot of worthy causes, all across the political spectrum. We can't take sides."

Espy stole quick glances at the group. The men she'd been following had shifted position slightly, enough so that even though she still couldn't see faces, she could see that there were two other people in the back room. A man and a woman. Probably the two people who'd been talking.

She put the book back, circled to the other side of the shelves to get closer.

"You'll tell him?" the booming voice said.

Espy edged closer, pretending to scan the shelf in front of her. A word caught her eye: *Crosley*. She pulled it off the shelf, pretended to study the cover. There was the man and his little car again. Two men. A book about the Crosley brothers who Mrs. Claypool had mentioned earlier in the museum.

"Did you see the organ?"

Espy looked up and saw the woman from the cash register smiling at her.

"I'm sorry?"

"The organ. At the back of the terminal. It belonged to Mr. Crosley. Actually, it belonged to his wife, Gwendolyn, who died of tuberculosis at forty."

"No," Espy said. "I didn't."

A man's face suddenly appeared over the manager's shoulder.

Robert Teresi.

"Espy?" Teresi said. "My mother said you might be here."

His mom was right; he had lost weight. Maybe a hundred pounds.

"Good to see you, Robert."

They shook hands. "I can't believe you're wearing that dress."

Before Espy could respond, a young blond woman strode right up to Teresi and snapped, "Is he here? Did you ask him?"

"He's back there, I think," Teresi said. "But I haven't had a chance to talk to him yet. Just met an old friend of mine."

He nodded in Espy's direction.

The woman said, "Oh my God, you're wearing my dress."

"Well. Actually, we're wearing the same dress," Espy said, though of course it looked completely different on them. The woman was a half-foot taller and she'd had the dress shortened a little, maybe tailored...

Robert introduced the woman as "Kaci," who said only, "This is not happening."

"I knew you two would find each other," said the booming voice. Espy turned and saw the man walking from the back room.

He was big. A neatly trimmed white beard, a full head of white hair...

He was the man who commented on her dress earlier.

"Do you know how much money I spent on this?" Kaci asked furiously.

"It's just a dress, honey." The big man shook his head.

She folded her arms across her chest. Espy realized she was not much more than a girl. A lovely, physically mature girl. "It's not just a dress. It's a Valenti, for your information. Which I had tailored."

"I'm sorry," the big man said, trying not to smile. "But getting upset won't do you any good."

"Come on, Robert," the girl said, and stomped out of the gift shop.

Teresi started after her.

The big man's arm shot out. He caught Teresi by the wrist.

"Son," he said. "That's my granddaughter. She's nineteen."

Teresi's eyes widened. "She said she was twenty-three."

"Nineteen." The big man smiled. "You understand what I'm saying?" The look on his face, despite the smile, made very clear what he was saying.

"Absolutely," Teresi said.

The big man let go. Teresi smiled uncertainly and dashed off.

The big man said, "She's got a temper. I apologize for anything offensive she might have said."

"Not necessary," Espy said.

"Kind of you." He smiled. "I wanted to apologize, too. For what I said before...about your dress? I wasn't making fun, it's just that seeing you wearing the same thing as her..."

"I understand," Espy said.

Which was when she saw the red, white, and blue ribbon hanging around his neck, the very edge of a medallion, peeking from underneath his tuxedo jacket.

All she could see of the design was the eagle's eye.

The man put out his hand.

"My name's Crane, by the way," he said. "Stuart Crane."

Stuart Crane. Head of the Society of the Cincinnati.

Espy shifted the book she was holding to her left hand and held out her right.

"My name's Harper." She said it slowly, clearly, so there couldn't be any possible misunderstanding. "Esperanza Harper."

"Pleased to meet you."

She didn't see the slightest recognition in his eyes. The man was either a very good actor, or...if he wanted to play games...

They shook hands.

His grip was firm. Espy made hers firm as well. She hadn't bought that exercise machine for nothing. She'd been working out hard these last few months. She had real muscle. She felt like using it on this man.

He was a foot taller and a hundred pounds heavier, but he was old. She was in her prime.

She squeezed his wrinkled flesh for all she was worth.

Crane didn't seem to notice.

"What brings you here this evening?" he asked. "Are you a member of the society?"

"No. My mother. She's on one of the organizing committees."

"Harper." Crane knit his brow. "Is your mother Penelope?"

"That's right."

Crane smiled. "Alice," he said, turning to a woman who stepped from the back room. "This is Penelope Harper's daughter."

"Alice Crandall. Pleased to meet you," the woman said. "Your mother is a treasure."

Alice Crandall. The wife of senatorial candidate and society member Garrett Crandall. They ran the Democratic Fund for Direct Action, which was tied to the society in some way, involved with the illegal gambling money and whatever they were doing with it. She didn't look like a crook or a murderer. She had white hair shaped into a reserved style, a wizened face.

Crane also introduced two of the men she'd been following. They turned out to be Kent Holwadel, who worked with Tunde on the Democratic Fund for Direct Action, and Garrett Crandall himself. Both looked distinguished and wealthy, and they were almost courtly in their manner. Espy had a tough time connecting these men to the case, to killing her father and Agent Kauffman and threatening her own life. Something didn't fit.

She found herself fighting the urge to be flattered by the attention of these powerful men while trying to learn more about the society. Crandall told a funny story about coming to the terminal as a child and almost getting lost.

Then the lights flickered.

"That's dinner," Crandall said. "Ms. Harper, a pleasure to meet you."

"We must get together," Holwadel said.

"Yes, sure," Espy said. Right after she finished exposing this international conspiracy. The members of the Cincinnati she'd met tonight, however, seemed distinctly unconspiratorial. As the men trooped away to dinner, Espy felt more confused than ever.

"Great men, don't you think?" said a man standing in the doorway of the gift shop. He wore the eagle medallion around his neck and a Ben Franklin version of the Revolutionary War-era outfit. With his wire-framed glasses he even looked a little like Ben Franklin, a thinner version with a military-style haircut.

Espy said, "They seem nice."

"Not them," the man said. He pointed at the book she was still holding. "The Crosleys."

"Oh." Espy said. "I haven't read it yet."

"I'll buy it for you." He reached into his vest pocket and pulled out his wallet. Apparently noticing Espy's surprise, he said, "I'm Jed Seagrave. And you're Esperanza Harper."

The man in the picture she'd seen of society members sportfishing in The Bahamas. He'd been standing in the background, the one who hadn't been fishing.

Jed Seagrave.

He said he'd just run into Crane, who mentioned her name. Which Seagrave had recognized immediately.

"You had a letter in one of the journals I subscribe to," he said. "May of last year, I believe. *The Journal of Law and Religion*. At least I think it was you. Esperanza Harper is not that common a name."

Espy blushed. "I'm impressed you remembered."

"You had some valid points," Seagrave said. "I took note."

They followed the crowd, shuffling slowly into the banquet hall,

Espy carrying the book Seagrave had bought for her, Seagrave with his hands clasped behind his back, looking very Ben Franklin-esque indeed.

She tried to remember what she'd learned about him. Not much. On the board of one of those companies tied to MGT: Aiken-Scuffs. President of the Young Patriots Association. And he read *The Journal of Law and Religion*. An eclectic set of interests.

"What is it you do, Mr. Seagrave?" Espy asked.

"Nowadays? I lecture at a number of universities in the D.C. area."

"Interesting," she said. "On what subjects?"

"Among other things, the Cincinnati. I'm a member through Major Abiah Seagrave of the fifteenth Pennsylvania regiment. Who played, by the way, a key role at the battle of Saratoga. First significant American victory of the war. In many ways, the most critical battle of the war; certainly one of the most overlooked, in terms of its importance."

"I'm guessing," Espy said, "that you're a history professor."

"Guilty as charged." He smiled ruefully. "I'm boring you already."

"Not at all. I've read quite a lot about the Revolutionary War myself. And the Cincinnati."

The last slipped out before she could stop it. She looked for something other than curiosity in Seagrave's eyes and couldn't find it.

"About the society?" he said. "And what have you found out?"

You're fixing golf tournaments, she thought.

She gave him a few basics, what she'd given Matt Thurman the week before. Which led her to a question about the society's current activities.

"I look at our job as providing inspiration, role models who exemplify the rights and responsibilities that come with being an American."

Inside the banquet hall, Espy saw a podium toward the back of the room. Nearby, she saw two waiters arguing. One of them gestured angrily toward a set of double doors—through which the staff walked in and out with trays. The one getting yelled at kept looking toward the tables set up in the dining room.

She almost jumped out of her skin when a booming, amplified voice intoned out of nowhere, "If you could all find seats, please." The voice belonged to Stuart Crane, who stood behind the podium at the front of the room, signaling for quiet. The Society's flag hung behind him.

"Well. I hope we can talk further, professor," she said to Seagrave. Which was the truth. He not only was eager to chat, he seemed to be on the periphery of a lot of the things she had come tonight to find out about.

"I hope so too," he said.

"But I'd better go find my—"

Table, she had been about to say, when she saw it. Table fourteen. There was her mother, and Mrs. Teresi, and Mrs. Claypool. And Robert. And Kaci Crane.

And Leonard, and Tunde, and Chris Holloway.

What she didn't see was an empty chair. She sighed. "Kaci Crane has not only taken my dress, she's taken my seat."

Seagrave looked at the table, a little smile on his face. "Stuart's granddaughter has never been good at following directions." He gently touched her elbow. "Come sit with us."

He gestured toward the head table, where Garrett Crandall, and his wife, and the governor, and Kent Holwadel, among others, were talking. There were three empty seats. One for Crane, who was still at the podium. One for Seagrave. And one for her, if she wanted it.

It was almost too perfect. She'd come to learn about the Cincinnati and she was being offered a seat at their table. Literally.

"Are you sure?" she asked.

"Quite sure," Seagrave said. "I'm sure you'll be a better conversationalist than Kaci. Though please don't tell Stuart I said that." He smiled.

She found herself smiling back.

Stop it, the voice in her head whispered.

They killed your father.

"Although our talk may have to wait a few moments," he said. "I have a speech to give."

❖ ❖ ❖ ❖ ❖

Seagrave pulled out her chair and announced to the table that she would be taking Kaci's place.

Alice Crandall chuckled. "Stuart will have a fit. But we're all glad to have you."

At the podium, Crane thanked the people who organized the affair, thanked the Museum Center, and thanked Jed Seagrave for suggesting the place.

The crowd gave polite applause.

"Don't clap yet, folks," Crane said. "Jed tends to go on a bit."

Laughter.

Seagrave smiled too. A tight, that's-not-really-funny kind of smile. Poor Professor Seagrave. Espy had a feeling that in this crowd of politicians and high-powered business executives, he got teased quite a bit.

Crane talked about the society's programs—patriotic, educational, historical. He made a plea for the audience's support, both in money and time. He called on them to mentor the young people in their lives, and then mentioned some things the society was doing in that regard. He pointed to the Young Patriots Organization as an example, and then he glanced at Seagrave again.

"And right there, I suppose," Crane said, "is as good an introduction as any to the man who's been running that organization for the last few years. Colonel—I know he hates when I call him that—Jed Seagrave. Jed?"

Seagrave rose as the audience applauded.

Colonel?

Alice must have seen the confusion on Espy's face.

"I don't think Jed's ever held a weapon in his life," she said. "He was in administration, something technical, as I understand it. Not active duty."

Espy nodded. Still...

Her guard went up, just a hair.

Seagrave reached the podium.

"Thank you, Stuart, for those kind words. But you're right—I do hate being called Colonel." He leaned into the microphone. "It only reminds me of how long it's been since I could fit into that uniform. I'm sure the dinner tonight won't be any help in that regard."

More laughter.

Seagrave pulled a stack of index cards from his pocket. Set them on the podium and adjusted his glasses.

"Excuse me, ma'am," said a waiter suddenly standing next to her. He had a bottle of wine in each hand. "Red or white?"

Neither, Espy was about to say. She was working. Except...one glass wouldn't kill her. "White," she said.

"I've been asked to talk this evening about both the Society of the Cincinnati, and the event we're here to celebrate, the passage of the United States Constitution," Seagrave said. "It is more than two hundred years ago now, that our ancestors, the creators of this society, helped birth a nation, a republic grounded in the revolutionary premise that all men are created equal. Many of us here this evening know the names of those founding members by heart. George Washington, of course. Baron von Steuben. Major General Charles Knox. Captain Thomas Shaw. Generals Huntington and Hand. They are role models to us, a source of inspiration, as Cincinnatus himself was to them. Heroes."

Seagrave took a sip of water as the crowd applauded.

"I would like to begin by pointing out a little-known aspect of that heroism."

Half a minute into the speech, she could tell Seagrave was good.

"Valley Forge. December 1777," he said. "I ask you to picture the scene. General Washington and the Continental Army, in retreat from Philadelphia. Winter is hard on their heels, and the taste of defeat is bitter in their mouths. Eleven thousand men enter the camp; until they build shelters they must sleep around the fires to stay warm. Their uniforms are in tatters. As for food, they have none. And the Continental Congress has no funds to buy more. They are starving. What is more, their families back home, who they left to join Washington's Army, are starving as well.

"Mass desertions are expected. Mutiny is feared. There is, in fact, a plot among some of the officers to replace Washington as commander. And yet...in the spring, the army emerges not in tatters, not in rebellion, but as a cohesive whole, a hardened, trained fighting force. What holds them together?"

Seagrave gazed at the crowd, his jaw set firm.

"That vision of independence, to be sure. The vision of a world where all men are entitled to their pursuits of life, liberty, and happiness. Yet I think another vision provided an equal incentive to these soldiers. A vision placed within their minds by General Washington, for this very purpose."

He leaned forward on the podium.

"It is a vision," Seagrave said, "of the lash."

Someone coughed.

There was no other sound in the entire room.

"It is a vision of the firing squad. Of the hangman's noose. Of what would happen to those who deserted the army and were captured. We have no exact statistics for those times, though we do have anecdotal reports. Men flogged within an inch of their lives. Men shot by the very compatriots they had broken bread with only hours earlier. There is an instance of a man decapitated, his head placed upon a pike outside a fort, to serve as warning. Executions by the hundreds, executions ordered at Washington's command, executions of men he knew were on the verge of desperation. Men who sought only, perhaps, to rejoin their families, to see their wives and children. To provide for their wives and children. And yet he had them killed. Why?"

His eyes scanned the room, as if waiting for a hand to be raised.

"In the name of the greater good," Seagrave said. "Washington was willing to perform not just the noble acts of heroism, but the necessary ones. We picture him crossing the Delaware, jaw thrust forward. I suggest this picture of heroism is incomplete without knowledge of the lash, of the noose, of the firing squad. Of the hard times that demanded hard choices. Times that call not for mercy, for a yielding heart, but for a spine of steel, and a fist of iron. Times that demand absolute, unqualified victory."

Seagrave looked down at his index cards.

"General Ulysses Grant. Many of us here think of Grant fondly, not just because he was an honorary member of the society, but because he had the good sense to name his horse Cincinnatus."

A few people chuckled. Seagrave paused a second, waiting for more people to realize it was a joke. Or maybe they did, but like Espy, they were too caught up in what he was saying to laugh.

"History has been unkind to Grant. He was a drunkard, we are told. He was a brute. Unqualified for the high office he came to hold. Many of you here this evening were, I'm sure, taught to remember him that way. Far fewer were taught the nickname he acquired in the first years of the Civil War. He was known as 'Unconditional Surrender' Grant, a name given at Fort Donelson, where he led the Union to its first major victory of the war. He defeated a West Point classmate, who after flying the white flag, asked Grant for his terms of surrender. None, Grant told him. I offer no terms. Surrender unconditionally, or the battle continues. The death and the dying continue. Grant said this to his friend. No surrender. Not at Donelson, not at Shiloh. Grant, like Washington, did not shy away from carnage. Was not afraid to get his hands dirty in the name of a greater good—the abolition of the abomination that was human slavery."

Seagrave's voice rose on the last sentence. He paused to take a breath, another sip of his water.

And someone clapped. Someone else joined in, and then another someone, and another, and soon the whole room was applauding. Seagrave was perhaps twenty feet away from Espy—close enough that she could see his eyes glittering with pleasure.

He obviously was enjoying the attention.

"Grant understood, as Washington did, that there are times when negotiation is not only uncalled for, but counterproductive. When your enemy must be cowed, not for a day, not for an hour, but for all time. I think this is an integral and misunderstood part of heroism. I am certain it is a large part of why we chose to make Winston Churchill an honorary member of the society in 1952. It was his heroism, the line he drew in the sand, this far and no farther, the indomitable spirit he displayed in the face of the Nazi terror. An understanding that evil must not be allowed to fester, that it must always be called by its proper name and confronted. Something we would all do well to remember, particularly given the anniversary we as a nation commemorated on September eleventh.

"To my mind, this is the day when we, as a country, first became aware that evil was loose in the world once more. It is a day we can equate to the Nazis crossing into Poland, to the Soviet tanks rolling in the streets of Hungary. The sound of the towers falling was as a wake-up call to our generation."

He paused to look around the room. People were nodding.

"And yet..." He shrugged. "I feel, sometimes, as if that call has gone unheard. Our government's response to what happened in Israel yesterday being just the latest example. Now..."

He turned to Crane and smiled.

"Stuart asked me not to bring politics into this, and I want to re-assure him that I won't. I haven't had enough to drink yet to talk politics."

Laughter sprinkled all around the room. Seagrave laughed too.

His eyes glittered again. Not so much with pleasure; with malice.

Crane was laughing as well, yet his laughter, to Espy, also seemed forced.

There's something going on there, she thought. A deeper, sharper edge to what she had thought was mutual kidding.

"I won't point fingers," Seagrave said. "I'll leave that for Garrett."

More laughter; Seagrave nodded toward Crandall.

"Thank so much, Jed!" Crandall called out, and the laughter continued.

Seagrave let it go on, until it had worn itself almost completely out.

Then he started in again.

"What I will do is suggest that these murderers who mask them-selves in the cloak of religion, who murder their own children as some sort of sacrifice to their god—must be dealt with in the same way Churchill dealt with the Nazis. The way Truman dealt with the Japa-nese. It is my belief—"

"Champagne?"

Espy half-turned to a waiter standing behind her.

"Thank you, no."

But he was pouring it anyway.

Right into her wine.

She turned all the way around in surprise. The waiter was the same one who'd been trying to get her attention earlier that evening.

Who'd dropped the tray of dishes in the main hall.

Who'd been arguing behind the podium.

Who'd looked somehow familiar to her.

Up this close, she at last realized why.

He looked like Matt Thurman.

An awful lot.

Of course, that was impossible.

Matt Thurman was dead.

BOOK TWO: SOLDIERS

Union Terminal
Western Avenue
Cincinnati, OH
Friday, September 21, 9:02 P.M.

"MY mistake," the waiter said. "I'll get you a fresh glass."

He turned and walked away.

"That's not necessary," Espy said, but he walked away very quickly, not toward the kitchen, but toward the banquet hall's exit doors.

When he reached them, he stopped and turned back to look at her. Matt Thurman.

Up on the podium, Seagrave was talking.

"...threaten our one consistent ally in the region, we must display the same sort of heroism. Not just we as a country, but we as individuals must be prepared..."

She excused herself and headed for the banquet hall doors and pushed through them. The main hall was empty.

The History Museum was closed. So was the gift shop.

The waiter stood at the back of the terminal and then headed toward the rest rooms.

Espy followed.

Past the rest rooms and down a staircase.

"Harper," a voice said. "Espy."

She turned and there he was.

"Finally," Matt said, and took the wig off. "You know how long I've been trying to get your attention?"

❖ ❖ ❖ ❖ ❖

She looked shell-shocked, Matt thought. Dumbfounded.

Probably the way he looked when Rawson grabbed him at the corner across from Espy's apartment, shoved the barrel of a gun in his back and led him to a parking garage, pushed him into a tan Ford and said, "Drive."

They drove forty minutes out of downtown Cincinnati, into Kentucky, on Decoursey Pike, headed in the direction of Cold Spring, according to the last sign they'd passed.

"So you going to make me dig my own grave?" Matt had asked.

In a deadpan voice, Rawson said, "We have no reason to kill you. We just want to talk. Cooperate and you walk away a free man."

"That's why you hired somebody to kill me in prison?" Matt asked.

Rawson shook his head. "I don't know anything about that."

Another lie, Matt thought. He's going to kill me, and then he's going to go back to Cincinnati and kill Harper. Which was when he realized that somehow he was going to have to turn the tables.

Maybe run the car off the road, he thought.

And at that second, Rawson put the gun up against his head.

"Pull over," he said, and poked the metal barrel of the gun into his scalp.

Matt did as he was told.

The car was an automatic, the gearshift on the right side of the steering wheel. Matt slid it into park.

"You might be tempted to try something stupid. So I just want to make clear what's gonna happen if you do. Okay?"

"I'm not going to try anything."

"I just want to make it clear," Rawson said. He shifted the gun to his left hand, put his right on top of Matt's.

Matt was by no means a small guy. His hand was by no means small either.

But it looked like a girl's under Rawson's.

"I'm going to break every one of your fingers. You'll never play golf again. Hell, you might not even be able to use your hands."

Matt's heart pounded in his chest. "I won't try anything."

"Okay, good. I want to be sure though," Rawson said as he grabbed the pinky finger on Matt's right hand and yanked it back so hard it snapped like a toothpick.

Matt screamed, more out of surprise than pain.

Rawson smiled. "I did that one quick. Believe me, it hurts a lot more when I twist it as it snaps. That is painful. Believe me."

"I believe you," Matt said. He held his wrist, tried to shake away the pain.

"We understand each other now? We're in sync, in terms of communication?"

"Yes," Matt said.

He drove for another half hour, his finger swelling and changing color as they headed farther and farther east, into the Kentucky hills, into the middle of nowhere. Neither of them said a word. There was nothing to say. They both knew what was going on. Rawson was going to kill him and dump his body where it would never be found.

Run the car off the road, Matt thought. Just do it.

But Rawson still had the gun at his head.

There was nothing he could do.

Talk. He could talk.

"So how'd you do it?" Matt asked. "How did you fix those golf tournaments?"

Out of the corner of his eye, Matt saw Rawson's face in the shadows. He was like a machine. No emotion. No sign he was human. "I don't know what you're talking about," he said.

"It's got something to do with the greens, doesn't it?" Matt asked.

Rawson didn't move a muscle, but Matt sensed a reaction. A sudden uncomfortableness.

It *was* the greens.

"So," Matt said. "Was that putt Driscoll made on thirteen—"

A siren sounded behind them.

Matt looked in the rear-view mirror and saw a Blue Lincoln. Unmarked car with a siren.

Where did he come from?

Rawson looked back at the cop, then at Matt. "What's he want? What did you do?" His voice, still low, sounded menacing.

"Nothing," Matt said quickly. "I wasn't speeding."

Rawson shot a quick look behind them again and then turned back around, his huge arms and shoulders filling the seat.

The siren sounded louder, more insistent, as the cop closed in.

Matt said, "What should I do?"

"Pull over," Rawson said. "Try anything, I'll kill you and the cop."

Matt nodded, and pulled onto the shoulder.

The cop got out of his car. He was big. Not quite as big as Rawson, but a strapping guy. Matt watched him approach in the driver's side mirror, very aware of Rawson in the seat next to him. The gun on his lap.

In the mirror, he saw the cop reach down to his own gunbelt, unsnap the holster. Matt squinted. Was that standard procedure? Was the cop on to them? Maybe that's why he pulled them over. The car was stolen, something like that.

No. That didn't make sense. The cop would wait for backup. He wouldn't tackle them alone.

So why unsnap the holster?

The cop came closer. When he reached the rear bumper of Rawson's car, Matt recognized him.

The cop was Jake.

Jake—his own big brother come to save him. Again.

Rawson said, "Your license. He's going to ask for your license, he'll see your name, and I'll have to shoot him."

"No," Matt said quickly. "He might not recognize my name."

"There's an APB out on you, genius. Of course he'll recognize your name."

But Rawson took his finger off the trigger and slid the gun out of sight.

What now, Matt thought? Truth was, he didn't even have his license. The police had taken away everything when he was arrested. But he didn't mention that, didn't want to put Rawson on edge.

And then Jake was standing at the side of the car.

"Hey, guys," he said, leaning into the window.

"What's the trouble?" Rawson asked.

"No trouble," Jake said. "Just wanted to make sure it wasn't either of you left a wallet back at the diner."

Matt said, "Wallet?"

"Back at Gloria's. The diner." He pointed down the road. "One of you leave a wallet? Brown leather, got about fifty in cash in it, a few cards."

"Wasn't us," Rawson said.

"You sure?" Jake asked. "Take a look."

He reached down to take something out of his pocket.

He came up holding a gun.

He shoved it through the window and shot Rawson point-blank. Dead center in the forehead.

A warm, wet liquid splattered the side of Matt's face.

❖ ❖ ❖ ❖ ❖

Harper dragged Matt out of the hall, into the shadows. "Where have you been?"

"With my brother."

"Your brother? Why didn't you call? I thought you were dead. Do you have any idea..."

She went on for a good thirty seconds before Matt could get in a word. Before he could tell her what had happened, how Rawson had surprised him, how Jake had surprised them both. He told that part, was about to launch into the story of where he'd been all week when Harper held up a hand.

"Time out," she said. "How did your brother find you?"

"Luck."

"That's an unbelievable stroke of luck."

"Not really. He was in front of your building already."

"Why?"

"Because he was looking for you. He found out about Kazmir, about that gambling thing. He wanted to talk to you about it."

"Okay. But why didn't you call? Why did you leave me hanging?"

"It wasn't exactly my choice, all right? Jake was calling the shots. We had to be sure I was safe from, well, everybody. Listen, we found out how they're doing it. Fixing the golf tournaments. It's got something to do with the greens. This company called—"

"Next Century Course Development."

Matt said, "Well, yeah. How'd you know that?"

Harper waved off his question then pulled her keys from her purse. "Here. Go to my apartment. You remember where that is, right? I'll meet you there when this is over, we can talk."

"Whoa," Matt said. "You can't go back in there."

"Why?"

"Because you're sitting right next to him."

"Who?"

"The guy who killed Kazmir. I saw him drive up, and I almost flipped out. Jake had to practically put me in a headlock."

Harper said, "I'm sitting next to the man who killed Bob Kazmir?"

Matt nodded. "The guy with the glasses. Looks like Ben Franklin."

"Jed Seagrave," she said. "Jed Seagrave killed Bob Kazmir? He's a professor."

"He's a lunatic. He shoved a flask down my throat and framed me for murder. Now can we please call the cops already?"

CINCINNATUS

"NO," Espy told Matt. "We can't call the police."

"Why not?"

"For one thing, they're not going to arrest him on your say-so."

"What about all this other stuff? Next Century and Kazmir and the gambling?"

"I don't have any proof yet. Do you?"

"No. But it's there. Has to be. Something to do with the system Next Century installed. Me and Jake would have found it if we had more time." He raked his fingers through his curly hair. "We went to The Pines, dug up the green."

"This is a lot bigger than a gambling ring," she said, and gave him the sixty-second version of what had been happening for the last five months. What had happened in the week and a half since he had disapppeared.

"And you're not calling the cops?"

She pursed her lips. "Not yet. I have to talk to Agent Shurig. For now..."

"I know. Go back to the apartment and wait."

"Exactly."

Matt sighed. "But we'll put this guy in jail soon? I want my life back."

"He killed my father. He'll be lucky to make it to jail."

She slapped the keys into Matt's hand, and before he could say another word, turned around and started back up the stairs.

300

She went half a flight before realizing that if she went back to the table now, in the mood she was in, Seagrave would know something was wrong. She had to calm down. She had to pretend she'd been fixing her makeup, using the bathroom, whatever. She had to go up there and pump Seagrave and the others—whoever else was in on this thing— for the truth. She had to be calm, clinical, dispassionate.

She had to go sit next to the man who killed her father and make polite conversation.

She went to the ladies room. Went to the sink and stared at herself in the mirror.

As always, she saw her father's face in hers.

Saw him smiling at her, as she came out of the jetway holding the flight attendant's hand, the first time her mother let her fly to L.A. by herself. She was maybe nine years old and scared to death she was on the wrong plane, that she was going to get kidnapped, that her dad would forget to pick her up, that everything was going to go wrong, and then she saw him and everything was completely fine, and she ran to him and he hugged her and whispered in her ear...

"Make sure your mother knows this was your idea, not mine,"

...and she pictured a different time, the two of them older, sitting down at the corner table at the little diner near the OSU campus, a couple months before graduation, right after she told him she was go-ing to intern at the Justice Department that summer, which had been completely her idea, of course.

But his inspiration.

They were a team. At least she thought they were.

Everything I have, you have.

But that wasn't true. Why was he going to Kirtland Air Force Base?

She had no idea.

But Seagrave did.

She wanted to splash cold water on her face, to give herself a jolt, and realized she couldn't. She'd smudge her makeup.

She almost did it anyway. Let her eyeliner run. Let it streak down the sides of her cheeks, like war paint.

❖ ❖ ❖ ❖ ❖

Seagrave had finished his speech. A waiter was clearing dishes from the table. He blocked her from Seagrave's view as she approached.

The waiter moved.

Seagrave saw her and smiled.

"There you are, Ms. Harper. Alice was just about to come looking for you."

"I just needed some air," she said.

Seagrave stood as she pulled out her chair and sat.

"I'm sorry I didn't get to hear the rest of your speech," she said.

"No need to apologize," Seagrave said. "I probably went on too long."

Alice Crandall, on Espy's left, shook her head. "Don't be silly, Jed. You know Stuart was teasing before."

Espy put her napkin on her lap. "So...*Colonel* Seagrave?"

He nodded. "It was awhile ago."

"But you served?"

"A few years. No battlefield glory for me, though. Mostly field support. Mostly, to tell you the truth, desk jobs, here in the States."

"Such as..."

He smiled. "Chief paper-pusher for some field commanders. Nothing interesting."

A waiter announced the next course—stewed fowl with oysters, in a white sauce. A recipe from the society cookbook, attributed to the wife of Colonel Icarus Johnson, of Richmond, Virginia.

A bowl of stew appeared in front of Espy a split-second later. Bowls were appearing all over their table, which received the VIP treatment, not only being served by a dozen waiters, but being served first. No other table was being served yet. Not even table fourteen.

Where her mother sat, talking to Tunde.

"I'm afraid you've missed the salad," Alice Crandall said.

"That's all right," Espy said. "I'm not big on salad."

She wasn't big on fowl, either, she decided after a few bites. Mostly because of the oysters. She cared for seafood about as much as she cared for the sea.

"I took the liberty of getting you a fresh glass of wine," Seagrave said.

"Thank you." She took a sip.

"You're in the Justice Department, isn't that right, Esperanza?" Alice Crandall asked. Kent Holwadel sat next to her.

"That's right."

"And what exactly do you do there?"

Espy took a sip of wine. A small sip. Careful. You're in the lions' den here.

The problem was, she wasn't sure exactly who the lions were.

"I'm part of a special program the DOJ is running with the Financial Crimes Enforcement Network."

"FINCEN." That from Kent Holwadel, leaning around Alice Crandall's shoulder.

"Yes. FINCEN. And I work in the tax division. Checking out corporate fraud, that sort of thing. Not all that exciting."

"You must work with SARs, I imagine," Seagrave said.

She nodded, tried to keep her expression neutral.

"SARs?" Alice Crandall said.

"Suspicious Activity Reports," Espy said. She explained briefly what they were and why they were so potentially important.

"Designed to help catch terrorists," Alice said.

"Yes," Espy resisted an urge to look at Seagrave as she answered.

"Speaking of terrorists—you know, Jed, what you said before?" That from Kent Holwadel, leaning in to join the conversation. "About Washington and the lash, and keeping people in line?"

"Yes," Seagrave said.

"Well, you know what struck me just now? In a way, isn't that partly what these people want to do?"

Seagrave shook his head. "I'm not following you, Kent."

Not following, and not all that interested in doing so, Espy thought. Seagrave's condescension toward Holwadel was painfully obvious.

"Washington puts the lash to his troops to make them toe the straight and narrow," Holwadel said. "Isn't that the same idea behind, say, telling people not to steal or you'll cut off their hands? To make them toe the line?"

Seagrave shook his head. "Not the same at all. Washington's measure is a temporary one. The terrorists want a state ruled by those laws at all times; theft punishable by amputation; adultery by stoning...that sort of thing...where the punishment is greater than the crime."

Kent wiped his mouth with his napkin. "Well. It's their country. Whatever they want to do—"

"You miss my point," Seagrave said. "They want that state here."

"Some Muslims do," Espy said. "Not all."

"Muslim family court," Seagrave said. "A few years back, there was a congressman—"

"I remember that," Alice said. "Allowing Muslims to use Muslim law to decide family-related issues. Whatever happened to that idea?"

"It's a law," Seagrave said. "That's what happened to it."

"It's a law being challenged," Espy said.

"Not by the DOJ," Seagrave said. "I believe the government's position is freedom of religion."

"It is," Espy said.

"And you agree with that?" he asked.

"To a certain extent."

"Don't dodge the question. You agree with it, or you don't."

"I'm not dodging. It's a complicated issue."

"In some respects. In others, it's crystal clear."

"What is this you're talking about?" Holwadel asked.

"A family court run according to the laws of *sharia*. In Minnesota, I believe."

"For Muslims only," Espy said.

"Of course for Muslims only," Seagrave snapped. "Where the word of the prophet is law. The prophet who thinks a Muslim woman's voice counts for half a man's in court; who thinks adulterers should be stoned, thievery punished by amputation. We are going to allow this in America? It's an abomination. It runs counter to everything this country was founded on. Equal protection under the law. You come to America, you become an American. Not a Muslim-American, not an African-American, not an Irish- or Italian-American, an American. Period."

Seagrave was nearly shouting. Conversation around the table and at the table behind them stopped.

"Easy, Jed," Crane said with a tight smile. "Don't use up all your strength during the appetizer. We have a whole meal to get through."

Seagrave nodded, offered a tight smile of his own. "Sorry," he said, looking around the table. "It's a sore spot with me. As you know."

"Of course," Espy said.

His outburst gave her a peek at the man behind the Ben Franklin mask, the man who beat Kazmir to death, the man who killed her father.

He was obviously very passionate about certain things.

If she hadn't been sure of it before, she was now.

Fixing golf tournaments was only part of what was happening here.

There's something else going on.

Espy had the feeling she was getting close to finding out what.

❖ ❖ ❖ ❖ ❖

The main course—roast pork, potatoes, green peas—came and went.

The conversation moved from Muslim terrorists and Al-Aqsa to the economy, and to the president's shortcomings in that area too. And then to movies and books and then dessert was served—a chocolate cake, with red, white, and blue frosting.

During coffee, Espy turned her attention to Seagrave again.

"So. Jed. Where do you teach?" she asked.

"No one place in particular," he said. "Visiting professorship. That sort of thing. I'm not anywhere this semester. Taking some time off."

"Ah," Espy said. "And doing what?"

"Some traveling. Working with the Young Patriots."

"Jed doesn't like to talk about himself, Esperanza," Alice Crandall said. "In case you hadn't noticed. So I'll tell you. He teaches in D.C. mostly. Where were you again last year, Jed?"

Seagrave took a sip of coffee. He didn't look happy. "The National Defense Intelligence College."

Alice said, "It's for professionals in the intelligence community."

"Interesting," Espy said.

"Not really," Seagrave said. "The courses are largely technical in nature."

"Oh don't be so modest." Alice Crandall leaned closer to Espy. "Three of the joint chiefs of staff are his former students."

"Impressive."

"The new director of the CIA, as well," Alice said.

"Excuse me," said a waiter. He put a little silver pot to the right of her plate, between her and Seagrave. "Your tea, ma'am."

"Thank you," she said.

"Please." Seagrave took the pot before she could. "Allow me."

As he poured the tea, he said, "Am I remembering right, Esperanza, that your office was involved in what happened up at The Pines? The murder?"

She managed to keep the surprise off her face. She hoped.

"Yes," she said. "Unfortunately, we are involved."

"Terrible thing," Seagrave said.

She took a sip of tea. It was strong, just as she'd asked for.

Alice Crandall said, "You're talking about what happened to Bob Kazmir?"

"Yes," Espy said.

"Poor Bob," Kent Holwadel said. "Heckuva guy. Heckuva golfer. We played down on the island every holiday season."

"Poor Bob? Poor Dina. She's going to be lost without him," Alice Crandall said.

"At least she's still got her money," Holwadel said, half under his breath.

Alice Crandall tittered.

"Now now, Kent," said Crane, who shook his head, chuckling. "That's terrible. True, but terrible."

Every one of them knew Kazmir. Were they all in on this? Did they know Seagrave had killed him? Did they know why?

Who were these people?

They were the Society of the Cincinnati. Descendants of the original members, Washington's inner circle. His most trusted officers. Patriots. Defenders of the republic. Good guys, never mind the fact that two hundred years ago people thought they were plotting to seize

307

power themselves, make George Washington—

It suddenly hit her.

She looked at Garrett Crandall, the soon-to-be-senator, already being groomed for higher office....

At Stuart Crane, chairman of the contracting firm that was, for all intents and purposes, running the American war effort....

At Jed Seagrave, who'd spent the last twenty years teaching the most powerful men in the military....

She pictured her father, shaking his head.

There's something else going on, he had said.

And it had been right in front of her the whole time.

Cincinnatus had inspired the original members of the society.

But it seemed to her that the men and women at the table were taking cues from another Roman entirely. Julius Caesar.

Two thousand years ago he'd seized control of the most powerful military machine on the planet and used it to overthrow a republic. To establish Empire.

History, she feared, was about to repeat itself.

BOOK TWO: SOLDIERS

Union Terminal
Western Avenue
Cincinnati, OH
Friday, September 21, 10:48 P.M.

"I still can't believe it. Stuart Crane."

Jake, in the front seat, shook his head.

Matt was in the back, halfway wiggled out of the costume he'd paid a guy five hundred dollars for a few hours earlier.

"He's in there," Matt said. "He's all buddy-buddy with the guy. Seagrave."

Last week, as soon as they started researching the society and Crane's name came up, Jake had said, "No." Out loud and definitively. "Can't be the same guy."

But it turned out to be the same one.

Matt focused on Seagrave. On hauling him off to the police station.

"Use your head," Jake said. "You're an escaped fugitive. You're wanted for murder. He's a—what, professor?"

"Yeah."

"Guy hangs out with Garrett Crandall and the governor and all these society types. You go to the P.D. and say, 'yeah, it was my driver, my fingerprints are all over it, but I didn't do it, I was framed, and they were going to kill me in jail, so when this guy offered to help me escape—'"

"All right, all right. I get the picture," Matt said. It was the same picture he got from Harper.

"Soon, don't worry," Jake said. "See what this FBI guy of Harper's has to say."

When Matt finished dressing he said, "So what are we waiting for? Let's go to her apartment. She said she'd meet us there."

"We're not going anywhere until she walks out that door, safe and sound."

309

"You really think they'd try something here? With all these people around?"

"As opposed to a golf course or an Air Force base? Yeah. I think they might."

Matt could see his point. These people were capable of anything.

BOOK TWO: SOLDIERS

Union Terminal

Western Avenue

Cincinnati, OH

Friday, September 21, 10:54 P.M.

ESPY texted Shurig.

Coup, she typed. Society plan is a coup, I think. Stuart Crane, Garrett Crandall, a man named Jed Seagrave. Maybe others.

The letters on the little screen looked a little blurry.

She blinked to focus them.

Strange.

She finished the message. Hit send.

As she put the phone in her purse, she suddenly felt a little nauseous. The oysters in the fowl, she thought. Maybe she was allergic. She walked back to the table, her legs a bit unsteady.

Seagrave looked at her closely, his face full of concern. "Are you all right?"

She looked at him. He looked a little blurry too.

"Fine," she said, and reached for her tea.

Her hand knocked into it. The tea sloshed in the cup, spilled on the table.

Something is wrong.

"Esperanza?"

Alice Crandall's voice. Sort of.

It sounded slow—like an old tape recording. Es-per-an-za. That was her name. Es-per-an-za Mar-ce-li-na Har-per.

Seagrave put a hand on her arm. "I don't think she's all right," he said.

"I'm not," Espy said, as clearly as she could. Which didn't sound clear at all.

The words sounded like mush. Her tongue felt like mush in her mouth.

311

"You don't look well." Mrs. Crandall put a hand on her shoulder.

Espy's hands dropped to her lap.

And stayed there.

She couldn't move them.

Her vision blurred again. The whole table blurred. The little flag in the center of the table, her half-eaten piece of cake, her tea...

Her tea.

She looked at Seagrave, blurry Seagrave—

Please. Allow me.

—and saw, in his blurry eyes, a glint.

He drugged me.

Seagrave drugged me.

Help, she tried to say.

And started to fall forward.

Seagrave caught her.

"We need a doctor," Mrs. Crandall said.

"Let's get her outside," Seagrave said. "Some fresh air, then straight to an emergency room." He stood up and turned toward the kitchen. "Quicker out that way, I think," he said. "Let's get you to your feet."

He lifted her straight out of her chair.

He was stronger than he looked.

A security guard appeared in front of them. "Is there a problem? Can I help?"

It was the guard she noticed on the way in, the one who looked like Rawson, only of course it wasn't Rawson, Rawson was dead, but he was the same type, a weightlifter type...

A military type.

A coup.

"That would be wonderful," Seagrave said. "Thank you."

The bodybuilder snatched Espy off the ground as if she was a child. Held her in his arms and started walking.

She was looking at the ceiling. Then the ceiling changed. The air around her changed, grew much warmer. The noises around her changed too. People were talking louder, dishes clattering...

The kitchen.

"Make way," she heard Seagrave say. "Please. Make way."

Then they were out in the fresh air. The stars above her spun in the dark sky. The whole world spinning...

The whole world coming to an end.

Seagrave was going to kill her.

She started to cry. Only she couldn't even manage that, a full-on sob.

All she got was tears, running down her face.

She must have made some kind of noise. Seagrave turned to look at her.

"Shhh," he said. "Everything's fine."

No, not fine. Her own fault. What a terrible actress. A terrible liar.

He'd seen through her at dinner, the way she kept trying to find out more about him. Her clumsy attempts to guide the conversation.

She heard Seagrave call his driver, tell him to bring the car around to the back of the terminal. They'd be waiting. And hurry, please.

Harper was still crying. Trying to make some commotion, draw attention.

Then a young woman's voice: "Uncle Jed?"

Crane's granddaughter. Green dress. But wrinkled. Her hair a mess.

"Kaci, what are you doing back here?" Seagrave said.

Then a man stepped from behind her.

"What's happening?" Kaci asked. "Is something the matter with her?"

"Esperanza?" the man said. Robert.

"She fainted," Seagrave said. "We're taking her to a hospital. Just to be sure."

"Is she going to be all right?" Kaci asked.

"Your grandfather was looking for you," Seagrave said. "Better get inside."

Kaci said something, but Espy could barely hear anything. The voices blurred. She couldn't understand them.

Couldn't manage to say anything herself.

Barely conscious.

Then a car. Tires squealing and then stopped....

A car door opening.

Being lifted again.

Then someone between them and the car.

Someone in bare feet, breathing hard.

"Excuse me," Seagrave said. "We have to get her to a doctor."

"Excuse *me*," a woman said. "That's my daughter."

BOOK TWO: SOLDIERS

Barton Lane

Lancaster, CA

Friday, September 21, 8:18 P.M.

SHURIG'S stomach was full of sarma, a Croatian dish, a kind of stew, different types of meat (he hadn't dared ask exactly what) and vegetables (he'd recognized onion and cabbage, but there were others) sitting in a thick tomato sauce. It was edible. Better than he'd hoped for when he'd been sitting in the little spare room, smelling it cook. A boiling pot of cabbage, staple food of poor farmers around the world. His grandmother had made cabbage. Shurig had actually thrown up from eating it once. He'd gotten nauseous for a minute this afternoon, though that had as much to do with the mess he was in as the smell. What was he going to say to Goran when he came home? What was he going to say to the both of them at dinner?

The first part turned out to be easier than expected.

Goran had known he was going to be there. He had called home at some point during the afternoon, and she gave up the truth. Gave up Shurig. Although no harm, as it turned out, because Goran had decided to wait until they could speak in person before telling anyone else about Shurig's visit.

During dinner Shurig had done most of the talking, and the conversation had gone pretty much the way he had expected it to go, and now he and Harper had, Shurig hoped, a few more days to work with.

He stepped out of the house, shutting the door behind him.

The street, which had been dead that morning when he arrived, was alive now.

Dogs barking. Music blaring. Kids playing nearby, screaming with laughter. There were guys leaning on a car half a block down, passing around a joint, it looked like. Their music was so loud that Shurig could literally feel it vibrating the sidewalk. Feel it in his bones.

315

No wait.

That was his phone.

He pulled it out of his pocket and looked at the screen.

O'Neill again.

Okay, Shurig thought. Time to deal with this guy.

"Lieutenant."

"Agent Shurig. You took the day off, I hear."

"That's right."

"So did I." O'Neill almost chuckled. "Although in my case, it wasn't voluntarily."

"What's that mean?"

"It means that officially I'm no longer part of the investigative team."

"Wow," Shurig said, because he didn't know what else to say, except maybe 'stop calling me.'

"I suspect your boss had something to do with it."

"Kennedy."

"Yeah. Although I guess it doesn't really matter, since the case seems to be pretty much wrapped up."

"Seems that way."

"Which is why you took the day off."

"Is there a point to all this?" Shurig asked.

"You mean why am I calling you?"

"Yeah. That's what I mean."

"Well...I'm curious about a couple things. Number one, you were as sure as I was Al-Hasra had nothing to do with Hernandez's death. What changed your mind?"

"The evidence. Obviously."

"Yeah. The evidence." O'Neill didn't even bother keeping the scorn out of his voice. "I thought you might say that."

"You were right."

"So you really think the case is solved?"

"Like you said...that's why I took the day off."

"And drove up to see Tomasevic's wife."

Shurig, who had been walking to his car, who had his keys out and was about to press the door open button on them, froze where he stood.

"I'd ask if you two had a thing going on, but I know you don't, because Tomasevic joined you."

Shurig stood by his car, listening, thinking what to say.

"I went to talk to Tomasevic this afternoon," O'Neill said. "I wanted to know what might have been on those computers at Fox that Al-Hasra, supposedly, might have found out. I get there, and the guy can barely sit still. He's nervous about something. Anxious."

To get home, Shurig realized. To talk to Maya, to talk to me. Find out why I was at his house.

It was all falling apart.

O'Neill was still talking.

"I decide I want to find out why this guy is hopping around like the Energizer Bunny. So when he leaves...I follow him. And when I get here, I find you."

Shurig looked around.

There was a car parked half a block behind him.

A light came on inside it.

O'Neill, sitting behind the wheel, phone pressed to his ear, that smirk of his obvious even from a distance.

"Let's talk about it," he said into Shurig's ear, and then hung up.

Shurig hung up too, and walked to his car.

O'Neill rolled down his window.

"I'm getting tired of doing all this legwork because you and Harper don't want to let me in on your little secret." He pressed a button on the armrest next to him; the doors unlocked. "There's something else going on here, Agent Shurig. Now get in and tell me what."

Shurig turned around. Turned away from O'Neill.

He had to think. But it was hard, with the music blaring, with the kids laughing, with the taste of the sarma still in his mouth...

What to do? He didn't have time to make any phone calls, time to talk to anyone or think things through. The lieutenant had backed him into a corner.

He turned and saw O'Neill looking at him.

Past the lieutenant's car, he saw the lights on in Maya and Goran's house.

Past that, the next block over, he saw more lights; more houses. Maybe they belonged to more section eighters, maybe not, but even the section eighters had kids, and they wanted better lives for those kids, that's why they were here in America, to give their kids a shot at something more, but right now...

If guys like him and O'Neill didn't do what was necessary, there wasn't going to be any America. At least not any kind of America Shurig wanted to live in.

We don't need any heroes at this point.

You're wrong Sam, Shurig felt like saying out loud.

We always need heroes. To do what has to be done.

"Let's go," O'Neill said.

"We don't need to go anywhere." Shurig pulled the CD out of his pocket with his left hand, the CD he had Goran burn for him before dinner. The CD with all the cloudbytes.com files on it. "This is what you want."

O'Neill stretched his hand through the window to take it. His fingers closed on the CD.

Shurig's fingers closed on his wrist.

He yanked O'Neill through the window, just far enough to drive his free hand into the bridge of the lieutenant's nose, slamming it up into his brain. A killing blow.

When Shurig let go of O'Neill's wrist, he slumped back into his seat.

Shurig reached inside the car and turned off the dome light.

He looked up and down the street. No one had seen anything: calculated risk, but one he'd had to take.

He opened the driver's side door, and shoved O'Neill over.

Buckled himself in, started the car...

And sat there a moment, hands on the steering wheel, trying not to scream.

"Sonuvabitch," he said, shaking his head, looking at O'Neill. That was the last thing he wanted to do. They were on the same side, for God's sake, him and the lieutenant. They...

Focus, he told himself. Focus.

He popped another blue pill. Buckled O'Neill's seat belt.

Okay. This was a problem, but nothing he couldn't solve. Same way he'd solved Goran and Maya, slumped over the dinner table, music playing, back door busted open, her jewelry missing, his FBI badge gone...gunshot victims. A break-in gone bad, obviously. So what had happened to O'Neill?

He'd kept investigating. Looking for something the rest of us had missed. And he'd found it. But an Al-Hasra operative had gotten the drop on him and...

Wait a second. No bullets: he hadn't used any bullets, Shurig realized.

The scenario needed work.

His phone rang. Ah.

"Colonel," Shurig said, picking up. "I was just about to call you."

"We have a situation, Michael," Seagrave said.

Shurig nodded.

"Tell me about it," he said.

Book Three

CINCINNATUS

The die was now cast; I had passed the Rubicon.
Swim or sink, live or die, survive or perish with
my country was my unalterable determination.
— *John Quincy Adams*

Union Terminal
Western Avenue
Cincinnati, OH
Friday, September 21, 11:30 P.M.

IT took a good three seconds—one...two...three...

—for her brain to absorb what she was seeing. Who she was seeing.

Her father.

"Dad!" She jumped to her feet and ran to him, wrapped her arms around him, smiling and laughing and sobbing all at the same time.

"You're alive," she said. "You're really alive!"

"I am," he said. "And isn't it silly that I live in Los Angeles and you two live all the way out here?"

"It *is* silly," her mother said. "We should do something about it."

"Let's be a family," Espy said. "Let's drink to it." She raised the glass of champagne in her hand, and her mom and dad raised theirs, and the three of them clinked their glasses, and Espy drank and the bubbles...

Tasted funny on her tongue.

Tasted wrong.

The room began to spin.

"You all right?"

"I don't think I am," she said, and tried to sit down before realizing she was already sitting down.

Her father melted away.

"Oh no," she said. "Daddy..."

"See you soon," he said.

And disappeared.

The room spun so fast she felt sick, like she was going to throw up.

And she did.

"Again," someone said. A man's voice. "Do it again."

She did—all over the street in front of her.

She was sitting on a curb. Head between her legs. Someone sitting behind her, propping her up. Her mother, she knew without even looking.

"Good. Get it all out." The same voice speaking.

A bright light shined down on her. Framed in it was a man's face—blurry, indistinct. Coming into focus, just a little...

Matt. No. Bigger. Broader. And the voice wasn't Matt's...

Behind the face, coming into focus...an eagle. Staring down at her, from inside a circle of stars. From the society's flag.

She was outside Union Terminal. The front entrance. A crowd of people milled around, talking in hushed voices. Staring at her, trying not to stare. She saw Mrs. Claypool, Mrs. Teresi, Robert. Leonard and Tunde. Alice Crandall and, behind her, Stuart Crane, talking to the governor.

She didn't see Seagrave anywhere.

"What do we have?"

A woman in a paramedic's uniform stood over her.

"She was drugged." The man who'd been kneeling in front of her was Jake, Matt's brother. "I induced vomiting."

A male paramedic stood behind the woman. And behind him the lights on an ambulance flashed, lighting up the area in red and yellow.

"What makes you think she was drugged?" The female paramedic knelt next to Espy, felt her forehead, looked into her eyes.

"That's what she told me," Jake said. "Somebody put something in her drink."

"Is that what happened, miss? Can you tell me?" the woman asked.

Yes, Espy was about to say. That's exactly what happened. And I can tell you who did it. Jed Seagrave. And he killed my father too. He—

The male paramedic moved closer.

He was Asian. Not a big guy, but built. Biceps popping out of his dark blue paramedic shirt. He had a crew-cut; sharp angular features. He looked like a dangerous guy.

A military kind of guy.

"Is that it?" he asked. "You were drugged?"

Espy stared at him. His nametag: Sanders. He reminded her of the security guard. The one who had carried her to the car. Seagrave's man.

"Honey?" Her mother's voice, from behind her. Thick with emotion. On the verge of breaking down. "Can you talk?"

Espy managed a nod. "Yes," she said.

"I'll get the stretcher," the male paramedic said. "Don't worry, ma'am. We'll have you at the hospital in no time."

There was a hint of reassurance in his voice.

There was none in his eyes.

"I don't want to go anywhere," Espy said. "I'm fine."

"You're not fine," said Jake, who was standing next to Sanders. "Go. Let them run a couple tests."

"No!" Espy said, louder than she intended. So loud it hurt her head. "I'm not getting in that ambulance."

Not with him, she thought, staring at Sanders. He was Seagrave's man too. Just like the guard. Just like Rawson. A military man. A military coup.

"You really should go," her mom said. "at least let them—"

"I'm fine," Espy said, though she knew she wasn't. Not only was her stomach gurgling, her arms and legs felt like they were encased in bags of sand and her head was pounding. "It was the oysters," she said. "In the stew. I'm allergic."

She put her hands on the curb and stood up. Started to, anyway. She wobbled a little. Her head spun. Her stomach lurched. Bile surged into her throat.

"Easy, honey," her mom said.

"You look a little green," the female paramedic said. "Let's sit back down."

Espy managed to stand straight. "I'm fine. See?"

And then she threw up again.

❖ ❖ ❖ ❖ ❖

Three more times, she threw up.

Matt watched her with the binoculars from the backseat of Jake's car, in the far end of one of the terminal parking lots. It was painful to see, nearly as painful as watching Seagrave drive off in his limo twenty minutes ago. Matt wrote down the license number and hoped that Jake and Espy were right, that they'd catch up with Seagrave and make *him* the wanted man. Trust that he hadn't thrown away his best chance to get back some semblance of a normal life.

The two weeks living in the RV Jake 'borrowed' from the impound lot, two weeks at the Tower Mobile Home Park in a little town called Washington Court House, had given him time to realize he hadn't had a normal life for a long time—since the shoulder injury, since taking the job at The Pines, since Nancy moved out.

When Espy finally stopped puking, the paramedics drove away. Jake and Harper's mom guided her back inside the terminal. The crowd around the entrance thinned, as did the cars in the parking lot.

Matt watched the big clock over the terminal entrance.

Time passed. Five minutes. Ten. What were they doing in there?

Jake had told him to stay in the car, but that was when the parking lot was full. It was now nearly empty. Besides...

Matt was getting tired of Jake telling him what to do.

He was about two hundred fifty yards away from the terminal entrance. The length of a good par three. Like, say, sixteen at The Pines.

Back in the day, he could have reached that door with a single swing. *Matt Thurman, 15-Year-Old Phenom, Stuns Field to Take Trophy.* Big picture on the front page of the *Columbus Dispatch* sports section.

They'd run the picture again last week, right next to his mug shot.

Kid Golfer's Road to Ruin

The terminal doors opened. Someone emerged. Three someones. Espy. Flanked by Jake and her mom.

She still looked wobbly.

Jake and Mrs. Harper had cleaned her up. Wet blotches on her dress, her makeup wiped off. She looked pale, exhausted, sick.

"Is she going to be okay?" Matt asked when they got to the car.

"Seagrave drugged her," Jake said.

Matt opened the back door. He and Jake maneuvered Espy into the back seat and laid her down. She was like a limp rag doll.

One that smelled like vomit.

Matt held his breath and squeezed into the back seat alongside her. They didn't quite fit. Her head ended up in his lap.

Espy's mother got in front. "All right, we're alone," she said. "Now someone tell me what's happening."

"I'll tell you what I know, Mrs. Harper," Jake said, starting up the car. "Your daughter—"

"Penelope," she said. "Or Penny. Whichever you prefer."

"Oh. Okay. So what's happening, as far as I can tell—"

"It's a coup," Espy said, out of nowhere.

Matt looked down. Her eyes were still closed.

"It's a what?" he said.

"A coup. Something to do with the military. Garrett Crandall. Remember I told you there was something else going on besides fixing golf tournaments. That's it. That's what they're planning."

Espy's mom turned and looked at Matt, and then down at her daughter.

"What who is planning?"

"The Cincinnati," she said. "This is what Dad and I have been working on. This is why they killed him. Because he found out about it. Kirtland Air Force Base. It's all tied together."

Jake looked in the rear view mirror. Caught Matt's eye. Gave him a do-you-have-any-idea-what-she's-talking-about look.

"The Cincinnati?" Espy's mother said. "The people at the banquet?"

"That's who I mean."

"Alice Crandall? Stuart Crane?" Espy's mother leaned across her seat to look at Espy. "I can't believe it. I don't believe it. I've known these people for years."

"They killed my dad."

Matt looked down at her in his lap. "You said that before. But I still don't get it. Why—"

"That was my dad in your jail cell." She opened her eyes and looked up at Matt. "Who helped you escape."

"Whoa."

"He was an FBI agent."

Her mother added, "His name was Sam Hernandez."

"Long Beach—that Sam Hernandez?" Jake asked.

"Yes," Espy said, with her eyes still closed.

"So what's this about a coup," Jake said. "They're going to run a coup from New Mexico?"

"I don't know," Espy said. "Kirtland is where Altair is. That's who my dad was going to see. Altair is part of a company called Enovation, which also owns Next Century."

"Kazmir's company," Matt said.

Espy sat up so fast her head almost clipped Matt on the chin. "What do you mean, Kazmir's company?"

"Well, not his exactly," Matt said, trying to remember what the woman he'd spoken with had told him. "He worked as some sort of consultant for them, helped them sell the systems to the bigger courses. The Pines, Oakmont, places like that."

Espy eased herself into a sitting position, all at once looking wide-awake. "That makes sense. How'd you find that out?"

Jake said, "Went to The Pines, talked to the head grounds guy."

"Gary Blackstone," Espy said.

Matt nodded. "Kazmir and him go way back."

"Will someone please tell me what's going on," Espy's mother said.

Harper explained about the fixing of golf tournaments, how it could have something to do with the greens and the irrigation systems beneath them. How members of the Cincinnati may be involved, using the gambling money for something she did not yet understand.

"Down," Jake said, his voice suddenly changing. "Both of you in back, on the floor. Penny, get down too. Now."

Matt was moving before his brother finished talking. He grabbed Espy's arm and dragged her down to the floor, practically on top of him.

"Hey!" Espy said. "What's the matter?"

"There's a guy standing in a doorway a couple buildings down from your apartment." Jake drove the car slowly, checking out the situation. "He looks like the paramedic. From the banquet."

"I knew it," Espy said, getting up on her knees.

Matt yanked her to the floor.

"Hey!" she said again. "Stop doing that!"

When Jake told them they were past the building, Espy shoved Matt away from her and climbed onto the seat.

"He looked like the paramedic?" she said.

"A little," Jake said. "He was Asian, anyway."

"So I wasn't being paranoid."

"Maybe not."

"Go to my house," Penny said. "Hyde Park. Esperanza can borrow some of my clothes."

"No." Jake said firmly.

"Definitely not," Matt said.

It took Penny a second to get it. Then her eyes widened. "You think they're there, too?"

"They know she left with you," Jake said.

Penny sat back in her seat, gazing at the road ahead. "So what do we do?"

Good question, Matt thought.

"Good question," Espy said. "Let me make a call."

Alameda Street

Compton, CA

Friday, September 21, 11:18 P.M.

SHURIG walked along Wilshire, headed west, away from O'Neill's car, which he left in MacArthur Park, where in another few hours it might get chopped up for parts. If not, LAPD might notice it sitting there abandoned in a day or even two.

He had left O'Neill's body a few hundred feet off Five Deer Trail in the Angeles National Forest, liberally doused with two eight-ounce squeeze bottles of Golden Blossom honey. Good stuff—at least the bugs crawling all over the lieutenant seemed to think so. By now, bigger things were no doubt getting their share of the Golden Blossom. By the time someone found the body, it wouldn't be much more than bones.

And the operation would be long since complete.

So that was two problems down. Problem number three was getting back to his own car. The plan was to take a bus to his apartment, where his ride would meet him and take him back to Lancaster, well before morning light.

Shurig was moving quick, wearing his best badass look, so no one would be tempted to mess with him. This was not a neighborhood where a person was safe walking alone. Although part of him wished someone would try something. He needed to let loose, break out his old Bravo moves, work off some tension. His shoulder felt stiff but he'd have more than enough to offer your average street gangsta. Or two.

His phone buzzed in his pocket. Harper. Again. Third time she'd called in an hour.

He did a quick mental review of what he and the Colonel had discussed: the plan. Isolate and annihilate. Maintain operational secrecy, above all.

He picked up.

"Hey. Sorry to call so late. I left a message before, but—"

"I got jammed up," he said. "Anything happen at that reception?"

"A lot," she said, and told him.

Shit, Shurig thought, when she got to the part about Enovation. Parent company to Altair and Next Century.

The news got worse. The golfer was still alive. The man she called Rawson was dead, which was not a big surprise; they all knew something had gone wrong when they hadn't heard from him in a while. At least now Shurig could think of the guy by his real name—Dale Metcalf, a Bravo squad buddy. Well, *buddy* was the wrong word because none of them had been close, except Shurig and D.B., but they all shared a certain attitude about things, a belief in how the world worked, part of which they learned from the Colonel, part of which was something innate, an understanding of the terrible things that had to be done sometimes in the name of the greater good, an understanding that precious few people shared, which was why Metcalf's death— raging asshole that he was most of the time—made Shurig unhappy.

And then it got worse. Harper and the golfer were now with the golfer's brother. A cop and clearly a capable guy, not just some bozo with a gun. He'd taken down Dale and spotted Jason at Harper's apartment. This was a problem.

"Agent Shurig? You there?"

"Yeah," he said. "Sorry. Still waking up."

Right then a car cruised past, music booming. Two guys in it gave him the cold stare as they trolled by.

"Listen, let me call you when I get back home," he said.

"I thought you were home."

"Right, right," he said. "I mean when *you* get back home—"

"I'm not going home. That guy in front of my apartment?"

"Right. Sorry." He took a deep breath. Focus. Focus, focus, focus.

He pulled one of the blue pills out of his pocket and swallowed it.

Isolate and annihilate. That had been the plan. But the plan had to change.

He needed to talk to Seagrave again.

"Okay. Give me five minutes, then call me back."

The car that had passed him pulled a U-Turn and cruised back toward him.

Might not mean anything. Then again...

The car stopped next to him. Right in the middle of the road.

"I'm going to have to call you back," Shurig said. "Half an hour or so. Okay?"

He hung up without waiting for a reply.

"What's up?" the driver said. The guy was Hispanic, a little Asian thrown in too, maybe a little African-American. Shaved head, muscle T, a little soul patch, a big tattoo on his left arm, hanging out the car window. Faded tattoo—the glare from the streetlights above wasn't bright enough for Shurig to read it.

He closed his phone, and put it in his pocket.

"Nothing," Shurig said.

"Nothing." The driver laughed.

The passenger door opened.

A guy stepped out. Hundred percent African; no American in there at all. Black skin; wiry frame. Nigerian, maybe. Wearing jeans. No shirt. Wide-eyed; google-eyed. Hopped up on something. He strutted around the edge of the car, one hand held down at his side.

Shurig saw the blade as the guy cleared the front of the car.

The driver opened his door and stepped out.

"You got some money we can borrow?" he asked.

"Sure." Shurig said with a smile. "Come and get it."

BOOK THREE: CINCINNATUS

❖ ❖ ❖ ❖ ❖

Forty minutes later, he was on the 105 bus, on his way back to his apartment. Feeling jazzed. Energized. Nothing like a little exercise to get the blood flowing. And speaking of blood...

He rolled up his sleeve to hide the stain, just in case anybody boarded. Doubtful. This time of night, this route...he'd probably ride the whole way to Hollywood by himself. Fine with him. His own little rolling office. He'd checked in with the colonel, checked in with his ride, and now he was on the phone with Harper and her gang.

She sounded completely exhausted. Poor kid. He felt sorry for her, a little bit. Actually, he felt sorry for her a lot. Sorry for what had happened to her dad, for what was inevitably going to happen to her. He had a second there when he wanted to call the Colonel and say maybe we can just put her someplace out of the way for the next few days and then reassess the situation. We're on the same side, really, when you get down to it.

But he knew what the Colonel would say: Operational secrecy was paramount—before, during, and after. Harper walking around, asking questions, sticking her nose where she could cause trouble was a threat that couldn't be tolerated. And he would be right.

So Shurig said goodbye to Harper.

She passed the phone to the cop. Jake.

He sounded juiced, ready for action.

A coup? Shurig said. I don't know. I wasn't there, but Harper's smart. If she thinks so, it's worth looking into. Kirtland Air Force Base. Yeah. I'll handle it. In the meantime...yes, I agree. Get everyone someplace safe. Someplace where you can...Wilmington? Ohio? Never heard of it. But sounded good. Right off the highway. Holiday Inn. The Roberts Center. Right.

Then he hung up and called in the address.

His ride was parked in front of the apartment.

Njomo climbed out of his car. "Hey, I've been here for half an hour. The police drove by, and I had to pretend I was—"

"Shut up," Shurig said.

Njomo shut up.

"Let's go," Shurig said.

They went.

Njomo had been doing exactly what Shurig told him to do since the night Kauffman had been killed. He was afraid that Shurig would tell the Colonel how close Njomo had been to cutting a deal with Kauffman, the first time they'd met, when Njomo hadn't known he and Shurig were on the same side. Unfortunately for Njomo, Seagrave already knew everything that had happened. Shurig didn't keep secrets from the Colonel.

Njomo, though, was a different story. Shurig was happy to let the man go on thinking they had a quid pro quo here. It made his life a lot easier.

Plus there was something about the guy that set his teeth on edge. A lack of character maybe. No backbone. The way he kept picking at his teeth with the fingernail of one pinky. Maybe out-and-out prejudice. Njomo looked a little like the girl in Ghaziliyah. Big dark eyes; same color skin. *Salaam. Salaam aleikum.*

Shurig slept the whole way up to Lancaster. Njomo let him out a few blocks from Tomasevic's house, and Shurig walked the rest of the way, trying to be inconspicuous.

The dining room light was still on at Tomasevic's house when he got there. The curtains were drawn, but he could see (or imagined he could see) Goran and Maya sitting at the dinner table. Well, not sitting, but...they were there.

And then Shurig recalled the look on Maya's face in that split-second after he shot Goran, when he turned the gun on her....

Isolate and annihilate.

Maintain operational secrecy.

He got in his car, drove away with the lights off, slowly and quietly.

Roberts Center Holiday Inn
Wilmington, OH
Saturday, September 22, 1:45 A.M.

THE last thing she heard was Shurig's voice, telling her he was headed to Kirtland, that he'd handle things, that she should just take it easy. Then Jake took the phone away. She was too tired and queasy to be upset, though she knew she ought to be, the way he insisted on talking to Shurig, his whole obnoxious, take-charge attitude. As if she hadn't been the one who'd started this whole thing, as if she wasn't capable of taking care of herself.

She leaned back and closed her eyes.

Next thing she knew, a car door slammed next to her ear.

Matt's face—six inches from hers.

She wasn't sitting anymore. She was stretched across the back seat, her cheek pasted to the vinyl. Matt sprawled across the car floor, his head propped on an elbow.

"How you doing?" he asked.

She pushed herself into a sitting position. "Not good," she said. Her head was pounding and there wasn't a single square inch of her that didn't ache.

Her mom was still in the front seat, leaning against the passenger side window. Snoring, albeit a dainty, ladylike snore.

"What time is it?" Espy asked.

"Almost two, something like that." Matt climbed up on the seat next to her. "Jake went to get rooms. Should be back in a second."

She closed her eyes. Leaned against the car window.

Then she jerked up straight. "He went to get what?"

"Rooms," Matt said. "He wasn't sure about going back to the RV. Wants to check it out in daylight first. Tomorrow."

She looked out the window. The sky was pitch black. They were in a parking lot in front of a new-looking Holiday Inn right off I-71. A big bright display sign next to the highway said Roberts Conference Center. It flashed various messages and cast colorful shadows across the cars in the lot.

Beyond the hotel—fallow fields. Pretty swanky place right in the middle of farm country.

"Where the hell are we?" she said.

Matt sighed. "Someplace safe for the night."

❖ ❖ ❖ ❖ ❖

Espy was mad. And she wasn't shy about letting Jake know it. Matt thought she ought to cut his brother a little slack, considering that he'd saved their lives. Matt carried the stuff they'd bought for Espy and her mom when they stopped at Meijer—jeans and t-shirts for each of them, a purse for Espy to replace the one she brought to the reception.

They ambled down the hall, looking for their rooms. Matt was leading the way, listening to the argument behind him.

"I never agreed to this," Espy said.

"You were asleep," Jake said.

"Well I'm awake now."

"Fine. You're awake. Can we talk about it tomorrow?"

"I want to talk about it now. I need to go back."

"Back to Cincinnati?" Jake had that 'are-you-crazy' tone in his voice. "In case you've forgotten, there are people who want to kill you back there."

"Here we go," Matt said, stopping in front of a door. He opened it and flipped on the light. The room had a standard hotel layout: bathroom, closet, two twin beds, a desk, and a bureau with a TV on top. It looked nice, smelled new.

Penny, who appeared to be sleepwalking, immediately glided onto the far bed, and turned over, nestling into sleep without even pulling back the covers.

"You need anything?" Jake asked.

"A ride back to Cincinnati," Espy snapped.

"We're right in the next room," Matt said, setting the bag of clothes on Espys bed.

"What time are we leaving tomorrow?" Espy asked.

"I'm setting an alarm for ten," Jake said. "I'll come and get you."

"Ten." She frowned. "How far is Cincinnati?"

"Too far to walk," Jake said. He passed Matt and headed out of the room, rolling his eyes as he went.

"What's his problem?" Espy asked, turning her anger on Matt.

"In case you didn't notice, he saved your life."

"My mother saved my life."

"Your mother would have put you in that ambulance."

"He would have too."

"You wouldn't even have been conscious if he wasn't there. If he hadn't gotten you to puke up some of that stuff Seagrave gave you."

Espy pursed her lips. Let her hands fall from her hips. "How far is Cincinnati?"

"Forty miles. Little more."

"I want to be out of here at nine," she said. "You tell him that."

"Hey. In the first place, I don't take orders from you. In the second place—"

"When you were deciding to come here you should've woken me up. This is the most idiotic—"

"We were trying to keep you safe. Sorry for caring."

She held up her hand. "Whatever. The point is, I don't want to be stuck here for the next ten hours."

"Why?"

"Because there's going to be a military coup, that's why," she said, her burst of anger so loud that it woke her mother.

"Esperanza?" Penny said, lifting her head from the pillow.

"It's okay, Mom," she said. "Everything's fine."

Her mother put her head back down on the pillow.

Matt took the opportunity to escape. Espy obviously was upset and there was no reasoning with her.

"Hey!" she said, as he grabbed the doorknob.

Matt stopped but didn't turn around.

"Look," she said. "I'm...sorry."

Matt nodded.

They stood in silence for a moment.

"Thank you," she said. "I appreciate what you've done. Really." She paused. "And I haven't had a chance to say it, but I'm very glad you're still alive. I thought—"

"I should have found a way to let you know," he said with a shrug. "We'll get you to Cincinnati. Early. I promise."

She nodded. "Tell your brother I...appreciate everything he's doing."

"You can tell him yourself. Eight in the morning, right?"

She took a couple of steps toward him, looking a little embarrassed by her tantrum.

"Make it nine."

He smiled.

Though she looked absolutely beleaguered—tired and sick, wiped out from the drug—he was struck by how pretty she was, standing there. A tough little gal with the whole world on her shoulders. He wanted to put his arms around her.

❖ ❖ ❖ ❖ ❖

And then he did. And she let him. At first, she kept her hands at her

339

sides, but then she brought them around his back. A short, spontaneous hug turned into a much longer one.

He wanted to kiss her, to throw her on the bed, but her mother, on the next bed, made pushing things in that direction impossible. It was enough just to hold her, feel her strong little body in his arms.

He'd thought about her quite a bit in the days when he was hiding, waiting for Jake to figure out what to do. He'd thought, too, about Nancy.

Nancy was from Tampa. Matt met her the year he was on the Nationwide tour at a post-tournament party. She was a stunning blond, every guy's dream, an amazing body, like a Barbie doll come to life. He whisked her out of the party, and they drove out to Ybor City, had a fancy dinner, went dancing, kept drinking, went back to his hotel and did things he hadn't known were physically possible.

He was hooked. That's how it started; that's how it stayed for a long time. His pro career was going well, and he had the most beautiful girl he'd ever known. The tour took him away, the tour brought him back, and she was there. Except...really, she wasn't. He began to realize that the things she did and said didn't come from her—they came from some idea she had of the way girls who looked like her were supposed to act. The clothes, the walk, the talk were part of a role she had to play. Even when she moved to Ohio to be with him after the injury, part of her was never really there.

Espy was completely different. She was so real she scared him—since she first picked him up at the Crosley Tower. She was always serious, always focused, always herself. She sometimes made him feel stupid, like some dolt who could hit a golf ball but wasn't worth much otherwise. Of course, he'd felt that way about himself since the injury had derailed his career.

And now here she was—in his arms.

Then just as quickly as she embraced him, she broke away.

"Oh my gosh...sorry about that," she said. She traced a finger around her lips, as if to wipe away her momentary lapse of control. She wouldn't look him in the eye, the first time she'd ever seemed shy.

"Don't apologize." He reached for her but she stepped back, raised a cautionary hand.

She raked her fingers through her hair. "I need a shower. I must look awful." Before he could beg to differ, she held up her hand, still not meeting his eyes.

"You look great to me," he said.

She smiled and nodded, started pulling the clothes from the bag on her bed. "Well, that's sweet." And the note of control, even hardness, had returned to her voice. She was not someone who let herself go—at least for very long.

Her mom, still asleep on the bed, let out a snore, which broke Harper's cool again. She giggled.

Matt laughed too.

"Crazy night," he whispered.

She nodded, seemed on the verge of saying something, then didn't.

"What were you going to say?" he asked.

She finally met his eyes. "Your brother's car."

He rubbed his jaw. There was no figuring out this woman. "My brother's car?"

"You know where the keys are?"

WILMINGTON. A Holiday Inn on the interstate.

Seagrave was pleased when Michael called it in and was pleased to relay the information to Jason. It was almost enough to make him believe in fate—that there was a God up above making everything come out nice and neat.

Almost.

It wasn't that Seagrave didn't believe in a Supreme Power. He just felt that a being powerful enough to create the universe had better things to do than make out report cards for every member of the human race. He did believe that the Judeo-Christian religious ethic, as it had permeated western civilization, was responsible for that civilization's ascendance in world affairs: its emphasis on the family unit, on respect for your elders, on personal responsibility. The last in particular rang true with Seagrave.

Which was why he was angry with himself. His behavior at the banquet had been inexcusable. He had planned to meet Harper and determine what threat she posed to the plan. Instead, he behaved like a B-movie villain; thankfully, the situation seemed back under control.

Wilmington.

He checked his watch.

Jason should be there right about now.

Seagrave was in the rear cabin of Stuart Crane's Gulfstream V, jetting back to Washington. The cabin had been modified for use in Garrett Crandall's senatorial campaign. The window opposite his leather chair had been replaced by four television screens—a way for Crandall to know what the networks were saying about him and the campaign.

Seagrave used the screens for similar purposes.

He had been scanning the networks and several foreign stations since boarding twenty minutes ago. He searched for patterns. While not a believer in the hand of God per se, he'd come to believe in synchronicity, the idea that what appeared to be coincidence was often a manifestation of a larger, underlying authority.

On one screen he watched a discussion on BBC-1. The topic: Al-Aqsa, and the ongoing repercussions of the mosque's destruction. The panelists talked about how the collapse of the Dome had led directly to the collapse of the Israeli/Syrian peace talks. Earlier the channel had run footage of the Egyptian cleric Husayn al-Rani, noting that the catastrophe on the Temple Mount had swelled the ranks of those receptive to his "hand of Allah" message. The footage was from an impromptu speech al-Rani gave at Hurghada airport. Seagrave had watched it on Al-Majd. It was one of the more riveting moments he had ever seen on TV, even though he had to follow the transliteration of al-Rani's words, rather than the Arabic, which was poorly recorded.

The man shed tears over the destruction of the mosque. He shed tears over the riots sparked by the disaster. He saved his most affecting moments for the end of his speech, when he asked his audience to consider the mosque's destruction a sign of God's displeasure. A warning that for Muslims, too, a day of judgment would come, when the good they had done would be balanced against the evil. He begged his audience to do what good they could, not just for each other, but for the children of Abraham all over the world, Muslims, Jews, Christians alike.

It was a lot of tears, Seagrave thought. Perhaps too many. Enough, almost, to make one doubt the man's sincerity.

Now, on the BBC program, the panelists had changed subjects, discussing the impact of Al-Aqsa's destruction on United States domestic politics and on the upcoming mid-term elections. The consensus seemed to be that the president's actions had reinforced his impotence in the mideast crisis.

Seagrave smiled. As if the man could be any more impotent than he already was.

Someone knocked on the door.

"Come," Seagrave said, muting the volume again.

It was Gene Carter.

"Jed," Carter said. "Mind if I come in?"

"Please," Seagrave said, and indicated the chair next to him. Carter was the number two man at the NGA's Innovision Directorate. The National Geospatial-Intelligence Agency was part of the Defense Department and specialized in satellite mapping and imaging. A student of Seagrave's, twenty years ago, Carter was ill-equipped for his position. He was in his mid-forties, balding, out of shape, a once-handsome man whose job was literally killing him. The man wasn't cut out for this kind of stress. Seagrave would be surprised if he made it through the year. Though the next three days were all that really mattered.

"It's about Cashier," Carter said. He said he'd had a long talk with Major General Tom Van Croft, current director of the DIA, the Defense Intelligence Agency. DIA, NGA, CIA, NSA, FBI—keeping track of the acronyms floating around America's intelligence community these days was almost as hard as getting those agencies to cooperate with each other.

Which was why Seagrave had pushed Carter for the NGA job. Carter and Van Croft were close friends. They spoke frequently. Over the last few years, a lot of the ideas—a lot of the words, even—Carter used in their conversations originated with Seagrave.

As had Cashier. The idea for the operation, anyway; the name, to be fair, had been Carter's.

Carter said, "Tom feels, and I agree, that it might make sense to let the NSA know about it now."

Tell the NSA about Cashier? Seagrave thought. The NSA, the National Security Agency, was a yet another governmental intelligence group. The agency focused primarily on code breaking and on collecting information.

Telling that agency, Seagrave thought, was close to the stupidest thing he'd ever heard. When your whole plan depended on secrecy, the one thing you absolutely did not do unless you had to do it was tell anyone about it.

He knew Van Croft was jockeying for position among his peers in the intelligence community. Once Cashier went live, everything would change, and the general wanted to start from a position of power.

Van Croft was in for a rude awakening. Things would change, all right, but not in the way he expected. And bringing the NSA in on Cashier at this point would do no good at all.

But Seagrave could hardly tell this to Carter, who knew only one part of what was to come.

Seagrave said, "Cashier is your plan as much as mine. If you want to bring in the NSA, then, by all means, let's put it in motion."

Carter looked relieved. "I'm glad you feel that way. Tom was pretty insistent on it."

"Of course," Seagrave said.

Because Van Croft has already told the NSA, Seagrave added, though not aloud. With Cashier just two days away, the general surely had told them already, to allow them time to position themselves to take advantage of the event.

Seagrave wished Carter and Van Croft didn't have to be involved in the Cashier operation, but he couldn't do it alone.

When he finally got rid of Carter, Seagrave turned his attention back to the television screens. The one in the upper right caught his eye.

It was tuned to Al-Ikhbariya: Saudi television. They were broadcasting hundreds of thousands of Muslims making a pilgrimage—called the hajj—to Mecca, to the most holy of Islamic sites. The pilgrimage usually is performed during Dhu al-Hijja, the twelfth month of the Islamic calendar. But due to recent events, such as the unexplainable weather and the destruction of the temple, and fueled by Husayn al-Rani's "hand of Allah" message, huge numbers of Muslims were making an additional pilgrimage during Ramadan in hopes of holding back that hand.

Exactly as Seagrave had planned.

It was an awe-inspiring sight, so many believers gathered in one place at one time, beseeching Allah to show mercy, to forgive them. As he watched, Seagrave did not feel merciful or forgiving. He felt only eagerness to take the next steps toward fulfilling what he thought of as his mission.

Interstate 71
Eighteen Miles Northeast of Cincinnati, OH
Saturday, September 22, 7:02 A.M.

MATT drove, Espy sat next to him. Cool air blew through the open window, her elbow resting on the edge. The sun rose in the eastern sky, showering pink rays on the morning traffic. They'd been on the road for a half hour. Matt could make it back to the hotel before nine, before Jake woke up. He ought to be happy about that.

But he didn't look happy. He hadn't looked happy since he'd snuck out to meet her in the hotel hallway with Jake's car keys.

"I don't know about this," he'd said.

"Come on, Matt," she said. "Jake's not going to want me to go back to Cincinnati. He's going to want me to sit around while he and Shurig decide what to do next."

"I guess so."

"We're going to have a fight, and I don't have the energy for it. I really don't."

It wasn't just fighting with Jake; it was fighting with her mom.

"Please," she said again.

Finally he said, "Okay."

And that was the last thing he'd said.

When they started driving, he just stared straight ahead and sipped his coffee. Espy tried a couple times to start a conversation and failed miserably.

Now she watched the scenery fly by. Looking at Matt every few minutes to make sure he was awake. She pictured their embrace last night, wondering, if the circumstances were different, if it would have led to more, actually feeling very sure it would have led to more.

They pulled up in front of the Federal Building. Matt stopped the car, put on the hazard lights.

"See?" Espy said. "It's not even eight yet. You can be back at the motel before he wakes up."

"Yeah," Matt said. He looked up and down the street. "I don't see anybody."

"Neither do I," she said. The street was completely deserted.

"Of course, I'm not Jake," he said. "I don't know what sort of hiding spots people like that might use. I mean, they might—"

She grabbed her bag and opened the car door. "Thanks for everything," she said. "I mean it. I know you're worried about Jake."

"That's not who I'm worried about," he said. "This doesn't seem right, just leaving you here."

She patted his hand. "I'm just going to run in and get my computer."

"And then what?"

"A hotel, I think. I'm not sure." She stepped out of the car. "I'll call you."

"You don't have my number."

Espy bit her lip. "You have mine, right?"

"Oh yeah. 588-5377." He reached into his back pocket and pulled out an envelope. "Take this."

"What is it?"

"Cash," he said. "The rest of what your father gave me. In case they're tracking your credit cards or whatever."

"Thanks." She stuffed the envelope in her bag and turned toward the building.

"I'll wait," he called after her.

She turned and looked at him.

He pointed to the building. "They might be up there. In your office."

She shook her head. "You need i.d. to get into the building."

"These guys? They can get i.d., don't you think?"

She didn't have an answer for that.

"Okay," she said. "Be right down."

At the building, a security guard squinted at her identification and passed her bag through the metal detector. She took the elevator to her floor, walked through the silent reception area and down the empty hall, reached her office, and turned the knob.

Which she shouldn't have been able to do. Because the door should have been locked.

But it was open.

A man sat behind her desk.

Leonard.

❖ ❖ ❖ ❖ ❖

"Good morning," he said, and leaned back in his chair—her chair, actually. "Glad to see you're feeling better."

She could think of nothing to say, but she didn't conceal her alarm.

"You're wondering what I'm doing here," Leonard said. "I could ask you the same thing."

She sat down in the chair opposite her desk with a thud.

"I've been in since six," he said. "Looking over your work. And I'm pleased to say you were right."

She tapped her purse, cradled in her lap. "About what?"

"United Apparel. 'Stop cheating. Pay your taxes.'"

"Oh." She managed a smile. "Good."

He leaned forward and ran his hands over a stack of files scattered across her desk. Espy hadn't noticed them. "It's all here. Good work."

She gazed at the files, stunned, and then looked at Leonard. "You've been going through my case notes."

"I hope you don't mind."

"Actually, I do," she said, trying to control her anger.

"I'm sorry," he said. "It won't happen again. I don't think. I believe I have a much better handle on what's been happening these last few months. Why you've been acting so strangely."

He rested his hand on the open lid of her computer—which she also noticed for the first time. Sitting on the filing cabinet behind her desk.

Now she was angry. And a little afraid. Given Leonard's ties to the society, to what she was investigating, she wondered if they were alone in the office, if his invasion of her files and computer was prelude to something more.

"I don't think I've been acting strangely," she said.

He raised his hand. "Please. Let's be truthful with each other." He cleared his throat. "Bob Kazmir. You never stopped working on the case. Did you?"

She opened her mouth again, to lie, to say of course I stopped, what on earth are you talking about.

But she couldn't do it.

"Even yesterday, after you promised you would stop, after you gave me your word, you went on Factiva and looked up a company called..." he looked down at a legal pad, "Next Century Course Development."

"Yes," she said, because what else could she say? "I'm sorry."

"And what's Next Century? Some kind of golf course company, as far as I can tell, and the only reason I can think you might be interested in a golf course company is that it's relevant to the Kazmir case, though for the life of me I can't figure out how."

His gaze meant business. He was through being nice. "You want to tell me how?"

She shook her head. "No."

"That's an improvement. At least you're not lying anymore."

She looked down at her lap, at her hands folded on her purse, like a schoolgirl in the principal's office.

It was all falling apart.

"It just didn't add up," he said. "You're very smart, Esperanza. Very intuitive. But you completely botched the Kazmir case. How was that possible? I kept wondering that, all last night—well, I was also wondering about United Apparel, I have to admit, that whole thing with Chris Holloway—and I couldn't sleep. So I came in, poked around. And not only do I find you're right about United Apparel, I find the Factiva search, and I realize that not only did you lie to me yesterday, you've been lying all along. And that got me wondering why."

He paused, perhaps giving her a chance to tell him.

She didn't.

He continued. "Why was working on the Kazmir case important enough to risk your job? It was just a gambling investigation. And you were treating it like life and death. It didn't make sense."

He looked her in the eye.

"Unless that golfer who killed Kazmir was telling the truth about being framed, and then I thought maybe the golfer's lawyer was right, that you were there that night, and I tried to put all that together in my mind, who might have been where when, and you know what it reminded me of?"

"I have no idea."

"The grassy knoll."

Espy frowned. "The Kennedy assassination?"

"Exactly. Oswald saying he was framed. People thinking there were other shooters on a grassy knoll, near the motorcade. And then Oswald was killed. Because he could identify the real killers. Which, if David Abraham is right, was going to happen to Thurman too."

"There's no conspiracy here," Espy said. "If that's what you're driving at."

"Then what is happening? Why were you using Factiva yesterday?"

"Like you said...I botched the case. I wanted to make it right."

He tapped a finger against his cheek, as if considering whether or not to believe her. "So what does Bob Kazmir have to do with Next Century Course Development?"

Espy floundered for a second. Then she remembered what Matt had told her in the car. "He did some consulting for them. I'm not sure exactly what."

He arched an eyebrow at her.

"Word of honor." She raised her right hand. "Now, can I have my computer please?"

He took a minute to respond, then passed it to her.

"So where are you going?" he asked.

"Home. To do some work."

"So I'll see you Monday?"

"Absolutely," she lied. "I'll see you Monday."

❖ ❖ ❖ ❖ ❖

If you're in New Mexico, I'll see you Monday.

That was where she was headed. To Kirtland. To meet Shurig. That was where Shurig told Jake he was going, from what she remembered overhearing of their conversation last night. What she thought she remembered hearing. She'd been pretty out of it. Matt would know for sure.

She walked out and saw him sitting on one of the concrete planters in front of the building. "What took so long?" he asked.

"Long story." She looked around. "Where's the car?"

"In a parking garage. Down the street."

Espy looked at her watch. "You'd better get going if you want to be back in Wilmington by nine."

"I don't want to be back in Wilmington by nine."

Espy got a sudden sinking feeling in her stomach. "What do you mean?"

"I mean I don't plan on going back there."

She tried not to get upset. "What do you plan on doing?"

"Borrowing some of that cash back from you."

"Why?"

"Because." He smiled. "I'm going to Florida."

CINCINNATUS

SHURIG'S phone was ringing.

It had been ringing for a while, he realized.

He gave it another few rings while he collected himself, then picked it up.

"Shurig."

"Michael. It's Jason. I'm here."

Wilmington. Shurig's heart sank, just a little bit. Harper. Poor kid.

"You find the packages?" Shurig asked, sitting up in bed, flicking on a light.

"No."

"What?"

"Only two of them are here. The smaller ones. That's why I'm calling."

The smaller ones—meaning the two least important ones. The cop, and the mother.

Shurig checked the clock. 5:20. 8:20 there.

"That doesn't make sense. Where are the others?"

"I don't know. Do you still want me to do the pick-up?"

Meaning do you want me to kill them.

"You should probably check with the customer." Meaning Seagrave.

"I can't reach the customer. That's why I'm calling you."

Of course he couldn't reach Seagrave. The Colonel was in Washington by now. Finalizing things. He wouldn't be reachable for hours.

"Let me think," Shurig said.

Kill Harper's mother. Kill Thurman's brother. What good would that do? What did they know? What could they prove?

"Let me make a call," Shurig said. "Let's talk again."

"I don't have all day," Jason said. Meaning, obviously, he was in a hurry. Probably exposed, uncomfortably so.

Shurig called Harper.

She didn't answer.

He didn't know what to do. He had no hard data. All he had to go on were his instincts. What were his instincts telling him? Nothing.

His instincts were all screwed up.

Twenty minutes went by.

His phone rang again.

Jason.

"So?"

"Grab the blue package. The other...you can leave." Meaning kill the cop, leave the woman alone. Harper's mother.

He felt good about that.

❖ ❖ ❖ ❖ ❖

Shurig put on coffee, sat down at the table.

Maya and Goran sat across from him, eating sarma.

Shurig stood up, went into the bathroom, splashed cold water on his face. Sat back down at the table.

Sam sat across from him, eating a Jumbo Jack.

"That's it," Shurig said out loud, and stood up again.

He had to get out of here.

He went into the office; no one was there. He went into Westwood, stopped at Cassel's coffee shop. The door was locked. They opened at noon. What kind of coffee shop opened at noon?

He stopped at Stan's, got an orange juice and a jelly donut. He walked onto the UCLA campus. There was a guard on duty at the gate. Shurig showed his badge, and the guy waved him through.

He was hoping he'd spot Leila, though he wasn't sure why he wanted to see her. The only people he saw were joggers.

Then O'Neill stood next to him. Partially chewed face and all.

Shurig began to run.

Detox, he thought. He needed a clinic, a nice long rest. He'd been pushing too hard, for too long. The pills didn't help. He had to lay off. But he couldn't, just yet. Too much to do. He had to stay alert. Focused. Isolate and annihilate. Maintain operational secrecy.

Hard to do when Harper was running loose, flapping her mouth about a military coup. What made her think that? Something she heard? From whom? Sam?

Shurig stopped running.

Something Sam had sent her.

Vwest.

BOOK THREE: CINCINNATUS

Fountain Square
Corner of Fifth and Vine Streets
Cincinnati, OH
Saturday, September 22, 8:01 A.M.

FLORIDA.

He'd decided while he was waiting for Espy.

She was right: a military coup? He couldn't just sit around watching TV.

Jake would be mad—not just about the car, about the chances he'd taken, and the even bigger ones he was about to take. You want to get caught? You want to spend the rest of your life in prison?

Well no, but...

He didn't want to spend the rest of his life in an RV park either.

"Why Florida?" Espy asked. Before he could answer, she said, "Next Century."

"That's right."

"Look," Espy said. "Don't take this the wrong way. But this is an investigation. A very dangerous investigation. And you're not an investigator."

"Right. I'm a golfer. And we need to figure out how they fixed these tournaments. And that's what I want to do. Figure it out."

"But you're wanted for murder. The cops are after you."

"Yeah, well, somebody's after you too."

"That's different."

"I've been thinking about this. We already have most of the pieces. We know the Cincinnati are tied to Kazmir, we know Kazmir's tied to Next Century, we know Next Century installed these systems all over the country. On tournament golf courses. All we have to do is find proof there's something not quite right about them, and then..."

"Find proof?" Espy said, that sharp edge he didn't like creeping into her voice. "You think these people at Next Century are just going to hand that over to you?"

"They might."

"And why would they do that?"

"Because I speak the language. I've been around these people all my life. Plus..." he grinned at her..."I have a plan."

She folded her arms across her chest. "Go on."

"I'll tell you on the way," he said. He started walking toward the car. The sidewalk and streets had begun getting busier, and he figured they shouldn't be standing in such an open place.

"I can't go to Florida," Espy said, hurrying to catch up with him. "I'm going to New Mexico."

"Shurig's handling that, isn't he?"

"Altair is key. Altair is—"

"Why your father got killed. I get it. But that's military. They're not going to talk to you."

"Altair is a civilian company."

"Doing government work."

He could see her thinking, considering his point.

They stood by the car, Matt unlocking the driver's door. "Come with me," he said. "We'll go right to Next Century, find out how they're doing it, you'll go to the cops, show them the gambling evidence you got on your computer, they'll arrest Seagrave, and—"

"How are you going to get there? Drive your brother's car?"

"If he'll let me. I'll have to ask him."

Espy rolled her eyes. "I'd like to hear that conversation."

Matt pulled out the cell phone Jake had given him.

"Better use mine," Espy said. "The signal's encrypted. No one can listen in."

She pulled the phone out of her purse and cursed. "The battery's dead. And the charger's at my apartment."

"We can buy another charger," Matt said. "Hell, we can buy another phone."

Espy plopped the phone back in her purse. "I don't like the idea of talking on an open line."

"I'll make it quick," Matt said.

Jake didn't pick up.

He tried again. And again five, ten, and twenty minutes later.

The phone just rang and rang.

South La Verne Ave.
East Los Angeles, CA
Saturday, September 22, 9:45 A.M.

IT was a neat little house, on a street full of little houses, some neat, some not-so neat. A little patch of green lawn out front, concrete on either side, a four-foot wide path separating one house from the next. There was a flagpole in the ground to the right of the door. The Stars and Stripes hung from it, at half mast.

There were flowers woven into the metal handrail next to the front steps.

Shurig stood at the front door, took a deep breath, and rang the bell.

The door opened. A little girl looked up at him.

"Hello," she said.

Shurig smiled. "Hello." He pulled out his badge. "My name is Michael Shurig. I'm with the FBI. Is your mom or dad home?"

The girl said, "No."

"You're Olivia, aren't you?" Shurig asked.

She smiled then, shyly. "How'd you know that?"

"I knew your grandfather. He showed me pictures of you."

"Oh," she said. "He was with the FBI too. But the terror people killed him."

"Yes." Shurig said. "They did."

"But now they're dead too."

"They are," Shurig said, which was true. Or would be true in a few days.

"Can I come in for a minute, Olivia?" he said, kneeling down so they were at eye level. "I need to check out a few things in your house."

She shook her head. "My momma said to never let strangers in the house. That's what my grandpa said too."

"And that's very smart. But I'm not a stranger. I'm with the FBI. Just like your grandpa was."

She leaned against the doorframe, a sour look on her face.

Shurig could see into the house: an entryway, brass hooks hanging on a wall, baseball hats and coats hanging from them. Beyond that, he saw a mission-style wooden table, matching wooden chairs, the dining room. Beyond that, the kitchen counter, a sink, wooden cabinets.

He didn't see the computer. But he knew it was in there somewhere.

Shernandez@vwest.com. That e-mail address, he'd been informed, was a sub-account, one of six appended to the main account of the Vwest DSL subscriber, a man named Hernan Villarosa, who lived in this very house.

It had taken Shurig all of one phone call and a minute and a half to get that information out of the Vwest tech people.

You had to love the Patriot Act.

"This is very important," Shurig said. "It has to do with catching the terror people. You want me to catch them, don't you?"

"I thought you said they were dead."

"Well." He forced a smile. "Most of them are. There are still a few left though, and I want to catch them. So can I please come in?"

Instead of opening the door, she took a step back, which was when Shurig realized he had raised his voice. That he'd been close to yelling at her.

"I'm sorry," he said, although really, he wasn't. He was angry. Impatient. He wanted that computer, which Sam had used and might contain more information like he'd found on the Tomasevics' machine, more clues about Sam's knowledge of the operation.

His job was clear.

He was suddenly very aware of the gun in his shoulder holster.

"Excuse me."

He looked up and saw a woman standing behind the little girl.

A very short, stout woman who looked very familiar. "Can I help you with something?" she asked, in a thick Spanish accent.

"I hope so. You're Sam's mother, aren't you?"

She narrowed her eyes. "Yes."

"My name is Shurig." He flashed his badge. "Agent Michael Shurig."

She broke into a big smile.

"Ah. Michael Shurig. *Si, si*. Of course." She opened the door. "Come in."

She led him into the kitchen and made a pot of coffee. She put a plate of sticky buns—fresh from the oven—on the table in front of him. She sent Olivia into the next room to get a photo album and spent a tearful twenty minutes showing him pictures of Sam as a young boy.

She told him all the nice things Sam had said about him.

Finally, she showed him Hernan Villarosa's computer, the family computer, and left him alone.

He made little progress. He had a hard time concentrating.

Maya kept interrupting him.

"You are finding things?" she asked.

After ten minutes, he gave up, asked if he could borrow the machine for a day or two, have some of his tech people look at it.

"For my son's friend?" She smiled. "*Si*. Of course."

Shurig brought the computer to the car, set it down on the seat, and put his head on the steering wheel.

When he raised his head, Sam was in the seat next to him.

Shurig started the car, and revised this morning's plan.

He'd been on his way to his tech people (his tech person, actually), just like he'd told Sam's mom.

Now though, There was another stop he needed to make first.

❖ ❖ ❖ ❖ ❖

He was leaning against the wall of the parking garage when Doctor Haileigh pulled in. She didn't see him till she got out of the car, and started for the elevators.

"Agent Shurig?"

"Yeah. Hi."

"How's the shoulder?"

"It's fine." He rubbed it a little. "It's just...thing is, I'm having trouble sleeping."

"That doesn't surprise me."

"I was hoping maybe you could prescribe something."

She knit her brow. "I can't do that."

They reached the elevators. Haileigh pressed the button.

"I really need something to help me," he said. He hated the pathetic tone of his voice.

"I understand," she said. "First your partner getting killed, then Sam. It must be awful."

"Yeah," he said. "It is."

The words 'I killed him' were somewhere between his brain and his mouth. Struggling to get out. Even though he hadn't even known it was going to happen, even though Seagrave hadn't given him a clue that they were even contemplating something like that...

It was his fault.

His responsibility.

"The bureau must have support services," Haileigh said. "Someone you can talk to."

"I'm talking to you."

"I can't help. I can refer you—"

"Please," Shurig said. "I don't think I've had more than four hours sleep these last couple nights. Total."

She looked at him and sighed. "You FBI guys. You think you're bulletproof."

"I used to," Shurig said. "Not anymore."

❖ ❖ ❖ ❖ ❖

She gave him six pills—green ones. Take one at bedtime. One only. It'll knock you for a loop. Do not mix with alcohol or any other drugs. Shurig thanked her profusely, said he'd give her a call when he got back into town.

"Where you headed?" she asked.

"A tropical island paradise," he said.

She laughed. "Yeah. Right."

"Just a work thing," he said. "No place special."

When he got in his car, he sat for a minute, wondering whether or not he could afford to take one now. Half of one, maybe. A quarter. When he got home. Except home was only fifteen minutes away. He could be in bed, asleep, get a few hours before he had to leave.

He broke the pill in half, then in half again. Swallowed it.

His phone rang.

"I just got off the phone with Jason," Seagrave said. He updated Shurig on the situation. "So where are they? Harper and the golfer?"

"I don't know. She's not answering her phone."

"Where are you?"

On my way home, he was about to say. To get some rest. Then he saw the computer sitting on the passenger seat next to him. He'd completely forgotten about it.

"Michael? Are you there?"

"Yes, sir."

Focus, Shurig told himself. Focus.

He reached into his pocket for one of the blue pills.

They weren't there. He'd left them back at the office.

"I'm just...a little tired," he said. "A little stressed."

"I understand. We all are."

Shurig told the Colonel about the computer he'd confiscated from Hernandez's mother and what he planned to do with it.

"Good," Seagrave said. "Carter's in with Van Croft now. As soon as they finish, we're on our way to the island. You understand what I'm saying?"

"I do." Seagrave on his way to the island, Cashier was a 'go.'

There was no turning back.

"We need to find those packages, Michael. You need to find them."

"Yes sir. I will."

He hung up. Focus, he told himself. Isolate and annihilate. Maintain operational secrecy.

He yawned. Once, and then again.

He stopped at a drive-through and picked up a large coffee.

❖ ❖ ❖ ❖ ❖

Twenty minutes later, he pulled into the Star Maker Motel near Burbank. It was a two-story concrete dive that hadn't been renovated in a long time.

He took the outside stairs to room twenty-one. Banged on the door and saw rust from the metal railing had rubbed off on his hands. He brushed it away.

No answer.

He banged on the door again. Louder.

"Coming!"

He heard movement inside the room.

"Who is it?"

"Open up, Manny," he said. "I got a present for you."

Silence.

"This is not the best time."

The door cracked. Njomo peered through.

"Could you give me half an hour?" he asked.

"No."

"Fifteen minutes."

"Now." Shurig held up Hernandez's computer. "Colonel's orders."

Njomo sighed and opened the door.

He was wearing boxers and nothing else.

Shurig pushed his way inside.

The Star Maker was as run-down inside as out. A weatherbeaten orange couch and mismatched red fabric chairs, a rickety-looking coffee table. A bathroom to Shurig's left; a half-open door to his right. The bedroom, he presumed.

Shurig set the computer on the desk. He explained what he wanted Njomo to do with it.

Njomo said, "I don't have the time or equipment for an exhaustive search. Not here anyway."

"Do the best you can," Shurig said.

"Come back in an hour or so, I should—"

The toilet flushed. Then the sound of running water.

The bathroom door opened.

A girl walked out. Asian girl. She looked about thirteen.

"Not the best time," Njomo said. "As you can see." He reached into his pocket, pulled out a wad of bills. "Mai!" he yelled.

A second girl walked out of the bedroom. Identical to the first. They both looked at Shurig and smiled tentatively.

"Maybe another time," Njomo told them. "Here. For your trouble."

He gave the girls a few bills.

Shurig smirked, watched them leave. Then he turned to Njomo. "Sorry to break up the party," he said. "Now get busy."

❖ ❖ ❖ ❖ ❖

Shurig laid down on the bed and closed his eyes, fell almost instantly to sleep. Then he heard his name.

He opened his eyes. Njomo was standing in the doorway, eyes wide with excitement. "Come see," he said. "We've hit the jackpot, my friend."

Shurig followed Njomo to the computer. There was a picture on the monitor. A little girl.

"Olivia," Shurig said. "Hernandez's granddaughter."

"That would explain why he used her."

Shurig rubbed his eyes. "I'm not following."

"I'll show you." Njomo closed the picture. There was a window behind it, an open folder, with a list of files that ran off the screen. Image files, judging from the extension at the end of each file name.

"You see?" Njomo said, pointing. "There are dozens of them."

"Pictures, you mean," Shurig said.

"Oh, they're more than pictures. Have you ever heard of steganography?"

Greyhound Bus Terminal
Gilbert Avenue
Cincinnati, OH
Saturday, September 22, 2:12 P.M.

THEY left the car in a parking garage downtown. Better safe than sorry, Matt said. Especially since Jake still wasn't picking up his phone. She got the sense Matt was glad to get rid of it, that he was feeling guilty.

She was feeling something else.

Not only couldn't they reach Jake, she couldn't reach her mom, either. She left messages, she had the cell company check the number, she called Mrs. Claypool and Mrs. Teresi and every one of her mother's friends she could think of and asked casually if they'd heard from her and the answer was the same: no.

Espy was worried.

She sat down on a blue plastic chair in the bus terminal and considered her options. She was still considering them when Matt came back from the ticket window and sat down next to her.

"There's a bus that goes through to Fort Lauderdale leaving in an hour."

She shook her head in disgust. "We can't afford that kind of time."

But they'd been through every option. They couldn't get her car because Seagrave's cronies were probably watching it and even if they could get to it, they wouldn't get far before they were spotted.

They couldn't rent a car because her credit card could easily be traced and probably was being monitored. Matt had no identification at all. Jake could trace the progress of his own car through the state highway system. They even talked about chartering a small plane but that, too, would require showing identification. As a last resort, here they sat at the bus terminal, where at least they would feel safe.

Espy, however, agonized about the time it would take to get to Florida on a bus. "This just won't work," she said.

"I guess we could hitchhike," Matt said with a smile.

Espy bit her lip, started to say something but stopped.

"What are you thinking?" Matt asked.

"Maybe we ought to go back," she said.

"You think something's wrong?"

"I know something's wrong. The only question is what."

"So what do we do? Call Shurig?"

She thought about it for a moment and then nodded. She held out her hand. "Let me borrow your phone."

❖ ❖ ❖ ❖ ❖

This had to be some kind of joke.

He'd taken the green pill, drunk half a bottle of wine, eaten himself into a stupor, and still...

He couldn't sleep.

He laid on the couch, staring up at the ceiling. Listening to the silence and then suddenly listening to his phone ring. He didn't recognize the number.

"It's Harper."

He sat up straight. "Where have you been?"

She told him.

"Okay. Where are you calling from now?"

Bus station. The golfer's phone.

He got up and wrote down the number while she kept talking.

She was worried about the packages; couldn't reach either of them. She sounded panicked. He needed her to calm down. He pictured her and the golfer, sitting in the bus station, while she cried hysterically. People would notice. The cops might notice. The last thing they needed was the golfer back in custody, shooting his mouth off. The colonel had made that clear.

"Don't worry," Shurig said. "They're safe. I talked to Jake this morning."

"You talked to him? Was he mad about the car?"

"Furious," Shurig said. "Hang on a second."

He put her on hold. Called Seagrave.

"Got them," he said. "Both of them. Cincinnati. The bus station. There's another number we need to watch, by the way."

Seagrave wrote it down. "I'll take care of it," he said.

"What do we do about Harper?"

"What are her plans?"

"She's not sure," Shurig said. "She wants my opinion."

Seagrave thought a moment. "Here's what you tell her," he said.

"And the golfer?"

"The golfer too, yes."

❖ ❖ ❖ ❖ ❖

They finished talking just as Carter and Van Croft came out of the latter's office, laughing and shaking hands. They sobered up when they saw Seagrave.

He shook hands with Van Croft, thanked him for his support, said they couldn't have done it without him.

"You're welcome," Van Croft said. He was a big man, had played linebacker at Yale. He towered over Seagrave and made sure to stand in a way to remind the Colonel of it every time they were together.

At least it seemed that way to Seagrave.

"I'm looking forward to Monday," Van Croft went on.

"We all are," Seagrave said.

"You'll call me as soon as you go live?"

He was looking at Seagrave, but he was talking, really, to Carter. Not so much asking a question as issuing a reminder. Call me the instant it happens.

Seagrave couldn't blame the man for being anxious. Nor would he blame Carter for having the phone by his side in the lab, while they were watching the countdown. Waiting for Cashier to go live.

If things went according to plan, they would be two of the most powerful men in the American intelligence community.

Unfortunately for them, the plans had changed.

Carter's car was waiting for them outside. On the way to the airport, Seagrave pulled out the card he'd written the golfer's phone number on.

He handed the card to Carter. "I need a favor, Gene."

Carter took the card. "You want a location trace?"

"Yes. Hourly reports."

"Not a problem." He tucked the card inside his coat pocket.

"And intermittent service disruption. Starting now."

Carter frowned. "That's a little bit harder. A lot of man-hours, a lot of resources, but it's possible. What's this about?"

"Let's just say it's relevant," Seagrave said. "I wouldn't ask if it weren't."

Greyhound Bus 326
Four Miles South of Knoxville, TN
Sunday, September 23, 12:45 A.M.

MISTAKE, Matt thought.

They should have risked taking the car.

In the seats in front of them, a baby was getting its diaper changed—for the third time in the past couple hours.

"What a nightmare," he mumbled, leaning back, trying to get away from the stench and the wailing in front of him.

"Your idea," Espy said.

Rather than argue about it, Matt tried calling Jake again.

No service.

He saw a half dozen people talking on their cells. He'd had a signal five minutes ago. Tried calling Jake. It rang once and went to a dial tone.

Weird.

Espy was working on her computer, which was pretty much all she'd done since they boarded.

"Finding anything?" he asked.

"A couple news articles, an old press release." She turned the screen so he could see it.

For Immediate Release:

NGA Innovision Directorate Awards Contract

Matt leaned closer and read the first paragraph of the text.

Vice-Admiral Tomas Migdalski, Director of the National Geospatial-Intelligence Agency (NGA), announced today that the software designer firm Altair Technologies has been awarded a $25 million contract to develop new, multi-platform solutions for the agency's image-acquisition systems. According to Migdalski, the contract, awarded through NGA's Innovision Directorate, represents the agency's continuing commitment to re-taskable, user-configurable systems.

Matt said, "I have no idea what that means."

Espy leaned back and rubbed her eyes. "I don't really get it either."

Not that it mattered, he thought.

She was going to Florida. Not New Mexico.

The decision had been Shurig's. Matt had overheard part of the conversation. Shurig said it made more sense to try to get information out of a private company than the United States Air Force. Go to Next Century, he said. Espy had very reluctantly agreed, though she was still focused on investigating Altair at Kirtland.

She yawned again. She looked wiped. She had pinned up her dark hair with a clip and still looked pale from being sick last night.

"You ought to take a break," Matt said.

She took a deep breath, rubbed her eyes. After working for a few minutes she turned to Matt, who had been watching her. She pulled a book from her bag.

"Why don't you do something constructive with your time?" She handed the book to him.

He tried to hand it back to her. "This is a long book. I don't read long books."

"Then look at the pictures," she said, already focused on her computer.

Matt looked at the cover again.

Crosley: Two Brothers and a Business Empire that Transformed the Nation.

He settled back in his seat.

❖ ❖ ❖ ❖ ❖

Ten minutes later, he was snoring. The book lay on the seat between them.

Okay. So the guy was not a reader.

As she looked at her computer screen, the alert box popped up again: Disk mirroring cannot connect to server

Every fifteen minutes it was doing that, like clockwork. Must have been something the tech guy set up. Disk mirroring? Maybe some kind of backup function. Just as well it couldn't connect—she didn't want everyone in the department to see what was on her computer.

She was also having trouble connecting. The 3G card worked, but not well. Maybe because of the crack in the plastic, a bad connection, or something else, but the signal was very spotty. Made the research she was doing difficult, made getting onto cloudbytes almost impossible.

Right now she was following up on that press announcement she'd found earlier, looking up information on the NGA. The National Geospatial-Intelligence Agency; formerly NIMA, the National Imagery and Mapping Agency. All these government acronyms—impossible to keep them all straight.

Thankfully, she didn't have to. She was trying to figure out what NGA's Innovision Directorate did. According to the agency website, their job seemed to focus on long-term planning. Positioning the agency for the future. Okay, she got that. Innovision. Intelligence-gathering. Presumably by using Altair's software. But how did all of this relate to the coup?

Maybe Shurig could help. He was going to visit Altair on Monday, he told her. Taking some time off to do it. Espy asked about O'Neill: any word? There wasn't, which she found strange, given how much of a pain in the ass the lieutenant had been. And now for him to just disappear...

"Like the earth swallowed him up?" Shurig had said, to which she had replied 'exactly,' at which point he, for some reason, laughed.

She clicked around the NGA site, noted a few names, a few other projects before the letters on the screen started to blur. The battery was going. Though there was probably an outlet somewhere on the bus, she wasn't going to crawl around in the dark looking for it. Running the power cord across the aisle, or in between seats. Morning would be plenty soon enough. They still had a long, uncomfortable way to go before Fort Lauderdale.

Which was a mistake. She knew it in her head, felt it in her heart. The answers were at Kirtland. At Altair. They'd killed her father to stop him from going there. Even though she still didn't know why.

Everything I have, you have.

I don't think so, Dad, she thought.

Espy woke up twice in the night. Both times Matt was snoring on her shoulder. She pushed him off; he rolled back. Second time she saw the phone, halfway out of his pants pocket.

She reached across and grabbed it.

Signal.

She dialed her mother's cellphone. It rang. Twice.

The line went dead.

No signal.

She gave up and went to sleep.

CINCINNATUS

A woman came out of the elevator, talking on the phone.

"...absolutely not. You can bet no one else is meeting their price either. You hold firm."

She had long blond hair, pulled back from her face, hanging down the back of her navy blue pantsuit that fit snug across her chest, across her butt. Her heels added a good couple inches to her height, which made her close to six feet tall. Espy felt like a midget.

"No," the woman said. "Wait. Call back this afternoon. Late this afternoon. Let them sweat a little."

She looked up and saw Espy and Matt, standing in front of her.

"Hang on, Deb." She punched a button on the cell. "Can I help you?"

"I hope you can," Matt said, smiling.

Espy hoped so too. They arrived in Fort Lauderdale late that morning, immediately found a motel—the Casablanca—a half-mile from the Next Century office. Though they both could have used a few hours of sleep, they wasted no time in executing their plan.

It was Matt's plan. Espy conceded that slapping her badge on somebody's desk and demanding answers stood a good chance of getting them absolutely nothing.

They went shopping. For clothes (the blue blazer, pink shirt, khakis, and shoes she now wore), scissors (with which she salvaged the mess Jake had made of Matt's hair), sunglasses (to disguise, as much as possible, his face), and hair gel (to slick back those parts of the hair she couldn't salvage).

Now here they were. Matt looked every inch the part he was supposed to play.

"Are you with Next Century Course Development?" Matt asked.

"Kim Wiest Grosser," she said, thrusting out her hand. "Vice-president of marketing."

Matt shook her hand. "My name is Martin Babcock, and I'm an agronomist with Gambal-Mahoney."

The woman's reaction was almost comical.

"Gambal-Mahoney," she said, raising an eyebrow, taking a step back.

"You've heard of us?" Matt said.

The woman put her phone in her purse and closed it. Forgetting, apparently, about 'Deb.' "Of course," she said. "Everyone knows Gambal-Mahoney."

Matt exchanged an I-told-you-so glance with Espy. Gambal-Mahoney had been his idea: "They're the A-league in course design these days," he had told her. "Right up there with Nicklaus Course Design."

Judging from the woman's reaction, he was right. The reaction also told Espy that however Next Century's systems were fixing golf tournaments, Kim Wiest Grosser had nothing to do with it. No one could fake the gleam in her eye and the unnaturally wide smile on her face. Her title may have been marketing, but she was in sales, and she smelled a potential killing.

Selling individual courses a Next Century system was one thing; getting a company that designed courses all over the world to consider them was something else entirely.

"We've been hearing good things about your company," Matt said. "Do you have some time to talk to us?"

"By all means," the woman said, smiling. Brushing her hair back from her face. "We've made improvements to the technology that I'd love to tell you about."

Espy said, "I'm Carli Hernandez. I'm with Gambal-Mahoney as well."

"Wonderful," Grosser said, without taking her eyes off Matt. "Let's go inside, shall we?"

❖ ❖ ❖ ❖ ❖

The offices were tiny. Two desks parked across from each other, a row of filing cabinets in between. Framed photos of golf courses—landscapes, not golfers, not tournament shots—served as decoration.

Grosser sat behind the desk on the left; Matt and Espy (as Martin and Carli) took chairs in front of her. She pulled a brochure from a desk drawer.

"This highlights some of the differences between our systems and others on the market," Grosser said, handing the brochure to Matt. "What it doesn't talk about, are some of our latest developments."

Matt glanced at the brochure and passed it to Espy.

There was nothing helpful in it—testimonials, a list of courses where the system is used, general info about the company. Nothing about how the system could help you cheat your friends or win millions on a long shot.

Grosser and Matt talked about Next Century's latest 'technological innovations,' about the importance of a good agronomist, about the PGA, the courses, the tournaments.

"So what do you do at Gambal-Mahoney, Mr. Babcock?" Grosser asked.

"I'm fairly new, to be honest," Matt said. "Floating between departments. Mostly out of the Shanghai office."

Grosser knit her brow. "I didn't know Gambal-Mahoney had an office in Shanghai."

"It's more of an outpost right now. But we're growing."

"I can imagine." She was practically licking her lips.

Espy leaned forward. "What we need to get from you," she said, "is a close-up look at one of your systems."

Grosser nodded. "We can arrange a course visit."

"Actually, I was thinking along the lines of a floor model. That sort of thing."

"Floor model?"

"Prototype," Matt suggested. "I'd like to get a feel for the hardware."

Grosser tossed back her hair. "I'm sorry. We don't have one here."

Espy asked if they could tour the factory, a question Grosser found humorous. She told them that manufacturing was outsourced to a contractor in Mexico.

Which spoiled their hopes of seeing a system first hand. Matt and Espy looked at each other, clearly disappointed.

"I could give you a quick look at the plans, if you'd like," Grosser said, sensing something was wrong. "I have them right here—wouldn't be a problem to get them out. I'll get them out."

She was at the filing cabinet before either of them could say a word.

The plans looked like architectural drawings. Espy couldn't figure out what they were supposed to represent, the writing far too small to read.

Matt leaned over them intently.

A couple minutes passed. Grosser cleared her throat.

"I, um," she began, "I can't really let you study them that closely, Mr. Babcock. Some of that information is proprietary, and—"

"Radiant sensor array," Matt said, pointing. "What's that?"

Grosser leaned over him and took a look. "Well," she said, smiling. "I imagine there's some kind of radiant heat component to the array.

Matt said, "Who might know for sure?"

Grosser obviously felt the tables turning, her big sale slipping away. "You know, I really don't feel comfortable—"

"I bet the manufacturer would know. Whoever makes the part. Would that information be in there?" Espy asked, gesturing toward the filing cabinet.

Grosser glanced quickly in that direction, then turned back to Espy. "I'm sorry, Ms. Hernandez, but I don't—"

Espy pulled out her DOJ badge.

"Harper," she said. "My name is Harper."

She gave Grosser a song and dance about Next Century's corporate parent, Enovation, being in deep trouble with the DOJ. Suspected money laundering. Using the time-honored method of putting invoices on the books for services and/or goods never received.

"We had a tip," she said. "About this 'radiant sensor array.' We're not really sure it exists."

Grosser couldn't open the file cabinet fast enough. She pulled out a folder and flipped through the paperwork, her fingers shaking.

"I think maybe you're right, Ms. Harper," she said. "I have a manufacturer, country of origin, but no mailing address. No contact information either."

Espy, not surprised, nodded. "Give me what you've got."

"Aiken-Scuffs," Grosser said. "Bahamas."

A little bell rang in Espy's head.

Aiken-Scuffs. Bahamas.

"Bob Kazmir," she said.

Grosser's eyes widened. "You know Bob Kazmir?"

"I know he did some work for you," Espy said. "He had a house in the Bahamas, didn't he?"

Grosser shook her head. "Not him. Dina. His wife. Dina Petropolis. It was her family's house. Been her family's house for twenty years."

Dina.

The conversation from the night of the banquet rushed back to her.

Poor Dina. She's going to be lost without him.

Poor Bob. Heckuva guy. Heckuva golfer. We played down on the island every holiday season.

"Where exactly in the Bahamas was this house?" Espy asked.

"An island called Cat Cay. Spelled like 'kay,' pronounced like 'key.' The entire island is a private club."

"Never heard of it," Matt said.

Espy had.

In the parking lot, Espy told Matt about the picture she'd seen in the article on Crane, sport-fishing with Crandall, and Holwadel, and Seagrave, off the coast of Cat Cay.

"Which is in the Bahamas," Matt said.

"And it's also where Aiken-Scuffs is based."

"The Bahamas is a pretty big place."

Espy admitted that was true. But it didn't feel like a coincidence to her.

❖ ❖ ❖ ❖ ❖

Matt's phone rang. He looked at the number. Didn't recognize it. He handed her the phone. She looked at the display and punched the answer button.

"Agent Shurig," she said. "I thought we'd lost you."

"Not a chance," he said. "I'm right here."

"What do you mean right here?"

A horn honked.

A car pulled into the parking lot in front of her.

Shurig was in it.

Casablanca Motel
Marin Road
Fort Lauderdale, FL
Monday, September 24, 11:03 A.M.

HARPER had come very close to hugging Shurig.

Which seemed to annoy the golfer.

Interesting.

The three of them got in his car. Shurig made sure Harper sat in front. She told him what they'd just found out: the radiant sensor array. The Colonel would want to hear about that, right away. He'd also want to hear about this Grosser woman. It seemed to Shurig like they had a loose end now. Seagrave would want that taken care of. Shurig was tempted to handle it himself, post-haste—drop Harper and the golfer at their motel, make some excuse about checking in with local bureau personnel, and then tying up that loose end.

But Grosser worked at Next Century and might have some connection to the Colonel. Jason was here now; he could handle Grosser, if Seagrave thought it necessary. Today, even, once he finished his other work.

Shurig glanced in the rear view mirror then and caught the golfer's eye. He didn't look happy.

Just wait, Shurig thought. You have no idea what true unhappiness is.

"So tell me again how you found us?" the golfer asked.

"Your phone."

"This piece of crap?" He held it up. "I haven't been able to get it to work for the last two days."

"It's been putting out a signal," Shurig said. "I've been tracking you all the way from Ohio."

"How does that work?" the golfer asked.

Shurig shrugged. "Something to do with cell sites and your transponder ID."

"Sounds like the stuff NGA does," Harper said.

Shurig resisted the urge to slam on the brakes.

Instead, he asked, "What do you know about NGA?"

"Not much," she said. "Except they gave twenty-five million dollars to Altair Technologies a couple years back."

Now Shurig had to resist the urge to call Seagrave and put them all on speaker. Harper had the whole thing staring her in the face.

Cashier couldn't come a moment too soon.

"Maybe it's been you tracking us that's messing up my phone," Thurman said.

Shurig said, "I doubt it."

"Have you heard from my mother and Jake?" Harper asked.

"The packages?" Shurig shook his head. "No."

The golfer leaned forward in his seat. "What do you mean, packages?"

"Sorry." Shurig forced a smile. "That's bureau speak. Terminology we use for the bodies we're guarding."

"But you haven't heard from them?" Harper said again.

"Not exactly. I did get a message from Jason last night. The guy I sent to pick them up. He says everybody's fine. Not to worry."

Harper, though, was very worried. He could see it in her eyes.

"So why are you here?" Thurman asked. "I thought you were going to Kirtland."

"Something came up," Shurig said. "Turned up, actually." He reached into his pocket for the envelope.

Sam was suddenly sitting there in the front seat between Shurig and Harper.

"Take it," Shurig snapped, thrusting the envelope at Harper. He stared straight ahead, focused on the road, as she ripped it open.

BOOK THREE: CINCINNATUS

❖ ❖ ❖ ❖ ❖

At the motel room, Shurig sat on a desk chair spun around backward. Thurman leaned in the doorway between bath and bedroom. Harper stood next to the coffee table, reading the fine print, though all the information she needed was in the box at the top of the page. Shurig was getting impatient, but he didn't want to force things. Harper was smart; she didn't need someone to point out the obvious.

Thurman said, "No question what we ought to do."

Harper nodded. "None."

She handed the paper back to Shurig. He didn't need to look at it. It read:

Location: Cat Cay

Property: Lot 12B, the house (inclusive of all land, relevant outbuildings, and water facilities) more commonly known as Twin Beaches

Owner: Aiken-Scuffs LTD

Former Trustee: Stuart Parkes Crane

Current Trustee (as of 11/24/90): Jedediah Seagrave

It was a copy of a deed from the Bahamian Documents Information System. Shurig told her he found it while looking up information on Seagrave. In truth, the Colonel had provided it as a way to move things—and people—along. As it turned out, though, it was more like icing on the cake.

"Cat Cay." Harper shook her head. "This can't be a coincidence."

Shurig said, "I don't think so either."

"So how do we get there?" Thurman asked.

"The question is *can* we get there," Harper said. "It's a private island. And it's in the Bahamas. You need a passport."

"You have your DOJ badge?" Shurig asked.

"Of course," Harper said.

"We ought to be able to make that work. Temporary investigator's permit, something like that."

She frowned. "Okay."

"What about me?" Thurman said.

Shurig kept his mouth closed.

He would leave it to Harper to point out the obvious.

❖ ❖ ❖ ❖ ❖

Be reasonable, Matt.

Be serious, Matt.

Don't be stupid, Matt.

Espy had said the same thing so many times her voice was probably still bouncing around the room. Shurig hadn't said anything. Guy creeped him out—acted like he wasn't there half the time. Off in his own little world. She didn't seem to notice. Worse yet, she was defending him.

"He looks like the walking dead," Matt told her after Shurig left the room.

I'll be in the car, Shurig had said. We'll go to one of the marinas, rent a boat. Won't be hard. I checked it out.

Seemed to Matt he could have found a way to sneak them all on the island while he was checking things out.

"Cut him some slack," Espy said. "He's probably seriously jet-lagged. On top of everything else."

"On top of what else?"

"He was there," Espy said. "Standing next to my father when he was killed."

"I still don't see why he can make it work for you but not for me."

"Because I'm an employee of the U.S. government."

He felt her hand on his shoulder.

"It's a three-hour cruise," she said. "The weather's perfect. We'll be back by the time it gets dark."

"Unless something happens."

She patted him again and looked at him with a tenderness he hadn't seen before. "Thanks for worrying about me," she said. "Really. Thanks."

"Well, I *am* worried. I don't want you to get hurt."

"You heard what Shurig said—Seagrave's in Washington. Crane and Crandall are campaigning. We're going to check in with the local authorities, walk around the island, look at the golf course, look at this Twin Beaches place, ask some questions, come back. No big deal."

"I don't like it."

"Don't worry," she said. "Shurig'll be there."

❖ ❖ ❖ ❖ ❖

After she left, Matt sprawled on the bed and turned on the TV. The Weather Channel. A woman giving the local forecast. Seems it was going to be sunny in south Florida. Go figure.

The image switched. A guy sitting at a news desk.

"For the second straight day, a series of freak sandstorms has paralyzed traffic to and from the historic city of Medina in Saudi Arabia," he said.

A new image: it looked, for a second, like a scene from *The Wizard of Oz*, the black and white part, the twister in the distance, moving toward Dorothy's house.

Except in this movie, there were two twisters.

And they weren't moving.

The news guy said, "For more, Luisa Copeland, in Jeddah."

A woman stood at the side of a highway, wearing a veil. She wasn't Arabic, though; she was Hispanic. She was cute. She looked a little like Espy.

"More of the same, Bill," she said. "And authorities still have no idea—"

Matt shut off the TV.

More of lying in bed by himself, watching TV. He was tired of it. Tired of just being the golfer—the ex-golfer, really. What good was golf when he couldn't play anymore? No more kidding himself, the shoulder was never going to heal well enough to let him compete again. It was the only thing he ever wanted to do...loved doing.

What else could he do? Go to college? And study what? Be a cop, follow in dad's footsteps like Jake had? He wasn't the cop type.

He rubbed his shoulder.

Espy had left him the envelope full of cash. He went out to find something to eat but found a liquor store across the street instead. That seemed more his speed. More what he was good for.

He bought a pint of Jack Daniels. Made a long, winding loop of the motel corridors and finally found an ice machine. It was out of order. Of course.

Circled back down the hall to his room and saw somebody standing at his door.

An Asian guy in a t-shirt, dark blue jogging shorts, and a fanny pack. A camera dangled from a strap around his neck. The guy pulled out a card key.

"I think you got the wrong room," Matt called out.

The guy turned.

"Oh," he said, and looked embarrassed. "This your room?"

The guy had a heavy accent. Sounded Chinese, almost comically so.

"Yeah," Matt said.

"Oh." The guy's card key didn't look anything like Matt's. "Sorry," the guy said and made a little laugh. "Very sorry." He walked away.

Matt shoved the bottle in his pocket and pulled out his own card key, put it in the lock. The light flashed green. He pushed the door open—

And something flashed in the glass. A reflection. Something moving behind him. Fast.

He started to turn around when something punched him in the back, pushing him face first into the door, which flew wide open as he flew into the room. He didn't have time to react before that same something slammed him in the back again, and again, and the door slammed shut behind him, and then he was slammed down to the floor, face first, arms splayed out in front of him, and something grabbed him by the hair, and yanked his head backward, and he made a noise somewhere between a moan and a grunt.

The Asian guy was sitting on his back. He pulled Matt's hair with one hand and with the other yanked at the zipper on his fanny pack.

He pulled out a hypodermic and then bit down on the plastic cover over the needle, started to pull it off with his teeth.

The guy, Matt realized, was trying to kill him.

It was unreal. Like watching a movie, like this was happening to somebody else.

The guy grunted. He was having trouble getting the plastic cover off. Matt couldn't imagine he'd have trouble for long.

The guy was going to kill him. Unless he did something. Do something.

He tried to get to his feet. The guy yanked his hair back even harder. Matt yelled. The guy slammed his face into the floor. Matt tasted carpet and sand, and then something slammed into the back of his neck that hurt more than anything had hurt in his life and he screamed into the carpet, which did no good whatsoever, and pushed off the ground with all his might, and felt the guy on his back lose his balance, just a little. He pushed again, and felt a sharp, stabbing pain in the palm of his right hand.

The needle.

No, a shard of glass. The liquor bottle. Pieces were scattered on the floor next to them.

Matt grabbed the biggest one he could reach and drove it into the guy's leg.

The guy howled in pain; more importantly, he moved. Just for a second, but it was enough, and Matt pushed his weight in the same direction. The guy fell off. Matt stumbled to his feet.

The guy yanked the glass out of his leg. His face showed no sign of pain, no emotion at all.

"Help!" Matt yelled. "Somebody! Help!"

The guy charged him. High kick to the chest. Matt tried to get out of the way but couldn't move fast enough. He sprawled backward. The guy attacked again—throwing fists and feet—and then Matt was kneeling on the floor, gasping for air.

"This is way more trouble than you're worth," the guy said, in perfect, unaccented English. He spun his fanny pack around again, reached inside it, and pulled out a phone.

Matt tried to get to his feet. The guy kicked him in the side of the head.

He saw stars—literally, stars. Blue ones, red ones, orange ones, dancing right in front of him.

"Come on," the guy said, walking to the bed. "Pick up already."

Matt got to his hands and knees. The stars faded; things rolled into focus. The carpet. The guy's feet. Sandals. Leather sandals, with metal straps.

"Hey," the guy said. "Little problem here."

Matt raised his head. The guy had the phone in the crook of his neck and Espy's computer on his lap. He had something metallic in his hand.

He jammed it into the side of the laptop. There was a soft crack and then a puff of smoke.

"Not the computer," the guy said into the phone. "That's taken care of. It's Thurman. I have to move him." He moved the computer and stood up. The leather sandals went with him. So did the metal straps. Mostly. One strap stayed right where it was, about two feet in front of Matt's face, buried in the carpet.

It blurred. It gleamed.

It wasn't one of the metal straps.

It was the hypodermic needle.

Matt reached to grab it and his head spun.

He put his hands down flat and tried to steady himself.

"Because he's all marked up," the guy said. "He put up a fight." He paused. "Yeah, very obvious. Bleeding like a pig." Another pause. "No. That's too far."

Matt reached out and missed again.

"That's a good idea," the guy said. "Hold on."

Focus, Matt told himself, staring at the needle. Concentrate.

Things were still very blurry.

The guy suddenly yanked him back by his hair. Stared at Matt's face.

"Definitely," the guy said. "That'll work. Almost looks like he was hit by a steering wheel. Plus he was carrying a bottle. Stinks of it. I know." He laughed. "It's perfect."

Perfect, Matt thought. Make it look like he'd been in a car accident: another DUI. Who'd believe he wasn't?

Nothing he could do about it.

Nothing but focus. Concentrate.

He grabbed the hypodermic and jabbed it square into the guy's thigh, pressing the plunger down at the same instant.

The guy looked down and his eyes went wide.

"Sonuvabitch," he said, and dropped the phone.

He yanked the needle out of his leg and stumbled toward the bathroom.

Matt lunged and tackled him around the ankles.

The guy lost his balance for a second but didn't fall. He yanked a leg free and kicked Matt in the head. "Let go," he said.

But Matt didn't. The guy kicked him again, struggling to drag himself and to the bathroom.

Then he slowed.

He sank to his knees.

Gasping for breath.

Then pitching forward, face first.

He closed his eyes.

Matt lay there too, still holding onto one ankle. Wondering what had been in that hypodermic. Beginning to realize how much he hurt, all over his body, but mostly his chest. And his face. And his head, where the guy had kicked him. It was still ringing.

No.

That was a phone.

The guy's phone. On the floor behind him.

Matt crawled over and picked it up. Punched the answer button. He could hear someone breathing on the other end of the call.

He was sure the other guy could hear him too.

Seagrave?

He moaned a little. Like he was hurt.

"Jason?" the voice on the other end said, and Matt almost dropped the phone.

It wasn't Seagrave.

It was Shurig.

Desidero Amatoris, Private Motor Yacht
25 Degrees 33 Minutes North, 79 Degrees 31 Minutes West
Monday, September 24, 1:45 P.M.

THE line went dead.

Shurig stared at the phone.

Many possibilities occurred to him. None of them good. Worst-case scenario, also the most likely—that was the golfer. On Jason's cell. Which meant Jason hadn't completed his mission, which meant Jason probably was dead. Worse...

Shurig had a feeling the golfer had recognized his voice and therefore knew whose side Shurig was really on. Now...

What to do about that?

Shurig sat below deck, in the front cabin. He could see Harper through the window of the sleeping compartment. She was on the front deck, leaning back in one of the cushioned bench seats, legs up in front of her, face turned toward the sun, either asleep or more likely, just daydreaming. He'd been up there with her for a while, talking things through. What to do when they got to the island; how the dominoes would fall once they were able to prove the tournaments had been fixed. The gambling, the murder, the society, Altair, the coup. He had to admit, she'd put a lot of the pieces together. Not all of them, but enough that he was glad he'd tracked her down.

About what needed to happen next, he wasn't glad at all.

He called the Colonel to break the news about Jason.

"This is one lucky fellow," Seagrave said. "We're talking about luck, not skill here?"

"Yes," Shurig said.

Seagrave paused. "The smart thing for Thurman to do is to go to the authorities. Produce Jason's body. Tell his version of what happened at The Pines. Bring my name into it, let things proceed from there."

393

"That would be a disaster," Shurig said.

"Not necessarily. But something to be avoided. The question is, will Thurman do that? Will he go to the police?"

"No," Shurig said.

"Why not?"

"Harper." Shurig explained his sense that feelings between Thurman and Harper seemed to be getting personal.

Seagrave laughed. "So he's going to come charging to her rescue?"

"That's my guess," Shurig said.

"Well. That may work out after all. I have some questions for Ms. Harper. Thurman's presence may help persuade her to answer them."

"He'll never make it to the island. No one's going to charter him a boat. He's got no i.d., can't name a single member of the club, probably doesn't even have enough cash—"

Seagrave clucked his tongue disapprovingly. "Don't be so negative. I suspect our golfer's good luck is going to continue."

"Sir?"

"We have pictures of him, don't we?"

"Of course."

Seagrave laid out how things would unfold. Thurman's luck would hold out for a while longer. The next few hours, at least.

And it would end. Abruptly. Once and for all.

❖ ❖ ❖ ❖ ❖

Espy woke up feeling nervous. She'd dozed off in the sun and looked around to get her bearings. Surprising. Very unlike her to nap. Must be exhausted.

She thought about Matt, who continued to surprise her too. She'd seen him at first as an arrogant jock—or an arrogant, alcoholic ex-jock. Almost pathetic. But he'd shown much more character and resourcefulness than she expected, handling the pressure and the danger with grace. And there was something sweet about him. Tender. Innocent.

She thought about their embrace. What was that about? And why did she find herself missing him, feeling sorry he was stuck back in the motel?

She needed to focus.

She checked her watch: going on three. They'd been on the boat for almost two hours. The trip was supposed to take two and a half; "depending on the winds," the pilot told them when they boarded.

Shurig, she assumed, was napping below deck. The guy needed sleep even more than she did. The pilot was above her, in the wheelhouse. Bahamian guy. He'd said hello when she and Shurig came on board. Hadn't said anything since.

"How much longer till we get there?" she called up to him.

He took one hand off the wheel and pointed straight ahead.

Just visible in the distance was a speck of color—a bit of green against the blue water. An island.

She climbed the ladder to the wheelhouse.

"We made good time," she said, coming next to the pilot. "I'm Esperanza Harper."

He smiled and shrugged.

Getting information out of this guy, she realized, would be impossible.

"So you've been here before?" she asked as casually as possible.

"Oh, many times."

"Tell me about it. This is my first trip."

"It is small."

"And it's private? Privately owned?"

He nodded.

They were close enough that she could begin to pick out details—a narrow white beach, behind it a seawall of white concrete. Behind the wall, among the palm trees, houses. Some big, some small, some that looked like mansions.

She felt like she was sailing into an issue of *Travel and Leisure* magazine.

"How many people live here?" she asked the pilot.

"In season...a couple hundred."

"So how many now?"

His brow furrowed. "Not many."

Shurig climbing up the ladder to join them. He didn't look like he'd slept. He looked, in fact, more tired than before. More stressed.

"How much longer?" Shurig asked.

"Ten minutes, maybe. Docks are on the other side." The pilot turned the boat to the left, bringing it parallel to the island. He pointed in the same direction. "We'll go through the cut—there."

Espy saw what he meant a minute later. The island narrowed, the row of houses coming to an end, the palm trees thinning, the ocean becoming visible on the other side, and what she thought was just a continuation of Cat Cay revealed itself as a separate land mass, made up mostly of rock. A few scattered patches of sand, some scrub, some stunted shrubbery. A lighthouse stood on the end of it.

"Gun Cay," the pilot said. "No people there."

As they passed through the channel, Espy saw a concrete platform at the end of Cat Cay. Looked almost like a loading dock for industrial equipment. Very much out of place. She asked the pilot what it was used for. He shrugged.

They came back down the other side of the island. Fewer houses, bigger buildings. A gravel landing strip with a hut next to it. Finally, off in the distance, a set of docks. Several sets. Capable of holding a hundred or so boats, she guessed.

She counted four.

Definitely not in-season, she thought.

They turned at the first set of docks, motored down to the end. Shurig jumped out of the boat and tied off. Then he helped Espy step out.

The marina sat at the bottom of a gently sloped hill dotted with all sorts of buildings. Wooden, concrete, stucco, most painted off-white or light blue, nestled among stands of palm trees and concrete planters filled with bushes. They stepped off the docks onto concrete, where Espy saw a big white sign:

Members in Residence

Cat Cay Club

At the top of the sign, a drawing: a black cat, back arched, stood on top of a key. Cat Cay. Underneath were a series of metal slats for nameplates. Only one nameplate filled a slat: Services Manager

Shurig pointed to a two-story white wooden building with a *Customs* sign above it. They climbed a half-flight of steps to the front door, which was locked. Espy peered through the glass. Lights off. No one inside.

Something wasn't right. Where was everybody?

"This is strange," she said.

Actually, it was more than strange. It was downright spooky.

Across from the building, they saw a line of two-seater golf carts. Shurig walked up to one of the carts and looked inside.

"Keys are in it," he said. "Let's take a drive."

❖ ❖ ❖ ❖ ❖

He needed a few minutes to mentally prepare. There was no rush— ten minutes one way or the other wouldn't change what was about to happen today, or more importantly, tomorrow, wouldn't change the look Harper would give him when he put an end to not only her illusions, but to the whole idea of a happy ending.

That was why he decided on a tour of the island.

He took her down South Cay Road, which like all the other roads on the island was a concrete path, meant only for golf carts, the service truck, and fire engine. Passenger cars were not allowed on the island. She noticed right away that all the houses had names, not numbers. She paid close attention to the signs as they went past, looking for Twin Beaches. Which was on the other end of the island. Don't be in such a rush, Shurig wanted to tell her. You'll get there soon enough.

They drove past the eastern edge of the golf course, circled around it to the southern tip of the island and started north again. Past the old Rockwell place, past a few of the newer, bigger mansions. She said a few things about "poor Matt," asked a few questions about what else Shurig had found out about Seagrave. He gave her a few details she already knew. They talked about O'Neill's strange disappearance.

Finally, she fell silent—took in the flowers, the trees, the ocean, the sand, and the eerie, unnatural quiet.

"This isn't right," Harper said. "We've been here almost half an hour and we still haven't seen anyone."

He shrugged. "It's off season."

"Right," she said, but clearly didn't accept that explanation.

It's time, Shurig thought.

Which was a good thing.

They'd reached their destination.

On the western edge of the golf course, they stopped at a tidy white clapboard hut that served as the clubhouse for the island's nine-hole golf course.

Shurig pulled onto the grass.

"I hear tennis," Harper said.

"Coming from over there." Shurig pointed down the fairway, past the green, to a grove of carefully landscaped palm trees, and the tennis courts beyond. Even from this distance, he could see two people playing.

"People," she said. "At last. Come on."

They strode together across the grass. Harper wore a determined look on her face. A familiar look, one he'd seen many times during the last six months.

Shurig turned and saw Sam. Keeping pace, walking right alongside them.

Shurig walked faster.

Do the right thing, Mike, Sam said.

That's what I'm doing, Shurig answered.

Harper suddenly stopped.

"That's Seagrave," she said. They were fifty feet from the courts. The one closest to them was empty, and on the other...

Shurig squinted. "I think you're right."

"But you said he was in Washington."

"He was," Shurig said. "Last time I talked to him."

"When you...talked to him?" Her face paled, her jaw dropped. The shock turned quickly to horror as the realization took hold.

He nodded. "This morning. I think he flew in a couple hours ago."

Harper slowly backed away. She said...

"You."

CINCINNATUS

MATT thought about going to the cops. Walking to the front desk and telling them to call 911, there was a dead body in his room. When they showed up, he'd tell them the whole story. He'd use Seagrave's name; he'd use Shurig's name. He'd tell them that a woman named Esperanza Harper, who worked for the Department of Justice, was trapped on an island in the Bahamas with some crazy guys who were planning a military coup.

More than likely they would ship him back to Ohio. He'd be handcuffed in a cell somewhere, and Espy would be alone with Shurig.

So he cleaned up his face as best he could, putting ice on the cuts to stop the bleeding. He left the dead guy in his room, hung the Do Not Disturb sign on the door, and left.

Before coming to the motel, that dead guy had been sent by Shurig to kill Jake. And Espy's mom. Matt assumed the guy had succeeded. From a thousand miles away, that was all he could do.

He hoped he could do more for Espy.

He hurried to the nearest marina and looked for a boat to rent. Take me to Cat Cay. This minute. I have a thousand dollars to spend.

People looked at him and backed away; others just laughed. His right eye was swollen and purple. He had a gash above his left eye and on his chin. He looked like hell. He found a pharmacy and bought an eyepatch. Pirate Matt. He went back to the marina and tried again. Went up to two thousand dollars. People started asking for identification. When he couldn't show it, they waved him off. He went to $2,500. He found no takers.

He went to another marina. He started at a thousand there. Same story.

He spent two hours going up and down the inland waterway, marina after marina, dock after dock, boat after boat. Nobody bit.

He stopped at a shack selling Jamaican meat patties, sat at rickety picnic table, and ate while trying to figure out what to do next. It was 3:30. How much longer could the stiff lie in his room without being discovered? How much longer would Shurig keep Espy alive? If she wasn't dead already? He had to have a boat. If he couldn't rent one, he'd have to buy one.

As he considered his options, a blue convertible pulled up alongside the docks. A guy climbed out, scanned the docks, saw Matt, and walked right toward him.

Matt stood up.

The guy was short and thin. Dark-skinned. Arabic. A cop? No. Not in that car. Not wearing plaid shorts and an off-white button-down shirt.

The guy said, "Are you the man who wants to go to Cat Cay?"

Matt got ready to run. "How'd you know?"

"Some friends of mine. Back at the marina."

He gestured north, up the inland waterway.

"How'd you know I was here?"

"I didn't. I've been looking."

"I have a thousand dollars," Matt said. "If you can get me there this afternoon."

The man kept his smile in place. "I heard two."

"Okay. Two."

He counted the money into the guy's hand.

The guy said, "Let's go," and offered his hand, saying, "I'm Manny Njomo."

Tennis Courts
Cat Cay, Bahamas
Monday, September 24, 4:20 P.M.

SHE wanted to kill.

One second she was shocked, frightened, backing away, the next she charged him. When she slammed into him, he fell backward. She landed on top, kneed him in the gut, and reached for his eyes, trying to claw her fingernails right into them and—

She was flying backward through the air.

She landed hard, her head snapping back and smacking the ground. It took her a minute to get her bearings.

When she did, she saw Shurig standing over her.

"You all right?" he asked.

"Murderer," was all she could muster.

"I didn't kill—" He stopped talking, looked past her. "That's exactly what I'm doing," he said. "This is the right thing. You'll see."

Espy staggered to her feet and looked behind her. Nobody there.

She looked at Shurig, who stared in front of him, as if seeing a ghost. His lips moved but he made no sound.

Then,

"Michael!"

Seagrave strolled toward them, a towel around his neck, a tennis racket in one hand, a gym bag in the other.

"Everything all right?" Seagrave asked.

"She's a little upset," Shurig said.

"Understandable." Seagrave squinted at her. "Ms. Harper. I'd say good to see you again, but I'd be lying. I wish you had left well enough alone."

Seagrave's tennis partner joined them, saying, "Who's this, Jed?"

"Gene Carter," Seagrave said, "Esperanza Harper. Ms. Harper is with the Department of Justice."

"DOJ is in on this?" Carter asked.

Seagrave shook his head. "Ms. Harper has been working independently. She has, unfortunately, ferreted out certain aspects of the operation."

"Cashier?" Carter asked, wide-eyed.

Seagrave's face darkened. "Yes, though not the name until just now."

"Sorry," Carter said. "But how are you going to handle this?"

"Better you don't know," Seagrave said. "Don't you think?"

"People know I'm here," Espy said. "When I don't show up they're going to come after me."

Carter frowned. "Is this true?"

"As a matter of fact, I think it is," Seagrave said. "No cause for alarm, though. Let's head back, wash up, change for dinner. Six o'clock good?"

❖ ❖ ❖ ❖ ❖

Espy and Shurig headed north in the golf cart, up Gun Cay Road, according to a sign they passed. Neither spoke.

In the cart ahead of them, Seagrave and Carter talked animatedly. How, she wondered, was Carter involved in Cashier. Interesting name. There was an old saying—cashier an officer. Something like that. Meaning to get rid of. Dismiss. But who were they going to dismiss? And how were they going to do it? Arrange an accident? An assassination? March the army into Washington? Where did the society fit into this? So far the only one whose guilt she was certain of was Seagrave's. And Shurig's. Judas.

The contrast between her thoughts and the scenery couldn't have been greater. Immaculately trimmed shrubbery lined the road, along with bright, colorful flowers—red, yellow, orange—everywhere she looked. All of it under a canopy of palm trees.

And still no people.

"Where is everybody?" she asked. "And tell me the truth this time."

"We put out a bulletin," Shurig said. "Medical emergency. Contamination at the water plant. Evacuated the island for the next forty-eight hours."

"Why the need for privacy?"

Shurig didn't answer. Espy could guess: forty-eight hours. The time-frame for Cashier.

Why did they need everybody off the island? She was missing something. Cat Cay wasn't just a vacation spot, not just a place where the Cincinnati owned a house, where they went fishing every winter. It was important, in and of itself; although she couldn't imagine how. And how it related to a coup.

The cart slowed. Carter and Seagrave turned left, off the road. Shurig followed. Turned into a driveway. A sign on a faded white fence-post about a foot high—green piece of wood, with white lettering—said Twin Beaches.

It was halfway between mansion and bungalow—comfortable-looking. Set back about fifty feet from the road, at the top of a rise, protected by two four-foot walls of faded orange concrete. A concrete sidewalk ran from the drive through the lawn and up a short flight of steps to the house's front door, which was flanked by two bay windows. Up the hill from the drive was a swimming pool, and beyond that, the ocean. Behind them, the ocean, too, maybe a hundred feet away, across the path, through a sparse grove of palm trees. They were on the narrow end of the island, which at this point wasn't more than a few hundred feet wide.

Twin Beaches. The name fit.

"We'll see you at dinner, Ms. Harper," Seagrave said in that gallingly courtly manner she despised.

"After what happened at the banquet? I don't think so."

"Your choice. But we're having bluefin. Freshly caught. Quite remarkable, if you've never tasted it."

Espy shook her head.

Shurig led her inside the house—rugs laid over Mediterranean tile floors, comfortably furnished, a lot of exposed wood, the ceiling beams, the stairs, the closet doors. He took her to the last room at the back of the house. It was two rooms, actually—a sitting room, with French doors that opened onto a patio overlooking the ocean, and a bedroom with a full bath.

"There's clothes in the drawers." Shurig pointed toward the bedroom. "Help yourself. You can even go for a swim. The ocean, there's a pool too..."

"Why are you doing this?" she asked

He didn't answer.

"How much is Seagrave paying you?"

"This isn't about money."

"Then what? Power?"

"The barbarians," he said. "They're at the gate."

"The barbarians?"

He shot her a grim look. "You want me to get you for dinner or not?"

"For the last supper?" she said. "No thanks."

❖ ❖ ❖ ❖ ❖

She needed to get out. With her father dead and Shurig a traitor, who could she call for help? Were Jake and her mom still alive?

Maybe someone from the DOJ. Leonard. That whole thing with Tunde and the Democratic Fund...after what had happened Saturday morning, she felt like an idiot. She'd been wrong about them, which meant she could have gone to Leonard with the original notification about Kazmir's winnings and her suspicions about fixing golf tournaments. Tell him about the phony bank accounts. Get him on board instead of hiding everything and screwing up her job.

Voices sounded in the hall. Footsteps pounded outside her door.

It burst open and a man came literally flying into the room.

Matt.

Twin Beaches
Cat Cay, Bahamas
Monday, September 24, 8:09 P.M.

SO much for charging to the rescue.

He rose to his feet and saw Espy—with a look of horror on her face.

"What happened to you?" she asked.

He told her. She smiled when he got to the part about the hypodermic, about Jason lying there on the floor, dead.

"Good," she said, her voice wavering.

Then the smile wavered.

But before she broke down and cried, she got up, busied herself putting cold towels on Matt's swollen face.

❖ ❖ ❖ ❖ ❖

Matt thought about Jake and found himself wanting to cry too. But he couldn't cry. Maybe it was a guy thing. Maybe it was because he couldn't picture Jake dead, couldn't see anybody getting the drop on his brother. But Jason had gone to Wilmington to "pick up the packages" first.

So the packages were gone.

"They're dead," Espy said.

"We don't know for sure."

She stifled a sob. "First my dad, now my mom."

He put his arm around her and her head leaned on his chest. She cleared her throat. "Growing up, I missed my dad so much. Always trying to impress him, make him proud, just get his attention, you know?"

Matt nodded, though he didn't really know. Compared to her, he'd had it pretty easy. More than he realized.

Her voice grew firm again, the tears gone. "Maybe that's all this is—a silly girl reaching out to her far-away dad. This whole mess."

"It's a lot more than that," Matt said. "You've risked everything."

"And lost it," she said. "Everything is lost. Everyone I love."

He patted her shoulders, feeling completely useless.

She laid down on the bed and stared at the ceiling, her big dark eyes glassy with tears but starting to harden, to focus. He tried to think of something to say but nothing came to mind. He couldn't see a single bright spot in the situation. Other than that they were still alive. For the moment.

Espy began to fill the silence, talking about Cashier, trying to figure out what it was, specifically. Why Cat Cay was important. What her father had found out and why he hadn't told her. She was, Matt realized, thinking out loud. He didn't mind being a sounding board, and he was preoccupied with thoughts of his own.

How do you fix a golf tournament, what was a radiant sensor array...

He wondered if he'd ever get a chance to find out.

At some point Espy stopped talking and fell asleep. Matt couldn't.

He pulled a blanket over her and walked into the sitting room.

He peered through the window at the stone patio behind the house, a low wall separating it from a slope leading down to the sea. A table and chairs.

Shurig sat at the table. Staring at the ocean. Hands in his lap, a beer on the table next to him. Still wearing his sunglasses.

Shurig saw Matt. He raised his right hand, formed it into the shape of a gun, and pointed it over his shoulder. Right at Matt.

Bang.

Matt stepped away. He plopped on the couch in the sitting room, stared for a while at the blank TV screen.

BOOK THREE: CINCINNATUS

❖ ❖ ❖ ❖ ❖

He woke to the sound of the ocean. A dim light shining through the curtains. And pain—all over his body, everywhere that Jason had hit him but especially...

His shoulder. It felt like it did the first time he injured it—not on a golf swing but on a night out with Nancy, the night before the first round of the Miccosukee. They'd gone line-dancing at a country music club, he swung her around and felt a ping in his shoulder. No big deal. But when he got up the next morning he knew something was very, very wrong.

What a screw-up he'd been. If he'd only concentrated on his game instead of having a good time. Enough, he thought. Living in the past wouldn't help. He had to focus on staying alive. Getting out of here.

The bedroom door was shut, Espy still sleeping. He walked to the door leading into the hall. Locked. Went to the window, drew the curtains, and almost jumped fifty feet high.

Shurig was still sitting at the table. In the same spot. In the same position. Still staring out at the ocean, his beer (couldn't be the same beer, could it?) still sitting on the table next to him.

He raised his right hand over his head, and without turning, waved.

Matt stepped back from the curtain, turned to see Espy in the bedroom doorway.

Wearing a t-shirt and shorts, she looked wide-awake.

"Where'd you get those?" he asked, gesturing toward the clothes.

"Bureau in there. Looks like there's some men's stuff too."

Matt found a pair of khakis and a polo shirt. They fit, more or less. When he came out of the bedroom, he saw Espy looking through the curtains. At Shurig.

She lowered the curtain. "We need a weapon," she said. "A knife, something sharp. Something to even the odds."

No harm in looking, he thought, though unless they found a gun, he didn't think it would do them much good against Shurig.

He searched the bedroom, she went through the bathroom. Nothing. They rifled through the sitting area.

He scanned the bookshelf, which was cluttered with knick-knacks, seashells, figurines. Just below eye-level, on the second shelf from the top, he found a small metal tube lying on its side. There was a corkscrew on the end of the tube.

Not exactly a lethal weapon, but it was something.

"Hey," Espy said.

She'd opened a drawer in the TV cabinet and found a black plastic box.

"A DVD," he said.

"Read the label." She popped out the disc and tossed him the box.

Radiant Sensor Prototype Demonstration
Cat Cay Special Projects Lab
March 1951
Tape 1 of 4

"Whoa," was all he could manage.

Espy popped the disc into the DVD player, and they moved to the couch.

The disc began with black-and-white numbers counting down from ten to one. Then the screen filled with type. White against a black background.

Prototype Demonstration
Cat Cay Special Projects Lab
March 2, 1951

The type abruptly vanished.

Replaced by two men, both around sixty years old, both wearing suits and ties. They looked stiff. A little nervous. They stood in a big room in front of a long, low countertop, behind which was another long, low countertop, behind which was a wall of archaic-looking electronic equipment. Things with dials and levers and tubes, wires running everywhere.

One man was very tall, the other very short.

The tall man stepped forward and, in a deep voice, said, "Hello. My name is Powel Crosley."

Special Projects Lab
Cat Cay, Bahamas
Friday, March 2, 1951 3:32 P.M.

LEWIS raised a hand. "Wait a minute," he said.

He stood behind a camera ten feet in front of his brother.

"The microphone sounds like it's overloading," Lewis said. "I'm going to lower the gain a little."

He turned a dial on the preamp perched on a table behind him.

"I'll back off," Powel said. "A few steps should do it."

"I suppose," Lewis said. He'd had all of a half-hour's training on this equipment. It had been a long time since he served as a field engineer for any of the company's radio broadcasts, never mind filming.

Lewis positioned himself behind the camera, raised his hand, counted down from three, said, "Action."

"Hello, my name is Powel Crosley. I am the founder of the Crosley Corporation of Cincinnati, Ohio. For the past thirty years, we have had the honor and privilege of serving not just the American consumer but the American way of life."

The audio still sounded distorted to Lewis, but he probably couldn't make it much better. Powel spoke like an old-style radio announcer, nearly shouting into the microphone in his deep, booming voice, e-nun-ci-a-ting every syllable. And, in fact, he'd been one of the country's first radio announcers, a quarter century ago, back when he and Lewis were getting started in radio, trying to figure out how they could launch the radio boom, back in the days before networks, back when they broadcast out of Powel's living room, back before Lewis' daughter Ellen was born, back before Powel's Gwendolyn died. Back when they were young.

They weren't young anymore.

Their day was passing. Part of the reason they were making this film—for the men and women who were going to come after them.

"...technological advances," Powel was saying, "that during the world war we shared with the forces of freedom. Yet even as war raged overseas, even as we devoted our corporate resources to aid in the defeat of totalitarianism, the Crosley Corporation was aiding in the development of a revolutionary new technology, one that literally has the power to reshape the world. One whose potential applications, for both commercial and military purposes, rivals that represented by atomic energy. For these reasons, the development of this technology has occurred in secret, within the walls of the laboratory you see behind me."

Lewis pulled back to show the lab.

Powel motioned toward the man behind him. "I would like to introduce the man whose work has served as the foundation for this technology—Mr. Edward Leedskalnin."

❖ ❖ ❖ ❖ ❖

Leedskalnin stepped into the frame, and Lewis pulled back farther. Powel looked old and tired. Leedskalnin looked worse. Gaunt. Sick. There'd been something wrong with him for about a year now. Lewis had tried to get him to go to a doctor, but he wouldn't.

He would thump his chest. "Energy. You understand, yes? In here... balance is not good. But I will fix. Like before. Tuberculosis, yes? You remember?"

Lewis remembered. But he remembered Gwendolyn too. Leedskalnin hadn't been able to fix her. And he hadn't been able to fix himself this time either.

"I wish to thank you gentlemen watching," Leedskalnin said. "I wish to thank all people from my adopted country. Greatest country in all of history. I come here from Latvia forty years ago, I know no one, I do not speak your language, I have no money. And now...I have friends. I have a place in this world. I have accomplished, I believe, great things. With the help of these friends. So..."

Leedskalnin smiled.

"I am giving back. What Mr. Crosley calls 'my technology,' though I have told him this is not mine. This is ancient knowledge belonging to great minds, of times past. From countries all across globe. From Egypt. From India. From books, and people, and things I have studied all my life. Knowledge of energy, in the world around us, inside us, in the stars."

He pulled something from his inside coat pocket. It was cylindrical, maybe a half inch in diameter. It looked, more than anything else, like a cigar tube, with the top quarter cut off and an augur bit glued on.

Actually, Lewis thought, seeing it up close, in the lens...

It looked like a corkscrew.

"Magnetic current," Leedskalnin said. "This idea is the key to all my discoveries. There is energy running through this—" he held up the tube—"as there is energy running through us. Energy running through the earth we stand on, through the air we breathe. We can sense it, yes? And so can this. And once we know how to detect this current, and use it...nothing is impossible. Nothing. To lift a thousand tons of coral. To build a machine which runs and does not stop."

He talked about magnetic current, north and south poles, and cosmic forces, and what truly held the planet together. A grid formed by magnetic lines. He talked of how he had managed to tap into the grid to generate forces that defied the laws of gravity.

Powel watched and nodded.

Scientists and engineers had been working in the lab for almost a dozen years. Working in secret, all of them, sworn to secrecy, flown down under cover of night. Leedskalnin came every few weeks, stayed a couple days, managed to both inspire and frustrate everyone.

He showed them miracles.

He showed them how to replicate his work.

They were further along than Lewis had been that first night at Rock Gate Park, after Leedskalnin had shown him his castle. After they ate dinner and Lewis asked him how he cured his tuberculosis, Ed marched him down to his workshop and demonstrated how he'd moved ten thousand tons of stone by himself. Had explained the power Lewis had felt standing next to the well—and what it represented.

It was virtually the same explanation he was giving now.

Someday the world would change again, the way it had changed at Menlo Park, Dearborn and Kitty Hawk. Leedskalnin's secrets wouldn't stay secret forever.

And when that happened, Powell, and Lewis and Ed wanted to make sure they were in the hands of the right people. They wanted Leedskalnin's technology to be used to defend freedom, not destroy it. They had worked to preserve it for the last dozen years.

From here on out, though...

That job belonged to the Committee.

Lewis checked the time remaining on the reel—a minute. He held up one finger. Powel cleared his throat.

"Excuse me, Mr. Leedskalnin." He addressed the camera. "Gentlemen, we will now change reels and continue our demonstration, moving from the theoretical to the practical."

"Ah yes." Leedskalnin said, nodding vigorously. "The practical."

He pointed the tube toward the countertop behind him.

A pen that had been sitting there flew up through the air, straight at him.

Leedskalnin caught it and smiled.

And that was the last frame.

Lewis stepped away from the camera. "Let me change reels."

❖ ❖ ❖ ❖ ❖

The screen went to black.

Matt held up the tube with the corkscrew on one end and started to show it to Espy, to tell her that maybe he'd found a weapon here they could use—

And the door opened.

Matt pocketed the tube.

Seagrave walked in, Shurig a step behind him.

"Good morning, Ms. Harper." Seagrave said. "Mr. Thurman, I didn't think I'd ever see you again." Then he saw the TV. "Watching something?"

Shurig walked to the cabinet, ejected the DVD, and handed it to Seagrave.

He nodded. "I'd forgotten about those. Well. No matter."

"What does Powel Crosley have to do with this?" Espy demanded.

"Quite a bit, actually." Seagrave went to the window and drew the curtains. Light poured into the room. "It's going to be a glorious day. Let's not talk about the past."

Espy planted her fists on her hips. "Fine. Let's talk about Cashier."

"The coup, you mean?" Seagrave looked at Shurig and chuckled.

"You think that's funny?" Espy asked.

"Ms. Harper, you have a very active imagination." He shook his head. "What on earth gave you the idea we were planning a coup?"

Twin Beaches
Cat Cay, Bahamas
Tuesday, September 25, 8:26 A.M.

HARPER looked shell-shocked. Seagrave wished he had a camera. He glanced at Thurman, who stood by the bookshelves, hands in his pockets. He looked surprised, too, but there was something else in his eyes. Calculation. He was planning something.

Seagrave surveyed the shelves. The old prototype was missing. Silly to have left it there, though even sillier for Thurman to take it. Seagrave wasn't sure it even worked anymore, and certainly Thurman had no idea how to use it.

"Michael," Seagrave said. "I believe Mr. Thurman has the prototype."

Shurig held out his hand.

Thurman looked at Shurig, then at Harper, and then back at Seagrave.

"I'll count to three," Seagrave said. "Then Michael will shoot you."

Shurig, a step ahead of him, had already drawn his gun.

"One," Seagrave said. "Two."

Thurman cursed and pulled the prototype out of his pocket. Shurig took it and put it in his. The golfer looked visibly deflated—weakling. No backbone. No willingness to fight for...

An idea came to Seagrave.

The plan had been to deal with the golfer now, but after spending several hours cooped up in the lab with Carter and Njomo on such a glorious day, Seagrave felt restless. He had a few hours to kill before Cashier went live and he needed to return to the lab. Why spend that time inside?

He said, "You look unhappy, Mr. Thurman. I have an idea—a way to cheer you up."

Thurman and Harper looked at each other.

"A round of golf," Seagrave said. "Nine quick holes. Interested?"

Thurman's eyes narrowed.

"I'll take that as a yes," Seagrave said, and headed for the door.

❖ ❖ ❖ ❖ ❖

The Colonel rode with Harper; Shurig took the golfer. Made him drive the cart; told him to shut up when he started to talk. Shurig didn't want to hear Thurman or even be reminded Thurman was still alive. He just wanted this whole thing over and done.

He wanted to go back to the patio and drink another beer.

He wanted to close his eyes and go to sleep for a long, long time.

He wanted to talk to Leila again. He'd tried calling her early in the morning. Somehow, though, he'd messed up the time zones. Gotten things backward, calling her around six, which turned out to be three her time, not nine.

"Sorry," he'd said, forcing a chuckle. "Can't believe I did that. I'll call later."

"No, no, it's all right." He imagined her sitting up in bed. "I was hoping you'd call," she said. "Any news?"

"News?"

"The report. On Al-Aqsa?"

"Oh. Right. No news, sorry."

Silence.

"So...what else is going on? What have you been doing?"

Meaning 'why are you calling?'

Shurig took off his sunglasses. "What have I been doing?" He shut his eyes and rubbed them, opened them, and opened his mouth to answer...

And Sam was sitting at the table.

O'Neill sat next to him, crunching an ice cube.

Maya and Goran too, staring at him.

"I'm sorry," Shurig said.

For what's about to happen, he wanted to say.

Instead, he said, "I have to go."

He hung up.

The phone rang a second later. Leila calling back. He didn't answer. It rang every few minutes for the next half hour or so. He got tired of hearing it.

He pitched it into the ocean.

The only thing in his pocket was the tube as he drove Thurman around the golf course.

"So it's not a coup?" Thurman said.

"The Colonel will tell you what he wants you to know."

"The Colonel. Right." Thurman put a mocking tone in his voice.

Shurig wouldn't stand for that. "Listen, you don't know how the world works. You get to sleep at night because of guys like the Colonel. And me. Guys making sacrifices, so you can play golf."

At that instant the ocean to the east, blocked by palm trees and houses up until that point, suddenly became visible again.

"There," Shurig said, pointing. "You know where we are?"

Thurman shifted nervously in his seat.

"We're five hundred miles west of San Salvador," Shurig said. "Where Columbus landed. Five hundred miles, five hundred years, and nothing's changed. You know what I'm saying?"

The man clearly had no clue. Looked sorry, in fact, he'd even spoken. Shurig was going to explain the reference further, and then realized there was no need.

Thurman was quiet now, staring straight ahead.

Shurig could close his eyes and pretend he wasn't there.

❖ ❖ ❖ ❖ ❖

No coup. So what then?

Out of the corner of her eye, Espy sensed Seagrave studying her. Waiting for her to ask that question. Probably had prepared his answer.

Throw him a curveball, she thought.

"You gave me that book," she said. "Why?"

It took Seagrave a second to get the reference. "Tempting fate, I admit. But...I wanted you to understand. To see things as they did. As I do."

"But what do they have to do with Twin Beaches?"

"Powel Crosley built the house. Back in the late 1930s."

"He was a member of the society."

"No. He shared our values, though. Our goals."

"Which is why he gave you Twin Beaches."

Seagrave smiled. "One doesn't have to be a member of the society to share its aims," Seagrave said. "At the banquet the other night. Less than half the people there were members. And yet they paid over two hundred dollars a plate because they share the society's goals. People all across the socio-economic and cultural spectrum do. For example, your boss. Kennebeck?"

"Leonard."

"Good man, from what I hear. I imagine you two work very closely together."

"What's your point?"

"He's not here with you now. Why is that?"

Seagrave tried to make the question sound casual, but Espy sensed there was more to it. He was interested in Leonard.

"I could ask you the same thing," she said. "Why are you here without Crane and the others?"

"The two have nothing to do with each other," he said. "I'd like to know why you told your father about Bob Kazmir and not your boss. Or did you tell your boss some things too?"

Espy thought a moment. She couldn't see any harm in telling Seagrave what he wanted to know. In fact, if she could make him think she was giving up and would cooperate, maybe she could buy some time.

"Tunde," she said, doing her best to sound discouraged. "Leonard's wife." She explained about the connection to the Democratic Fund for Direct Action, one she now knew didn't exist. Something else she'd been wrong about.

Seagrave paused, taking in the information. "You know," he said, "up until recently I wasn't aware you were involved in the case. I thought it was just your father. The fact that you actually started the investigation...both of you managed to keep that a secret."

"Not secret enough, obviously," she said.

He sighed. "Understand, I never wanted to kill your father. He forced my hand. I had to make a quick decision. If he had gone to Altair, Van Croft would have cancelled the entire operation."

"Who?"

"Tom Van Croft. General. Head of a defense agency, one of our primary resources. Cash, political support...he likes to think he's in charge. And in a sense he is. If he thought operational secrecy had been compromised, well...." He shook his head. "I did warn him, you know. Your father. Sent a note like the one I sent you. Neither of you are very good listeners."

Espy, suddenly, had had enough of the cat and mouse.

"So what's it about, really? If it's not a coup, then what? Money? Keeping the society's nest egg safe? Building new vacation homes?"

Seagrave's back arched as he shifted in the seat. "We've spent all this time together, and yet you don't know me at all." Then he leaned forward and pointed, to the left.

"Pull up," he said. "We're here."

❖ ❖ ❖ ❖ ❖

The name Windsor Downs Golf Club was carved into a plaque on the side of a white wooden hut that Matt supposed was the clubhouse. Seagrave chipped on the practice green on the left side of the building while Matt tested the clubs Shurig had given him. Decent enough clubs. Decent enough course. Only nine holes, and the fairway looked brown in spots, but the sightlines were good, the distances short, and if the greens were in decent shape he'd get himself a decent score.

How decent, of course, depended on the shoulder. And, for that matter, the eye, the leg, the fingers. Seagrave's boys had messed him up pretty good. Still, even injured he would kick Seagrave's ass. Silly thought, given that he might be killed before the day ended, but at least he'd have some satisfaction.

The Colonel's swing was stiff and awkward and ugly. Matt figured if he managed par on every hole, he'd beat the guy by a half dozen strokes, at least. That ought to count for something. Someday. Somewhere. The pearly gates, maybe.

He stepped up to the tee, tried a few practice swings himself. Not good. The shoulder hurt. He rolled it a little, trying to loosen up. The finger that Rawson broke couldn't grip the club.

Espy stepped up alongside him. "You really doing this? Playing golf when..."

"When they're getting ready to kill us?" he snapped. "Yeah, seems nuts. If you've got other things we can do, like getting off this island, stopping Seagrave's plot, killing that psycho Shurig, let me know."

Espy took a step back, a hurt look in her eyes.

Matt said, "Sorry." He rubbed his shoulder. "So...yes. I'm playing. Me and Seagrave on a golf course. Just like all of this started. All we need is you walking up the fairway in your gray suit."

❖ ❖ ❖ ❖ ❖

Seagrave gave him honors.

Matt stepped into the tee box and looked at the first hole. A par 4, dogleg left with water on the right starting about fifty yards off the tee, a small sand trap guarding a small green. Looked about 250 yards. He ought to be able to drive the green and have a shot at a birdie.

Seagrave stood to one side. Next to him stood Njomo, who had appeared a few minutes before and huddled with Seagrave.

Shurig and Espy stood a couple dozen feet farther back.

Despite the pain in his hands, Matt savored the feel of the club. At last, something familiar. A place where he had the upper hand on Seagrave.

He set a tee in the ground, set a ball on top of it. Positioned himself. Rolled his neck. Tugged at his glove. His lucky routine. The same routine he'd used since he was a kid and won the Ohio Amateur. *Matt Thurman, 15-Year-Old Phenom, Stuns Field to Take Trophy.*

He brought the clubface to the ball, took a deep breath, and then started his swing. First time he'd swung a club, it occurred to him, since that night at The Pines with Kazmir, which felt like a lifetime ago, except that as he brought the club back, something in his shoulder went ping.

The same ping he'd felt that night.

He brought the club forward, and the ping intensified into a much sharper pain, which kept him from following through.

Matt winced as he watched the ball fade right almost immediately. It sailed about a hundred fifty yards and hit the edge of the fairway, then bounced into the rough.

It bounced again and rolled into the water.

"Bad luck," Seagrave said, and stepped up to the tee box.

Matt mumbled a curse. This was going to be harder than he thought.

Windsor Downs Golf Course
Cat Cay, Bahamas
Tuesday, September 25, 9:21 A.M.

MANNY Njomo.

Espy didn't realize who the guy was until Shurig mentioned the name as they stood on the second tee, watching Seagrave line up his shot. Matt had already hit his to the center of the green. Seagrave's lips tightened. Obviously the Colonel cared about winning.

"You were at the apartment," Espy said to Njomo, who cocked an eyebrow in bemused surprise. "The night Ben Kauffman was killed. You were the guy they were investigating."

"Guilty as charged."

"You were moving money around for Al-Hasra."

"For the Arab-American Amity League. Not that it matters at this point."

Right: it didn't matter. Njomo had nothing to do with Al-Hasra. He was part of what was happening here—Seagrave, the society. Except...

In her rush to figure out what had sent her father to Altair, Espy realized she'd overlooked something. The Evidence Response Team investigating her father's death said they had evidence Njomo was involved with terrorists. Proof they'd found on some servers in Denmark. Some big international operation.

"Icepack," she said.

"What about it?" Again with the raised eyebrows.

She told him.

"Evidence?" He shook his head. "What they had was suggestive, at best. Bank account numbers."

Bank account numbers? This was the first time she'd heard about that.

❖ ❖ ❖ ❖ ❖

Double-bogey on one, to Seagrave's par. Par on two (barely, a twenty-foot putt that almost lipped out), to Seagrave's bogey. Par on three (where his twenty-footer for birdie came up half a foot short) for both men. Which meant that three holes in...

Matt was down a stroke. Unbelievable.

Seagrave's swing was stiff as a board, but the man knew the course. Knew the sweet spots on the fairway and the tough spots in the rough. Knew the greens too—sank his ten-footer on three as if he'd hit it a hundred times before. Stiff as he was at the tee, Seagrave had a smooth stroke on the green.

They walked together toward the fourth tee. Matt rubbed his shoulder, where the pain had begun to spread.

"I enjoy playing with you, Mr. Thurman," Seagrave said. "Studying your approach to each shot, which clubs you choose. It's been a long time since I've played with a golfer of your caliber."

Matt peered at Seagrave. "Bob Kazmir?"

Seagrave nodded. "We played together quite often. In fact, Bob was with me the day this all started. Right back there." He pointed toward the third green. "More than a quarter century ago. Hard to believe."

They walked on in silence for a moment, Seagrave caught up in his memories, Matt wondering how he and Espy could escape.

"There'd been a meeting back at the house," Seagrave said. "I hadn't—things hadn't gone the way I expected. I came here to hit a few balls, and Bob wandered by, and the next thing I knew we were playing. And right on the third green, that's when it came to me."

Seagrave stopped in his tracks, held up his right hand, held the thumb and forefinger about an inch apart.

"This much. That's how close I was to birdie. The ball rolled to the edge of the cup, and just wouldn't go in. Bob won the hole. We were playing for money, of course. With Bob you always played for money. And it occurred to me how much difference an inch here or there could make. How much money was at stake, how much each stroke was worth, and that if you had a way to effect those shots..."

His voice trailed off.

They walked to where the others were waiting: Shurig, Njomo, and Espy, who shot him a question with her eyes: Find out anything yet?

Working on it, he said with his gaze, as he walked past her, heading for the tee.

Njomo stepped aside to make room. He was holding something in his hand—a PDA.

❖ ❖ ❖ ❖ ❖

The fourth hole was about three hundred yards with a dogleg left to the green. Matt hit a half-drive, half-pitch shot off the tee. Favoring his shoulder again. A pitch and he was on the green; two putts, he was in the cup. Par. Seagrave made the green in two as well. His putt for birdie curved right, came up short by a couple feet.

His bid for par curved too, missed the hole by half an inch and rolled half a foot past the cup.

Under other circumstances, Matt wouldn't have allowed a 'gimme,' but the look on Seagrave's face as he approached the ball...

He was getting mad. Matt wanted him happy. Talkative.

"Go ahead and pick it up," he said.

Seagrave did.

As they set off toward the next hole, though, he still wasn't happy.

"You were standing too close," Matt said. "To your putter. You were right on top of it, practically. That's why the ball went off-line both times."

Seagrave glared but then gave a courtly nod. "Thank you. Bad habit I have. I work on it when I can."

"Everybody has bad habits. Especially when they putt. Mine is I grip the club too tight. I know I'm doing it, but, you know."

"Bob was always telling me to check my stance. Could be very annoying at times. Lecturing me like that. But I know he meant well."

Matt cleared his throat. "He lectured me too," he said. "When I was just starting. I'd be going through my routine, getting ready to putt, and he'd start shouting at me 'too tight, Thurman. Too tight. Hold it like a baby bird, remember?'"

Matt recalled that during the first couple years he knew Kazmir, the guy had actually been nice to him. Helpful. It had continued even after Matt won the amateur. Then it stopped. When? He couldn't remember. Why?

"Baby bird," Seagrave said. "Yes. He said that to me more than once."

"He was the one who helped you get those systems installed at all the big courses."

Seagrave's expression turned serious. "Obviously."

Why, Matt almost asked. Why would he do that? Kazmir spent his whole life around golf, why would he degrade the game, make his whole life's work worthless, but the answer was obvious.

Money.

He'd cheated the game. He'd even cheated Seagrave. Gotten greedy.

Gotten his head bashed for it.

"So those sensors," Matt began. "How, exactly—"

"Please, Mr. Thurman." Seagrave stopped walking. "Do us both a favor. Stick to golf. It's what you're good at. Don't play detective. You lack the intellect."

Matt shrugged. "Just asking," he said.

"I'm sorry," Seagrave said. "It's just that I have a lot on my mind, and your constant prattling...it's distracting. And really not necessary. Nor was that act of generosity on the last hole. I can handle myself on the course, thank you."

And saying that, he stalked off toward the fifth tee.

Matt watched him go. His attempt to get information from Seagrave failed. He'd half-expected Seagrave to lay out the whole scam. Show off what he had done. Why else was he keeping them alive?

Seagrave stepped up to the tee. Five was a short par three; Seagrave smacked a drive right down the center of the fairway that kicked up onto the green, giving him what looked like an easy birdie putt.

He smiled as he stepped aside to let Matt hit.

Matt could read that smile. He'd seen it—or something like it— on the face of every hacker he'd played in a pro-am. On the face of every weekend duffer who ever challenged him at The Pines. Hey, Hot Shot. You're not so tough. I'm kicking your ass, and I barely even practice.

Well. We'll see about that.

He set his ball on the tee.

Five holes left. Maybe the last five holes he'd play in his life.

No sense in holding back.

He felt the sun shining on his arms, and took a deep breath of the warm ocean air. It's eat-your-Wheaties time.

Yeah, he thought, and swung.

A full swing. The shoulder screamed, the fingers roared, but he swung straight and true and followed through. The ball flew like a guided missile, straight toward the green. Straight for the hole.

Landed, bounced once, and rolled right in.

"Wow," Espy said. "I've never seen one of those before."

Matt turned to see the expression on Seagrave's face.

What he saw was the man's back, as he stomped off down the fairway.

BOOK THREE: CINCINNATUS

Fairway/6th Hole
Windsor Downs Golf Course
Cat Cay, Bahamas
Tuesday, September 25, 9:51 A.M.

BEAUTIFUL day. Glorious day. The Colonel was right to get out and enjoy it. Shurig stood on the edge of the fairway on six, which paralleled the eastern shore of the island, trying to do the same. Only there was a problem. Harper.

She was staring a hole in his back. Staring at the gun, probably, tucked in the waistband at the back of his pants. Thinking about trying to take it from him.

He had to give her credit. She hadn't given up yet.

She was Sam's kid, for sure.

Sam—who suddenly stood in front of him, a dozen feet away, looking at Shurig and his daughter, wanting Shurig to stop what was about to happen. But he couldn't. People were going to die today, and he was going to have a hand in killing them. A couple here, a few million there...

He couldn't change a thing. He wouldn't want to change a thing. The Colonel's plan was right. Necessary. Long overdue.

Then Sam was gone and Harper stood next to him. Stepping toward him.

"Don't," he said, holding a hand out.

She stepped back, her face, Sam's face, molded in anger.

"Tell me again why you're doing this," she said.

"Five hundred miles, five hundred years...and everything's the same. Exactly the same."

She bit her lip. Matt was right—Shurig was losing his mind.

"The Nina, the Pinta, the Santa Maria," Shurig said. He pointed east, to the ocean. "It wasn't a science experiment. You know that, right? You're a history person."

431

She looked at him like he was crazy. Maybe he wasn't being clear enough. Maybe he needed to focus.

"Hang on," he said, and reached into his pocket for the pills.

He pulled out the prototype instead.

Whoops. He'd meant to leave it back at the house. It was vibrating, the attractor actually starting to move in his hand. Trying to spin. It was drawing energy from the field up on the green, probably had been doing that the whole time, and he hadn't noticed.

"You really need help," Harper said, backing away. "Can't you see that?"

He shoved the tube back in one pocket. Grabbed the vial from the other. "No, no, this is important," he said. "I want you to understand."

"I'm listening," Sam said.

"Not you. Hey!" He reached toward Harper, who backed away. "Stand still, dammit!"

She froze.

"Thank you. Now just give me a minute here...."

He fumbled with the vial. Tried to open the lid. Snapped it too hard.

Pills flew through the air.

The green pills.

Where were the blue ones? He could have sworn—

"Michael?"

Shurig saw the Colonel—fifteen feet away and closing fast. An angry look on his face.

"Is everything all right?" Seagrave asked.

Shurig bent down to pick up the pills. "Just dropped my meds. My pain prescription. For the shoulder. Everything's good."

432

❖ ❖ ❖ ❖ ❖

Espy watched him scramble around in the grass.

She'd waited all morning for something like this to happen. Shurig and Seagrave, both distracted at the same time.

The Colonel walked past her, carrying a club in one hand. She hung back, pretending to be scared of Shurig.

Then she lunged, grabbed Seagrave's club, hoping to yank it away. Hit him in the knee, hit Shurig in the head, and...game over.

But Seagrave held onto the club. Tightly. Espy yanked again, harder.

Seagrave let go. She fell backward, landing hard.

He laughed.

Espy staggered to her feet, holding the club high. Ready to hit him.

Then Shurig sauntered up to her, held out his hand, a determined look on his face. She gave him the putter.

"Please," Seagrave said. "No more foolishness."

He walked away, Shurig joining him.

Matt stepped up alongside her.

"Are you okay?"

She shrugged. Anger and fear and frustration boiling up.

"That's not the way out of this," Matt said. "Not without a gun."

He told her about Kazmir, about Seagrave saying they'd been fixing tournaments for twenty-five years.

Twenty-five years? That didn't sound right. It didn't jibe with the information she'd uncovered. More like ten years, she thought, a decade of longshots paying off, of bank accounts bearing the names of those original members of the society, bank accounts dead-ending at Alderney.

"Mr. Thurman?" Seagrave called. "Your shot." Matt and Espy exchanged a glance as he walked away.

Espy grudgingly followed.

Shurig approached her. "Sorry," he said. "I just want you to understand. I'm trying to do the right thing."

"Sure," she said, dismissively.

When she'd met him in L.A., he'd seemed very no-nonsense, very together. Now he seemed to be teetering on the edge.

Maybe, she thought, she could push him over.

❖ ❖ ❖ ❖ ❖

Six was the longest hole on the course. Five hundred yards. Matt had gone long off the tee, never mind the pain, and made the green in two. He nearly had another eagle, needing to make a thirty-foot putt, slightly uphill, not much break. When he hit it he was sure it was going in but at the last instant, it veered off-line. He missed for birdie too, hit it too hard, and cursed. He tapped in for par. Seagrave managed par as well. Which left Matt up by two strokes, with three holes to play.

He played it safe on seven—played for par and made it. As did Seagrave. Both did the same on eight.

Nine was a short par three. Matt rubbed his shoulder as Seagrave stepped to the tee.

"Two strokes, am I right?" Seagrave asked. "That's what I'm down by?"

Matt nodded.

"Two strokes, you have a par three here. A hundred twenty yards." Njomo was reading the information off his PDA, which he'd been using during the last few holes to keep score and give them yardage.

"Congratulations, Mr. Thurman," Seagrave said. "I don't see how I can possibly make up that margin."

Matt didn't either.

Seagrave hit a solid drive to the far edge of the green, about forty feet shy of the cup. Matt's was better, rolling within ten feet of the hole.

He turned to Seagrave, a smile on his face.

Seagrave, strangely enough, smiled too.

They walked to the green. Seagrave's ball was closer than it had looked at first—thirty feet from the hole, maybe. But not a high-percentage shot.

Seagrave studied the green. Then he rose, drew back the club.

And paused, mid-swing.

He looked at Matt.

"Not standing too close to the ball, am I?"

Matt said, "Looks good."

"And this is for birdie. That will put me one stroke behind?"

He was talking to Njomo, who stood on the far side of the green, looking at the PDA. Njomo concurred.

Seagrave settled over his ball. "I'm feeling very lucky," he said. "Very lucky indeed." He drew back the club and stroked his putt.

He hit it too hard. It was going to break right and slide well past the hole. He'd end up with a ten-foot putt for par—if he was lucky.

Except the ball didn't break. It ignored a little dip in the green like it wasn't there. Traveled right on through, straight for the cup.

And then went in.

"I had a feeling," Seagrave said.

Matt stared at the green, trying to figure how that putt had gone in.

Seagrave pocketed his ball and strutted off the green. "You're up," he said.

Matt took his stance. There was no break to the green from his angle. He had a straight line to the hole.

He checked his grip. Too tight. He loosened his hands. He looked at the putt once more, then stroked it. Feather-light. Dead-center. Right on target. Mr. Baby-Bird, meet Mr. Birdie.

Except the ball didn't slow down

It hit the cup, lipped out, and rolled on. Three, four, five feet past the hole before stopping.

Now he was even more confused. "No way I hit it that hard," he said.

"It looked good to me too," Seagrave said.

Matt stalked to his ball. A five-footer for par. He could do that in his sleep.

He looked at the shot. There was a slight break now in the green. Hit it solid, he wouldn't need to take that into account.

He settled into his stance, took a deep breath and relaxed.

He stroked the ball. It stopped a foot shy of the hole.

"Oooh," Seagrave said. "Close."

He was smiling. Matt was about to tap in for bogey to tie the game.

Behind him, Njomo fiddled with the PDA. The sight of it bothered Matt. Still. And now he realized why. It reminded him of that morning at The Pines. When he'd come upon Kazmir, kneeling over the thirteenth green. Holding a PDA.

And in his mind, pictured Seagrave's miracle putt, the ball not breaking when it should have. His own ten-footer, not slowing down. His eagle on six that veered off-line.

"Wait a second," he said, and stood up straight. "Wait just one damn second."

BOOK THREE: CINCINNATUS

9th Green

Windsor Downs Golf Course

Cat Cay, Bahamas

Tuesday, September 25, 10:35 A.M.

SEAGRAVE and Njomo burst out laughing.

"My goodness, it took you long enough to figure it out," Seagrave said.

Matt was so angry he didn't trust himself to speak.

"Mr. Thurman, really." Seagrave shook his head. "I just thought you might like to see the device at work."

"Bull," Matt said. "You wanted to win."

Espy walked up to them, said, "What's going on?"

"They have them. Right here. Under the greens. Those sensor things."

He'd been looking at the question like an intellectual exercise. How do you fix a golf tournament? Yeah, maybe there was something else going on here, something else they were doing with the money, but to get that money...

Cheating wasn't a strong enough word to describe what they were doing. They were stealing. Not just the money, but the time, the years of practice every guy on the tournament had put in to get where they were, the sacrifices they'd made, the things they hadn't done with their lives.

And it wasn't just the guys who lost. It was the winners too. Gary Wadman, Craig Driscoll...how long were they going to look at video of the tournaments they won, try to duplicate whatever magic had seized them that day?

"This Cincinnatus crap," Matt said, stepping forward. "This great American patriot bull you've been spouting, it's nothing but—"

There was a noise behind him, and then an arm clamped around his throat.

437

Shurig.

Matt tried to pry the arm away but couldn't. He gasped for air and kicked. Heard Espy yelling.

It was like the chokehold Rawson put on him at The Pines, only tighter. The world began to fade.

An instant before it went to black, the pressure, all at once, eased.

Matt dropped to the ground.

"Take a deep breath," Seagrave said. "It's only a game."

Espy helped him to his feet. "Tell me how it works," she said to Seagrave.

He nodded toward Njomo, who held up the PDA.

"He was a scorer too, right?" Matt asked. "Kazmir?"

Seagrave nodded.

"What's that mean?" Espy asked.

"Scorers get one of those."

"Actually, a different model," Njomo said. "Required us to not only switch out the equipment, but layer in our code alongside theirs."

"Whatever," Matt said. "The point is that scorers have the PDA on the course, they send back information as the round progresses— not just everybody's score, but where the ball lands, the length of the shot, that sort of thing."

"But how does it work?" Espy said. "When you want somebody to miss?"

Njomo pressed a few keys on the PDA and held it out.

Matt took it. "'In' and 'out'?" he said. "That's it?"

Njomo's eyes narrowed. "Are you aware of how many hours of coding that simple screen represents? How many years of my life?"

"But what exactly happens when you press those buttons?" Espy asked.

"Nothing," Njomo said. "Unless the system is on. Which requires a command from the lab or direct access to the sensor array. Once the

438

system boots and the sensors recalibrate, which can take anywhere from two to three hours depending on any environmental change that might have occurred since the last power-up, then what you have is a radiant field. The sensors not only control the strength of that field, they map acceleration and direction, so you can input your desired outcome."

He took the PDA from Matt. "In. Out. You see?"

Matt nodded. He did. Sort of. "What's a radiant field?"

Njomo looked to Seagrave.

"It's some kind of magnetic field," Espy said. "That's what Leedskalnin says on the tape."

"Despite what you may have heard Mr. Leedskalnin say, I assure you it's not a magnetic field," Seagrave said.

"So what is it?"

Seagrave said, "For lack of a better phrase, I suppose you could call it an anti-gravity device."

Espy and Matt exchanged a glance.

"I'll demonstrate," Seagrave said. "Manny, I don't think Mr. Thurman's going to take that last shot, so could I..."

Njomo nodded and punched buttons on the PDA.

"Anti-gravity?" Espy said, more to herself than to anyone in particular. "That's not possible."

"Ready," Njomo said.

Ten feet from them, a foot shy of the hole, Matt's ball, which he'd left untouched after his realization, rose slowly off the ground.

"You see?" Seagrave said. "Anti-gravity."

The ball hovered, a foot in the air.

Seagrave stepped forward and snatched it.

CINCINNATUS

THEY were back in the cart. This time, Seagrave drove. Matt and Shurig in one cart behind them, Njomo in another. Seagrave hadn't said a word since they left the course. Neither had she. Anti-gravity. Edward Leedskalnin had discovered anti-gravity. It still didn't seem possible. And then he brought in the Crosleys, who had provided for the stewardship through the Society of the Cincinnati, who had misused it to fix golf tournaments.

But there was something else going on. Cashier. Which wasn't about money. Which wasn't about a coup. So what was it? It had something to do with Seagrave's pal Carter, who she hadn't seen in a while.

"Where's your friend from the tennis courts?"

"Gene returned to Washington early this morning," Seagrave said. "He's seeing to some things for me."

"He's with the government, then?"

"Geospatial-Intelligence. Part of the NGA."

The article. The one she'd found on the bus.

"They contracted with Altair...some kind of software..."

Seagrave gave her the slightest nod.

"That's what Cashier is? Software?"

"Cashier is my attempt to put history back on course."

"Sounds like a big job. How are you going to manage that?"

He smiled. "About five hundred miles due east from us—"

"San Salvador. Nina, Pinta, Santa Maria. I heard."

"They were at a crossroads," Seagrave said. "Columbus. Isabella. As are we. They went around the problem. I prefer to confront it head-on."

"What was the problem?"

440

"Constantinople had fallen, severing the overland route between Europe and Asia. They were searching for a sea route. You remember?"

She did: vaguely. Columbus had no thought of finding the New World when he set off. He'd been looking for a route to India.

The cart slowed. Twin Beaches came into view. Seagrave turned into the drive.

"The spice trade—the whole of the Far East. With the Turks controlling the isthmus, trade, travel, contact itself became not just prohibitively expensive, but dangerous. The west was too weak to confront the sultan then. We're now in a much better position."

He stopped the cart and climbed out. Espy remained in her seat.

"The sultan," she said. "You're talking about the Arabs?"

"I'm talking about terrorists. Radical Islamic terrorists. Please. Evil must always be called by its proper name. Called out and confronted."

His words from the banquet.

The others pulled up behind them. She was vaguely aware of Shurig, Matt, and Njomo climbing out of their carts.

She remained in hers. "Terrorists?" she said. "Cashier is about terrorists?"

Instead of answering, Seagrave called to Shurig. "Keep everyone here a moment. I need to make a call."

❖ ❖ ❖ ❖ ❖

He went into the living room, shut the door. Called Carter.

"Gene. Tell me what's happening."

"I've only been here a little while. Can't be sure of anything yet."

"Tell me what you do know."

"Well, someone's definitely curious, that's for sure."

Seagrave tensed. Not a complete surprise, but not good either. "Someone?" he said. "Be specific."

"I can't yet. They're being very cautious. The queries are coming in over the new DOD backbone, and they're routing through the whole NSA infrastructure before they got to us, so tracking them—"

"Stop with the damn acronyms." Seagrave shouted. He took a deep breath and got hold of himself. "Give me some actual information."

"I'm trying. We don't know where the queries are coming from. We know they're focused on Altair, almost exclusively. One or two redirects on Enovation."

Seagrave cursed again, under his breath.

This was the problem with sending Carter and not going himself. He wanted the level of detail he could only get by reading the text of those queries. Was the problem DOJ? The missing packages? He had to know. Of course, it was more important to be here, but ideally he would be in both places. At the same time.

Truthfully, it didn't matter where the queries were coming from. Nothing could stop Cashier now. The only question was...

Operational secrecy.

He could handle things on this end. As far as who was asking the questions—another story.

"Jed?"

"Forgive me. I was just thinking. And forgive me for being so abrupt with you. It's a very stressful time. You understand."

"Of course."

"So—queries only on Altair and Enovation? Nothing about the bank?"

"No."

"Good. Can I suggest we get hold of someone there, on the ground, make sure they're not receiving inquiries as well."

"That's a good idea."

Seagrave shook his head. Carter. What an imbecile. Of course it was a good idea.

"And you might want to consult with Tom. We'll want our tracks covered on all this. Operational secrecy."

Carter was silent a moment. Easy enough to interpret what that silence meant. The man had always been a little squeamish. He knew what Seagrave meant by 'covered tracks.' Van Croft would know too. More importantly, Van Croft would act, should it become necessary. He presented a secrecy risk.

"Gene. We just want to make sure plans are in place," Seagrave said. "We'll take no action, of course, without discussing this at greater length."

When they hung up, Seagrave looked out the bay window at the front of the house, saw the others waiting for him. Thurman looked nervous, as well he should. Harper quizzical; that was understandable. She had questions. So did he. They needed to talk. More importantly, though, he needed to get downstairs. Get started. Enough fooling around. He went out the front door, stood on the top step, and caught Michael's eye.

"Bring them," he called.

❖ ❖ ❖ ❖ ❖

Espy tried to sort through what she'd learned: terrorism? Cashier was about fighting terrorism?

She also wondered why she and Matt were still alive. Seagrave obviously wanted the chance to beat Matt on the golf course and show off his device. He also seemed to need some information from her—how much she knew and who she had told before being captured.

When they entered the dining room of the house, she saw Seagrave in the kitchen standing next to an old-fashioned dumbwaiter. He stepped aside as Njomo approached, pried open the doors of the dumbwaiter, and reached inside.

And then the whole wall began to move.

The paneled doors of the dumbwaiter slid away, recessing into the floor below, the ceiling above, revealing a dimly lit passageway, maybe ten feet long. At the end of it, she saw massive stone steps, leading down into darkness.

Seagrave stepped inside the passageway. "You want to know what Cashier is really all about?" he said. "Then follow me."

BOOK THREE: CINCINNATUS

Twin Beaches
Cay Cay, Bahamas
Tuesday, September 25, 1:18 P.M.

THE stone steps led a long way down through a narrow passageway. A secret passageway, which only made sense. Secret passageway, secret society, secret island hideout...

"Where are we going?" Matt asked.

"The lab. The one we saw on the tape. It's here. Right in Crosley's house." That was Espy, on the steps in front of him. Following Seagrave and Njomo. Shurig was a few steps behind, bringing up the rear. Still wearing the sunglasses he'd put on while they were in the cart.

"The Special Projects Lab," Seagrave said.

Matt ran a hand along the wall as he descended. The stone was rough and cool. Then the stone, for a second, seemed to vibrate beneath his palm.

"What kind of rock is this?" Matt called out.

"It's not rock, really," Seagrave said. "It's coral. The entire island chain here—from Bimini on south—is built on it. One of the main reasons they decided to locate the lab here. That, and its isolation from more populated areas. Lessens the potential for any sort of catastrophic accident. The forces being experimented with here are very powerful—primordial, you might say."

When they reached the bottom of the stairs, they found themselves at one end of another stone passageway. At the other was a massive, weathered-looking steel door, set directly into the rock.

"How do you think they'd feel?" Espy said, breaking the silence. "Leedskalnin and the Crosleys. If they knew what you were doing with their legacy? Taking this amazing scientific discovery and using it to cheat—"

"They'd understand," Seagrave said. "They'd approve, in fact."

445

"So they were big gamblers?" Matt said.

Seagrave punched buttons on a keypad next to the door. "Cashier is not about money," he said. "The money is a means to an end. Cashier is about principle. The things we stand for. The things we're willing to fight and die and kill for."

"Things that let you shoot a man in the head from a thousand yards away," Espy said.

"Maybe you ought to take the eagle off your society flag," Matt said. "Replace it with a snake."

The door slid open.

Seagrave let Njomo precede him, then turned. "Flag?" he said. "The society has nothing to do with this."

❖ ❖ ❖ ❖ ❖

It was the lab she and Matt had seen on the video. Modernized, all new equipment, racks of blade servers, sleek silver and black machines that made the ones in the DOJ building look like antiques. Conduit ran from the servers to a horseshoe-shaped console at the front of the room. On top of the console was something that looked like a long window shade—a very long window shade, an off-white piece of vinyl about two feet high, stretching from a thin metal post at one end of the console to a much thicker post at the other. Strange-looking thing.

Even stranger—Seagrave's claim about the Cincinnati having nothing to do with Cashier, with fixing the tournaments. He had to be lying. All those other long-shot winners, whose accounts dead-ended at Alderney Financial. All those names. Knox. Hand. Pickering. Shaw. All those companies. MGT, Aiken-Scuffs...

Aiken-Scuffs.

"That piece of paper." She looked at Shurig. "The one you showed us at the hotel. From the Bahamian registry."

"The deed." Matt said. He looked at Seagrave. "You were on it. You and Crane."

Seagrave didn't respond. He hovered over Njomo, who sat at a chair behind the console, reading an LCD screen. Shaking his head.

"Still can't pin it down exactly," Njomo said. "Probably just a power surge. We've had that happen before, and—"

"Field fluctuation," a computerized voice announced. "Warning. Field fluctuation."

It was the same voice, the same words, that sounded when they entered the lab a moment earlier. Field fluctuation. Hearing it, Seagrave had looked concerned. Njomo had looked more than concerned. It wasn't hard to guess why. Primordial forces—Seagrave's words echoed in her head. She should have been a little concerned herself, Espy supposed. But...

Not the Cincinnati?

How was that possible?

Njomo pressed a button on the console. The voice stopped.

"Not a power surge, obviously." Njomo told Seagrave. "Some kind of equipment malfunction. Hard to tell without running a full diagnostic."

Seagrave sat down in a chair next to him, drummed a finger on the console. "How long will that take?"

"Half an hour, at the most."

Seagrave rapped his knuckles on the console. "No. We'll proceed. Let's power up phase one now, please."

Njomo didn't look happy. For a second, Espy thought he might protest. But he began keying instructions on the console.

Seagrave turned to face her. "You were saying?"

"The deed. You're both on it. You and Crane. Trustees for Aiken-Scuffs."

"I took over from Stuart. Almost a quarter century ago. Took charge of the house, the lab, the technology, and their legacy, of course. Most important of all, their legacy. Their principles."

"They—meaning the Crosleys."

"And Leedskalnin. They set up the corporation, chose its members, established its mission. Defend the Republic."

"And the people they chose just happened to all be members of the Society."

"Not all. Not then, not now."

Espy tried to read his face. "You are. Crane is. Holwadel—"

"Crane's father owned a house here. He knew the Crosleys. He was the link. But as I said, one needn't belong to the society to share its ideals."

"Cincinnatus," Shurig said, out of the blue.

Espy started. It had been so long since Shurig had spoken, she'd forgotten he was there.

"Yes," Seagrave said. "Cincinnatus. You're right, Michael. Exactly right."

His words said one thing. The look he gave Shurig said another. Seagrave knew his man was falling apart.

"So Crane and the others are part of this?" she asked.

Seagrave smiled. "I didn't say that."

"So you're going behind their back? Bringing the government in?"

"I didn't say that either." He sighed. "The plan has evolved, Esperanza. My thinking has evolved along with the challenges we face as a nation. It's taken me twenty years to reach my conclusions and determine how to implement my decisions."

"Ready here," Njomo said.

"Then let's begin," Seagrave said.

Espy wondered what she was about to see, and why, in fact, she and Matt were being allowed to see it.

❖ ❖ ❖ ❖

Matt tried to follow the conversation between Espy and Seagrave. Aiken-Scuffs had built the device—the sensor—that Next Century sold, that Bob Kazmir used, to fix the golf tournaments. Aiken-Scuffs wasn't the Cincinnati society; it was the Crosleys. They started it, Seagrave was in charge now. Seagrave—who gave the crazy speech at Union Terminal. The lash. Killing people to set an example. Cashier was his plan.

Njomo touched a series of icons on the console, and the big LCD screen turned a dazzling white then a dark, velvety black. It went to red and green and blue and then finally black again. A series of gray and white stripes rolled past, left to right first, then right to left, then top to bottom, bottom to top.

"Screen is functional," Njomo said.

Seagrave said, "Let's activate the phase-one feed sources."

The screen went black for a second, and then full-color images, each about a foot square, began scrolling across the screen, moving from left to right, almost too fast to follow. Then they slowed and, finally, stopped.

A dozen separate pictures now filled the screen—pictures of people caught in mid-stride, pictures of city streets and deserts and businessmen and soldiers.

The people in the images started moving.

A man in a business suit, facing forward, almost as if he was looking right into a mirror, began straightening his tie.

A half-dozen soldiers in full battle gear—olive uniforms, flak jackets, combat helmets—shifted position behind a barricade.

Waves crashed on a beach. Men in robes and headdresses walked along a busy street, laughing.

"These are surveillance cameras," Matt said.

"That's corrrect." Seagrave pointed to the image directly in front of him. "That is downtown Riyadh."

Espy, standing next to Matt, said, "Saudi Arabia?"

"Exactly." Seagrave pointed to the beach. "And here we have San-ganeb Marine National Park. The Sudan. And this," he pointed to the image with the soldiers, "is, believe it or not, Waziristan. Placing that particular camera...very difficult indeed."

Matt said, "You're fighting terrorists with surveillance cameras?"

"Thanks to the Altair engineers, these cameras have some very unique capabilities." Seagrave nodded to Njomo. "Give our friends a demonstration."

Njomo tapped in a few commands. The image from Riyadh—the city street, the two guys walking past—suddenly had a red border. The two men—one in a business suit, one in a long white robe, wearing some kind of headdress—were talking to each other.

All at once, Matt could hear every word they were saying.

"...*ana men almaghrib.*"

"*Amreeka.*"

"*Amreeka?*" The man in the robe shook his head, and smiled. "*Ah.*"

The men moved on, out of sight of the camera, their voices fading away.

"We could keep listening," Seagrave said. "Follow their conversa-tion to a distance of about two hundred feet with no significant deg-radation in signal quality. We have enhanced visual capabilities as well."

He nodded to Njomo again, and the Riyadh image went from full-color to blurry black and white, with splotches of red and green.

"Infrared," Seagrave said. "I think that's the limit of this installa-tion. But more critical locations have additional capabilities."

The infrared images wavered, and the picture returned to normal.

Espy leaned closer to the screen. "You did this with the Saudis?"

Seagrave shook his head. "No. All on our own."

"Where'd you hide the cameras?" she asked

"They're not hidden," Seagrave said. "See?"

He pointed to the image directly in front of her, where a young man walked toward the camera, holding out something.

A bank card.

Matt pointed at the screen. "That one's inside an ATM."

"They all are," Seagrave said.

Espy said, "Cashier."

"Clever, don't you think?" Seagrave said.

"I'm linking in DIA," Njomo said. "With your permission."

Seagrave nodded. "Let them see what their money bought."

Espy said, "You went to all this trouble, you fixed these golf tournaments, you killed people, to position surveillance cameras?"

"This is only phase one," Seagrave said. "Van Croft's vision of Cashier. A network of surveillance cameras positioned strategically across the Middle East. A substitute for the ground assets our intelligence agencies no longer seem capable of providing."

"So what's phase two?" Matt asked.

Seagrave ignored him. Spoke to Espy. "To be fair to Tom and Gene, we may gain valuable information from these installations. But ultimately they leave the fundamental problem unchanged. We don't speak the same language. We barely inhabit the same planet. These people...these Islamists...they're not rational. Every rational argument we make, every rational carrot or stick we hold in front of them, they ignore. Which leaves us no alternative but to speak in a language they understand."

"What does that mean?" Espy asked.

"What did you think was happening back on the green? When the ball rose up in the air? What did it look like?"

Espy frowned. "Just what you said...anti-gravity."

"Wrong answer. Mr. Thurman?"

Matt had no idea what he was getting at.

Seagrave turned to Shurig. "Michael. Perhaps you can answer the question. What happened on the ninth green? What did it look like to you?"

Shurig lowered his sunglasses. His eyes were bloodshot. He looked like he hadn't slept in days, like he had sat on that porch behind the house all night, after all. Nursing his beer.

"A miracle," Shurig said. "It looked like a miracle."

Seagrave nodded. "Exactly."

BOOK THREE: CINCINNATUS

Special Projects Lab
Twin Beaches
Cat Cay, Bahamas
Tuesday, September 25, 1:54 P.M.

SAM was leaning on the console, facing Shurig.

If you want to know what I saw back there...

Not really, Shurig thought. I don't.

I saw a guy cheating. Wasting this incredible discovery. And what was worse, I saw you letting it all happen. I gotta say I'm disappointed.

Don't be, Shurig wanted to tell him. There was a lot more than gambling going on. It wasn't his decision to use the technology in this way.

Walk away, Shurig told himself. And he started to. Then the phone vibrated in his pocket again. Leila. Why did she keep calling? Couldn't she realize he was busy with the historic thing they were doing here?

Or maybe she did know. Maybe that was why she was trying so hard to get in touch with him. She'd figured it out—the whole thing.

He had to talk to her. Convince her to be quiet, or failing that...

Maintain operational secrecy.

He reached into his pocket for the phone—

And pulled out the prototype he'd taken from the golfer.

"Field fluctuation," the computer announced again. "Warning. Field fluctuation."

Njomo cursed.

The Colonel frowned.

"Hell," Shurig said, stepping forward, holding out the tube. "It's me."

❖ ❖ ❖ ❖ ❖

Seagrave took the prototype without a word, handed it to Njomo, who began making the necessary adjustments. The device clearly contained a

453

residual field of some sort, enough to trigger the proximity sensors, possibly even destabilize the system. Careless of Michael. And dangerous. The interlocking, intertwined fields that surrounded the laboratory, that made its presence here possible, were delicately balanced. If that balance was upset...

"I meant to leave it in the house. My fault," Michael was saying.

"Don't concern yourself. It's done with." Seagrave tried to look understanding. Encouraging, even. Not the sort of thing he was good at. Particularly since he didn't mean it.

Michael had become a problem.

Something had happened to him in Los Angeles. Barely a dozen weeks he'd spent there, and yet the rot had sunk into him. He was nothing but a shell of the man he'd been—the star pupil Seagrave had noticed at Fort Dix, had comforted after Iraq, had nurtured and groomed to perhaps one day take his place as custodian of the house. Of Leedskalnin's legacy.

Seagrave no longer envisioned that day. Probably for the best. He had many more good years ahead of him, and bringing Michael into the fold would inevitably have led to conflict. Like the one between Stuart and himself. Seagrave managed to overcome the problem with Crane through subterfuge, but it was less than an ideal situation. So there was no place for Michael here, truth be told.

"Colonel Seagrave?" Manny had set the prototype on the far left side of the console surface. Problem solved. He was looking at one of the screens. "Voice message coming in from the DIA system. You want me to handle it?"

"Not necessary." He could guess who it was. Seagrave slipped on a headset. "Gene."

"No, it's Tom."

Why was Van Croft contacting him now?

"Good to hear from you, Tom. You're getting the images, I take it."

"We are. Everyone here is very excited. Congratulations."

"To you too."

"Thank you. That question you asked Gene earlier..."

"The bank."

"Yes. I wanted to call myself. Let you know there was no activity on that front."

"More good news." But that wasn't why he was calling, Seagrave suspected.

"One more thing," Van Croft said. "Gene mentioned a woman. From DOJ?"

"We're handling that. Not to worry."

"Good. Let me know if you need help."

"Of course. And regarding those other queries. If you can source them, I'd be appreciative."

"We'll do our best."

After a quick goodbye, Seagrave severed the connection, pleased by the unusual good humor in Van Croft's voice.

"You're talking about Alderney Financial," Harper said.

Seagrave swiveled in his chair to look at her. "I'm talking about Sayeed-Pearson. A private bank, chartered out of Saudi Arabia. Recently, they underwent a period of significant growth, which included," he gestured toward the screen, "an expansion of their ATM network."

"Your surveillance cameras."

"Every one of these feeds comes from a Sayeed-Pearson uplink. Thirty-nine, I believe. With another dozen scheduled to come on-line in the next—"

"Sayeed-Pearson," Harper nearly shouted. "They held the accounts my dad found out about. From Icepack. The Arab League." She looked at Manny.

"The Arab-American Amity League," Seagrave corrected her.

"They're connected. The league and the bank."

"They're essentially the same thing," he said. "They were conceived at the time, created to serve each other—the bank to funnel funds to the cause. A single entity." He twined his fingers to demonstrate.

Harper looked confused, if still determined.

"Another connection between the two," he added with a smile, "is that they're both mine."

❖ ❖ ❖ ❖ ❖

Matt was sliding slowly toward the door. Espy didn't understand why. Shurig had the angles. Shurig had him blocked. Shurig had the gun. She'd tried to catch his eye during Seagrave's rant, tell him to forget about it, but he wouldn't look at her.

Njomo and Seagrave sat facing her. The viewscreen behind them still showed the same handful of images—people all across the Middle East, going about their business. Except for that one shot of the ocean. The beach. Was that Saudi Arabia too? No. Someplace in the Sudan, Seagrave had said. Still, most of the feeds she was watching were Saudi, which only made sense, because Sayeed-Pearson was a Saudi bank. Seagrave's bank. How was that possible?

"How are they both yours?" she asked him.

"I'm exaggerating. I conceived their joint creation, assembled the people to build them and circumvent the laws that prevent their existence. But as a day-to-day presence in either organization...." He shrugged. "I have influence. No formal role."

"You started the AAAL to spy on Arabs. That's your definition of amity?"

"Of course not," he snapped. "The AAAL, in those first few years, do you have any idea how much money we spent? How much we funneled to moderating forces all across the Middle East? Politicians, charities, schools?"

"You keep saying *we*."

"Myself and the other founding partners. Private individuals. Certain governmental organizations. Certain governments. Willing to help. Wanting to lift these people from poverty, to free their minds and spirits. But it didn't work. Fundamentalism continued to grow. Its leaders could not be swayed by appeals to reason. The cancer of their thought processes—the nihilistic, self-destructive...." He looked her in the eye. "We tried, Esperanza. It's important you understand that. Ten years, we tried."

She would've laughed, if she didn't think it would set him off. Seagrave wanted her understanding? Is that why she and Matt were still alive? He needed to explain all of this to someone outside the plan? To justify his actions?

"We couldn't change their minds," he said. "To get our message across we needed to abandon the rational ourselves. Turn to the language of the supernatural."

"You lost me there."

"The language of the prophet. The language of miracles." Seagrave turned to Njomo. "Manny, show me the Al-Musayjid ATM. On Highway 15."

Njomo's hands darted across the console. The images on the screen began moving again. Slowly at first, and then faster. Then they stopped.

A single image remained, centered on the screen. A parking lot. Wide-open spaces, desert, a two-lane highway behind the blacktop, a road sign posted directly across from the camera's eye.

But the road sign was blue.

And the writing on it was Arabic.

There was something blurry in the distance. Then the something turned into two somethings.

They looked like tornadoes.

"Sandstorms." Matt's first words in a long time. He'd given up on sneaking out the door. He was at Njomo's shoulder now, near the console.

"They're not moving," Espy said.

"They'll remain in the same spot for some time," Seagrave said. "Paralyzing traffic on Highway 15, the Jeddah-Medina road."

"How are you doing this?" Espy asked.

"A version of Mr. Leedskalnin's device. Larger, more powerful, but in essence the same thing. Buried several months ago by ground assets masquerading as part of a petrochemical exploration squad. Activated just recently, from the console here. Quite strong."

Espy felt her stomach sink. "How strong?"

"Very. For instance, last week, we put one in Jerusalem. A pushcart driven to a plaza near the Temple Mount."

The Temple Mount.

In her mind, she saw the golden dome fall again.

"Al-Aqsa," Espy said. "Are you trying to start a war?"

Seagrave shook his head.

"The war's already started," he said. "I'm trying to win it."

Special Projects Lab
Twin Beaches
Cat Cay, Bahamas
Tuesday, September 25, 1:18 P.M.

DONE.

Matt had an urge to step back from the console; he stifled it. No sudden moves. No drawing attention to himself.

Njomo turned and glanced at him, suddenly aware of his proximity.

"Get back," said Shurig, who obviously had become aware of the same thing. Guy had been off in space somewhere.

Matt moved away. He'd laid a hand on the console for a second to get a better sense of it—some sort of high-tech composite, clear as glass but a lot more solid. He'd thought of smashing it when he walked in the lab, but that would be impossible. Then he'd thought about trying to short-circuit the thing, but he doubted he'd be able to pull that off, either. He'd have to wait and see.

He faded back another step.

Espy was talking.

❖ ❖ ❖ ❖ ❖

"...by killing a few hundred people?" Espy said. "By destroying the Dome of the Rock? That's how you're going to win your war on terrorism?"

"In fact...yes." His voice oozed condescension. "The very rock where Mohammed ascended to Heaven atomized—what does that say to you?"

"That you're insane," Espy said.

"The path Mohammed took to eternal paradise obliterated as if by magic...what does that suggest?"

459

She still didn't get it.

"Perhaps this will make it clearer." He spun in his chair and made some quick adjustments on the console. The image in the center of the screen changed from the sandstorms to a tall, thin man, with a long dark beard, flecked with gray. He wore a knit skullcap and a long black robe, and he stood in the middle of a group of similarly dressed men. Muslims. Standing at a microphone, speaking in Arabic to a crowd.

"This is a broadcast from Al-Jazeera, taped a few days ago," Seagrave said. "The man is an Egyptian cleric named Imam Husayn al-Rani. He's had a low profile until recently, but things are changing."

Espy saw what he meant. The camera pulled back to show al-Rani and the men alongside him standing on the bottom steps of what looked like a government building. The crowd facing him filled the street and the sidewalks beyond. A couple thousand people, at least.

"He's talking about Al-Aqsa here. Suggesting to his audience that the mosque's destruction is a sign of God's anger with the Muslim people. At our suggestion, over the next few days, he'll make that connection a little more explicit."

Espy glanced at him. "Why is he taking your suggestions?"

"Because we're paying him."

"He's an American agent?"

"He's a lunatic. We found him preaching on a Cairo street several years ago. It took us—well, me, really—almost three years to teach him the elements of public speaking. He's gotten quite good. Attracting larger crowds. Getting the message out—a message many are more inclined to believe because of the considerable disruption to traffic the whirlwinds are causing. Thousands of pilgrims, stranded along the Jeddah-Medinah highway. Halfway to Mecca and running out of time."

The hajj. The pilgrimage to Mecca millions of Muslims undertook every year, usually during the month of Dhu al-Hijja, now being taken during Ramadan to appease an angry Allah.

Millions of Muslims.

"Al-Aqsa was a whisper," Seagrave said. "The whirlwinds, a warm-up. Now, let me show you Cashier. Phase Two."

❖ ❖ ❖ ❖ ❖

"Easiest to start with a map," Seagrave said. "Manny?"

The broadcast of al-Rani vanished. The screen went black, and then filled with a flattened map of the world. Njomo zoomed in on the Middle East. Egypt. Israel. Shifted the focus farther south, and then zoomed in again, on Sudan and Saudi Arabia, separated by the Red Sea.

Espy saw three glowing red dots on the map. One on the coast of Sudan, one directly across the Red Sea, on the coast of Saudi Arabia. The third, slightly farther inland on the Saudi peninsula.

Seagrave pointed to that one first. "This is Basrah."

Next he pointed to the dot on the coast of Saudi Arabia. "Jeddah."

And finally, he gestured toward the glowing dot on the coast of Sudan. "Maghersum Island. Its existence, to borrow a phrase, is truly a godsend. Not that we couldn't have devised a different scenario, but this one is just so poetic, really. The Red Sea. Pharoah's Army."

She stared at the screen.

"'We drowned the people of Pharoah'," Seagrave said. "'For they were all oppressors and wrongdoers.' That's a direct quote, from the Koran. Al-Rani has been using it for awhile."

We drowned the people of Pharoah.

Seagrave touched the console; the map disappeared. The screen filled with an image that Espy, at first, had trouble understanding.

The background was easy enough—a cityscape, at nighttime.

Scattered lights in the distance, against a pitch-black sky. Some taller buildings—towers, two to the left, one to the right, white buildings, all three of them, with bands of color around them.

The foreground was harder to figure out.

At first Espy thought she was looking at a stadium with rows of empty white seats. Circles of them, ringing the stadium interior. There were three buildings in the immediate foreground, rising over the stadium. Mosques.

Then she realized that what she had taken for empty seats were, in fact, people. Muslims, in their white prayer robes. Row upon row upon row of them.

The hajj.

"This is a broadcast as well. From Al-Ikhbariya. Saudi Television. Sunset prayers at Mecca, which is," he adjusted the console again, and the map reappeared, "right about here. About ninety miles inland. Quite a distance, but reachable."

A chill ran down Espy's spine. Her entire body felt frozen.

The screen cleared; the map reappeared. The glowing red dots.

"Phase Two," Seagrave said. "My version of Cashier. Each of these three installations has installed within it a modified version of the Leedskalnin device. One we can trigger from this console. We'll perform that triggering in sequence, beginning here."

He pointed again. "Maghersum Island. Which happens to lie along a transform fault line in the Red Sea. So that as the wave generated by the device propagates, we receive the benefit of a sympathetic pulse, so that by the time it reaches land on the Saudi coast the crest should be well above two thousand feet. We will need every bit of that height, as the Jeddah device's primary function is not to increase the height of the wave but to push it forward across the coastal plain. The Basrah device will act in a similar manner. So by the time the wave reaches Mecca, we should still be cresting at twelve-thirteen hundred feet. Which will leave us a margin of error of about thirty percent. Either way, the oil fields will be intact."

Espy, still stunned, said, "A tidal wave. You're going to flood Mecca."

"A display of God's displeasure," he said.

"You'll kill a million people."

"Tens of millions, I would think."

"You're a monster."

"Some people said that about Truman. After Hiroshima and Nagasaki. And yet, the war ended. And how many lives were saved? How many American lives? How many soldiers returned home to their families, whole in body, mind, and spirit, because of Truman's willingness to do what had to be done?"

Espy couldn't think of anything to say. The enormity of what she had been trying to figure out for months overwhelmed her.

Seagrave raised a finger to bring back her attention. "It's more complex than you think. I've thought these things through. Really I have."

She gazed, stupefied, at all the people on the screen. People who soon would be dead.

"It is my intent to serve the Republic," Seagrave said. "In its hour of need."

Special Projects Lab
Twin Beaches
Cat Cay, Bahamas
Tuesday, September 25, 1:37 P.M.

HARPER turned to Manny. "You can't let him do this."

"I'm happy to help," Manny said. "I've had personal encounters with these savages. I am Iranian. My heritage I can trace back for hundreds of years. My father was a policeman in Iran. Not SAVAK. Police. A captain. A well-respected man. When Khomeini came...do you want to hear what they did to him? Do you want me to lay it out in graphic detail? The savageries they performed?"

"Or perhaps we should run the newsreel footage from Long Beach?" Seagrave added. "It's all over the Internet. I'm sure it won't take long to find."

"That's not necessary," she said.

"Perhaps you'd like to see footage from 9-11? See the buildings fall? See people taking a stroll out the window, screaming as they go?"

He took a deep breath, his heart pounding.

He was suddenly tired of arguing. It was pointless. He had hoped that Harper might see the logic of his position. The necessity for this shock treatment, the futility of conducting any other kind of war. It also occurred to him that perhaps he'd been showing off. More B-movie villain behavior. She seemed to bring it out in him.

On the other hand...

Why shouldn't he preen a little, show off his intellect, his hard work, all of which would go entirely unappreciated, entirely unknown, forever. A thousand years from now, no group of young officers would form a society in his honor. No one would remember him. He didn't even have a son to survive him, or a daughter, someone who he could trust to remember this day, and what happened, and what role Jedediah Seagrave

III played in these momentous events.

He would die and be buried, and in all probability, disappear from the collective memory of human civilization. Oh well.

What he did here today would live forever.

Provided...

"Operational secrecy," he said, looking at both Harper and the golfer, who was shifting weight on his feet in a way that suggested he was planning something. He grabbed Harper's wrist, not hard, but enough to get her attention. "Tell me what Leonard knows."

She yanked back her arm. "What do you mean?"

"The man you work for. What does he know about this?"

"Nothing."

"What does he suspect?"

"I don't—"

"There are queries being made. Focusing on Altair. Enovation. Of all the possible sources for these queries, the most likely one seems to be him."

"He thinks the Kazmir investigation never went forward."

"And you've told him nothing?"

"No."

Seagrave stared at her. Considered her words. Her expression.

"You're a terrible liar." He slipped on the headset. "I'm going to call Cincinnati. The Department of Justice. I want you to speak with him, tell him you've found..." He paused a moment. "Tell him you've found evidence of some sort of coup. Tell him that no one can be trusted. That he needs to fly down here right away."

"So you can kill him too?" She shook her head.

"I can kill someone else, if you wish. Michael?"

Shurig drew his gun and pointed it at the golfer.

Thurman's face changed color.

"Give me the number," Seagrave said. "His direct line."

"You're making a mistake," Harper said. "Leonard wanted to fire me, he thought I messed things up."

"I'll count to five," Seagrave said. "One. Two."

"I'm telling you the truth."

Seagrave frowned. Maybe she was at that. She did seem to be getting genuinely upset. Still...

Better safe than sorry.

"Five," he said, turning to Michael.

Which was when the golfer made his move.

Thurman lunged forward. Faster than Seagrave expected.

Michael pulled the trigger.

It must have been a high-caliber round. It hit Thurman and sent him hurtling backward, slammed him against the wall.

Harper said something—a noise, not words. Thurman hit the stone, and then slumped to the ground.

"You sonuvabitch," Harper said. "You—"

Good God, enough already.

"Her as well, please," he snapped.

Michael nodded. And shifted his aim.

❖ ❖ ❖ ❖ ❖

He knew this was coming.

He'd known it since Maya and Goran. Since O'Neill. Since the trip to Next Century, and the boat ride here. He was the executioner. He'd had plenty of time to prepare for it, and yet...

Sam stepped up alongside his daughter.

Both of us, huh? Sam peered at him. Keeping it in the family, is that it?

Harper looked him in the eye. "My father trusted you. He told me you were going to be something special."

"Shut up," Shurig said.

Special. That's exactly what I wrote.

Sam's voice again. Sam standing right there.

You knew the respect I had for you, right?

"Yes," Shurig said, in a small voice he barely recognized as his own. He'd seen it, he'd gotten access to all the files, from the router code he'd planted up at Fox, his file, Sam's file, Sam's phone numbers...

"You're going to be part of this?" Harper said. "The biggest murder in history?"

"Shoot her." Seagrave snapped.

Shurig aimed the gun again.

Her knees, he saw, were trembling. She was trying to be brave, but...

"Mike," she said. "That's what my dad called you, isn't it? Don't do this, Mike."

"I'm sorry," he said. "But operational secrecy—"

Leila stepped in front of him. Behind her—Goran. Maya. O'Neill.

D.B. stepped forward.

A little moan escaped his lips.

Seagrave rose from his chair. "It's difficult. I understand. Give me the gun."

Shurig kept it pointed at Harper.

"Go on," she said. "Do it. Get it over with."

He nodded.

Get it over with.

"You FBI guys," Dr. Haileigh said. "You think you're bulletproof."

"No," Shurig said, and turned the gun around.

Ate the barrel.

Pulled the trigger.

Special Projects Lab
Twin Beaches
Cat Cay, Bahamas
Tuesday, September 25, 1:49 P.M.

SHURIG toppled to the floor. The gun went with him. Seagrave grabbed it and pointed it at her.

She wanted to cry.

She wanted to beg.

She wasn't going to give him the satisfaction.

She saw his finger tighten on the trigger.

"Sit down," Seagrave said. "And be quiet. I need a minute to think."

She did as she was told, trying not to look too surprised.

❖ ❖ ❖ ❖ ❖

The problem was, he still needed her to talk to Leonard. If he killed her, tied up the other loose ends, went forward with Phase Two, only to have the entire operation exposed down the road, everything would have been in vain. Although—what could Leonard expose? Phase One? If that became common knowledge, what harm, truly, would that do? He doubted anyone in the world would be able to trace the origin of the wave to the Sayeed-Pearson installation at Magh-ersum. Which would be gone in a few moments anyway. Along with anyone there who might be able to relate what had really happened. So Leonard...and his investigation, and the packages, for that matter, if they were involved...

Were all quite irrelevant. Perhaps Van Croft would want to deal with them, avoid those potential exposure issues, but as far as Sea-grave was concerned, the real danger came from those who knew of the device's existence. Who might be able to glean knowledge of his involvement from the reports about Phase One, put two and two together, and cause problems. Embarrassment. Disaster.

They were the ones who needed to be taken care of. Aiken-Scuffs. The other board members. The Committee. Some of the other scientists on the project. A fairly small number of people—a manageable number, although without Dale, Jason, Michael...

Seagrave supposed he'd have to do some of the managing himself. "Colonel?"

He looked to see that Manny had put the Al-Ikhibarya broadcast on the viewscreen again. The Muslim devout, gathered at the Haram Sharif; an endless sea of white-robed believers, millions of them, bathed in the golden lights of the mosque, encircling the black cube of the Kabah—a magnificent sight. The finely tuned coordination of their movements as they stood, and bowed, and sat, and prostrated themselves...they were an army. The legionnaires of Rome, assembling for battle. The SA and SS, parading through Nuremberg.

Hail Caesar.

Sieg Heil.

Allahu Akbar.

"I know," Seagrave said. Manny was going to tell him that the crowd was at its peak, that soon they would begin to disperse. That wouldn't matter.

They wouldn't get far.

He pictured the scene in his mind. A wall of water, visible on the horizon. No. It was night there; they would hear it first. A rumbling noise, from far off in the distance. Some would have news of the wave as it struck the coast. No one would have seen the possibility it could reach Mecca. But when it did...

There would be panic. A stampede. People climbing over each other as they tried to escape. It would be on the news. Some footage would survive. Men in white robes running in panic from the deluge behind them.

As people had run in the streets, when the towers fell.

Revenge.

He took a step back from the console, so he could keep the gun on Harper and watch.

"Activate the Maghersum feed, please."

Njomo nodded. A second later, the screen went black. No surprise. It was night on the island. Njomo adjusted the camera sensors. The beach they had seen earlier became visible. The ocean was visible as well. Seagrave could hear the surf—a gentle series of waves, lapping at the shore.

Not to be gentle much longer.

He told Njomo to activate. The signal transit time was practically instantaneous, as was the device start-up protocol. One second, the world before them was peaceful.

The next, it exploded.

There was a crack like the sound of a thousand thunderclaps—a sonic boom.

Harper started.

Seagrave, his finger poised on the trigger, almost shot her.

On the viewscreen, the ocean seemed to split itself in half— become two waterfalls, each falling into the crevasse the device's activation had created, the slippage along the fault it had triggered. It looked different from the simulations they'd run. Again, not a huge surprise. They had very little control over the technology, when you got right down to it. Now that the device had been activated— devices, rather, by his recollection the Maghersum installation consisted of one at the bank site, three others spaced along the fault line itself—things would take on a life of their own.

The viewscreen went black. Seagrave was surprised, frankly, the camera had lasted that long.

"Athens is picking it up," Manny said, reading the console display. "They're calling it a potential nine point oh. Now Trieste. Same thing."

Earthquake early warning systems. Berkeley should begin broadcasting theirs, shortly. Official government warning would come in another minute. DOD would alert their ships in the area. Nothing to be done about that. Unfortunate. He pictured the look on Van Croft's face when the man realized a great many of the installations he'd just paid billions of dollars for were going to be wiped out after being online for all of a few hours.

"You'll be remembered as the biggest murderer in history," Harper said.

"Not at all," Seagrave said. "This will be seen as a natural disaster no one saw coming. At least in the Western media. The unfortunate souls swept away in it will call it a miracle. The fist of God, descending."

Speaking of which...

"Manny, please activate the other two feeds in Jeddah and Basrah."

As Njomo went to work, Seagrave kept the gun trained on Harper, who was clearly boiling over with frustration. Anxious to try something.

The viewscreen came to life again; two images appeared. On the left, Jeddah—a dimly lit pier, a wooden dock, with a large ship in the background. On the right, Basrah. A gas station parking lot.

The irony wasn't lost on him.

"Five minutes till Jeddah activation," Manny said. "Fifteen till Basrah."

"Can you set those to trigger automatically?" Seagrave asked.

Njomo frowned. "Yes, but...why? Our timing will be more precise if we coordinate the actual travel time of the wave, rather than the theoretical model."

"I want to be safe," Seagrave said. "Just in case anything happens."

Njomo did as he was told.

"All set."

"Thank you." Seagrave said, stepping forward.

He pressed the gun to Njomo's head and fired.

There was a little pfft! sound, like the kind an empty ketchup bottle made when you squeezed it. Then there was a little, as it were, ketchup.

Njomo slumped over in his chair. Seagrave swung the weapon back to Harper.

Who looked at him open-mouthed, wide-eyed.

"The man would give up his own mother for money," Seagrave said. "Trusting him to maintain operational secrecy—that would be a mistake."

He put one foot on Njomo's chair, and pushed it back from the console. The chair rolled past Harper, all the way to the far wall.

"So you're going to kill everyone?" Espy said.

"Not everyone. In fact, remarkably few, all things considered." The board of Aiken-Scuffs, although Harper didn't need to know that. "The miracle of outsourcing. A component added in one location, another someplace else, a wire connected, a program installed, and the next thing you know...boom." He smiled. "Or rather...abracadabra."

He raised the gun.

"The only two people left, in fact, who know about everything are myself. And you. Regrettably..."

He stopped talking because Harper was smiling.

Why was she smiling?

"Abracadabra," she said. "You were right."

"Not a time for riddles, Esperanza."

"But perfect for miracles."

He had no idea what she was talking about until someone grabbed his shoulder.

As he turned he saw the golfer standing there.

Impossible.

The next thing he saw—or rather, felt—was the man's fist.

Special Projects Lab
Twin Beaches
Cat Cay, Bahamas
Tuesday, September 25, 2:00 p.m.

MATT timed his swing perfectly.

Best punch he ever threw in his life.

Seagrave stumbled backward, grunting in pain. Matt grunted too; the burn on the inside of his palm, the blistered stripe of skin an inch wide where he'd been holding the prototype when he charged Shurig, still throbbed. Pain that had almost made him scream out loud when he woke up a minute ago, surprised to find himself alive. The last thing he remembered was pulling the tube out of his pocket. What he figured must have happened, Shurig fired, and the prototype had grabbed the bullet out of mid-air, same way that it had grabbed the pen on the video. Now he knew why the little guy had put on gloves. The tube got very hot when it—

A rock hit him in the face. He stumbled backward.

A second hit him square in the chest and he stumbled again.

The world went a little blurry.

The rock, Matt realized, was Seagrave's foot.

"Idiot." Seagrave wiped at his bloody lip. "We're not playing golf anymore."

Matt put up his hands to defend himself. Seagrave spun on his heel, and Matt moved back to dodge his foot, but then Seagrave spun again, and hit Matt in the side with a brick. His other foot.

Matt crumpled to the floor.

He was aware of movement above him and looked up to see Espy flying backward through the air. She landed on the floor, gasping. Clutching her stomach and writhing in pain.

Matt pulled the prototype out of his pocket again, and it was hot already, burning his hand a second time, but he didn't care. He charged Seagrave, whose eyes widened when he saw the device, and he backed away from Matt, and then Matt lunged, but Seagrave grabbed him and sent him flying through the air. The prototype flew from his hand. He smashed into something that gave way beneath him, and then something that didn't.

The hard, cement floor.

And the viewscreen, which he'd carried to the ground with him and was lying beneath him. He rolled over and tried to push himself to his knees.

And stopped.

There was something wrong with his leg. He couldn't—

"Warning. Field fluctuation."

The computerized voice.

Beneath him, the floor was wet.

Why was the floor wet?

He looked up and saw the prototype—a dozen feet to his left, a foot from the long, curving wall at the front of the lab.

It was floating in mid-air. Hovering, like the golf ball.

Only it was glowing.

The golf ball hadn't glowed.

The wall behind the prototype was glowing too.

And it was doing something else.

It was leaking.

Little drops of water, splashing to the concrete floor. Drip drip, drip drip.

That couldn't be good.

The prototype. Michael's mistake. Njomo had deactivated it, but the golfer must have found a way to switch it on again.

And now it was overloading. Overheating.

Thankfully the damage to the viewscreen hadn't affected the console's operation. The devices in Jeddah and Basrah were still set to trigger automatically. As far as the stasis fields protecting the lab...

Seagrave studied the readout and shook his head. Njomo might have been able to manually adjust the fields to prevent their collapse, but that sort of fine-tuning was beyond his expertise. The walls were going to come down, sooner rather than later. And truthfully...

Perhaps it was better this way.

He'd found out some interesting things about himself in the last few days—not pleasant, the process of self-discovery. He realized he would have been tempted to brag at some point, to pull someone aside—perhaps at a state function, perhaps the democratically elected president of Egypt, or a Saudi congressman, or a woman he wanted to impress—and tell them the role he had played in those few weeks that had changed the world. The role he had played in determining the course of human civilization.

The old pirate saying "dead men tell no tales" came to mind. As did another phrase that had been running through his mind these last few days.

Isolate. Annihilate. Maintain operational secrecy.

It seemed as if he wouldn't be immune to the dictum either.

Out of the corner of his eye, he sensed movement. Harper, getting to her feet. She looked green. And no wonder. He'd hit her square in the solar plexus.

"What's happening?" she asked, still struggling for breath.

"The prototype is affecting the stasis fields around the lab," Seagrave said.

"Warning," the computerized voice said, as if on cue. "Field destabilization."

Water poured in faster now. Directly in front of him, Thurman struggled to get to his feet. The viewscreen beneath him had gone to black. Useless. Seagrave knew enough about the console's operation to reroute visual to the display in front of him, and he brought up a half-dozen relevant camera feeds. Mecca, Basrah, Sarum, several from Jeddah. One image caught his eye—a feed from near the docks at Jeddah, a ship, a big freighter, with people scrambling to get off, pouring down the gangway, screaming, the boat listing over behind them, because the water was going out. Ebbing away from the harbor.

Ever since Indonesia, people knew what that meant. Water going out...

Tidal wave coming in.

But would he live to see that wave hit Mecca? He checked the readouts. Quite possibly. The walls looked likely to survive just long enough. In fact, if he was interpreting the numbers correctly...

The two things would happen at almost exactly the same time. The fist of God descending, and the lab's destruction. He had to smile at that.

Synchronicity.

❖ ❖ ❖ ❖ ❖

Seagrave was distracted, watching the console. Matt was having trouble getting to his feet. She was having trouble catching her breath. It didn't matter.

Espy picked up a chair and charged. As Seagrave turned, she screamed, hoping to rattle him a bit. He ducked aside at the last second, as if he'd seen her coming the whole way. But that didn't matter. He wasn't her target.

She was aiming for the console.

She slammed the chair on top of it. With all her strength.

The chair bounced off and hit her in the face.

Seagrave laughed.

Espy turned and saw he had the gun pointed at her.

She dropped the chair and kept coming.

Seagrave took a step back...

Then sighed and lowered the weapon.

"Oh go ahead," he said. "If you must."

And he held out the gun to her.

"We're all going to be dead in a few minutes anyway," he said.

He looked happy about it.

She ripped the weapon out of his hands and pressed it to his forehead.

"Stop it," she said.

"I can't. No one can. You heard what Manny said. The devices are set to go off automatically."

She held the gun at his temple a few seconds longer.

Then she stepped back and slammed the handle of the revolver against the console screen. It didn't even crack.

She turned the weapon around, grabbed it with both hands, and squeezed the trigger. Once. Twice. A third time.

The bullets all ricocheted off the console and struck the stone wall.

She turned to Seagrave. "How do you shut off the power?"

"I have no idea. Look around if you like."

She raised the weapon again, took aim, and shot him in one knee.

Seagrave screamed, and buckled to the floor.

Espy stepped forward, and put the barrel of the gun up against his other knee.

"Where's the power?" she said.

Seagrave clutched his leg with both hands. Blood poured through his fingers.

She'd gotten him in the center of the knee, Espy saw. Good shot. Her father would have been proud.

"The power," she said.

"You can disconnect every cable in this room. You can shut off power to the entire island, if you want," Seagrave said through gritted teeth. "The devices are set to trigger. Automatically. There's nothing you can do to stop them."

"I'll count to three," she said. "One. Two."

"Stomach wounds are the most painful, if that's what you're after," Seagrave said. "Is that what you're after? Pain? Revenge?"

She stared at him a moment, then cursed. Looked at the console again. There was no visible cable anywhere in the room. Nothing to cut or short-circuit, unless she could somehow get to the inner workings of the console itself.

There was nothing she could do.

She looked at Matt.

❖ ❖ ❖ ❖ ❖

He was a few feet away from her, on the other side of the console. Half crouching, half standing, his right leg extended to one side, his left tucked underneath him. The water was up past his ankles.

The heat from the prototype warmed his neck. Warmed the whole left side of his face.

It felt like he was getting a sunburn. A very bad sunburn.

That pain, though, was nothing compared to the one in his shoulder. When Seagrave had yanked his arm, had thrown him, something had come loose. It hurt just to breathe.

He was helpless.

"Warning. Field destabilization. Warning."

Espy looked the same—first time he'd ever seen her out of ideas. He didn't have any either. All he could think about was all the things he hadn't done—gone to the cops after killing that guy in the motel, gone to the FBI with Jake after they killed Rawson.

Or stayed in the RV and watched television while the world burned.

No. That was no way to go out.

Neither was lying on the floor, in a puddle of water.

He looked up and noticed that the wall directly behind the proto-type, the coral itself, was discolored.

The device was now hot enough to burn stone.

He pushed past the pain and got to his feet.

He ripped off his t-shirt and wrapped it thick as he could around both hands.

"What are you doing?"

That was Seagrave's voice. Matt ignored it, and stepped toward the wall. The little sun in front of him.

"Matt?"

That was Espy. Good thing.

He was going to need something else to think about. Something else to concentrate on.

He had a feeling he was about to find out how real pain felt.

❖ ❖ ❖ ❖ ❖

Thurman was actually trying to touch the prototype? Why? Was he so enamored of Harper that he'd risk permanent disfiguration to save her?

Moving the device wouldn't change anything. The fields were al-ready destabilized, it was only a matter of time until they fell. Why prolong the inevitable? He certainly didn't intend to. On the other hand...

Seagrave wanted to watch as long as he could.

He dragged himself upright and into the nearest chair. Rolled forward until he could see the display. There was the Sarum camera feed. On the right of the screen, to the north—the lights from Jeddah. To the left, he saw sand. And a stream of people, running. From the thing that dominated the picture, directly in front of the camera.

The wave.

Seconds away. The roar drowning out all other noises. Just a few more seconds, then the feed would go dark. The wave would begin the 'miraculous' portion of its trip, its journey across land, pulled forward by Leedskalnin's device. A journey no one would ever be able to account for, to explain why the wave hadn't just died out when it made landfall.

Crane and the others might be able to explain. If they uncovered his involvement in the project.

Nothing he could do about that now. He certainly wouldn't be around to eliminate that possibility. He'd have to trust that if they put together the plot, they would see he'd acted, ultimately, in their best interests. In the best interests of civilization. The proof would be in the pudding. The tasting of it. The fading of those nihilistic cavemen who brought the towers down, the death of their murderous creed, their so-called scripture with its ritual stonings, sacrifices, beheadings, amputations—

Thurman screamed.

Seagrave saw he had grabbed hold of the device. Incredible.

The cloth around the man's hands was smoking.

"Matt!" Harper had come around the console toward him.

Thurman warned her away. Through gritted teeth.

Then, to Seagrave's astonishment, the man started pulling the prototype away from the wall. From the grip of the fields that held it there.

Good God. Seagrave was impressed. Thurman had played nine holes half-crippled, and now he had the fortitude to—

The cloth caught fire. Thurman cried out again.

Seagrave turned his attention to the wave.

It had arrived, he was pleased to see.

The display showed nothing but black. The endless, bottomless, obliterating sea. Poised to destroy everything in its path.

It was done.

A shadow fell over the console.

He saw Thurman holding the prototype high over his head, and in that split-second, realized both the magnitude of his own folly, and the real reason Thurman had risked everything to seize control of the device.

On the display, the wave crested, and began its fall.

And at the same instant, Thurman—carrying the prototype— came crashing down as well.

The console erupted in a shower of sparks.

❖ ❖ ❖ ❖ ❖

The shell sizzled—burning plastic, for a second, overwhelmed the other, more horrific odors in the room.

The display flashed bright, brilliant white, and then went dark.

Matt toppled over backward and fell to the floor.

Seagrave, a look of absolute horror on his face, rolled his chair forward, reached out to touch the sputtering, crackling console.

Espy, at last, spotted a fire extinguisher.

All the way on the other side of the room.

She ran for it.

❖ ❖ ❖ ❖ ❖

Hah.

The shoulder felt better than it had felt in years. Since that first ping. Matt couldn't feel any pain at all.

He wondered if that was because he was no longer there.

He was someplace else.

Going through his lucky routine, on the fifteenth at The Pines. Rolling the neck, tugging the glove, taking his stance...

Looking down the fairway. Par five, four hundred forty-five yards. A long drive, he could hit the green in two, in on four at the most, make a birdie, make up a stroke. He wouldn't get back to par today, the light was going already, this would be his last hole, but it would be a nice way to finish off the round. Always good to end things on a high note, he thought, and brought the clubface to the ball. Started his swing, and then...

Here came Espy, walking up the fairway.

Carrying a fire extinguisher.

Was she crying? Why?

He stood in the tee box, waiting for her, watching her hurry toward him. Evening coming quickly now, the sky darkening, hardly any light left anywhere, the course melting away, the flag on the distant green fading into the shadows and then gone, the fairway gone, everything completely dark until there was only Espy.

❖ ❖ ❖ ❖ ❖

Seagrave drew his hands back. The console was still too hot to touch.

A single line of text flashed across the display:

ANOMALOUS INPUT

What on earth—

ANOMALOUS INPUT

RECALIBRATING

The Sarum feed came back on-line.

It took Seagrave a moment to make sense of what he saw.

Water everywhere. A blue curtain over the land, as far as he could see.

A curtain which, as he watched, began to retreat. To ebb back toward the sea.

Oh no.

The Jeddah devices hadn't triggered.

The harbor was destroyed, people were dead, yes, probably hundreds of them, but the miracle that was going to change the world, that was going to make everything he had worked for, planned for, sacrificed for, all these years worthwhile...

It wasn't going to happen.

A strange hissing sound made him look up.

Harper, on the other side of the console, spraying a fire extinguisher. All over the golfer. Pointless really.

Surely the man was dead. And good riddance.

He'd ruined everything.

❖ ❖ ❖ ❖ ❖

Long after the flames went out, Espy kept squeezing the trigger. Letting the white foam pile up on Matt's arms, his chest, his hands until, at last, the canister was empty.

Then she dropped it and knelt down next to him.

Come on, Matt. Say something. Move. Get up.

But he didn't.

Then she saw Seagrave heading for the back of the lab. Using the rolling chair like a walker, pushing it in front of him toward the exit door, dragging his wounded leg behind him.

Seagrave chose that instant to turn as well.

Their eyes met.

"Hurry," he said. "The field's going to collapse any second."

Espy picked up the gun from the floor where she'd dropped it, pointed it at Seagrave.

"Shoot if you want," he said. "If we don't leave now we're dead anyway."

"I'd love to shoot," she said. "I really would. For my dad and my mom, for Matt, for all those people you murdered today."

"Then go on. Get your revenge."

She shook her head. "I'd rather have justice. So let's go. You'll stand trial."

"I have many very powerful friends and access to millions of dollars. Don't be naïve. I certainly won't stand trial."

The wall behind him buckled at the top, a shower of water pouring in.

He was probably right about avoiding prosecution. She'd seen it happen.

Her finger tightened on the trigger.

"Iminent Field Collapse," the computer voice said, and the lab floor quaked beneath her feet.

Seagrave looked past her, to the front of the room, and his eyes widened.

She looked too.

The entire wall was shaking. Water leaked everywhere, pouring through the gaps in the massive coral stones. Imminent field collapse. Imminent hell about to break loose.

She turned back to Seagrave, the voices from before still echoing in her head. She pictured faces to go with them now. Her father. Her mother. Matt. Njomo, and Shurig, and Kauffman. And O'Neill. The dead at Jeddah.

She'd lay them all at Seagrave's feet.

She sighted down the barrel and took aim.

A rush of words spilled out of Seagrave's mouth. Espy couldn't hear them, drowned out by the roar of the water from the front of the lab— a gushing, rushing white noise identical, she realized, to the sound the wave had made, the instant before...

Ah.

She stepped back, and lowered her weapon. A little.

Seagrave reached out a hand. "Please."

Then he heard a moan from behind her. She glanced back and saw Matt flailing his foam-soaked arms in the air. He was still on his back, his eyes still closed, but he was moving. And groaning.

She rushed back to him, grabbed an arm and tried to pry him up from the ground.

"Come on," she said. "I've got you. We've got to go."

Matt grunted, maybe said "no," or tried to say it.

She pulled him up so that he was sitting, seemed to be barely breathing, his eyes now open slightly.

He grunted again, another "no," flopping his head from side to side.

"Let's go," she yelled at him. "You just saved millions of lives. I'm saving yours."

She slung an arm over her shoulder and with all her strength raised him up so that she could drag him, half-draped across her back, out of the lab. They slogged through the rising water, Matt nearly slipping through her grasp a few times. But she managed to keep him moving.

Then she saw Seagrave, scuttling toward the exit using the rolling chair as a walker. His face was pale with loss of blood but firmly set.

She still held the gun in her hand and thought again about shooting him. They were within a few feet of him.

"An eye for an eye?" he said, fixing her with a hard look.

"More like reap what you sow."

Then she kicked the chair out of his grasp.

He splashed face-first into the rising water, rose up gasping for air.

She kicked the chair again, sent it knifing through the water before it toppled over, far from where he could reach it.

He rolled onto his back, flailing in the water as it rose higher.

Then she stumbled forward, holding Matt, heading to the exit.

❖ ❖ ❖ ❖ ❖

Harper was gone.

He was thirty feet from the lab door, barely able to crawl. He'd never make it under his own power.

But maybe he could roll. Use gravity—ha!—the slope of the floor to reach the front of the room and one of the chairs. Use it to crawl out. Take one of the auxiliary tunnels, leave the island as quickly as he could. Settle scores later, when he was whole again.

His knee hit concrete, and he screamed, and stopped rolling.

The plan wouldn't work. The pain was too much. He was too weak from the loss of blood.

Okay. He propped himself up on his elbows, so that he was facing the front of the lab. There had to be another way. Another piece of equipment.

The floor shook again.

"Field collapse."

The wall at the front of the lab vanished.

One second it was there, and the next it was gone. Crashed to the floor. It made a huge rolling, thundering noise.

Behind the collapsed wall rose a dark and swirling wall of water.

The Atlantic Ocean. The Caribbean. Whatever. Millions of gallons, being held up by the last of the stasis fields.

He smiled. He had to. Here he'd spent the last few years calculating how to use the sea to his advantage, to play with it, and now, at the end...

It would be the sea, playing with him.

Synchronicity? Or the hand of some higher power?

He supposed he would find out soon enough.

The lights, abruptly, went out.

There was a roar like a thousand cannons going off at once.

Seagrave braced himself.

❖ ❖ ❖ ❖ ❖

She struggled up the stone stairway, pulling Matt along with her, hoping the steel door to the lab would hold against the water. She'd made sure she closed it behind her.

Inch by inch, she pushed forward. Matt's body seemed to grow heavier as she wrenched him up the stairs, her legs burning with the strain of every step.

When they nearly reached the top, the full force of the sea exploded through the lab, shaking the ground beneath her. She pitched forward into a wall, barking her head against the rough coral. Matt's body slumped on top of her, pinning her down.

She shook her head, hoping to stop the dizzy feeling that slowly enveloped her. She summoned her last bit of strength and heaved herself up, Matt's arm slung over her shoulder, the full weight of his body leaning on her.

Up they climbed.

Liquid dripped into her eyes. Not seawater. Blood. Flowing from her forehead. She pushed on, barely conscious, barely able to see through the blood burning in her eyes.

With a final yell she lunged through the open door at the top of the passageway and collapsed into the kitchen where the dumbwaiter doors remained open.

She rolled Matt onto his back and closed the doors. With luck, the water wouldn't reach this high into the house. Then she turned back to Matt. He was still half covered with the foam from the fire extinguisher. She wiped it away, trying to determine how badly he was hurt and how she could help him. Save him.

And she would do that as soon as she rested. For just a minute. As soon as the gray fog in her head cleared and she could make sense of things.

As soon as the feeling of complete exhaustion stopped tugging her down and down and down into unconsciousness.

Twin Beaches
Cat Cay, Bahamas
Wednesday, September 26, 8:45 A.M.

THUDDING. A persistent sound like someone playing paddleball at hyper-speed. Pounding that ball. Beating it hard and fast.

No.

Helicopter blades.

She turned over to find herself in bed—in the same suite she and Matt had been locked in, which brought back memories that seemed like ancient history now.

Had she managed to save Matt and care for herself? Put herself in this bed? Had they stopped Seagrave? All of it was a blur, like a dream she'd awakened from, the memory of which already slipped away.

She turned onto her back and blinked herself awake, memories clearing now.

He had almost pulled it off.

Practically by himself.

He controlled a bank—that explained why she ran into so many dead-ends, how he'd managed to set up so many phony accounts. Easy enough to break any rules under those circumstances. Collect as much money as you want, move it wherever you want, whenever you want, no questions asked.

She understood now how that had worked. More or less. She still didn't entirely understand the business about the Crosleys, and Leedskalnin. Where the Cincinnati fit in. What they had to do with Aiken-Scuffs, and the technology Seagrave had developed. Which put her in mind again of the devices. At Jeddah, and Bahrah, and who knows where else. They all had to be removed, before—

She heard a rumbling and looked up.

There was a man standing in the doorway. It took her a second to recognize him.

Stuart Crane.

He sat down on the edge of the bed.

"When you're ready," he said. "I'd like to hear about it."

❖ ❖ ❖ ❖ ❖

"Matt," was the first word she spoke. It felt funny in her mouth.

In fact, she felt dizzy. A little nauseous.

"Easy now," Crane said. "You have a pretty bad bump on your head."

She touched her head and felt something wrapped around it. Cloth. A bandage of some sort.

She couldn't manage another word, but he read the look on her face.

"He should be fine," Crane said. "He was airlifted off the island an hour ago. Bad burns on his hands and arms. Some on his chest. Concussion. It'll take some time for him to recover."

"Mom?" she said.

"Fine too. Safe. Everything's safe now."

She wanted to say more but sleep pulled her back down to the pillow.

❖ ❖ ❖ ❖ ❖

They sat on the patio, where Shurig had spent the night on guard. Sunlight sparkled on the sea in the distance, the sea that had washed away the lab, that had seem so threatening not long ago.

Late afternoon shadows stretched across the patio. She sipped iced tea, feeling her strength begin to return, her mind begin to function again.

She told him everything. Crane said nothing until she finished.

Then it was his turn.

"Your mother and Jake called me from a pay phone," Crane said. "From a town in Ohio."

They told him what was happening. Crane hadn't believed them, at first. Jed Seagrave? A killer? He wanted corroboration—not just on what happened to Kazmir, but the evidence Espy supposedly had gathered. They went round and round, trying to figure out where to get it. Eventually...

They went to Leonard.

"He showed us these," Crane said.

Crane had a folder on his lap. As he spoke, he set it down in front of him, and fanned the contents across the table. Inside was a stack of documents. Espy recognized the one on top right away.

The MI-5 memo.

She flipped through the stack.

Here it was—the paper trail her father hadn't shared with her. The bank routing information, the e-mails and memos and documents that had led him to Sayeed-Pearson, and Kirtland, and Icepack and the AAAL. But how...?

"Where did Leonard get all this?"

"From you," Crane said. "From your computer."

The first thought that ran through her mind was what had happened Saturday morning, after the banquet. Going to her office, finding Leonard going through her files...

Except she didn't have any of this information on her computer.

She shook her head. "This is the stuff I've been looking for. That everyone's been looking for."

"It was encrypted," Crane said. "Hidden inside a series of image files, from what I understand."

He pulled a piece of paper from the bottom of the stack and showed it to her.

It was a picture of Olivia.

"The technique is called steganography," Crane said, and went on from there. Espy listened as he talked, flipping through the pages, putting the pieces together in her mind. Document scans, e-mail texts, bank routing numbers, bits and bytes of Seagrave's conspiracy, hiding in Olivia's smile. The pages passed in a blur. The details didn't really matter to her. All that really counted:

Everything I have, you have.

It wasn't a lie.

It was a clue.

If she'd just been paying closer attention.

She flipped the page and found another familiar-looking document.

The paper Shurig had shown her earlier. The deed to Twin Beaches—lot 12B. Owner: Aiken-Scuffs. Former Trustee: Stuart Parkes Crane. Current Trustee: Jedediah Seagrave. Her father had found it too, obviously.

"I still don't understand," she said, holding up the document so Crane could see it. "What is Aiken-Scuffs?"

"It's a holding company of sorts. Edward Leedskalnin's technology being the main thing we hold. Aiken-Scuffs—Gwendolyn Aiken, Powel Crosley's wife, Agnes Scuffs, Edward Leedskalnin's long-lost love. That's where the name came from. It's more of a trust than a company, really. We own the house and the lab and the technology. There are ten of us at any given time."

"And Seagrave was one of you."

His face tensed. "He was...keeper here, I suppose you would say. Primary custodian of the lab."

"So what happens now? With the devices?"

"First thing we have to do is find out how many there are. Where they are. Then...." He shrugged. "We'll decide what to do."

"The ones in Mecca," she said. "You have to take them out."

"If we can get to them without arousing suspicion. Worst thing that could happen is people find out what Jed did, how many lives he's responsible for...that could start a war."

Espy nodded. She supposed so, but still...

Leave the devices in place?

Crane must have seen the look on her face. "We'll do the best we can. I promise you. Trust me on that."

"And if I don't?" The words were out before she could stop them. Crane looked straight at her for a moment, which was when Espy, for the first time since he'd showed up, felt a twinge of fear.

And then he smiled.

"You want to handle things yourself?"

"That's not what I meant."

"I didn't think it was."

Crane nodded, his smile morphing to a more thoughtful expression. He seemed on the verge of saying something else when the door to the house opened. A man—Asian, in his fifties, ascetic-looking—leaned out.

"Total field collapse," he said. "Months to clean it up."

Crane nodded. "Better get started then."

The man looked at Espy, frowned, and shut the door. Behind him, she saw more people—half a dozen at least—milling about.

She looked at Crane.

"Part of the team," he said. "Scientists, technicians..."

"You're rebuilding the lab."

"That's right."

"After what happened? Why?"

Crane seemed surprised at the question. "That technology is our trust. Our responsibility."

"Anti-gravity." Espy shook her head. "Seems to me something like that...it ought to belong to more than ten people."

"It does," Crane said. "As I said, we only hold it in trust."

"For..."

"You said you saw the video."

Espy nodded. "Leedskalnin wanted America to have it," she said. "So maybe you should honor his wishes."

"We should give it to the government?"

"Yes."

Crane was silent a long moment before speaking again.

"Let me ask you a question. What'd you think about Jed's speech? The one in Cincinnati. About Washington. Grant. The lash."

She peered at him, unsure where he was heading.

What did she think?

Truth was, after everything that happened, she could barely remember it.

"I'm talking about the necessary tasks of heroism," Crane said. "Doing the unpleasant things that need to be done. You think the government is up to that?"

"The question is—are the people up to that? America's a democracy, right? If the people—"

"Wrong. America's a republic. The people don't make the decisions themselves. They vote for who they want to run things."

"They didn't vote for the Cincinnati. Or Aiken-Scuffs. Or any of you, for that matter."

"But the Crosleys did."

"They certainly didn't vote for Seagrave."

"No. That was me. I'm the one who put him in charge here." Crane shook his head. "He was supposed to be Cincinnatus. He ended up Caesar. Thing of it is...he wasn't entirely wrong."

Espy's mouth almost fell open.

"About the threat. From terrorists. Extremists. Whatever you want to call them. It's just the scale of his response—out of all measure. Kill millions of people...that's crazy. Insane. We learned that the last time around." He shook his head. "You don't bomb the village if you want to save it."

"Eye for an eye," Espy said.

"Exactly."

He put his hands on the table and stood up. "You want a drink? I could use a drink."

He went into the house before she could respond. He came back carrying two glasses. Crystal tumblers, full of an amber liquid. He set one in front of her.

"What's this?" she asked.

"Whiskey. Mr. Crosley's private stash. The good stuff. We break it out every so often, when the occasion calls for it."

He raised his glass.

"You saved a lot of lives, Ms. Harper."

"Not by myself," she said, thinking of her dad. And Matt and Jake. Even her mom had helped in the end. And Kauffman and O'Neill had been killed trying to help. "There were others who helped."

"Here's to all of you."

Espy raised her glass.

Here's to all of you.

Their faces flashed before her eyes.

She tilted her head back and drank, quickly.

"So what are your plans now?" Crane asked.

Espy set her glass on the table.

The question gave her pause. She didn't know how to answer.

In the space where her life had been—her double life of the last few months, anyway, DOJ lawyer by day, FBI freelancer by night—there was now, Espy realized, a vacuum. How would she fill it? Could she go back to working on tax fraud cases? To the weekly status meetings with Leonard? Would he even want her back?

"Honestly," she said. "I don't know. I used to have a vision of what I wanted to do, who I wanted to be. Now...not sure."

Crane made a sweeping gesture with his hand. "Feel free to stay here as long as you want. I expect by this evening everything on the island will be up and running again. No better place in the world to relax than Cat Cay."

"Thanks," she said.

He swirled the cubes in his drink. "You know, I had a vision when I was younger. I was going to be president. The second coming of Teddy Roosevelt. Get up on the bully pulpit, all that."

"What happened?"

Crane shook his head. "My vision was off. As my wife pointed out. My personality, I'm not built for politics. Too much compromise, too much glad-handing. The point is, sometimes it takes an outside perspective to get an accurate vision of who you are, what you might be best at, what your potential really is..."

He looked at her directly.

"I have a vision for you, Esperanza," he said.

She raised her eyebrows.

"A job offer, as well."

Espy was too surprised to say anything.

"It's a good job. A lot of responsibility. Nice perks, too. A house" and he waved toward Twin Beaches "with a membership to the island, of course. Comes with another membership too. I think you know the group."

He smiled.

It took Espy a second to get it.

Then she found herself smiling too. He explained that she would be the first non-descendant of the original group of society members honored with so high a position. She also would be the first female

497

elevated to the inner circle of power and certainly the first member of mixed ethnic heritage. Given the heroism she had shown, her background in American history, and her work for the government, she had more than proven herself equal to the task. Such a dramatic departure from the society's traditions, he said, showed that the society recognized how the world and the nation had changed since the days of the Founding Fathers, who, he added, would approve of the decision to offer her the job.

"I don't know what to say," Espy told him.

"Sounds like you're saying 'yes.'"

The Cincinnati Country Club
Cincinnati, OH
Friday, September 28, 11:35 A.M.

WAITING for her friends to arrive, Penny pulled the letter from her purse and read it again, the third time she'd read it since it arrived.

Dear Mom,

Three time zones away, we both pined for the same wonderful man. I think I now understand the depth of your emptiness.

Stuart Crane by now will have told you the magnitude of the case Dad and I worked on. The danger you sensed was correct. And, while neither Stuart nor I can tell you its detail, it turned out to be much, much more serious than I expected.

With Leonard's approval, I have resigned my position with the Justice Department and will be moving to the D.C. area. I know I am ready for new challenges and new associations.

While this may sadden you a little, I am resolved to take your advice and live the rich, full life you have wanted for me.

Here is your ticket to Ft. Lauderdale. I will meet you in the terminal. Be sure to bring your passport and your golf clubs.

I am taking you to my (new) club in the Bahamas. I can't wait to show you your suite in my new vacation house.

So, hurry and get packing.

See you soon.

Lots of love,
Espy

Room 615

Jackson Memorial Hospital

Miami, FL

Friday, September 28, 1:30 P.M.

AMANDA Ovalle, RN, leaned toward her patient.

"How do you feel, Mr. Thurman?" she said.

Matt opened his eyes, did his best to smile. "Glad to be alive."

"A piece of mail just arrived for you."

Matt lifted his head slightly from the pillow. He said, "For me?" in a hoarse whisper.

"It was delivered by courier to the nurse's station."

"Who's it from?"

"All it says is 'Please hand deliver to Matt Thurman—from Espy.'"

~ THE END ~

APPENDIX

Most of the places—and a few of the characters—in *Cincinnatus* are drawn from real life. We thought you might be interested to learn more about them. You can see photos and find more links at www.cincinnatusbook.com

EDWARD LEEDSKALNIN

Edward Leedskalnin was born in Riga, Latvia, on August 10, 1887. He worked for his uncle as a stonemason, and when he was twenty-six years old, Ed was engaged to be married to his one true love, sixteen-year-old Agnes Scuffs.

Agnes cancelled their wedding one day before the ceremony.

Leedskalnin left Latvia with a broken heart and moved to North America, living in Canada, California, and Texas before settling in Florida City, Florida, and buying ten acres of land.

After allegedly curing himself of tuberculosis, Leedskalnin began building his Rock Gate Park, what we now call Coral Castle. He moved the castle to Homestead, Florida, in 1936, attracting many tourists. He died in 1951 at Jackson Memorial Hospital in Miami.

www.edleedskalninbk.com

CORAL CASTLE

Deeply saddened by the loss of his "Sweet Sixteen," the heartbroken

Leedskalnin, seeking to create a monument to his lost love, constructed one of the world's most remarkable buildings.

Carving and sculpting over 1,100 tons of coral rock without assistance or large machinery, Ed single-handedly built Coral Castle, a testimony to Agnes, his lost love. Just over 5 feet tall and weighing only 100 pounds, Ed cut and moved huge coral blocks, sometimes four feet thick, using only his crude hand tools.

It is well documented that no one ever witnessed Ed building his rock castle. It is said that he discovered supernatural powers. Ed said that he "knew the secrets used to build the ancient pyramids."

It is widely accepted that when Ed Leedskalnin died in 1951, his secrets died with him.

www.coralcastlebook.com

Coral Castle

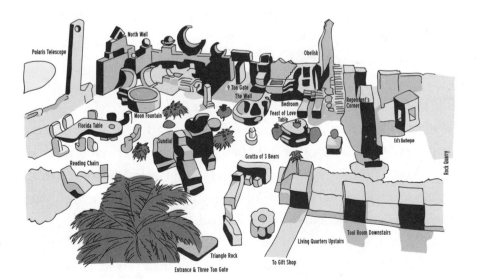

CROSLEY & THE CROSLEY BROTHERS

Set in Cincinnati during the vibrant Industrial Age, and filigreed with family drama and epic ambition, *Crosley* chronicles one of the great untold tales of the twentieth century.

Born in the late 1800s in Cincinnati, Ohio, Powel and Lewis Crosley were opposites in many ways but shared drive, talent, and an unerring knack for knowing what Americans wanted.

Their pioneering inventions—from the first mass-produced economy car to the push-button radio—and their breakthroughs in manufacturing, broadcasting, and advertising made them both wealthy and famous. Cincinnati's largest employer as recently as sixty years ago, the Crosley Empire rose and fell in a single generation.

Crosley is both a powerful saga of a heady time in American history and an intimate tale of two brilliant brothers navigating triumph and tragedy.

Older brother Powel's wife, Gwendolyn, suffered from and died of tuberculosis in the late 1930s.

David Stern and Rusty McClure are two of the co-authors of *Crosley*. Lewis Crosley and Powel Crosley, Jr. were grandfather and great uncle to co-author Rusty McClure.

www.crosleybook.com

THE SOCIETY OF THE CINCINNATI

With a mission "to preserve the rights so dearly won," the society originated when Major General Henry Knox invited twenty-three of the original fifty-six signers of the Declaration of Independence to an inaugural meeting in the New York City area, in May of 1783. A date that precedes the withdraw of the British.

The society is named for Lucius Quintus Cincinnatus, who left his farm to accept a term as Roman Consul and then served as Magister Populi for a short time, thereby assuming lawful dictatorial control of

Rome in order to meet a war emergency. When the battle was won, he returned power to the Senate and went back to plowing his fields.

In a similar fashion, General George Washington refused to serve as king of the new counry, and after serving two terms as president, he retired to Mount Vernon.

Noting the obvious parallels between the two men, British poet Lord Byron wrote, "George Washington is the North American Cincinnatus." Revering Cincinnatus to be his role model, George Washington was elected the first President General of the society and served from 1783 until his death in 1799.

Today, the public face of the Society of the Cincinnati is housed in Anderson House at 2118 Massachusetts Avenue, N. W. Washington, D.C.

The Society of the Cincinnati remains the oldest Military Society in continuous existence in North America.

The Crosley brothers had no known affiliation with the society, nor does the society have any affiliation with Twin Beaches, formerly Powel Crosley's home on Cat Cay. All members of the society depicted in *Cincinnatus* are fictional and have no relation to anyone in real life.

CAESAR

As general, Julius Caesar's conquest of Gaul and invasion of Britain extended the Roman world to the North Sea. His unmatched military achievements granted him power he used to eclipse the Senate.

Sending his legions across the Rubicon, Caesar began a civil war in 49 BC from which he emerged the first unrivaled Roman leader to be proclaimed "dictator for life." He was later sanctified as a Roman deity.

Hoping to restore the Republic, Senators assassinated the dictator on the Ides of March (15 March) 44 BC.

CALIGULA
Caligula, the third Roman Emperor's cruelty and insanity intensified so much after the death of his youngest sister with who he had an incestuous relationship that he was executed by his own guards.

FOUNTAIN SQUARE, CINCINNATI
Fountain Square in Cincinnati is also authentic, and the third flag down on the pole at the southwestern corner of the plaza is the flag of the Society of the Cincinnati flag. Just where Espy showed it to Matt.

CINCINNATI MUSEUM CENTER AT UNION TERMINAL
Cincinnati's magnificent art deco style railroad terminal building was dedicated on March 31, 1933, on a prominent location one mile northwest of the center of Cincinnati.

In November 1990, Cincinnati Union Terminal reopened as the Cincinnati Museum Center, an educational and cultural complex.

www.cincymuseum.org

CAMP WASHINGTON CHILI
A Cincinnati icon for over sixty years under John Johnson's leadership.

CINCINNATI, OHIO
Named in 1790 by General Arthur St. Clair, sent by President Washington to fight the Shawnee. He was a member of the Society of the Cincinnati.

CINCINNATI COUNTRY CLUB
One of the oldest American golf clubs. Its Grandin Road address and membership are among Cincinnati's most prestigious.

THE GREEN LANTERN CAFÉ
It is in northern Kentucky, right where Jake says it is.

THE CROSLEY TOWER
The tallest building on campus. It was a gift of the Crosley family to the University of Cincinnati.

CINCINNATUS STATUE
One hand returns the fasces, symbol of power; the other holds a plow, his return to farming, is located in Sawyer Point along the Cincinnati shore of the Ohio River.

MONTGOMERY INN AT THE BOATHOUSE
Cincinnati's most popular restaurant. It serves 800,000 people and the most ribs in the country annually.

ONE LYTLE PLACE
A riverside luxury high rise situated along the Ohio River in downtown Cincinnati.

THE ROBERTS CENTRE
Located in Wilmington, Ohio, it features the region's largest and most flexible conference facility.

SAKS
Saks at Fifth & Race in downtown Cincinnati offers the finest selections of designer items.

TOWER MOBILE HOME PARK
The largest mobile home park in Washington Court House, Ohio.

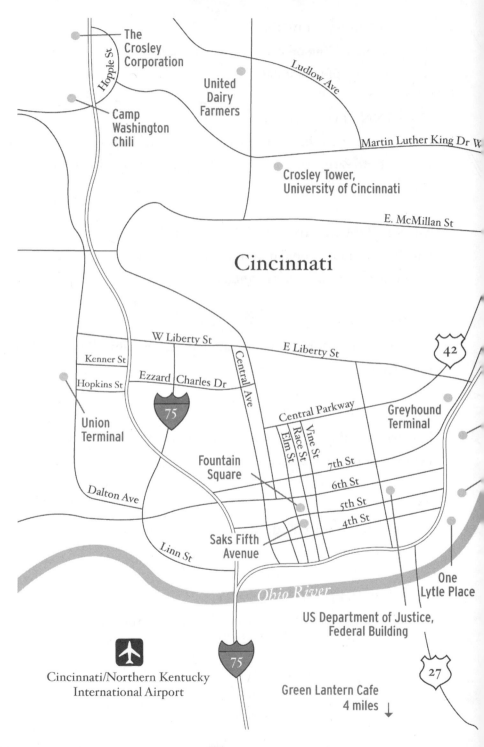

The Crosley Corporation

Hopple St

Ludlow Ave

United Dairy Farmers

Martin Luther King Dr W

Camp Washington Chili

Crosley Tower, University of Cincinnati

E. McMillan St

Cincinnati

W Liberty St

E Liberty St

42

Kenner St

Central Ave

Hopkins St

Ezzard Charles Dr

75

Central Parkway

Greyhound Terminal

Union Terminal

Elm St
Race St
Vine St

7th St

Fountain Square

6th St

Dalton Ave

5th St
4th St

Linn St

Saks Fifth Avenue

One Lytle Place

Ohio River

US Department of Justice, Federal Building

Cincinnati/Northern Kentucky International Airport

75

27

Green Lantern Cafe
4 miles ↓

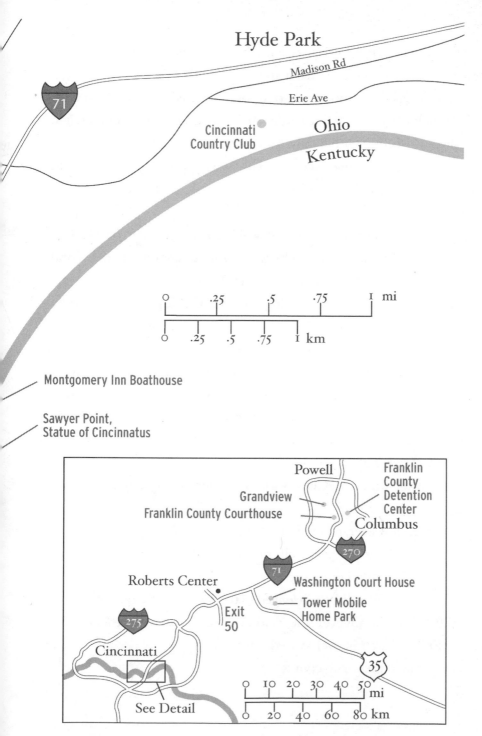

Hyde Park

Madison Rd

Erie Ave

71

Cincinnati
Country Club

Ohio

Kentucky

0   .25   .5   .75   1 mi

0   .25   .5   .75   1 km

Montgomery Inn Boathouse

Sawyer Point,
Statue of Cincinnatus

Powell

Grandview

Franklin County Courthouse

Franklin
County
Detention
Center

Columbus

270

Roberts Center

71

Washington Court House

Tower Mobile
Home Park

Exit
50

275

Cincinnati

35

See Detail

0   10   20   30   40   50 mi

0   20   40   60   80 km

CAT CAY, THE BAHAMAS

Cat Cay is an exclusive private island. Non-member yachtsmen admittance is restricted to the marina area.

In 1874 Queen Victoria granted the original deed for Cat Cay to Captain William Henry Stuart, rewarding his services. Later, Captain Haigh, of a distinguished English family, became the owner of Cat Cay.

Chicago advertising tycoon Louis Wasey purchased the island in 1931, converted the island to a private club, and sold lots to his friends.

Cincinnati multimillionaire Powel Crosley, Jr., one of Wasey's friends, built Twin Beaches, which remains today on its rock coral perch between the two beaches it overlooks.

Wasey also built a nine-hole golf course enjoyed by the Duke of Windsor who served as Governor of the Bahamas. The course is named Windsor Downs in his honor.

Several years after Wasey's death, Al Rockwell, the dynamic head of Rockwell International, formed a group that bought the island. Among Rockwell's group was fellow industrial military complex tycoon Fred Crawford, longtime chairman of TRW, who owned the Cat Cay home High Tide.

Co-author Rusty McClure was a member of Cat Cay for twenty years.

There is, however, no evidence that:

1) Wasey, Crosley, Rockwell, or Crawford were members of the Society of Cincinnati or its secret subcommittees;

2) Any Cat Cay members belonged to the Society of Cincinnati;

3) Ed Leedskalnin ever knew either of the Crosley Brothers;

4) Ed Leedskalnin ever visited Cat Cay.

www.catcayyachtclub.com

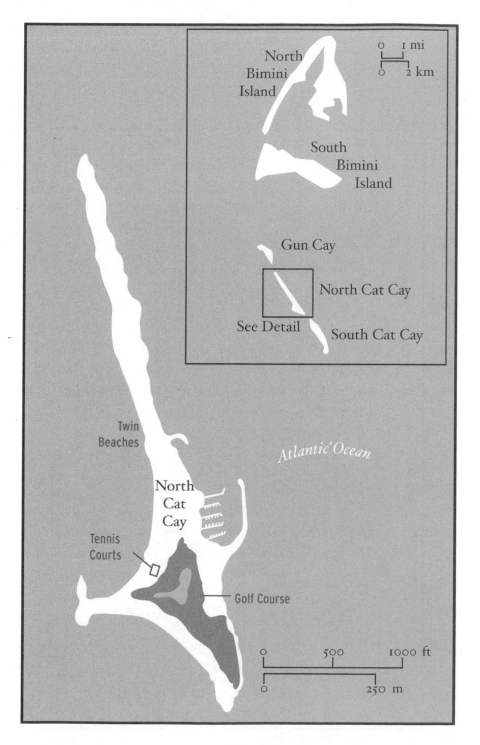

North
Bimini
Island

0   1 mi
0   2 km

South
Bimini
Island

Gun Cay

North Cat Cay

See Detail

South Cat Cay

Twin
Beaches

Atlantic Ocean

North
Cat
Cay

Tennis
Courts

Golf Course

0   500   1000 ft

0   250 m

MIAMI, FLORIDA

Jackson Memorial Hospital is the teaching hospital of the University of Miami at Coral Gables. It is where Ed Leedskalnin passed away in 1951.

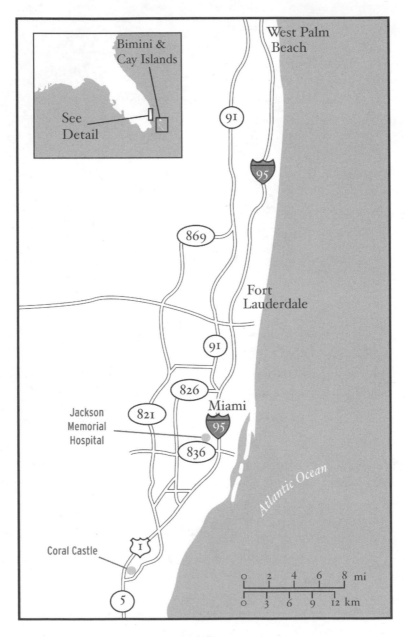

LOS ANGELES, CALIFORNIA

GENERAL WILLIAM J. FOX AIRFIELD
Known as "Fox Field" is used primarily for general aviation, is a U.S. Forest Service air tanker base, which becomes one of the principal hubs of firefighting efforts during fire season.

THE BLU MONKEY LOUNGE
The Blu Monkey Lounge at 5521 Hollywood Blvd has Moroccan style decor with multicolored silk bench couches, ottomans and rustic furniture. It's lit dimly lit patio features with cool lanterns and couches.

KERCKHOFF COFFEEHOUSE
Kerckhoff Coffeehouse on Kerckhoff Hall's Second Floor is UCLA's first coffee house. Opened in 1976, it remains a favorite student gathering-place. The leaded glass windows, wood-top tables, and copper counter-front we described are actual details that give the Coffee House its warmth and charm.

THE ISLAMIC CENTER OF SOUTHERN CALIFORNIA
The Islamic Center of Southern California is an independent organization whose function is to practice and propagate Islam in the United States of America by providing religious, educational and recreational facilities for members of the public at large. The emergence of an American Muslim identity is its prime goal.

MACARTHUR PARK
MacArthur Park is divided in two by Wilshire Boulevard. It comprises a lake, playing fields, amphitheatre and band shell which host music concerts. The LA Metro Red Train Line running beneath MacArthur Park can be accessed via the adjacent Westlake/MacArthur Park station.

STAN'S DOUGHNUTS
People in West LA will tell you that no one does doughnuts better than Stan's. This tiny little hole-in-the-wall is an LA landmark.

KIRTLAND AIR FORCE BASE
Kirtland Air Force Base, New Mexico, in southeast Albuquerque, nestled between the Sandia and Manzano mountain ranges, is a weapons development center. It is home to the Defense Threat Reduction Agency, energy and space vehicle research laboratories, the National Nuclear Security Administration and Sandia National Laboratories.

THE CARLYLE AT WILSHIRE BOULEVARD
The Carlyle at Wilshire Boulevard is the high rise epitome of luxurious living. Boasting "24-hour white glove concierge services," it is one of the most celebrated addresses in the world.

CALVARY CEMETERY
Calvary Cemetery is located at 4201 Whittier Boulevard, LA. Among notables buried there are Lou Costello of the comedy act Abbott and Costello and Eddie Collins, the voice of Dopey in Snow White.

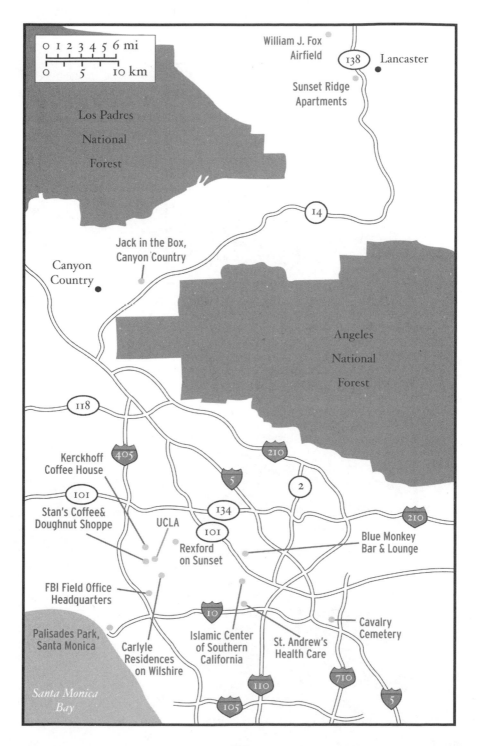

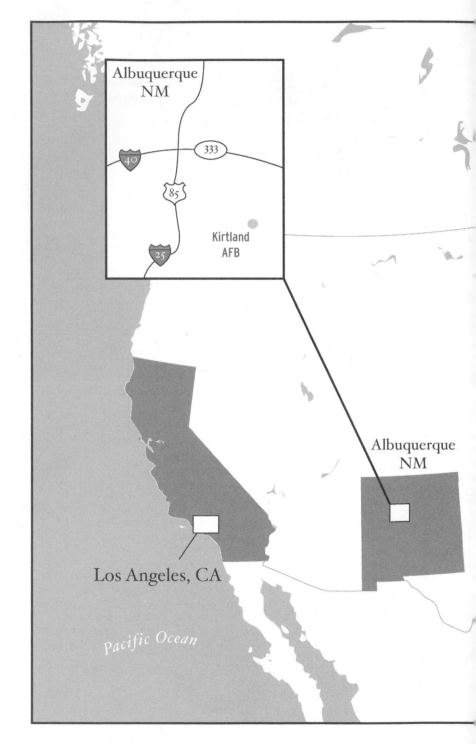

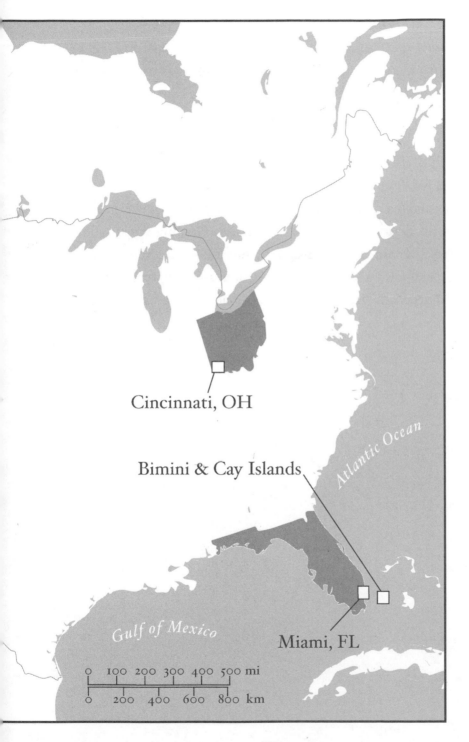

Cincinnati, OH

Bimini & Cay Islands

Atlantic Ocean

Miami, FL

Gulf of Mexico

0   100 200 300 400 500 mi

0   200   400   600   800 km

GENTLEMEN PREFER BLONDES

Gentlemen Prefer Blondes provided a worthy metaphor for the Penelope/Espy, mother/daughter contrast. This 1948 movie starred Marilyn Monroe as a gold-digging luxury liner performer who is introduced to a wealthy bachelor guest ... Mr. Crosley.

COLONEL JED SEAGRAVE

Colonel Jed Seagrave, who perished in a "sea grave" as he attempted to bring about a Draconian 25,000,000 casualty 'sea grave' probably earned his fictitious last name as much as Goldfinger earned his. The real Captain Edward Seagrave, serving in the Massachusetts Continental militia, answered the alarm of April 19, 1775, and made all his descendants eligible to join the Society of the Cincinnati.

7 & 7: THE LOST LOVES OF CINCINNATUS

Characters who suffered lost love

1. _____

2. _____

3. _____

4. _____

5. _____

6. _____

7. _____

... and their lost love

1. _____

2. _____

3. _____

4. _____

5. _____

6. _____

7. _____

Disguised plot reference to lost love

1. _____

2. _____

3. _____

4. _____

5. _____

6. _____

7. _____

HINT:

Place and play on words

A novel

A wonder of the world

A hit song

A movie

An encrypted reference

A vessel

ACKNOWLEDGMENTS

A book this big doesn't get written without a lot of help. Ours came from a number of different people and places, and covered a wide variety of topics.

For assistance on matters legal, judicial, procedural, and correctional, thanks go to Gary Wadman, Edward G. Biester III and M.R. Stern.

Michael Konick provided invaluable insight into the world of high-stakes gambling, both over the phone and through his many books and articles, careful perusal of which required hours of late-night reading.

Anne Durejs-Brossard brought the world Edward Leedskalnin inhabited to vivid life; were deadlines not looming, we would have broken out the Riga Black Balsam and drank to turn of the century Latvia and Latvians on more than one occasion.

T. R. Anderson delved deeply into Cat Cay history and provided valuable introductions of members. Lewis Crosley provided detail description of High Tide during the time his brother Powel owned it.

Kelly Stapleton helped lay bare the inner workings of the Justice Department; Louis Lappen provided assistance in this regard as well.

Shelly Giannini not only corrected a lot of initial misconceptions about the FBI, but concisely laid out correct bureau procedure for us in a number of critical story areas. Retired FBI agent Steve Kennedy made refinements.

ACKNOWLEDGMENTS

How did Jed Seagrave's team hide their money? A significant portion of Internet traffic over the last year and a half came from messages devoted to this topic (at least it seemed that way to us...)

Among those participating in the conversations; Lisa, Jack, and Martha Detwiler, Paul and Anne Gambal, Don Mahoney, Jory Luchsinger, Michael Turnbull, Teresa Mastrangelo, Rick Bendickson, Mary Roethel, and Bob Patrella. Thank you, thank you, thank you, one and all, for allowing us to bend your ears over and over again on this subject, and for the many inventive suggestions (and constructive criticisms) regarding same.

Thanks as well to the estimable Linder Pisarick, who provided low-rent housing and impeccable Slovak cuisine; to Lena Muenki, who provided assistance in both Arabic and correct caffeine consumption technique; to Jill Parsons, for (among other things) an unerring sense of story; and to Don Wallace and Sean Howland of the PGA, for demonstrating just how high-tech the world of professional golf truly is.

Kudos to Paul Latshaw for explaining the intricacies of golf course irrigation systems so that two liberal arts graduates could understand them.

Regarding steganography...

Brian Coleman not only alerted us to the mechanism's existence, but provided a crash course introduction to the basic concepts of computer security. Thanks as well to his team of experts for their insights.

Those who helped with the scoring and management of PGA tournaments include Lewis Chimes, Susan Palisano, Kevin Kennebeck and Frank Bork. People from Caesar's Palace who did not want to be named warrant mention with regard to golf tournament odds. Rick Byrum explained the fixing of NCAA basketball games at a most pivotal time.

For assistance with our (Call Jenny) phone number promotion, we thank Twenty First Century's Jim Kennedy, Russell Pinto, Platinum Marketing Group, Ohio Bell and Richard Hunt.

These people read the manuscript as part as part of a very carefully selected inner circle read group: Jack Gatesy, Dick Preston, Dee Preston, John Huston, Kaci McClure, Randy Nelson, Amy McClure, George Ruff, Steve Kennedy, Jim Kennedy, Amy McClure, Haileigh McClure, Joe Boeckman, Parker MacDonald, Kevin Votel, Jim Chandler, Brad Miner, Larry Norton, Pete Luongo, Kevin Kennebeck, Phil Meek, Dave Schoedinger, George Babyak, Don Shackleford, George Ruff, Jim Daniel, Jeff and Julie Wilkins, Jack Griener, C. L. Huddleston, Charlie Hoffman, Amy Pelicano, Amanda Cullison, Russell Pinto, Kim Wiest Grosser, Diana Gale, Steve Kronenberger, Mike Gorman, Andrew Graf, Gary Robbins, Warren Fishman, Dave Lauer, Stuart Crane, Mike Shurig, Susan Shurig, Gary Robbins, Bob Patrella, Lyndon Miller and Allison Brown.

Russell Pinto read six versions of the manuscript and provided invaluable input to many aspects of plot and character refinements.

For assistance with maps, we thank Sara Cousins and Kathleen Koscielak of the University California Berkley.

We are grateful to these people for their help in golf related matters: Marc Simon and Sheri Major of the PGA Merchandise Show; Lynn Swanson, The Greenbrier, Julie Ard, Boyne Mountain, Tom McKee, Grand Traverse Resort and Spa; Amanda Hawkins-Vogel, French Lick; Lindsey Southwell, Shanty Creek; Tom Galvin and Sarah Roberts.

Dr. Blake Michael, chair of the Religion Department of Ohio Wesleyan University, also guided us on religious issues.

We spent countless hours perusing libraries, bookstores, and websites; it's impossible to provide a comprehensive list of the many people whose work informed our own. Nonetheless...

We would be remiss in not mentioning:

The Hunt For Zero Point by Nick Cook. For those who think anti-gravity is pie-in-the-sky.

ACKNOWLEDGMENTS

American Islam by Paul M. Bartlett. For those who think Muslim-American is an oxymoron.

The Looming Tower by Lawrence Wright. For those who think 9/11 was inevitable.

1776 by David McCullough. For those who think it wasn't, and for his edification of Cincinnatus in *Truman*.

Two very helpful people were Coral Castle's Irene Barr and Ray Remierez.

Finally...

And we are indebted to the good folks at Clerisy Press for their invaluable assistance, expertise, wisdom, patience, and all-around proficiency; we refer, specifically to Jack Heffron and Richard Hunt.

Thanks to Tony Greco and Tom Lynch for their excellent work on the cover illustrations.

Thanks to Steve Sullivan for his steady hand laying out this entire book.

We are, as always, most grateful to our families for their support during the two years it took to write this book and the twenty years it took to conceive its plot.

— *Rusty McClure and David Stern*

ABOUT THE AUTHORS

RUSTY McCLURE is the *New York Times* best-selling author of *Crosley: Two Brothers and a Business Empire that Transformed the Nation.* He has a Master of Divinity degree from Emory University and a Harvard MBA. An advisor and investor in numerous entrepreneurial projects, Rusty teaches an entrepreneurial course at his undergraduate alma mater Ohio Wesleyan University. He is the son of Ellen Crosley McClure, daughter of Lewis Crosley. She is the sole surviving direct descendant of the Crosley brothers. He resides with his wife and daughters in Dublin, Ohio.

Rusty has served as a PGA scoring observer for twenty years. As a member of Cat Cay, a private island in the Bahamas, Rusty played golf on its Windsor Downs course.

DAVID STERN is the author of over two dozen fiction and non-fiction titles including the *New York Times* best-selling novelization *Blair Witch Project: A Dossier* and *Crosley: Two Brothers and a Business Empire that Transformed the Nation.* He has worked on a wide range of titles during his twenty-year career in the publishing industry. He has edited numerous national best-sellers and worked with many award-winning authors. He lives with his wife and children in Massachusetts.

Follow us on Twitter

www.twitter.com/RustyMcClure
www.twitter.com/EdLeedskalnin
www.twitter.com/coralcastlefl
www.twitter.com/powelcrosley
www.twitter.com/lewiscrosley
www.twitter.com/mikeshurig
www.twitter.com/matthurman
www.twitter.com/espyharper
www.twitter.com/oliviavillerosa
www.twitter.com/seagrave

Also, search for us on Facebook

Search:
Rusty McClure, Ed Leedskalnin,
Powel Crosley, Lewis Crosley,
Mike Shurig, Matt Thurman,
Espy Harper, Olivia Villerosa

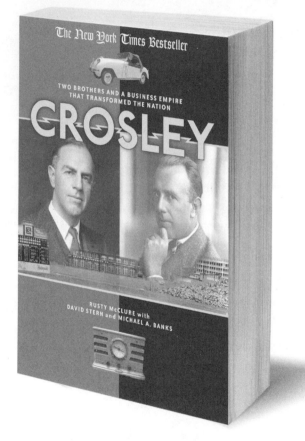

CROSLEY: TWO BROTHERS AND A BUSINESS EMPIRE THAT
TRANSFORMED THE NATION
Rusty McClure with David Stern and Michael A. Banks

With the publication of the national bestselling *Crosley*, readers for the first time get access to one of the great business, family, and baseball tales of the twentieth century.

Although Powel and Lewis Crosley were born into a humble world of dirt roads and telegraphs, their inventions and achievements led them to the vanguard as the driving force behind the world's largest manufacturer of radios, the world's most powerful radio station, to the World Series, to the World's Fair, and ultimately, to helping America win World War II.

Crosley is a once-in-two-lifetimes book, chronicling the conquests of Powel Crosley, Jr., one of the greatest innovators of the twentieth century, and Lewis Crosley, his brother, who engineered the successful culmination of all Powel's plans.

Powel and Lewis Crosley were opposites in many ways but shared drive, talent, and an unerring knack for knowing what Americans wanted.

A tale historically as rich as Seabiscuit, Tucker, and Wrigley—it firmly establishes the Crosleys alongside Ford and Rockefeller and Carnegie in terms of market domination, reputation, and wealth in their times. Get your copy today.

An Introduction to CROSLEY

"If it hadn't been for my brother, I swear I'd have been in jail several times....He kept me on the straight and narrow."
**~ Walt Disney, talking about brother Roy,
who managed his business empire.**

They were as different as two people could be.

One restless, always in motion, consumed by the search for the next big thing—a dreamer, a visionary, the very prototype of the American entrepreneur.

The other, a practical man, an engineer by trade, the consummate manager, rooted in work and family, home every night at five o'clock for supper with his wife and children.

One owned eight homes, half-a-dozen yachts, fourteen airplanes, the finest automobiles.

The other stuck with the same old Buick year after year, until it wore out, and did the same with his suits.

As boys, one dreamt of building a motor car. The other longed to be a farmer.

They were brothers, born two years apart—Powel (the visionary) and Lewis (the farmer). Their story, and that of the business empire they built, the empire that bore the last name they shared—Crosley—is the story of America itself during the first part of the twentieth century. The story of a rural people, a nation of farmers transformed by an unprecedented wave of technological inventions and innovations into an industrial colossus. For a quarter-century, from 1921 through 1946, from their Cincinnati, Ohio, headquarters, Crosley Corporation stood at the heart of that transformation, as radio manufacturers, broadcast pioneers, kings of the refrigeration industry, and maverick auto makers.

Powel was the public face of that empire, one of the most admired businessmen of his time. At the dawn of the radio era, he sat beside Herbert Hoover and David Sarnoff to set industry policy for decades to come. At the peak of the Roaring Twenties, he hobnobbed with the Ringlings and the Fleischmanns and rubbed elbows with Charles Lindbergh and Howard Hughes; in the depths of the Depression, he purchased his hometown Cincinnati Reds and led them to a world championship. He saw the shape of the future to come, the rise of the consumer culture, and rushed headlong to embrace it, building and bringing to market the products that culture wanted, some of which—the refrigerator, radio-FAX systems, the compact car—were years, often decades, ahead of their time.

A giant of a man—six foot four at a time when the average American male was five seven—he used his height to inspire, to dominate; he was impatient with those who didn't share his vision, or his brilliance; he berated those who didn't perform to his lofty expectations.

Lewis was the only man who could stand up to him.

Unlike Powel, the younger Crosley preferred to work behind the scenes. He ran the factories; he hired and fired the workers. Post WWII, when steel was in short supply, it was Lewis who climbed into a plane and went to find it. When the unions came to Crosley, when striking workers barred the gates to the factory and violence flared, it was Lewis who crossed the picket lines each day and negotiated an eventual settlement. When the elder brother wanted to diversify, it was the younger brother who figured out how.

Powel dreamt it; Lewis made it happen.

A story from their childhood sums up the brothers and their relationship and proved to be a seminal moment in their lives:

In August of 1899, Powel, all of thirteen years old at the time, decided he wanted to build a car.

In the bedroom of his College Hill home, he drew up plans. The body would be an old buckboard wagon belonging to their grandparents, the engine, an electric motor of his own invention. The buckboard's original seat was left in place; the steering tiller connected to a custom-designed linkage. A sketch Powel made from memory some years later shows a small wagon with a decorative wooden cowling at the front and a boxlike structure over the engine at the rear.

The boy shared the idea with his father, who promised him ten dollars—an enormous sum of money at the time, a month's rent on an apartment, half a week's wages for the average working man—if the car would run a block. The money seemed more like a bet, even a dare, than a reward, a way for his father to suggest that the car would never make it. Powel took the dare and prepared to build the car. He lacked only one thing.

Money.

The visionary had none. The earnings from his summer jobs, his various chores, had all gone toward the equipment that littered his bedroom, the generator he had designed to power electric lights for the family, and a hobby train for himself and Lewis. But down the hall, in the bedroom of that younger brother, the careful manager...

There was working capital to be had.

Lewis reluctantly but willingly offered the cash he had saved. And then, together, the two of them began working to realize Powel's vision. From the electrician at Pike's Theater in downtown Cincinnati (a building their father held the lease on), they obtained batteries; down the street, on the Hamilton Turnpike, Larry Deininger, the blacksmith who shod their grandparent's horses, built the custom parts Powel had designed. And after a few false starts, a few weeks of trial-and-error...

The first Crosley Car was ready for its maiden voyage.

In later years, when the story was told over and over again, in first the local, and then the national press, it was always 'Powel Crosley' who built the car. But in fact it was built with Lewis, who, the lighter of the pair, actually drove the vehicle his brother had imagined, rode it down to the College Hill Post Office at speeds upward of five miles an hour and back, at which point Powel collected the money from his father, repaid Lewis the capital he invested, and split the remaining profits with his brother.

The Crosley boys were in business. Throughout their lives, they would return to the notion of building a car. Something about this childhood episode—the urge to succeed as a carmaker, the need to prove himself to his father, or, perhaps, the desire to return to that moment of innocent triumph—reverberated within Powel until he died. Even after achieving extraordinary success, surely beyond what the brothers could have hoped for as boys growing up in College Hill, Powel needed to build a car. Late in life, a millionaire many times over, he still had something to prove.

The partnership of Powel and Lewis would endure for over fifty years, spanning the two world wars, from the rise of the horseless carriage to the dawn of the nuclear era. The arc of their story reaches from the depths of obscurity to world renown, from professional triumph to personal tragedy. The tale ends with the two brothers buried side-by-side in Spring Grove Cemetery, on a plot of land chosen for its view of College Hill and the boyhood neighborhood they shared.

It begins, as do the lives of all young men, with the story of their father.

CORAL CASTLE

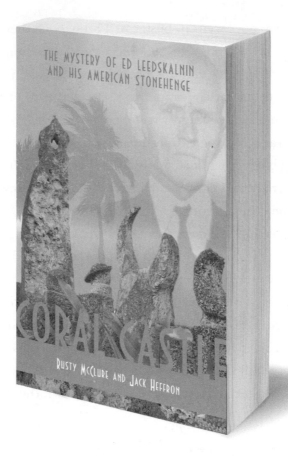

THE MYSTERY OF ED LEEDSKALNIN
AND HIS AMERICAN STONEHENGE

CORAL CASTLE

RUSTY McCLURE AND JACK HEFFRON

WWW.CORALCASTLEBOOK.COM

CORAL CASTLE is the first book to take an objective, journalistic look at one of America's most intriguing places—Coral Castle, located in Homestead, Florida, thirty miles southwest of Miami. It was built in the 1920s and '30s by an eccentric Latvian immigrant named Edward Leedskalnin. Working alone with primitive tools, he quarried, carved, and set in place more than 1,100 tons of coral rock, creating what is commonly known as the American Stonehenge.

How he accomplished this amazing feat remains a mystery. Some believe he was simply a talented stonemason and engineer. Many others believe he had somehow harnessed anti-gravity powers, which allowed him to lift and move the stones as if by magic. Several books have been written on Ed's other-worldly powers, and he has become a cult figure to those who believe in extra-terrestrials and in the magnetic grid theory. Skeptics have argued against these theories in magazine articles and on Web sites.

In *Coral Castle*, Rusty McClure and Jack Heffron survey the theories and tell the story through journalistic investigation, interviewing experts on all sides of the argument, bringing this fascinating tale to a mass audience for the first time.